PAMELA FRANKAU

(1908-1967) was the younger daughter of the prolific novelist Gilbert Frankau and his first wife Dorothea (Drummond-Black) Frankau, who divorced when she was a child. She was educated at Burgess Hill School, Sussex and thereafter lived with her mother and sister in Windsor. Declining a place at Cambridge she decided to devote herself to writing. Her first two fictional attempts were rejected and, forced to find employment because of her mother's illness, she took a job at the *Amalgamated Press*, making use of the journey to write.

This time she found success: *The Marriage of Harlequin* (1927) appeared when Pamela Frankau was nineteen. The next few years were prosperous — she was promoted to sub-editor on the *Woman's Journal*, found a ready market for her articles and stories, published three more novels and became friends with Noel Coward, John van Druten, G.B. Stern and Rebecca West. This halcyon period was short-lived. The story market slumped, Pamela broke off an engagement and, ill and unhappy, retreated to the South of France to finish *She and I* (1930). She later recorded these differing fortunes in an autobiography, *I Find Four People* (1935).

In 1940, Humbert Wolfe, whom she had loved for nine years, died suddenly. Devastated by his death, she travelled to America for some months. On her return she worked for the Ministry of Food — where she became a great friend of Lettice Cooper — and later the ATS. In 1942 she converted to Catholicism. Three years later she married an American professor, Marshall Dill Junior, and moved to California. Their child died in infancy and the marriage collapsed after seven years.

The best-known of Pamela Frankau's thirty novels include *The Willow Cabin* (1949), *The Winged Horse* (1953), *A Wreath for the Enemy* (1954, also dramatised for television) and *The Bridge* (1957). She also published non-fiction, three collections of short stories and was a critic for BBC radio.

For the last decade of her life, until her death from cancer, Pamela Frankau shared a Hampstead house with the theatrical producer Margaret Webster.

Virago also publishes *The* ̶̶̶̶̶̶̶̶̶̶̶̶̶̶̶̶̶̶̶̶̶̶ *Enemy*.

VIRAGO
MODERN
CLASSIC

NUMBER
311

PAMELA FRANKAU

The Winged Horse

WITH A NEW INTRODUCTION BY
DIANA RAYMOND

Published by VIRAGO PRESS Limited 1989
20-23 Mandela Street, Camden Town, London NW1 OHQ

First published in Great Britain by William Heinemann Limited 1953
Copyright Pamela Frankau 1953
Introduction Copyright (c) Diana Raymond 1989

A CIP catalogue record for this book is available from the British Library

Printed in Great Britain, by Cox and Wyman Ltd., Reading, Berks

Dedication

FOR you, there can be no doubt whose book this is, nor how it came to be written. Nor, I think, need I remind you of the hot grey morning on the highway—with the boat waiting at Pier Ninety—when first we talked of these people.

That was three years ago, Levitt was Levitt then, and Carey was Carey. But I was not the person who writes these words; nor were you the person who accepts them today. So I dedicate the finished endeavour to that you, and to this one, and to the alchemy for which I cannot find a name.

Martha's Vineyard—'52

INTRODUCTION

When Pamela Frankau died in 1967 at the age of fifty-nine, a woman fan of hers wrote to me. (I was Pamela's first cousin.) She had never met Pamela, but asked if she might have some small thing that had belonged to her "of no intrinsic value, such as a pencil or rubber". (She also included a cheque for a chosen charity.) She was, she said, "an ordinary slapdash housewife of nearly fifty, most happily married with five teenage children"— in other words, as sane as may be. But she went on to write of "that especial magic of hers which gets over to ordinary people like me".

That especial magic was something unique in Pamela herself, a magnetism which brought her a wealth of friends, love from both men and women, and made her life as stable as a roller-coaster. Magnetism of course does not preclude weaknesses — indeed it may partly spring from them: Pamela loved the gaming table to excess, and always spent or gave away more than she could afford: Celia West, the character in *The Winged Horse* with the strongest echoes of Pamela, remarks "One day I think I shall drop dead of starvation while hailing a taxi." But just as Pamela had the ability to draw people to herself, so she was able to create characters of equal and lively power. "She has a rare talent," her friend, G.B. Stern said, "for reaching down to pain and suffering so that vicariously it hurts."

It is not surprising that the chosen channel for her art was the written word, since both her father (Gilbert Frankau) and her grandmother (pseudonym, "Frank Danby") were in their day successful novelists. Jewish heritage on her father's side gave her a dark distinctive beauty; her mother, who loved clothes (also to excess) gave her elegance. That same paternal grandmother, who died in 1916 when Pamela was eight years old, passed on to her wit, generosity, and her taste for gambling. From all these inheritances she drew a quality that was erratic, even wild, at odds with those traditional elements in her upbringing — a devoted Nanny and a Sussex boarding school. These varying influences fused to produce a spark of total originality, a portrait painted in more dazzling colours than her forebears.

When she wrote *The Winged Horse* she was in her early forties, a good age for the writer, with a nice balance between energy and experience. Her entry in *Who's Who* mentions her first novel, *Marriage of Harlequin* (published in 1927) and then no more until*The Willow Cabin* (published in 1949). This leaves out some twenty books, written between the ages of eighteen and thirty-one. Of the eighteen-year-old, Pamela later wrote:

> Storytelling seemed an obsolete device. She liked her crackly, wispy little pictures of love with a dash of fantasy ... Love was the only thing worth writing about. Sex was the only adventure (possibly because she had not experienced it). But a story ... goodness, what an old-fashioned notion. Times have changed.

They had begun to change with one of the latest of those early books, *Tassell-Gentle* (1934) which has the first shadowy portrait of the man who was to be the most important in her life, Humbert Wolfe, and whose death was to inform *The Willow Cabin* with so much of its power: *Tassell-Gentle* is no wispy little picture of love, but a strong story, with a man who loses his memory in an air crash and, as it were, comes back from the dead.

The last of these early books was published two days before the outbreak of war. Called *A Democrat Dies*, it was a light political satire, and it vanished, blown away with so much else at that time. In the years that followed she lived through Humbert's sudden death, a desperate attempt to drown grief in dissipation, a final coming home (after a long and troubled spiritual journey) to the Roman Catholic Church, war service in the ATS, and an uncertain marriage. She wrote nothing until in the autumn of 1946 she sat down at her kitchen table in Cambridge, Massachusetts, and began the book that was to be called *Shaken in the*

Wind. This was her first novel as a Catholic, and as she admits, shouted her creed from the housetops: "The Catholics," she said, "have all the fun as well as all the answers." (When some ten years later she came to write *The Bridge*, the novel in which she explores the idea of purgatory, her approach was altogether different, more subtle, more complex.) She described *Shaken in the Wind* as "the toughest of assignments"; the years of silence had made her writing hand clumsy, and the characters and the construction fought her all the way; she wrote to her father, "This is more like an illness than a novel."

It was followed by her most successful book of all, *The Willow Cabin*. Writing with a fluency for which she'd been struggling, she drew on all her experience of life till then — pain, war, love, death — and produced what at the time became almost every woman's favourite novel, and many men's too. (And threatens, with its republication by Virago, to be so again.) The success of the book (over 30,000 in advance sales and a Book Society Choice) gave her the stamina, the rekindling of purpose to take up an idea that had haunted her for some years: the result was *The Offshore Light*, published in 1952. This was her own favourite and the public's least, and it was turned down by her American publishers, and finally published there under a pseudonym. It is the least characteristic of all her work, a story of a post-nuclear world, and a diplomat who lives partly in the world and partly on the island of Leron — a place of new-born innocence, which may or may not be imaginary. (Her father wrote — though he was sympathetic to the book, having himself written a novel on a similar theme — "The Leron part puzzles even me. Is it a schizoid's dream, or P. Frankau's reality?")

She was philosophical about the book's commercial failure, being too much of a professional to have false hopes of the public's reaction to experimental works from dependable authors; she knew that readers felt as if a long-looked-for friend had suddenly arrived, talking in an unknown tongue.

And then, *The Winged Horse* when she abandoned experiment and returned to her natural ground, with all her newly acquired fluency and skill. Her publishers, Heinemann, wrote the kind of congratulatory letter which all writers dream of — "You are scoring the first success of 1953 . . . splendid reviews . . . 'the magical touch' . . . 'outstanding work' . . . everything in your garden is looking lovely." In a delayed reply Pamela wrote "Forgive my unspeakable manners. I'm in the blackest of patches all round. But *delighted* to know how well the book is doing."

The blackest of patches speaks of a time when her marriage had failed, with the only child lost in infancy; and of the death of a greatly loved friend, Ethel Harriman Russell, from cancer. In November of 1952 she had returned from America just too late to see her father before he died. Their relationship had been complex, since he deserted the family when Pamela and her sister were small; but over the years he came to be someone whose advice and help she often relied upon, and his death at sixty-eight left the inevitable legacy of all deaths where there have been strong and conflicting emotions: an endless regret for things not said, the silence that goes on and on.

Gilbert did not live to read *The Winged Horse*; and though their methods and approach of writing were entirely different (Gilbert for one thing deliberately kept his wit out of his books, and Pamela unfailingly let hers in) he would have approved — particularly as it is a long full book. He had no time for short ones — he would, Pamela said, turn a novella in his hands "as if he'd found something nasty in the salad".

The book is dedicated — though not by name — to Margaret Webster, the theatrical producer and Pamela's last attachment. Give or take a little, the last years of Pamela's life held an unaccustomed calm: *The Winged Horse* stood at the frontier of that calm.

It is a story about lies and the truth, good and evil. It could well have as an introductory line on the title page those words from the Gospel according to St John: "The Truth shall make you free." Pamela was an habitually truthful person, and like many such was fascinated by the dissembler, the person with the flaw within. Through the whole book there runs this theme, lightly touched on at first with the central character of Harry Levitt, an American cartoonist, given to lying about his background, parents, marriage, for no better reason than that he finds it easier to lie than to tell the truth. This theme develops until it reaches crisis point, until the matter of truth brings a surprising revelation and a head-on conflict between the three main characters of the book: Levitt himself, Anthony Carey, the upright Englishman, and J.G. Baron, the newspaper tycoon, who brings Levitt from America to work for him. (Pamela, writing on methods of story-telling, says, "What do I mean by conflict? A man trying to get through a locked door.")

For anyone who has ever had a hard confession to make — and there must be few, truthful or otherwise, who have not — Pamela's chart of this particular journey is accurate to the point of pain. By an odd turn of circumstance, it is Carey, the ever-to-be-relied-upon Anthony, who finds himself the deceiver, Levitt the deceived. And from the beginning with the first temptation to hide, to lie — "A dark cloud of depression came without warning, like a black tent dropped on his head: it muffled all happiness", the journey goes on, the thing unsaid, growing larger and more obsessive with the passing of time. "He could . . . get back the minute that had passed. Odd, that it should be so important; when he had all the rest of the day in which to tell . . . Yes, that was comforting, no hurry, he said to himself." No hurry, but of course the words aren't spoken, and the obsession reaches nightmare point, true nightmare from which he wakes to the morning inquisition:

> Are you crazy? Why did you let it go as far as this? Look at the time you wasted; all the weeks and weeks that you've had; just that one little hurdle to be taken and you didn't take it. But it was *easy* then. You could have done it without thinking; why didn't you?

And then . . . "But of course you did that, you really did . . . It's all right, thank God. You're telling her, showing her. None of this has happened. You've turned time back to there, and you're honest again, you're safe."

But no, he is not safe; and only the tortuous skilfully handled events which bring the truth to light and give as it were absolution, can give, also, safety back to him.

This is the climax of the book, but to journey there one enters a world which is Pamela's world, a country of particular colour and light; one exclaims, "Oh yes; this is the place!" Her world, as all fictional worlds must, consists primarily of its people. When she wrote of the creation of character, Pamela said, "The term 'Reader-identification' wouldn't, even if it expressed itself in English, mean what I mean. It is only while writing that I need to identify myself with characters; not while reading. But I must believe they exist."

Oh yes, they exist. Take Baron first: J.G. Baron, Sir James Baron, Press lord, father of three children by two wives: Celia, by his first wife; Liz and Tobias by his second, both wives being dead — "of being married to J.G." his daughter, Celia, says. All evidence to the contrary, Baron is not based on the late Lord Beaverbrook: when the possibility of a film version of the book arose, Pamela wrote to Robin Maugham,

> "What I *don't* want him to be, though, is the Grand Old Man. He's a blend of Mr Barrett, Quilp [the tyrant and money-lender of *The Old Curiosity Shop*] and a couple of real people whose names I'll suppress in case the *Daily Express* is under your desk disguised as a mosquito."

Baron is important, not only because he tyrannizes his family and sets events in motion by hiring Levitt, but because he is the one character who continues to deceive himself — though towards the end of the book he reflects "For people like me, the Truth's the light that is too strong to bear."

Liz and Tobias, the two of his children who suffer most from "Baron fever" have varying descriptions of his many roles: "one can never guess," says Liz, "if it's going to be Citation of Family Characteristics in Front of Strangers (my worst) or ego-maniac outpourings to the Yes-Men. (Toby's worst; Toby called it His Early Struggles in the Collieries)." Pamela allowed that he had pathos — "when he can't remember his second wife, when he goes to say his prayer". Baron's prayer is funny and outrageous. He has made up his mind to go to Oxford to see his wayward son, Tobias, with his ''affected speech and romantic air''. Misgivings about this visit send him into a Catholic Church, where ''he was a little offended to discover a service in progress (on a Saturday too; their trouble is they overdo things''. His prayer ends

> ''Tobias is such a difficult customer; could you, if it doesn't shock you to be asked such a thing, make me *like* him a little better? . . . If you could arrange things comfortably, I'd be in your debt for ever. Excuse me, of course I'm in your debt already, that goes without saying. Amen.''

Tobias, the unloved son, is certainly affected of speech, but he has not only wit in the affectation — he describes Foliot, the secretary/housekeeper as looking like a cross between a Modigliani and a benign vampire bat — but is also a full character, touching in his youth and in his worshipful love for an older woman. Red-haired, romantic in looks, devoted to his sisters and doomed to enrage his father, he is also doomed, the young man flying (almost literally) too near the sun.

In a scene when Tobias and his sisters talk together out of earshot of their father, comes a snatch of *The Lykewake Dirge*. (''I have no urge to hear this dirge,'' Tobias says, but he listens.)

> When thou from hence — away art past
> Every night and alle,
> To Whinny-muir thou com'st at last:
> And Christ receive thy soule
>
> If ever thou gavest meat or drink,
> Every night and alle,
> The fire sall never make thee shrink;
> And Christ receive thy soule. . .

It is appropriate, for something of its spine-chilling quality pervades the book; and certainly touches Tobias: *The fire sall never make thee shrink* . . . but the fire when his fragile aircraft stalls on his return from a visit to his love in France engulfs the plane; and the light-hearted, haunted Tobias is dead.

And now he becomes the son that Baron had always wanted:

beloved, upright, to be mourned. To be remembered by a Memorial statue — which Anthony Carey, the sculptor, the always reliable Englishman — "Thank-God-for-Anthony" — is to design. And so it comes about that the design is the Winged Horse, the idea coming from the song which they all sing to Belloc's words

> And once atop of Lambourne, down toward the hill of
> Clere,
> I saw the Host of Heaven in rank and Michael with
> his spear,
> And Turpin out of Gascony and Charlemagne the Lord,
> And Roland of the marches with his hand upon his
> sword . . .
> For you that took the all-in-all the things you left
> were three.
> A loud voice for singing and keen eyes to see,
> And a spouting well of joy within that never yet was
> dried!
> *And I ride*!

Of this poem Pamela wrote to Robin Maugham: "It *has* a tune; I heard it sung by Beachcomber, unaccompanied, at one of V[ictor] Gollancz's parties, before you were born. Jolly good, too. We all joined in the chorus — even Charles Morgan. (This is, improbably, all quite true.)"

It is Celia, Baron's elder daughter, who challenges him on the hypocrisy of his mourning Tobias. Celia, with her broken marriage behind her, hot for truth, cannot endure the false image of the grieving father: she says, "I loved him and you didn't. You hated him. Please remember that I know that; and I don't forget it; not for all the sonnets in *Flash* or statues in the garden."

Celia is unafraid of him; she is one of the few who have escaped his shadow. She is truthful, fiercely independent:

> It was time for another fight, that was all. Alone . . . I've trained myself into the belief that I can, should, must take anything; that to put the burden down in any other place is weakness, that to be strong is to be alone.

Celia defies her father; Liz, the younger daughter (seventeen when the book starts, comically tragic: "love spoils everything" she mourns) is afraid of him — but Liz with her beguiling innocence deals in truth too.

How this is resolved should be left to the reader to find out; the story, far from being an old-fashioned notion, has compelling strength. The shadowed place of deception is exposed to full light — not quite as the reader might expect it to be; but Carey finds "peace going on and on inside him and about him"; and reflects "The words were said; fear's over."

But when all's said and done, what stays in the mind is not the story only, nor the company of characters, nor the poetry of Belloc, Kipling and the anonymous author of *The Lykewake Dirge*. It is an amalgam of all these; it is the alchemy by which the writer creates a world. Pamela's novels belong to their time: her characters remember nannies, nursery jokes ("*no* time to play with the giraffe"), and the flying bombs; whatever their varying fortunes they remain articulate, quoting where they will, their talk spiked with wit; and the world of good food and drink, homes of some grace if not grandeur, is never far away. But magic is timeless; and it is Pamela's own particular form which invests her books; this one, and those others which her readers may search out for themselves.

Diana Raymond, London, 1988

BOOK I

THE HARBOUR RECEDING

(March, 1949)

BOOK I

THE HARBOUR RECEDING

(i)

"TIME to be going," Levitt said. The girl stood up and put her hands on his shoulders. She murmured, "Don't think I care for this very much," distantly, as though talking to herself.

Holding her, he knew that she was already in the dimension of the past. So was this room, seen over the top of her head; his own room, given to her and changed with her possessions. He was staring at his sketch for a self-portrait; she had framed it and hung it above the mantelpiece. Not worth framing, Levitt thought, still absentminded in the embrace; it was a parade of his slickest talents, a ten-minute job; it made him uglier than he was. The few lines assembled themselves into a narrow head, a slanted look of laughter and that was all. It repelled him now because it would be here for a long time, the grinning nervous mask like the face of a fox.

"Let's get it over with," the girl said.

"I'm sorry, darling."

She said nothing.

"This is it, I guess," said Levitt. He picked up his brief-case with the brightly-coloured label standing out stiffly from the handle. The rest of the luggage was downstairs.

At the door he kissed his hand to her. He left her standing alone in the room. From the sidewalk, before he stepped into the taxi, he looked up at the window, knowing that she would not be there. She was gone. The house on 70th Street, the grey paint, the black front door and the green tree were gone.

New York was going. He had ceased to be any part of it. The only things that he owned now were the taxi carrying him across town to the pier, the five pieces of expensive luggage with

3

bright labels, the overcoat on his arm. It was a moment luxurious with adventure. He had not felt so much alone with Levitt, master of Levitt, before.

To the city, departing from him in the wild light between the rains of a spring afternoon, he kissed his hand, as he had kissed it to the girl. "Can't catch me," he said, "I'm off. Down to the sea in ships. Last time was an army transport. I thought I was a fool then. Why don't I think I'm a fool now? Everyone else does. They don't know. Do I know? I guess not; it can't be explained. It just became the thing that I had to do."

The girl had said, "You're flattered. You like thumbing your nose at common sense. You like proving to the people who know the answers that they don't and you do. You're besottedly in love with England and the English. And it gives you an Out from me."

His employer had said, "Just for the minute, you're a fashion, a craze like a popular tune. And we don't want to lose you. We want to go on building you. That's why we're offering you more money to stay, now. Right outside the terms of your contract."

"I know. I'm grateful. But——"

"Wait a minute. Do you realise that if the British assignment doesn't work out—and you come back to us for a job, we won't give it to you? Our policy never varies on that. We can afford," he said, with his secret monkish smile, "to cut off our noses to spite our faces."

"I know that too."

(He had seen the expression reflecting clearly the comment in the mind, "Stuck on yourself, aren't you, Levitt?") The tone of the voice had sharpened, "You may flop over there. Thought of that? British tastes aren't the same as ours. Satire's tricky stuff to sell to foreigners. And if you do flop—well, I imagine you know enough about J. G. Baron to understand that a year's contract doesn't mean a thing. . . . If there's trouble, he pays them up and pitches them out."

"So," Levitt thought, his taxi now held on the perimeter, one in a mob of taxis jamming the approaches to the pier, "they talk . . . and you don't tell them.

"Not to explain; the one thing that you refuse to explain; which is you; the gambler you, acting on hunch; less defiant of the rules than quick to catch the sound like a bell striking; the hour of destiny; your cue to say 'Yes' and to think 'I can'.

"The moment whispers 'I can'. I remember the first time that whisper came; years and years ago; when I was a kid, when I first took my foot off the floor of the swimming-pool and struck out with all four limbs together; and it was true that water bore me up. It has always been important," he said to himself, "to remember that feeling. When I'm afraid, it's important, saying to myself, 'You can swim, you know; you needn't sink.' This was the kind of talk that Levitt had with Levitt; not with the girl —nor any girl; not with the boys around the bar, only with Levitt.

"Where in all this——" he wondered, looking through the window at the pent-up mass, hearing the chorus of horns, feeling the traveller's unnecessary panic, "Where in all this is Baron? On board already, maybe; having a farewell party in his suite. That's what he'll be doing." He thought about Baron, the man who had bought him; the granite goblin with the light, baffled eyes.

"Why did he buy me? I still can't be sure. I don't know him yet; I can't even get his face clear when I think about it. There's a slit-eyed look. . . . Gnomish? Chinese? If there were such a thing as a Chinese gnome . . . and a pagan, curly look, and another look when there are just straight, angry lines. He's got at least three faces; maybe more. That neat body and those legs, kind of gay prancing legs; I can see those. Terrifying little creature; why?"

"Because he owns you, chum, from here on in. Baron owns Levitt."

"Does he know what he's bought? No, he doesn't. I didn't tell him my life-story. I don't tell it to anybody. I gave him some picturesque highlights and left the rest in the dark. And I think," Levitt said to Levitt, "that I'd better soft-pedal the fictions with J.G.B.; watch it all the time. 'Difficult to watch it, once I get started. The answer, of course, is not to get started.'

"Why can't I settle for the life-story as it was? Too dull. Born in Volo, Illinois; mother who did painstaking water-colours; father who saved to send me to college; brother a nice guy who got himself killed at Tarawa. He had the breaks till then. I never had the breaks till war came."

True enough. He had gone, with his artist's career unformed, into the army, into Italy, into the high spots of war. There he had begun to draw the comic strip for *Stars and Stripes*, and presently his name had sounded, the crested signature established itself and he was Levitt for the army. He had come home to nothing; he had drawn what struck him as the worst of that, becoming Levitt the recorder of post-war limbo, Levitt for the demobilised, the cynical and the uncertain. Out of his first gaily savage book of cartoons there had shot the career; the contract, the beginning of New York, the topless towers . . . Cut down, thrown carelessly away, in this leap after the next new thing.

"Damn it," he said to himself, stepping at last out of the taxi into the scrimmage, "*is* it the fool's way?" He began to walk up the steps, still arguing in his head.

"I've taken the fool's way from the beginning, haven't I? Fool's way for fun. I don't save a penny. I've lived high, wide and fancy from the first minute I knew I was in the money . . . and I'll go on spending.

"I spend it the way they spend it; on the luxuries that turn into the necessities." (These were the things that did not endure: dinners and drinks; theatre-seats at scalper's prices; air-tickets; bets; gasoline and champagne; the right suits, shirts, ties, shoes; presents for girls; girls. . . . The pattern of his expenditure was the pattern of theirs, and though he could not tell precisely whom he meant when he said 'They' he knew them by instinct. He had crashed their gate and learned their tricks, having as keen an ear and eye as an actor had. The caricaturist's gift was, after all, the mimic's gift. Levitt could, he thought, be anybody he wanted to be.)

Now all was slow and undramatic, a glass shed, an ante-room with signs pointing towards the gangways, an indoor prelude to the ship. He held out his ticket, the long pallid document with the scribbled words and figures, the contract to carry Levitt three thousand miles.

He walked up the gangway into the new world. A steward in a white coat directed him. The steward opened the cabin door and he stood in the slice of a room that would be his home for seven days. Overhead he heard the tramping, the shouts, the rattle of wheels; he looked through the porthole on to a black dockside wall, on to green weeds and a rope that dangled.

"There's a note for you, sir," the steward said. Levitt opened the envelope.

"Should be glad to see you after dinner tonight. Smoking-room at nine-thirty. J.G.B."

"I'd have thought," said Levitt to Levitt, "that he'd ask me to come to his suite . . ." He felt a little affronted.

(ii)

Van West knew the number of his wife's stateroom on A deck; his wife was J.G. Baron's daughter, and he had got the number from J. G. Baron's secretary. Celia would not have given it to him, even if he had asked her.

Now he knocked at her door, seeing himself standing here; the habit of seeing himself came easily to Van West. He saw a tall dark man with sad eyes, perfectly dressed, entirely wronged and justly miserable; a martyred man about to conduct an interview with great dignity.

"Come in." The light, abrupt voice with the laugh in it did what it always did to him. It had deeper notes; it was a haunting voice but he could not remember all of it when she was not there.

He walked in. The large stateroom was full of flowers and luggage. Celia leaned at the looking-glass, pulling a comb through her hair. He had this snapshot of her alone, not expecting him; he would remember it when she was gone; most of all the hair, fair and soft, like a child's hair, cut short with one square lock on the temple. Into the snapshot there would go the gold-topped bottles on the dressing-table; and he would sniff back the Lanvin scent; no, damn it, he would not; surely he had learned to hate these things.

She turned from the glass; he saw the face change with hostility; the pagan, curling lines straightened. It was a cold mask now, a Nordic mask looking at him; the eyes were a light and brilliant blue, oddly-shaped, almost square.

She said, "Hullo. What's the idea?"

"I wanted to see you again. I wanted to see Terry."

She shook her head, patiently, exaggeratedly. "What good'll that do anybody?" She lit a cigarette with one of her innumerable tricky lighters; her hand shook.

"See Terry—sure," she said. "I can't stop you. But don't kiss him. I don't want great hugs and scenes and sobs. See?"

He nodded coldly, not trusting himself to speak. She opened the door of the adjoining stateroom and called through to Nanny. He hated Nanny, the bustling, elderly Englishwoman who looked at him, when she looked at him at all, as though he were not entitled to take up the space on the floor. She gave him that look now as she led Terry in. Terry, aged four, was a fair, frowning little boy; he gave the impression of having urgent business somewhere else. When he spoke, his words were rounded and emphatic, all underlined, with pauses between the words. "Good-bye. But—I—thought—we—said—good-bye—already."

Van never knew what to say to Terry. He tried talking about the ship, but Terry was reluctant to admit that this was a ship. "It—doesn't—feel—like—one. It—doesn't—look—like—one." He sighed and began to play with the things on Celia's dressing-table. Nanny said, "He ought to have his rest, if you'll excuse me, m'm." Van kissed him and let him go.

"He doesn't like me," said Van. "He never has liked me. That's another nice thought."

"He can be quite repulsive," said Celia lightly, as though it didn't matter.

"Well?"

"Well?"

"Haven't you anything to say to me, Celia?"

"Nothing at all, I'm afraid."

He felt his eyes fill with tears.

"I love you," he said. "I want you back."

"Cut, please."

"God, you're hard. You're harder than hell."

"Don't let's have it again, Van."

"If I admit I've been wrong—I'll try—I'll do anything. I love you."

"Your love, my dear, has been concentrated for the past thirty-five years on Mr. Valentine West. With occasional deviations towards a bottle of Scotch, a girl who'll listen to you or a nice rich bunch of friends who'll put business in your way. Do I have to tell you again that I dislike you and despise you?"

He began to weep. Always he wanted not to weep in her presence; it was the defeat that made a woman of him, a man of her. She cried so seldom. It was damnably unfair, he thought, that she could treat him like a dog and still have the victory of composure. Seeing her turn away in disgust, he said, "I'm sorry," choked down his sobs and wiped his eyes. He said, "Sorry," again.

Still she said nothing. She stooped over a trunk and began to unlock it. He looked down with dazed familiarity upon the stooping figure, the wide shoulders and narrow waist; a few little lines creased the silk blouse at the belt; then there was the flat skirt, then the boyish legs. Artemis, he thought; something not sexed, untouchable; a lie, when he had by heart the detail of the body that had once belonged to him, when he could recall the response of that body; yet always it was there when he saw her now, the hint that she was not all flesh, but mixed with air and light, made in a substance beyond his hands.

She threw back the lid of the trunk; she turned to him. She was so pale that he could see the blue veins, and the line of the painted mouth was sharp. Even so, she could not be ugly.

"Any more?" she asked.

He said, "This can't be the end."

"It's got to be. How many times must I tell you? We've tried it twice. It doesn't work. It never will work. If you can only make the break in your mind, understand that there isn't a chance . . . then—don't you see?—you'll begin to settle for living without me. Don't hang on and clutch. It's gone. I've gone. Get it."

He stood there, watching her skin turn whiter. She had the thinnest of skins; he felt his fingers remembering the silken skin. Anger came back to help him.

"I'll break you," he said, "one day."

"You probably will. Watch those investments," she said, smiling crookedly. "Most of my capital's in, remember."

He wanted to hit her. Then he wanted to cry again. The telephone rang. She answered it, "Yes, all right. In a moment. I'm sorry, I was delayed. That is J. G.," she said to Van, "I have to go." She put on her jacket, leaning towards the looking-glass. Nanny came bustling in again.

"Could I start the unpacking for you, m'm?"

'Sure. Bless you; go ahead."

So it was all over, Van thought; not another second of her company. More dignified to leave now, but still he waited. The corridor was full of dodging strangers. She said "Good-bye" in the middle of it. The last he saw of her was her back departing through the door of Baron's suite, the fair head above the square black shoulders.

(iii)

"My daughter, the late Mrs. Valentine West," Baron said. Baron's family jokes did not vary, they were the clichés of a life-time; they could be distinguished sharply from his public words, his coarse or his agile phrases; they were stock, paterfamilias stuff, oddly out of date. She could remember his using this worn example when her mother was unpunctual.

Baron's guests were all men, with the exception of the pro-nounced young woman who was, Celia recalled, a night-club singer. She sat perched on the arm of Baron's chair. She was a long gold curtain of hair, a mouth, two authentically American breasts that looked as though shaped out of durable plastic, and two honey-coloured legs carefully arranged as an advertisement for nylons. From time to time Baron patted her thigh, absently, with the gesture of one patting a dog, and went on talking to the men. There were only seven men but they felt and sounded like fifteen. Each of the four who circled Baron showed the tendency of the American business man, after drinking, to fling his arm about his neighbour and cuddle him affectionately. Celia did not know their names.

She knew the other three. The tall monkish person drinking ginger-ale was Grant Parker. Van was his wife's nephew. He was a man of power. He owned the trio of publications, *Point*, *Steer* and *Democrat*. He looked lankier than ever because he was standing next to Hugh McLeod, the tiny, angry Socialist M.P. for South Kent, an improbable friend for Baron. Drooping at his ease beside these two was Gerald Lynn, who had gone on being a beautiful tired young man for years. He was an enormously successful journalist. He wrote with a pen dipped in sugar and talked with a corrosive cattiness.

"Celia, darling," said Gerald Lynn.

"Celia, darling," said Hugh McLeod.

"Celia, darling," said Grant Parker, sonorously mocking the other two. His voice was slow and melancholy, his eyes kind. He liked her and he did not like Van. He said, "I resent having to say good-bye to you. I have no reservations about saying good-bye to Baron. In fact, when I heard I was invited to his farewell party, I had my secretary telegraph 'Sympathise in every way with object of party. Will be there.' " He did not smile. But the look that he sent towards Baron was affectionate.

She too looked at Baron; the usual similes came up; Puck and Napoleon; Priapus and Puritan; they mingled in the neat little shape with the big head, the light eyes, the mobile mouth.

All Baron's supplementary ingredients were here; it was like looking at a whole platter served complete with vegetables, sauce, rolls and beverage. The trimmings were the chorus about him, the stewards on duty by the bottles, the dark flat-faced young secretary and the ringing telephone; the lines of telegrams laid out on the writing-table, the manila envelopes marked By Hand; Urgent; the recording-machine of newest make, and, of course, the girl.

Celia was aware of his uneasy glances in her direction while she talked to Grant Parker. She supposed that she must look as ill as she felt. It exasperated Baron when she looked ill. And the effect of Van was always the same, this hollow tremor inside, this sickness of spent anger. She could disguise any emotion in the cause of good behaviour, but she could not disguise the colour of her skin. A second glass of champagne would help, she said to herself, counting the times when she had stood in new company, as ill as this, with the echoes of Van sounding and the obligation to recover quickly, to tell nothing, show nothing.

"You're not going for long, I hope," Grant Parker said.

"Well, yes. I'm taking Terry."

He raised his eyebrows. Across his bony, thoughtful face she saw the doubts passing.

He hesitated again before he said, "You'll come back to America? Always you seem to me much more an American than an Englishwoman."

"Thank you."

"You take it as a compliment?"

"How d'you expect me to take it? Slap your face?"

He laughed.

"I'll come back," she said, "sometime."

"If I can help you in any way, Celia, I'd like to."

Baron interrupted. "Celia, I want you to meet Joe Cushman and Bob Shirley. Forgive me, Grant," He did this, she knew, because he saw that she was talking to the only person of importance in the room and that Grant Parker was enjoying her company.

"Going home for a visit to your family, I hear," said Cushman. That must be the way that Baron had decided to sell it. She wondered why he bothered to say anything at all. To go out of his way to protect the shiny Mr. Cushman and the plump Mr.

Shirley from the knowledge that she had left her husband. But that was Baron's trick. He could not leave things alone. He had to shape a situation so that Joe Cushman and Bob Shirley would feel comfortable with it. More, he himself would not feel comfortable until he had accounted for the speculations of every Cushman and every Shirley within earshot.

"How long have you been living over here now?" Shirley asked.

"Three years and a half, this time—I was here for two years before the war."

"You and your husband were in England all through the war, I understand," said Cushman. Maybe Baron had sold that story too; maybe they assumed it. It was easier to say "Yes." "Indeed," she said to herself, "what is the alternative to 'Yes'? I cannot reply, 'My husband, whom I left flat here in '39, got himself sent to England in '44; and wore me down until, misguidedly, I agreed to try all over again; Terry being the result of the misguided efforts." She did not want to say these things, she merely resented the necessity to lie. It was a relief to be haled away from Cushman and Shirley by Gerald Lynn.

"Darling, I cannot *tell* you what pleasure it gives me to know that we are travelling together. Fun of every *lôuche* variety will be had," said Gerald. Seen at close range, the golden limpidity of his youth had cracked and dried. The Praxitelean head had lost most of its hair; the cherub face was dissipated; the athletic waistline had thickened. She did not think that he cared. He cared for nothing and nobody; he sailed on; he was found in all the places where the rich, the titled and the people with names were found. She was fond of him, because he was all of a piece; all façade, no secrets nor shadows.

"Come and play with me. Over by the champagne, I insist. Tell me, dear," his voice became crisper, more paternal, "is it true that you're leaving Van?"

"Well, yes it is, but J. G. appears to have told some of those red shiny ones that it isn't. So keep your voice down."

"I can't *think* why he doesn't want everybody to know. I'd be *delighted*——"

"J. G. likes to keep the family troubles looking pretty."

"Common, I call that," said Gerald. "Department of What Will the Neighbours Say."

"On the other hand, no need to speak at all. I've no sympathy with the hair-shirt liar."

"Darling, *what* is a hair-shirt liar?"

"The over-truthful; the exaggerator. The hammer-and-nails insister. . . . You know the school: the one who *has* to tell; handing out the inside story to all, as if he were selling pamphlets on the steps of a church—it's a compulsion-neurosis."

Grant Parker loped up to them with the little red-haired McLeod beside him. "We are talking about the truth," Gerald said, "it goes in with fresh air and scenery; there you have my three *least* favourite things."

"The only truth that matters," said McLeod furiously, "is to be oneself."

"Liars have the most fun," said Parker and did not elaborate.

"Gold-spoon liars have fun," Celia said, thinking of Van, the braggart, the weaver of pretty stories; you could be as lightly impatient of his lie as of a tune that irritated you; tapping your fingers, waiting for the tune to end.

"Hair-shirt liars, according to Celia, tell the truth so often that it becomes a lie."

"Count me a hair-shirt liar, then," snapped McLeod and turned on his heel while Gerald murmured, "Very tiring, all that integrity."

The echoes of "All visitors ashore!" had died; now a ship's officer moved in apologetically, "I'm sorry, Sir James, but your visitors have just three minutes left."

Grant Parker took Celia's hand. He said, "Take care of yourself. And don't forget."

They were all out of the door now. Gerald Lynn had whisked himself away to send a cable; McLeod was gone. The girl was the last to leave; Baron was blowing kisses; her hand fluttered to her lips and back. Each stating, Celia thought, what each had received from the other, signing off the small obligation as though in figures.

Then there were only the stewards, straightening the chairs, emptying ash-trays, collecting glasses; the secretary busy with the latest telegrams; Baron, standing straddled, hands in pockets, gazing at her. Always, with her, he contrived to look as though he were waiting for an apology, even when there was none to be made.

"I'm sorry I was late," she said at once. "May I have another glass of champagne?"

"What?" He had heard, but it was his trick to say "What?" giving himself time to spy around any question. "Oh, yes, of course you can," he gave the permission as though she had asked for an outrageous privilege. He watched her, his large light eyes steely and cold, "Are you all right, Celia?"

"Certainly I'm all right."

"I thought you looked very white when you first came in." The badgered, accusing note in the voice was one that she had heard over years.

"Did I? I'm tired. Late last night and a morning of packing and fussing. Thanks," she said to the steward, drank off the glass and replaced it on the tray.

"I saw that you and Grant Parker had a lot to say to each other," said Baron. His uneasy curiosity was palpable as steam. He wanted to know if they had talked of Van.

"I like Grant," she said. "Case of millionaire's serenity. Rare. Shouldn't be rare. Ulcers are more usual and less attractive."

"I wasn't expecting him to turn up," said Baron.

"Why not?"

"I done him wrong," Baron said with an impish grin. "I done poor Parker wrong." He whistled "Frankie and Johnny". He plumped down on the sofa with a flourish of his legs. He smiled at her trustingly. These moods came suddenly upon him, they made for relaxation, Celia thought, as quiet intervals in an air-raid. She sat down and lit a cigarette.

"How did you do him wrong?"

"I bought Levitt," said Baron.

"Levitt? *The* Levitt? The cartoonist? You didn't!" She

was diverted into admiration. "Mean Levitt won't be drawing for *Point* and *Steer* any more? Well, that's a master-stroke. Did you bankrupt yourself in the process?"

"I didn't have to. He wanted to come."

"Why?"

"God knows," said Baron, still simple. There could, in other moods, have been a blast of pained pronunciamento. "Perhaps I'll discover tonight; he's on board."

"Kidnapped."

"And glad to be. I think you'll like him; I haven't made up my mind about him yet."

"Why d'you think I will?"

Baron said, "What? Oh, your kind of slick young man; looks like the Knave of Spades."

"And why are you doubtful?"

"What? . . . Well, I haven't got the hang of him yet. Might be just a smart-alec. He's a Californian."

"These," said Celia, "are, as I recall, large, simple and pleased with themselves."

"Levitt ain't simple," said Baron. "Yes, Mather?" The dark, flat-faced secretary had been hovering for some minutes; it was Baron's habit to keep him hovering.

"I thought you would wish to have this, sir. I know you were expecting it." His face became even flatter, the corners of his little mouth more carefully creased.

Baron took the cable, read it, cried sharply, "Oh, God!" and threw it down. He turned to Celia, pressing a hand on each of his cheeks, as though trying to hold his face together.

"It's from Anthony," he said. "Randolph's gone. In his sleep this morning."

The engines of the ship had begun to beat. Now there were the long blasts of the siren and they moved from the dockside. Baron sat still, hiding his face in his hands.

"I shall laugh aloud if I'm not careful," Celia thought.

"It can't be that much of a shock to you," she said mildly. "It's been dragging on for months."

He muttered, "Poor Anthony . . . poor Anthony."

"I cannot think," said Celia, "that it's anything but a relief to Anthony."

Baron took his hands away from his face; she saw no tears in his eyes.

"A *relief*? To lose his father?"

"Well, of course. Why not? Randolph has been dying, very slowly and painlessly, since December."

"My old friend," Baron murmured. He took a monogrammed handkerchief from his pocket.

"Oh, come off it," said Celia, surprised by the vulgarity of her own phrase, "you were never close friends and you hadn't a thing in common."

Deliberately she had invited the cold stare, the setting of the face into sullen slopes of anger. His hands trembled. He looked at her with undisguised hate.

"You will leave me," he said, "at once. And please don't return until I send for you. I would not have thought that even you could be so cruel."

"I want a bath, anyway," she said. "Will you be coming down to dinner or dining here?" He did not answer; he had covered his face again.

She said to herself, walking back to her stateroom, "Some of his acts—say sixty per cent of the hundred-and-one masks in his repertoire—are identifiable. This one beats me. No matter who dies, J. G. is bereaved. Death is an affront; death is unfair. Even when it hits Randolph Carey at the age of seventy-five.

"Why play it in front of me? Why not wait till I left and then do it for Mather? 'My old friend' . . . 'Randolph's gone' . . ." She shook her head; it was a long time since she had given up trying to read Baron.

Though she had assessed him, washed her hands of him and cut free from him—his pervasive quality remained. She still found it a relief to be out of any room where he was.

It was a relief now to be back in her own territory, to find the evidences of Nanny's faithfully chaotic unpacking and one of Nanny's frequent legacies, a page torn from the *Tatler*, marked with pencil crosses and stuck in the frame of the mirror. Nanny always read the *Tatlers*; they were sent from England regularly.

It was a full-page photograph. Two people stood posed beside a fountain. The woman was Catherine de Lille. Rarely photographed in these days, she contrived to look mysterious, far younger than her years; she was still startlingly beautiful, dark, nunlike, more statuesque than the figure on the fountain. The tall young man with the face of a frivolous Rupert Brooke was Celia's brother Tobias.

Celia read the caption. "In her garden at Senlis, Madame de Lille talks to Mr. Tobias Baron. Catherine de Lille's newest comedy, running successfully in Paris, will be seen on the London stage next month."

Celia smiled, frowned, thought it over. The legend of Catherine de Lille was like the thousand-and-one-nights, glamour that had become a cliché. The truth behind the legend was curious. That a woman who had, since her first youth, been stamped as a beauty, an English society beauty with the obvious destiny of these, should side-step the destiny was not remarkable. She might have been expected to retire, after two marriages, from the silly scene into a fake solitude, as palatable to the gossip-writers as Deauville or Venice; some publicised hermitage where she practised Yoga and painted bad pictures.

She had retired, but not like that.

She lived in a walled castle with a French husband years older than herself. She wrote novels and plays in two languages. She was classically talented. It might have been said of her, as of George Moore, that she had turned herself into a genius by taking pains. And it was not, in the eyes of the professional world, fair. Of her worth as a writer there could be no argument.

Of Catherine's own worth there was endless argument. "The reputation," Celia thought, "is that of a Circe, a snatcher; a collector of souls. Nothing could be further from the truth."

The last time that she had seen Catherine was at the end of the war when Van was with Shaef in Paris and they had driven out to Senlis to stay with the de Lilles. Celia remembered the shabby, limping deserter whom the servants had turned away from the kitchen door; and how Catherine had gone down after him towards the trees and the lake, brought him back, given him food. She, Celia, had been in the third month of her pregnancy. She remembered Catherine crossing the crowded room, the room that glittered with the faces, the uniforms, of that Paris and that year; saying to her, "You're tired, aren't you? Wouldn't you like to cut all this nonsense and have your dinner in bed?" She remembered the eager, vociferous little German-Jewish refugee, how bored the rest of the party had been with his monologues, how courteously Catherine had listened to him. She remembered the awful gay young woman who played the piano and sang her own embarrassing songs about sex; how Catherine alone had not joined in the savage comments afterwards.

She had got to them in her mind when Nanny came from their adjoining stateroom.

"He's half asleep already, m'm. Did you want to say goodnight?"

"Yes. I was looking at this."

"Beautiful, isn't she, still?" Nanny said grudgingly. "Lifted, I suppose. And so good of Mr. Toby. Hasn't he grown up? I wonder how they met. Of course, his being interested in the stage, and all. Still . . ." she clicked with her tongue. "I wonder what Sir James'll have to say, I really do."

"He ought to be pleased. She's a very great person, Catherine de Lille."

Nanny sniffed. "Must be fifty-five, at least. Let me see, now." She possessed an unhesitating acquaintance with the deviations of the peerage. "Married Lord Falchon in '22; and she wasn't young, I mean; we all expected her to marry before that. . . . The divorce was in '27, I think . . . married Sir Guy Blake in '29; sad, that was. Then she lived in Paris, of course; we didn't hear so much. . . . This Frenchman came along in '37. Oh, she's over fifty, m'm . . ."

"The son was at school with Tobias," Celia said, "Lionel Falchon, nice strenuous little boy."

Nanny clicked again. She had begun to fold up clothes in the wrong creases.

"All I can say is I'd rather see Mr. Toby in a picture with somebody his own age."

Celia gave it up. She said, "Sir Randolph's dead, by the way. J. G. got a cable from Anthony."

"Oh *dea*ᵣ!"

"Darling, he's been as good as dead for months."

"So straight, he was." Nanny sighed. "It's things *changing*, m'm; that's always sad." It was a more valid plaint than Baron's, Celia thought. She hugged Nanny, who at once became brisk. "Now, what do you want to wear? Nobody dresses up the first night, do they?"

"Nor any night, as far as I'm concerned. Black dress; not that one; don't bother. Just turn on the bath while I say good-night to Terry."

The next stateroom had acquired the nursery look, with toys and woollens, with Nanny's tea-kettle. Terry lay, arrogant and unconscious, with one arm flung straight above his head. She stood looking down at him.

She still had Tobias on her mind. Absurd, perhaps, to leap so rapidly to a conclusion that was parallel with Nanny's. Something of Catherine de Lille's legend clung to the picture, to the look of the two of them by the fountain. "It would be natural for Toby, after all, to love that way for the first time. He's a romantic; out-of-date, I suppose, in this day and age. He never had a mother to remember; I was his mother for a little while."

She kissed Terry's forehead and left him. Nanny was still unpacking. She had found the panel of photographs in their folding leather case and set them on the dressing-table.

"Your bath's ready, m'm."

"Thank you." Celia loitered; she sat down at the dressing-table and stared at the photographs. The first was of Terry, on the beach at Martha's Vineyard, with the sea behind him, half-naked in the sun. The next was Tobias, astride the terrace wall at Carlington. It was taken in a strong light, so that his hair looked white rather than red; there was beauty in the line of his bare throat and the shape of his skull. He was grinning at the world. "He looks exceptionally tall," Celia thought. "Funny for

Baron to father such long thin children." After Tobias there was her sister Liz; this photograph also taken at Carlington; Liz on the lawn. All the hack words went for Liz, Celia said to herself: dryad, flower, nymph and the rest. The camera had caught alike her grace and her profound melancholy. Both pictures were new; Baron had brought them with him to New York; looking for changes in Liz and Toby since her flying visit home last year, Celia saw only that their personalities were accentuated; that Toby looked yet more gaily defiant, Liz yet more tragic and afraid.

Anthony Carey's face stared at her from the last frame. Anthony was static and stable. When she was much younger, Anthony had reminded her of the stained glass St. Michael in the village church; a little too good and golden to be true. The Barons had made Anthony into a brother; or had he himself decided upon the rôle? It had happened too long ago for her to remember how it had happened. The Careys were their next-door neighbours; Anthony was an only son; Anthony was always in the house. Baron adored him.

At seventeen Celia had found him romantic; St. Michael was her first love. Now his good looks were as untroubling to the heart as a flat cornfield in the sun. He looked more like a squire than a sculptor. He was posed here beside a marble faun that he had made; the marble shape and the shape of Anthony had the same solid, well-proportioned strength. One of Baron's clichés in time of trouble was "Thank God for Anthony". Anthony had written this on the back of the snapshot before he sent it to her. ("Anthony can laugh at J. G. without malice. Fair enough; he's safe; he isn't a Baron; he has the luck to be a nice simple Carey.")

"Your bath's getting cold."

"Never mind." She rose and stood still, realising the steady movement of the ship down river. "We're away," she said.

Nanny looked at her carefully. "Four years' assault upon the nerve-ends finished. Hard to believe," Celia said.

"I hope you'll get some rest; not racket about till all hours.

Don't know why he had to come to the boat and upset us all like that, I really don't, m'm."

"Be fair. . . . Nobody was upset except Mr. Valentine West."

"He upsets you; it's always the same."

"Well, it won't be the same any more."

"And I don't know that it's a good idea, travelling with your father, either. . . . He makes you so jumpy. . . . And it'll be the same at Carlington, you see. How long do you suppose it'll be before we have some place of our own again?"

"Don't know, darling. As soon as I can fix."

"Well, you don't want to be thinking about fixing anything now; you've had quite enough on your mind lately. I'm afraid you'll have to put some more hot in that bath. Good-night, m'm."

(iv)

Levitt looked at his reflection in the glass. This was not one of the quick, habitual glances that he found it hard to forgo; the insecure necessity to keep an eye on himself. This was a deliberate study. As careful of his appearance as a girl meeting a lover, he had returned to his cabin, to comb his hair, straighten his tie, flick the clothes-brush over his jacket.

The man in the glass impressed him only moderately. He was tall and hard-muscled; a tailor's advertisement could use the mirror-smooth dark hair, the flash of eyes and teeth, the pointed nose, the neatly-modelled chin. Nothing displeased him in the easy attitude of the body, wearing its three-hundred-dollar suit, a thin English tweed with a red line running through the grey. But he saw Levitt looking at him out of the eyes; he saw the fox in the face.

This, he argued, was not just self-dissatisfaction; this was his talent. No matter whose the face, if there were a flaw to be found, his eyes could find it, and his pencil trap it on paper. He glanced at the menu that he had carried down with him from the dining-room. There were four pencil sketches on the back of the menu. Each had the neat, cruel twist: the American matron; her old tortoise of a husband; the sprawling, pretty, damply-eager girl at the next table; and the wine-steward with the gangster's jowl. He had made them his, made them themselves, made them ugly.

It was the thing that he could do.

It was not enough.

Why not? Why quarrel with it, at this moment of all moments? Simply because he had seen the hint of the fox?

"Not quite. I would like to make something different; something straight; something that isn't ugly. Beautiful, then? Important, at least; important so that I was remembered for it." He folded the menu card and put it in his pocket. He pulled down his waistcoat, gave the final twitch to his tie and went out.

The ship had a magic for him; his first Transatlantic liner. He liked her luxury. He went by glass showcases that held ties, scarves and sweaters, the expensive things that appealed to him. The orchestra was playing in the main lounge and he could see couples dancing there. He went the other way, through swing-doors into the smoking-room. Here there was cloudy, concealed lighting; scarlet leather chairs, chromium ash-trays. Sitting in the chair facing the door, alone, was a woman whom he had seen before.

"A week ago, at the Pavillon," Levitt thought; "odd, that she should be here." He had classified her as one of Them. She was dining, he remembered, with a man of dark, sorrowful looks; a thwarted lover.

This woman was not, within the conventional meaning, beautiful. She was arresting, because of her fairness, because of certain curling lines; because she made a dazzle of white and gold and blue. Was he staring? She smiled at him and raised her hand. He came on, to stand before her.

"Mr. Levitt? I'm Celia West, J. G.'s daughter."

"How do you do."

"You were at Henri Soulé's one night last week, weren't you?"

"Yes. It's odd," he said, "isn't it?"

"Can't see why it's odd," she said. "Only two alternatives after all. Even chances. We could have seen each other before or not. I didn't know who you were that time, either."

"How did you know this time?"

"From J. G.'s description." He would have liked to hear it. She said, "Do sit down, if you'd care to. He isn't coming."

"Isn't coming?"

"No. He asks you to excuse him. He's had a bereavement."

"I'm so sorry."

"You needn't be. Nor need my father. Or not quite as sorry as he is being. What will you have to drink?"

"You'll have a drink with me, please," said Levitt, not sure whether he liked or disliked her. She was undoubtedly They; in the calm manner, in the light, assured abruptness of the voice. He knew the name of the designer who had made her dress, the name of the jeweller who had made the one ring, the two diamond and ruby clips on the collar.

"I am," said Celia West, "deeply devoted to you. You're the only reason I ever buy *Point* and *Steer*."

"Bless you," he said, as he had learned to say.

"Just before my father was bereaved, he was telling me how he bought you from Grant Parker."

"Isn't this bereavement really serious?"

"No. An old Field-Marshal with whom J. G. found the greatest difficulty in maintaining ten minutes' conversation has died in his sleep after being comfortably unconscious for weeks. He's been our neighbour for fifty years, so J. G. feels—hell," she said lazily, "I don't know what he feels. You'll find out." She smiled crookedly. "At least I imagine you will. I imagine you'll join the chorus of J. G.'s young men."

"What does that mean?"

"They come for week-ends," said Celia West. "Their function is to say Yes."

"Hate your father?" he asked.

"Hate him," she said lightly; "he hates me, too. Makes it easy."

"Why do you travel with him?"

"First time I ever did since I grew up. The dates fitted, that's all. What are you drawing?"

"You."

She stiffened. "Must you?"

"Why not?" said Levitt, his pencil poised above the menu card.

"I don't know why not. Except that it makes me shy."

"You? Shy? Now I've heard everything."

She said, half-angrily, "I tell you, I am shy."

He looked at her. "Perhaps you are; inside."

"It isn't," said Celia West, "an attractive enough quality to be worn on the outside."

"This is coming all wrong," said Levitt, scribbling over the sketch. "What's my technique with Sir James now? Do I write a note saying I'm sorry?"

"Yes, if you want to suck up," she said indifferently.

"Does everybody suck up to him?"

"Sure."

"Tell me why he asked me to meet him here—not to come to his suite."

She looked at him quickly; the light, brilliant eyes narrowed at the corners.

"That's simple. He likes to be seen. He'll give a splashy dinner party soon. It won't be in the suite, but at the most visible table in the dining-room. J. G. thinks it only fair to give the passengers a view of him now and again."

"Come and dance," Levitt said. "Before you get to making a wax image of papa and sending the steward for pins."

She laughed and looked at him charitably.

"Do I want to dance?" she said, as though to herself.

"Don't you like to dance?"

"Sometimes. But I find it an embarrassing sport, particularly to watch."

"You don't have to watch."

"Can I trust you not to do all those shaming American things, like letting go hands and hopping up and down in front of me and walking off and stamping and smiling?"

He said, "You can. I'll be as sinuously correct as I know how. And I dance pretty, they tell me."

When she rose, she was almost as tall as he. He walked beside her, to meet the music.

(v)

"This sense of the curtain going up," Celia said to herself, "is one that I mistrust. I haven't known it in a long time, but I know the signs. One is the deceptive placidity; the ripple; the time-to-burn feeling. And another is the knowledge of being completely oneself, light-hearted, whole-hearted and safe."

(A storm warning made of calm weather? A point at which one would look back, saying, "That was the last time I was alone"?) "Better than anything else," she thought, "I like being alone."

She looked at him beside her; they were walking round the promenade deck.

"Oh, what are you afraid of?" she said to herself. "It is only that he makes you laugh and that he is cut to the pattern of looks that you inevitably choose. It is still Van's pattern of looks, let us face it. J. G.'s Knave of Spades. But a little tougher; something of the gangster to fill out the pattern."

"You're a Californian?"

"How d'you know?"

"J. G. told me."

"I was afraid it might show," said Levitt.

"But don't you like being a Californian? All the Californians I know like being Californians better than anything."

He said, "I was born with the wrong slant. I couldn't sob at the sight of the Sierras. I didn't find San Francisco the original from which Paradise was ineffectively copied."

"Unusual," Celia murmured.

"So my father hated my guts. Being a local business man of some size, and unable to speak of a cable-car without a choke in his voice."

"I know the kind. What happened?"

"I quit. The only interest in the story is that it's the perfect American cliché. He wanted me to take over the business; I wanted to be an artist. I ran away; thumbed my way East. It's got everything, hasn't it? I even changed my name. Got a job in a colour shop and worked my way through college. I was assistant art instructor at Columbia when war broke out—that's all."

"What's your real name?"

"Dangerfield—Ray Dangerfield."

"Why did you choose Levitt?"

"Worst pun I ever made. It was born of two beers and saying, to the image of my father, 'Take it or leave it'."

She thought, "No reason why it shouldn't be true. No reason why I should care if you are lying. What is it about you that threatens me and disturbs me? I should be proof by now against the slick façade, the tough sparkle, the gentleman who lopes like a smooth, dark hound. You're a state of mind rather than a man."

He had halted; he was watching her.

"Did you tell J. G. all that?" she said to the questioning look.

"Some of it. Why?"

"I wondered if he disapproved. He's a family-worshipper, Chinese style. One of J. G.'s punctual clichés—which you'll soon begin to know and love, I hope—is 'I don't know where I'd have been without my mother and father.' Tobias nearly got his skull cracked once for asking whether anybody could know where they'd have been without their mother and father."

Levitt laughed; it was an endearing laugh.

"Who's Tobias?"

"My young brother; half-brother, really. J. G. married a second time. Bright little girl, she died when Liz was a baby."

"Tough," Levitt said. "What did she die of?"

"Just of being married to J. G."

"And your mother?"

"She had the sense to leave him; but she died afterwards."

She wondered if her flippant tone shocked him. He was silent.

"Let us walk round the top deck once," she said to him. "Then I want to go to bed."

She forgot him for a moment in the sudden familiar drama of the night at sea; the lit smokestack, the curved shadows of the lifeboats, the dark above them and around them and below. The wind was strong.

"Of course you realise," she said, "that on the subject of my father I am not only biased but badly behaved. I can't discuss him without saying something awful."

"You're too honest," he said irritably. "I could tell you a lot about you if you cared to hear it."

"I wouldn't."

"Why are you shy?" he asked, putting his hand on her arm.

She thought about it. "Comes, I suppose, of having made a more complete mess of my life than most people manage to do by the time they're twenty-nine. Nobody else's fault; all my own work. Good-night. I'm going to bed."

"May I see you as far as the subway?"

She laughed, "All right."

They came to her door. "Good-night," he said. "Do I see you tomorrow?"

"I imagine so." That sounded brusque, ill-mannered; she added, "Yes, please." He kissed his hand to her.

"I want nothing new in my life, nothing," she said to herself as the door shut. The dark face, pointed with laughter, was still there, lightly intruding upon her wish to be alone.

(vi)

Levitt, waking gradually, watched the curtains drift inward away from the porthole, stand steady and fall slowly back. On the dressing-table his gold Cartier pencil made a maddening journey, as it rolled from one side to the other, rattled, and returned. The creakings all around the cabin were loud. He kneeled on his berth, watching the pattern of the heavy grey swell, looking away across the ridges to a misted horizon. "Ominous weather," said Levitt to Levitt. He lay down. He was still sleepy. Celia West had kept him awake.

"She's a disturber of the peace all right, all right. And how she hates the old man. I *could* envisage a time when I'd have to choose between father and daughter. Expensive choice.

"It is good fun, though, it always is good fun; the best fun. Like a light at the corner of the eye, or a smile inside: the beginning. And the danger is part of the fun. And the chances, I ask myself? The thing that I cannot put into words, the thing that is the tiger and the Dark Tower . . . ?

"It wouldn't be peaceful, ever. We're alike. Or is that the deception that the mind always practises when there's a physical wave-length operating? I could . . . though unwillingly . . . trust her," he decided. "She doesn't trust me. She was on to Mr. Ray Dangerfield of San Francisco.

"Perhaps the change of name was a little too much. Don't know what made me think of that one."

A far echo of his mother's voice reached him, "Harry Levitt, you know there's not a word of truth in all that; not a word; you just make them up as you go along."

There was a knock on the door—a dark flat-faced young man in a blue suit said, "Good-morning, Mr. Levitt. Sir James asked me to thank you for your note. He hopes to see you at twelve o'clock . . . would you come along to the suite? 3b on A deck."

(vii)

Baron was enjoying himself. He sat at the centre table with the relevant papers spread out before him. From time to time his fingers played a little tune on the table, as though it were a piano. In two chairs facing him were Hugh McLeod, the small red-headed firecracker, and the mischievous Gerald Lynn. They always fought and he was about to use them as a team. The spectacle of two smaller men than he, at logger-heads with each other and subservient to him, was an eternal diversion. And he liked rough weather; one could feel the ship this morning. At this rate, she would soon be rolling heavily.

"I want you two to get together on this," he said in his most benign voice. "You know all about it, Hugh. I'll just—to employ the repulsive army phrase—put Gerald in the picture. You know Glane, Gerald?"

The face of the dissipated angel went blank.

"Glane? No, dear, who is he?"

McLeod gave a raucous snort of laughter.

"*Who is he?* That's wonderful."

"It is—or rather it was—my native village," said Baron, grinning—"tiny place on the Kent-Sussex border; within the bounds of Hugh's constituency, God help it."

"Baron dear, how *could* it be your native village? Anyway," Gerald protested, "the term native village brings a depressing picture of straw huts, witch doctors and black women with no brassières. But quite apart from that, you were born in a Rochester slum, you never *stop* telling me so."

Baron said, "Ah, but my father came from Glane."

"And," Hugh snarled at Gerald, "it happened to be one of the most perfect villages in the English countryside until eight flying-bombs in succession destroyed it. I suppose you remember the flying-bombs?"

"No, darling. Mercifully I was with the Navy."

"Oh, for God's sake," Hugh snapped.

"Gentlemen, gentlemen," Baron murmured. "Here's how it is, Gerald. Hugh has an interest in rebuilding Glane for two reasons: one, it's in his territory; two, he's an architect and a town-planning expert."

"I'm glad you told him," said Hugh, "he is probably under the impression that my forte's fancy-needlework."

"I know all about your depressing town plans, Hugh. That looks like some of them on J. G.'s table."

"Gerald," said Baron, "don't be an ass. Listen to me. I've got an interest here. Glane is on my home pitch, just a mile or two from Carlington; it was very dear to me. What I'm organising,

via the *Sun* and the *Flash*, of course, is a fund for its restoration.
My own contribution will be anonymous."

"Oh, Baron—how can you bear that? But go on. Do you
want me to write a great stirring piece about its rising from the
ashes?"

"I intend to keep you on the job a little longer than that,"
said Baron. "The point being that we can't hope to have the
work completed under two years. All that time, we're going to
need public interest and public money. What I want is to
appoint you as Glane's—shall we say, guardian in the Press? Or
shall we call you Special Correspondent for Glane?"

"Either title suits me and both make me equally sick," said
Gerald, with his most charming smile. Baron knew the act.
Gerald would do the job well and he could not say no. Though he
wrote for the rival newspapers, refusing to sign an exclusive
contract, Baron paid him a retaining-fee, under which he must
write twelve articles a year.

"Come here, Gerald, take a look at this drawing." Gerald's
head with the thin gold hair bent over the table, close to Baron's
shoulder. "That's rather pretty," he said, sounding surprised.

"That's the finished product, we hope."

"Clever little man, Hugh, aren't you, really? . . . Oh, Baron,
it's useless to show me the plan; I'm allergic to plans; they only
muddle me in detective stories. . . . What photographs are
these? Oh, I see. Before the blitz and after; just like a permanent wave advertisement in reverse. . . . It *was* enchanting,
wasn't it? Of course *any* village green makes me burst into loud,
rending sobs."

"Have you thought," Baron said, aiming his remark at Hugh,
who sat hunched in a mould of fury, "that we should have a
memorial on the green?"

"Eh? No, I haven't. What sort of memorial?"

"A flying-bomb in rose-coloured quartz," said Gerald.

"Shut your trap now," said Baron. "It's right, Hugh. And it
occurs to me that we could run a competition there. Invite
sculptors to submit designs; set up a committee under the R.B.S.
Make a big noise about it."

"M'm," said Hugh, grudgingly, "not a bad idea."

"Baron, you're quite sure," Gerald pleaded, "that you want me. Oughtn't you to use somebody more *rustic*? One of those men who signs himself 'Countryman' or 'Vole-Watcher'?"

"Allow me to know, will you?"

"Yes, dear, of course."

There was a knock on the door. Baron said, "Oh, come in, Levitt. Glad to see you. Have you three met? No . . ."

"No. . . . Ye-es," said Gerald Lynn, giving Levitt a long, awakening look, "yes, indeed. . . . Quite a while ago. How are you?" There was an overtone there, Baron observed. He wondered in what circumstances they had known each other. Levitt grinned at him artlessly, shook hands with Hugh, negotiated the tilting floor to a chair.

"You'll be interested in this, I think," Baron said, "though of course rebuilding's hardly in your line. I'd call yours demolition-work, hmm?" He still wasn't sure about Levitt; too well-dressed? Too brilliantined? Too sure of himself?

"That's shocking," Levitt said, looking at the picture of the bomb damage.

"Something you haven't experienced yet," said Hugh.

"I was there," said Levitt mildly, "for some of it."

"I meant something your *country* hadn't experienced yet," said Hugh with a twist of his lips. Baron watched Levitt for a reaction; none came; he smiled absently, still looking at the pictures.

"Well, but they have to *pay* for us, all the time—so much worse, I think," said Gerald. "But then I'm an old skinflint. My *pocket*, that's where it pinches."

"Where it pinches the Yanks, too," snapped Hugh—"or doesn't that go for your generation, Mr. Levitt?"

Levitt raised deliberately sleepy eyes. "Not sure I believe in generations. They always seem to me like Cross-Sections of Public Opinion; you can make them what you like."

"You'd agree that there's such a thing as history, perhaps?" McLeod's voice had acquired a menacing coo.

"Why, sure. But I think we're trying to turn it out too quick.

In my country at least. All the 'Do You Remember?' 'I Can Hear It Now' productions implore the American people to make a past with the same speed and the same methods that you'll find at Willow Run." He stood easily, swaying to the movement of the ship, looking down on Hugh. "Won't be long now," said Levitt, "before some sociologist brings out a book called *This Is What We Were Like Last Thursday.*"

There was such a thing as being too clever, "And if you're too clever," Baron thought, "I'll have to keep an eye on you, Mr. Levitt. See what I can sell you when we talk later; that's the first step." He nodded to himself. Hugh was collecting the papers and photographs from the table.

"Time for us to have a word about these before lunch," he said to Gerald. They went. Baron said lightly, "Fantastic fellow, Lynn. But a genius at his job. When did you two meet before?"

"California, I think," said Levitt; "can't quite remember."

(viii)

Levitt saw Baron differently today. The thing that he looked for in this face was a resemblance to Celia. At first he did not find it; he saw a genial mask and grey curling hair. Then he began to see where the likenesses were; small likenesses; he greeted them affectionately. The shape of the brows was the same; although Baron's eyebrows were thick little eaves and hers so fine that they were the merest shadows of those eaves, arching high above heavy lids. He thought that he had not noticed the heaviness of her eyelids until now, looking at Baron's that were so much heavier. When Baron smiled, he found the origin of the pagan, curling lines; and the pucker at the corner of the mouth. This also he had forgotten of Celia overnight, the laugh that made her mouth suddenly crooked. When Baron's mouth did that it was a parody, because these lips were thin and hers were full.

All likeness fled at the eyes. He remembered her eyes clearly, the light brilliant blue, the square shape. Baron's eyes were round and grey and cold. Even when he laughed there was little charity in them.

"Very grateful for your note," Baron was saying. "Great loss, Randolph Carey; a great gentleman. I hope when you come to Carlington you'll meet his son. Anthony Carey's almost one of the family. He's got extraordinary talent. This is his work." He picked up a photograph from the table. It was a marble head, Levitt observed; Baron himself, idealised, competent, not impressive. "Careys have all been practical men for generations; soldiers; farmers; then you get a boy with this gift. . . . Here he is. Isn't that a remarkable face?"

At first it seemed to Levitt wholly unremarkable; any handsome young Englishman in a movie, even to the pipe. Looking at it a second time, he saw that there was one cryptic shadow, between the lower lip and the chin; as though the lower lip pouted. It was a queer shadow. Its result was a dilution of the straight-featured, smiling frankness; it made Carey sensitive and thoughtful, less of a cricketing hero.

Baron's words flowed past his ears. "Wonderful war record, that boy. Dug out three men with his own hands after he himself had been wounded at Anzio. . . . Well, here's the Gallery. . . . I never travel without it. My son Tobias in flying kit. Too young for the war, of course, done his training since. . . . Elizabeth, my younger daughter . . ." This picture, Levitt thought, was like a statement of youth, transfixed and vulnerable. "Here's Carlington itself; modern, of course. The original house was burnt to the ground. Stands on a lip of the land above Romney Marsh. Know Romney Marsh? . . . Celia, with the dogs; Bunter's dead—Prince is still with us. . . ."

One hint at least, Levitt thought, he had failed to catch until now: the hint that Baron could be such a sweetly-spoken bore.

As though he himself realised it, Baron looked at his watch and said, "How I do run on. Meant to talk turkey with you. H'm. I said demolition-work, didn't I? Well, the first thing you've got to demolish for my public is a certain attitude towards U.S.A.; based on myths; dangerous myths. We'll discuss it later. I'm lunching with the Captain."

Taking it as dismissal, Levitt moved; again he swayed to the roll of the ship.

"Getting rough," Baron said; "d'you care?"

"No, pretty good sailor," Levitt said nonchalantly.

"Then come back at six, will you? We'll forge our plan of campaign. That is, if you aren't otherwise engaged. Don't expect to own you body and soul on this voyage. Personable young man like you." He smiled, a different smile; for the first time he looked gentle; even the eyes were kind.

"Thank you," Levitt said, "I'd like to come."

He recorded Baron's loving glance at the family photographs. "Odd," he thought. "Why should I feel sorry for him all of a sudden?"

The door opened and Celia walked in, leading a small fair boy by the hand. "Do we disturb you?" she asked. "Hello, Mr. Levitt. Terry wanted to say good morning to you, J. G. Hold tight, Terry, this is getting difficult."

Why it should surprise him to see her with a child, he did not know. Baron had turned into a beaming grandfather, a sort of Santa Claus; beside the intense solemnity of the child, the heartiness was exaggerated. The "Well, well, *well*," and "Good sailor, eh, boy?" and "Think I've got some chocolates here," and "How's this for fun?" continued until Celia said, "I have to return him to Nanny for his lunch," and Levitt left with her, holding Terry's other hand. The child stared up at him suspiciously, then smiled.

"Like you," Levitt said.

"He looked horribly like J. G. just now, I thought."

"Can you lunch with me?"

"I'm lunching with Gerald Lynn. Shall we have a drink first?"

"Fine."

After the nurse had reclaimed the boy, he said, abruptly, "My kid died. When he was two," and saw her look of straight sympathy. "Tough on you; and your wife."

"We got a divorce," said Levitt. "Maybe if the child had lived, it would have worked out."

"Doesn't solve it," she said. They climbed the slanting companionway.

"It might have; for her. She was restless and lively, damn sight too lively to live. That's why she killed herself."

"You've had plenty, haven't you? . . ." Celia said, turning to him as they reached the deck. She added, "Those things usually come out at midnight; not on a rough sea before lunch."

"Sorry. I can talk anywhere. I could talk metaphysics in a swimming-pool."

The bar was built out over the sun deck; a greyish glass bubble today; with the bottles and the glasses playing a tune in their racks, the steady repeating thrum like a deep raw note on a violin. They sat down at the nearest table. He studied her; there was the dazzle again, the flying look that he had forgotten, the expensive look that he had remembered; different jewels from the same designer making much of themselves on a grey flannel suit; the pale blue sweater was conveniently matched to the colour of her eyes. "She's damn' pleased with herself," he thought, "not smug, but self-sufficient. I can imagine wanting to hit her." She ordered brandy and ginger ale; when Levitt asked for plain ginger ale she raised an eyebrow.

"That's not in character."

"I never drink in the middle of the day."

"I don't think I *never* do anything," she said after a moment. "What was J. G. selling this morning?"

"Nothing much. He made a little speech about Sir Randolph and Anthony Carey; then he showed me all the family photographs."

"God, how gay. Hope he turned on some charm with it."

"I think so. And there was one minute when I found myself being sorry for him."

She made her mouth crooked. "You did? Unnecessary labour; sending a man to do a boy's work. . . . All that's taken care of already. Nobody can be as sorry for J. G. as he can. Damn it," she said, hitting the edge of the table, "I vowed I'd be good about him today."

"He's obviously an obsession with you," said Levitt.

"Not always. I lay awake and wondered about it last night. Just why I'd been so savage, to you. . . . To somebody I didn't know. It seemed unforgivable. One doesn't, whatever one thinks of one's parent, sell him down the river quite so comprehensively to a stranger."

"Just part of your aggressive honesty," Levitt said.

"But I dislike aggressive honesty; and anyway, that isn't the answer. Point is, I've been living with a strain for nearly four years; you always think you can take that sort indefinitely. Then the strain lets up and you find yourself so jittery that you can't behave. And jitters always bring you to your King Charles's Head. And he's mine. And I apologise."

"You don't have to. I'll get a line on him myself tonight. We meet at six to forge a plan of campaign."

"You look out."

"What does that mean?"

"There's a trick he plays," said Celia, narrowing her eyes and staring ahead of her. "And I'm not being mean this time, it's just his game. He'll try to sell you something you don't believe in. He'll know you don't believe in it. If you buckle, he'll go on using you—and despising you, for ever."

"Is this an established J. G. Baron integrity test?"

"Lord knows what it is. But don't let him win. Don't take it. See?"

She flashed her smile at him and went.

(ix)

No drinks before Baron, Levitt said to himself.

When he came in, the suite had a stripped-for-action look, the photographs were all laid flat; the flower vases stood in corners on the floor; the roll of the ship was now long and determined, so that the image of Baron swung through a slowly-changing perspective. In his coloured silk dressing-gown he sat cross-legged on the sofa. He held his slim ankles so that he appeared to be brandishing his small feet in their red leather slippers.

With the dressing-gown, the pose, the eyes watchfully slitted, he was the Chinese gnome again.

"And now," he said, "let's try to work out this thing together. It's not the *Flash* campaign. The *Flash* doesn't need a campaign. You simply cover the news. The *Flash* evening cartoon is the most succinct news-commentary in the country.

"You're the boss. I don't care which side you take a crack at. Just look around and go ahead. Don't choose a target that you think will please teacher. Teacher doesn't give a damn. You're a lone wolf on this job.

"The satirist's talent, as I see it, is to make order out of chaos. Take the most chaotic situation in sight—domestic or international, set it up in perspective; make it orderly and recognisable. Once it's orderly, it's astonishing. It rocks them back on their heels. Their reaction ought to be 'Good God! I've been thinking about this vaguely, but I never realised things were as bad as that—or as ludicrous as that or as unjust as that.' That's all." He let go of his ankles and waved his hands with a magician's flourish, then grasped the ankles again.

"All clear on the *Flash* now?"

Levitt nodded.

"The *Sun*," said Baron, "is a different kettle of fish. Biggest circulation of any Sunday newspaper in the country. More than two million ignorant people read it once a week. When I say ignorant, I mean ignorant. Particularly on the subject of America. Matches, you might say, American ignorance about Britain. We-ell, I despair of teaching the Americans. But I don't despair of teaching the British. Via you. Give yourself a drink, boy; don't wait for me."

"Not yet, thank you, sir." ("Damned if I will before you do. I need my wits.")

"Can you preach to 'em, d'you think?" Baron asked, cocking his head on one side.

"What d'you want me to preach?"

"I'll tell you. I'm playing with the idea of a column; an illustrated column. I want Bob Cole to write it. Know Cole?

"I know Cole," Levitt said without enthusiasm. Cole was

primarily a hater. American-born, he lived half the year in England. He was a back-number, he drank, and it was odd that Baron did not know this, should be ready to use him.

"Cole will underline you," Baron was saying, "and you'll underline Cole. I want you both to get the clichés out of the British mind. This kind of cliché; I jotted some of them down while I was waiting for you."

He read lightly, tonelessly:

"America is the rich uncle with the short sight and the kind heart.

"America's the place of no poverty and no class-distinction.

"America's the only country free from shibboleths and taboos, the great benign pond where every kind of fish can swim.

"America is Hollywood.

"America's a kind of non-Imperialist Department Store, full of luxury goods and home necessities, entirely concerned with its own trade.

"All Americans are superlatively well-educated for free.

"Here, take the list; add to it as you like." He stretched out his hand with the paper. Levitt rose, negotiated the tilting surface and took it.

"Add——?" he asked. "From what I hear in England?"

Baron shook his head. "No, boy, no. From your own angle on U.S. I know what you think about your country from the way you picture it in *Point* and *Steer*. Your angle's my angle."

Levitt said, "I'm not so sure of that, Sir James." The dip of the floor obliged him to stand still, with his hand on the foot of the sofa where Baron sat. Baron twisted quickly to look at him. The smile was gone. Levitt saw that he was looking down into the truth of Baron's face, the granite goblin's face, coldly still. Now he knew what it was to be afraid of Baron.

This quality of fear, he thought, was especially distilled; it wasn't like the fear in a foxhole, the fear in a Dakota with anti-aircraft guns below. It was the same terror that Grant Parker could launch across a desk in an office room. It was the slow, cold pressure of power; it was the dominator at work.

For a long moment he stood, holding on while the floor tilted, getting that look and the chill of that look, saying to himself, "You can't scare me. I've fought Parker and I'll fight you. Even if you cancel my contract tomorrow, I've got money in the bank—I've got a public. I've got what men will buy," and none of these arguments worked upon the fear. He hoped only that he kept his impudent smile intact.

"Not so sure, eh?" Baron said at last, in a sing-song voice. "Well, let's take these jottings of mine, shall we? Sit here; it's easier with this roll. Now, what comes first? America—the rich uncle with the short sight and the kind heart. I'll break that down.

"Reason why the British hate the Americans at the minute is because they think they ought to feel grateful. They're being fed and clothed and financed by U.S.A. Nothing makes for hate like a sense of obligation. Haven't you felt that yourself?"

He was too near now, Levitt thought; you could smell his eau-de-Cologne, see the wrinkles under the chin, the little hairs in the nostril. It was difficult to fight at such close range. He pressed himself farther back into the corner of the sofa. He had the sensation that he was welding the whole of Levitt together, making himself into an embodied retort.

"As it happens, I've never felt myself under an obligation," he said sunnily.

Baron's eyelids drooped lower. "Lucky fellow." He was beginning to drum on his knee with the fingers of his right hand. "Well, one day you will and you won't like it. The British don't like it. But it's a myth. Once they get the truth, the fact that America's only building up Europe, just as she went into the war, by way of enlightened self-interest, that myth's exploded. They'll lose the sense of obligation.

"Get it? I want it rammed home, preached, re-preached. That this is America's world, America's year. And the next war, when it comes, will be America's war. They must realise that what they've got on top of them isn't a kind rich uncle getting rid of his capital, but an army commander who knows what weapons he needs."

Levitt lit a cigarette, glanced at Baron over the flame of the lighter. "I don't get it. I don't get your line, I mean. Is it suck up to U.S. or tear down?"

"What?... Oh, both,"said Baron; his fingers ceased to tap his knee; he glanced down the list—"That covers the non-Imperialist Department Store; needs no clarifying. What comes next?" he asked silkily. "Oh, yes." Like Levitt, he pushed himself back into his corner of the sofa; he fluttered the list to and fro; his voice stayed silky. "No poverty or class-distinction? Draw the negro. Draw the slums. Draw the restricted hotels. Draw the 'socialites' in provincial cities. Kid the social register. That'll learn 'em.

"No shibboleths or taboos? Give them the communist witch-hunt; the dry campus; the banning of religious teaching in State schools; the gambling laws; the Legion of Decency; any and all of the hundred and one rules and regulations that make Americans the most eager conformists in the world.

"Hollywood?... Hollywood's easy. Slaughter it regularly. The one dead horse that's worth flogging.

"And for America as the land of free, full, perfect education, give them the facts, that there's not a grammar-school boy in England who isn't three grades ahead of his contemporary over there. That, thanks to the State schools, there's hardly a literate seventeen-year-old who goes to college. He can't put two grammatical sentences together because he's never heard of grammar. He can pronounce paranoia but he can't spell Pontius Pilate. His head's a jumble of unrelated courses. Education for U.S. isn't a part of life; it's courses. And just like American *table d'hôte*, it's got several courses too many; it's a studied effort at indigestion."

He looked pleased with himself. He glanced at the list again, crumpled it, then smoothed it. Levitt waited. "One more thing you can do, take a crack at their fears and phobias—from infected dish-pans to Reds. What makes the American such a crashing bore about communism, as you and I know, is his belief that it's a bug, out to bite him. He's more scared than angry.

"Come to think of it, the Americans have invented more

bogies than any other nation on earth. They don't believe in ghosts; they don't need to; they've conjured their own. They've invented allergy, schizophrenia, sinus, the slipped disc, the flying saucer and the fellow traveller. Their life is one long hygienic shudder down the back." He rolled the list into a ball, threw it into the air and caught it.

"That's my angle, Levitt. And it's yours too. You love America as I do; we can't chastise when we don't love. Eh? Truth's our target. Affectionate home-truths, eh?"

Levitt wondered whether the slight buzzing in his ears were due to the fact that he did not believe them. The last outrageous twist of the argument surprised him into spontaneity. He said, "Are you crazy?"

There was silence. Baron sat very still.

"Sorry. But I don't think along those lines," Levitt said, "I don't love my country that way; or hate it that way. I'm not a social reformer. When I draw for *Point* and *Steer* I draw the thing that amuses me, or burns me up. But they're chance ideas, that's all. As to debunking America with Bob Cole for the great British public, I couldn't do it."

"Why not?" Baron mouth slanted; this new voice was like a steel thread.

Levitt thought longingly of a drink, decided against it and lit another cigarette. It was an effort to keep Baron waiting, to choose his words, not to rush in on the bayonets and get the suicide done quickly.

"I happen to think Bob Cole's bad news. I wouldn't want to work with him. And he's a mistake for your public. He's just a tired, acid old drunk. Nobody listens to him any more."

The rolling had reached its peak, and he felt as though he were being lifted up the side of the wall. Baron stretched a hand to the lamp above his head. In the near light Levitt saw the lips especially thin, the eyes darkened. Carey's stone head of Baron had more life, more charity. The lighting of the lamp was the only comment that Baron made.

"Aside from that," Levitt said, "I couldn't set out to tear

down America *lovingly* to the British. It can't be done. It doesn't make sense. They wouldn't understand.

"And it wouldn't look pretty anyway. I can pan my family at home; not abroad."

"Misplaced patriotism?" The voice whistled through the teeth.

"Maybe. You've been amusingly savage. I can be amusingly savage, too. But your policy is cock-eyed here. You must see that the campaign, if it had any effect at all, would make the British hate the Americans more than ever."

Baron's eyes were almost shut; the only movement was that of the fingers, tapping again upon the knee.

"You can't employ a weary old wise-cracker and a caricaturist as preachers, you really can't," Levitt said, conscious now of a whole fleet of burned boats at his back. "And if what you want is to hold up U.S. to the hate and ridicule of your two million ignorant Britishers—and that looks to me to be what you want, well—fine—but you'll have to count me out, I'm afraid."

Baron's silence lasted a long time. Levitt heard the breaking noises, the muffled thunder outside; the flick of the curtains that fell away from the porthole, the subsiding clink of bottles, glasses, flower-vases. Some small object was slipping forward and back on the little table at Baron's elbow; it made the same irritating rattle that his gold pencil had made this morning. It was a fountain-pen; when it rolled on to the carpet, he bent to retrieve it, glad to have something to do.

"D'you know the time?" Baron said, suddenly.

"It's just on seven."

"You must excuse me. I have to get dressed." He nodded, unsmiling, and rose. Moving neatly to the rise and fall of the ship, the small figure in the coloured dressing-gown feathered away.

In the corridor, Levitt stood still. He drew a long breath. He was not certain, as he went towards the bar, that he had in fact said those things to Baron; nor, if he had said them, how true or right they were. He was another person now that he was outside the door.

(x)

While he dictated, Baron walked. At intervals he stood still
and flung out his arms. Though for all other dictation he used
the recording machine, he found it impossible while composing a
leader. A smooth flow of words depended upon the smooth
pacing; a peak of oratory demanded the halt, the outflung arms,
the gesture of a priest at prayer. Now he made it, facing the blue
porthole, the sunshine, the calm sea.

"There is more to the project of rebuilding Glane than the
raising of a new and beautiful monument upon the crumbled
ruins of the old. It is, we believe, an act of faith in England
herself; a gesture of courage, a gesture of belief in the future.

"End copy. Mather, you can type that afterwards. I want the
names for tonight. Damn it, why do I give parties? You tell
me."

He sat down; he played his little tattoo on the edge of the
table. He liked to manipulate the grins of Mather; men like this,
low down on the ladder, enjoyed coarseness from those at the
top. Always, Baron made sure that they got it.

"Let's look: on my left, Lady Erndle. Always think of a
couple of andirons going to bed when I look at her and Joe
Erndle. . . . On my right, Madame de Frassin de Vièl. Despite
high cultural tone, likes to have her leg pinched. Who'll pinch it,
now? The right one, I mean; I'll take care of the left one.
Gerald Lynn? Hardly . . . any woman's leg is safe with Lynn,
wouldn't you say?

"But he's got a name; she'll like that. On Lynn's right—d'you
imagine he wants to talk stage-smut with Hugh McLeod's Coral
or would he rather have Celia? I'll give him Celia. Next to
Celia, not Hugh, they always fight. Hell, Hugh always fights
anyway. Can't think how Coral stands him; he must have
hidden talents, eh? I'll move him up next to Rosie Erndle; he's
such a stinking little snob, he may behave. . . . Gloria Coates
on his other side. Why are well-groomed tarts so often called
Gloria? Damned awful party, Mather." (He was entirely

satisfied with it.) "Those the menus?" His eyes moved placidly over the printed names.

Baron; Erndle; Lynn; Frassin de Vièl; McLeod; Coral Bishop; Gloria Coates; Levitt . . . a starry cluster. The only name without the spotlight of notoriety upon it was Mrs. Valentine West, and she had her own glitter.

He drummed on the table again. He did not want to send for Celia now, because he was in a good temper. On the other hand, his anxious curiosity was getting the better of him. This was the third day at sea and she had told him nothing.

He said to Mather, "Did you get that list of investments—my daughter's investments?"

"No, sir. Mrs. West said that Mr. West's firm was still handling them."

Baron said smoothly, "I see." He stopped strumming upon the table with both hands, and tapped his knee. All right, he said to himself; since he was now pitchforked into bad temper, he could send for Celia. Nothing to lose. He was reminded of a remark made by his first wife, many years ago, "I've got such a headache, I think I'll use it to go to the Royal Academy with." In solitude she often returned to memory with a light-hearted piece of nonsense such as this. Conjured by Celia, she came back like a pointed arrow to hurt savagely and be plucked out.

"Call through to Mrs. West, Mather."

Waiting for her, he composed as many lines as for a leader, but discarded far more than was his habit while pacing the room in oratory. Any talk with Celia was a foregone conclusion. It troubled him that she should still be the thorn in his flesh. She was one whom he could neither fool nor dominate. She did not accept his legend, as others did. Baron liked the legend. It armoured him in sterling clichés—"Heart of Gold", "Bark Worse than his Bite", "Good Friend and Bad Enemy"; "Great Little Man". It stretched him to the size of the Fleet Street Giants, the disappearing Titans. All the more disturbing, therefore, to feel upon occasion that the only two people who knew Baron were Baron and his daughter Celia.

The sight of her pleased his eyes; his mind thrust out its

defences lest it should be trapped; by the fairness and the flying look, the easy walk, the air of belonging to nobody. Her mother had had that air. Grudging and admiring, he observed her clothes; a dark blue flannel suit, a white shirt and a thin red scarf at her throat; all perfect and all, beyond a doubt, hideously expensive.

"Sorry I'm late," she said.

"You should have that sentence printed on a card and hung round your neck," said Baron. "Never mind. I've been working. Just done a very adequate leader about Glane . . ." He postponed his questions, finding that as ever he was a little afraid of asking them. She had seated herself in Mather's chair. She lit a cigarette.

"Who's your architect? Don't let him do anything cute . . ."

He showed her the sketches; her comments were decided and intelligent. She had her mother's taste, her mother's eyes. Presently she lingered on a photograph of the village taken from the hill. "Odd," she said, "the way that one starves for the English countryside after a year in America. There's a bit of me that is as excited as a child going to a circus—just for the look of the land."

"Well, Carlington's waiting for you. Carlington's your home," he said amply. "You couldn't have a better. For as long as you want it. And I hope, for Van's sake, that it will be a home for you both, one day."

"You do, do you?" she said gently, musingly. "Well, that's out."

"You mean that this separation is final?"

"As final as I can make it. He's still stalling on the divorce. But my lawyer's on the job."

Baron groaned; it was what he had expected to hear; he was not sure why he groaned; could it be because the pattern of escape reminded him of her mother's?

He said, "You know, I've always been fond of Van."

"Yeah . . . well, you can have him. He sobbed on your shoulder, I imagine."

"What? . . . did he tell you so?"

"Certainly not. He didn't have to. No string that one wouldn't pull."

"He's still in love with you."

"Nonsense."

"And he adores Terry."

Celia snapped, "Really, J. G.; you can't kid yourself on that. Van, you never seem to realise, is a balanced blend of sadism and masochism. Either he bullies the life out of Terry or he sobs over him; I've seen enough." Her hands were trembling. "I can't talk about it. I'm sorry. It makes me feel ill." She rose and paced the room. "Please let me alone," she said. "I'm through with it, and I've no more to say. If you're on Van's side, that's fine. Only don't talk about him. If you want a third-party witness, talk to Nanny."

"I shouldn't dream of talking to Nanny. Sit down. Would you like a drink? There's no need to get yourself in such a state. It's natural, isn't it, for me to want to know?"

"I guess so," she said. She came back to her chair, picked up the lighter and began to dismantle it. "Have you a spare flint?"

"I dare say Mather has. Why don't you use matches? There's a box beside you."

"I don't like matches."

He said exasperatedly, "Don't *like* matches? How can you like them or not? Might as well say you don't like string. Oh, Mather, give Mrs. West a glass of champagne. I'll take one too."

"Thank you, J. G." She raised the glass. "Here's to a happy death for Mr. Valentine West," she said.

It was the only type of remark that could shock him to his soul. He did not want to risk another argument. There was still the subject of the money ahead. He tried to approach it gently.

"Darling. . . . Weren't you going to have your bank send me the list of your investments?"

"No point," she said. "I'm not taking the account away from Van's firm."

"Why not?"

"It's a sound enough firm, even though it does happen to

contain Van. My lawyer's quite satisfied with it. He'll keep an eye. I'm delighted to see from your face that your affection for Van doesn't stretch to an affection for his handling my capital."

"Your mother's money . . . a sacred trust," Baron said. "You're too casual about those things. Why will you *never* take my advice? At least you took it about the property, I hope."

"Property?"

"The house on Martha's Vineyard. That was a wonderfully good offer. For a small, ramshackle place. You sold, didn't you?"

"I did not," said Celia.

"Are you crazy?"

"No, darling. I love that place. The house belongs to me. I'm keeping it."

"But Van said——"

"Don't quote Van, please. He never liked it. And it's mine."

The word "mine" exasperated him; as though she were striking a blow at Carlington.

He said, "Ridiculous. What use is it to you now? Serve you right if you found yourself stuck without a penny one day."

"Yes, wouldn't it?" she murmured placidly.

"You've got Terry to think of, you know."

"There's a trust—though not a sacred one—for Terry."

"What? . . . Oh, well, there'd better be. I shall be bankrupt in due course, if these bastards stay in office. Toby and Liz will be lucky if they have a penny between them."

"As to Tobias," Celia said. "Did you see the photograph in the *Tatler*?"

"What? Yes, I did. Well?" He tapped his knee. "What about it?"

"Has he known her a long time? She's the best possible company for him, I'd say."

Baron was outraged. "I will not discuss it, Celia."

Her look was amused and speculative. "Is it the stage connection that upsets you?"

"And, dear God, why not?" He banged the table. "Would

you want your son to be a mummer with a painted face—
mouthing other people's lines? Well, if he doesn't work when he
gets up to Oxford, he knows what to expect. Idle nonsense, all of
it. That affected intellectual crowd; Paris week-ends." Nothing
would induce him to speak Catherine de Lille's name; he
contented himself with, "It's a scandal."

"It doesn't sound very scandalous, J. G."

"Anyway, I don't want to discuss it, I've told you." He began
to fuss with the papers on the table. He chuckled suddenly,
seeing Levitt's file. "Take a look at these, will you?"

They were all sketches of himself. There was Baron as the
Devil, toasting the Prime Minister over a grid in hell; Baron as
God saying Let There Be Light; Baron as Eliza carrying the
squalling baby Britain across the ice, with the bloodhounds, the
Socialist Party, in pursuit; Baron as a signpost pointing One
Way Only; Baron as a cake with Baron eating the cake and the
appropriate caption; Baron as a candle burning at both ends.
All had the same wicked fluency, the arched black crest of a
signature.

"He writes his name as if it were a sneer," said Celia.

"What? . . . Yes, he does; you're right. Pretty stuff, eh?"

"Pretty stuff. He'll be one of the court jesters at Carlington, I
imagine."

"Court jester? Is that really how you think of me? A King
with a court?"

"Isn't it how you think of you? . . . I must leave you; I'm
lunching with the gentleman."

"With Levitt? What d'you make of him?" He himself was
still undecided.

Celia said, "I like anybody who makes me laugh."

"Think he's straight?"

"No."

"What? . . . Why don't you?"

"I just don't. Does it matter?"

"He talked straight to me," Baron said. "On Tuesday.
Discussing policy. He had the impertinence to tell me I was
wrong."

Her mouth slanted. "And were you?"

"Yes," said Baron, "but what the devil's that got to do with it?" Against his will he felt rewarded, as always, by Celia's laugh, a shout of natural laughter that belonged, he thought, to a person less tensely disciplined. He laughed too.

"Maybe you're right about him," he said. "Ever strike you that there's something wrong with people who have no family background?"

"No, darling. Not when I look at ours."

"You're impossible, and not funny." But he had forgiven her much in this half-hour. She could charm him still; with her mother's gift, the damned Hazelten charm. Though he liked the continuance of family characteristics, finding security in the fact of them, he deplored this one.

"Levitt," she said, "reeks of being alone, doesn't he? You know his child died and his wife shot herself?"

"Good God, no. He told me nothing; just said he wasn't married. Good God! I'm sorry . . ." He felt a rush of kindliness towards Levitt for having suffered the arch-enemy, the destroyer. "Poor fellow; poor old Levitt."

(xi)

"And you're thinking?" Gerald Lynn said.

"Did I look as though I were thinking? Any expression on my face is purely coincidental," said Celia, "I suppose—if at all —I was thinking about J. G.'s parties. London; Paris; New York; Monte Carlo, that was on the yacht; I couldn't have been more than fourteen. Always champagne; always a fussy little foreign woman with diamonds, and a dehydrated English countess."

"Dear Rosie, at least she's making a gallant fight against her own dehydration now; that's her third. Would you like another? Do, darling—make you *madly* gay . . ."

"No," she said. "And I think, judging from J. G.'s look of incipient generalship, we're about to go in to dinner."

She saw the other diners give them grudging attention as they annexed the large table with its flourish of lights and flowers. She found Gerald on her left; it was a relief not to find Levitt on her right, to have for neighbour the ashen Joe Erndle.

("But why do I not want to be close to Levitt? Because people don't bring themselves to this kind of party. They bring feverishly-trained exaggerations, with all the quieter features left behind in their rooms with their day-clothes.") It was more restful to look at Levitt across the table, not to hear every word that he said. He was seated between Coral and the metallic beauty, Gloria Coates.

"Going the usual way already," Gerald murmured. Hugh McLeod, thrusting his short angry little neck towards Rosie Erndle, was saying, "I happen only to be interested in Real Things and Real People."

"By which," said Gerald, "he means people who live a life of shabbiness, discomfort, poverty and dropped aitches. In my view life is real, life is earnest, even if you happen to be rich, well-dressed and well-educated."

"When I tell you, Lady Erndle, that I was flung upon the world at seven years old."

"Most people, Hugh, are flung upon the world at the age of nine months," Gerald crooned at him. "Must I be attentive to Madame Frassin de Ris de Veau, Celia?" he hissed out of the corner of his mouth.

"I think you must. In time . . ."

"*Have* you read any of her repulsive Asiatic books?"

"I read one," Celia said. "Or half of one. It was all about the Arabs searching for beauty. I'm allergic to beauty anyway."

"And I'm allergic to Arabs, so there we are."

Violette Frassin de Vièl, leaning towards Baron, declaring *les événements de l'est* to be *archi-serieux*, regularly touched the front wave of her blue hair with her finger-tip and withdrew it, as though testing the heat of an iron. She was tiny and fragile, with a face like a sugar-almond. "To look from her to Rosie Erndle," Gerald said, "is to look from Marie Laurencin to Munnings."

Rosie's clipped voice, authentically the voice of breeding, with the note of frenzy in it, cried out:

"Oh, my dear! With our poor political hands *tied* by monsters like you."

"Perhaps," said Gerald, "she'll strike Hugh in the face before the end of dinner. Nobody's behaving well; d'you observe Joe peering down the valley of Coral? He looks as though he were unwrapping a Christmas present."

"She needs little unwrapping, I'd say."

("Women shaped like Coral, curved like Coral, stripped for action like Coral, embarrass me always. I have to look away. Does Levitt have to look away? He keeps his shoulder turned and talks to Gloria . . .")

Gerald followed her eyes. "Chum Levitt's behaving quite nicely, on second thoughts," he said. "Wonderful how he's learned."

"Learned what?" ("And there is no need," she said to herself, "to feel this sudden tightening of the muscles round your ribs at the mention of Levitt.")

"Learned to behave," said Gerald, twirling the stem of his glass in his hand; watching Levitt thoughtfully.

"Since when?"

"It was just after his book came out, dear. Somebody brought him to Ben's ranch. We *nearly* died of him. I sobbed, but then I have a sweet nature. *You* know, darling . . . all the wrong clothes bought at *great* expense from Abercrombie and Fitch . . . *couldn't* stop talking . . . fresh as paint one minute and cowed to death the next; falling in love with California, and then with all of us in turn . . . then hating and snarling and doing our caricatures. *Maddening* everybody. We used to draw lots not to be left alone with him. The time I lost, he prattled for hours about the sexual taboos in Volo, Illinois."

"Why Volo, Illinois?"

"It's his home-town, darling. I despised him for being so mean about it."

"Are you sure it's his home-town?"

"Graven on my heart," Gerald said. "You have but to ask

him. . . . The *beauty* of this steak and vegetables . . . I feel as
though I were eating a Corot."

"Want a little mustard with your Corot? Go on about
Levitt."

"I never saw him again till now. He's grown up. . . . There's
a nasty lull on my left, darling. *Over* to the Arabs; see you
later."

Levitt's eyes met hers now and she wondered whether she were
looking at him angrily. It was an odd mixture, this in the heart:
ridicule, anger and pity. ("Mr. Ray Dangerfield from San
Francisco . . . you have grown up. Your clothes are right, you
are at ease; your manners are good and you are the most
pointless liar I ever met . . .") He winked at her.

"Don't call French food *edible*!" Coral was screaming. "It's
like saying somebody has a pleasant face."

"I always say——"

"*Always*, Rosie, darling? Don't you bore yourself to death?"

Again Levitt's eyes returned to Celia's. "And this," she said
to herself, "is the last thing I want; to sit here in the middle of
this nonsense and to see that the damned miracle has performed
itself. That your face has become what my eyes need and seek.
And less even than that, I want to feel sorry for little Harry
Levitt (of Volo, Illinois) at the ranch, with all the wrong clothes.
. . . That is to burn one's boats."

"Take a Gallup Poll——"

"Take Formosa——"

"Take two aspirin," said Gerald.

"Take my word for it," said Baron, "there's only one thing to
do with the Chinese."

"And I *never* have, would you believe it?" Gerald said to
Celia.

"Christianity is the only answer."

"No orthodox religion is the answer."

"This is the point," Gerald calculated, "where somebody
usually says, 'The Quakers'."

"Oh dear, I hope nobody will. Yes, Coral has," Celia said.
"What *does* Gloria mean by Living in Oneness?"

"Can't think, dear. I believe she graduated from Christian Science to Buddhism, or is it Pantheism? You know, the ones who are *always* persuading themselves that the Crucifixion either didn't happen or didn't hurt. . . ."

Celia laughed. "You're a Catholic, aren't you?"

"Yes," said Gerald, "the *worst*, but utterly devoted. . . . Now it's coming my way. Somebody will admire the Church for its stand against communism."

"And somebody will say it ought to keep out of politics," said Celia.

"But if it weren't for the ignorant Irish," Gerald added. "Oh, and with any luck we ought to get 'What I always say is, what's the good of confessing your sins one day and doing them all over again the next?' "

"I was terribly impressed with the Pope," said Rosie Erndle. "Terribly, terribly impressed with the Pope."

"There, that'll do just as well," said Gerald happily.

("And all the time there is only that face; the dark eyes; the visible bones. And the picture of Harry Levitt on the ranch in the wrong clothes. What is he telling Hugh and Gloria now? The story of Mr. Ray Dangerfield? It is a story; when he tells a story he makes that small movement of the hand, that introductory flourish. I despise myself for noticing these things.")

"I'm like a violin string," said Coral, "exactly like a violin string."

"Only *wider*," murmured Gerald.

There was the quick, high chatter of Madame Frassin de Vièl: "*Mais il faut constater*, Sir James, *que le caractère Arabe*," and then a sudden stop in the talk across the table; Gloria Coates putting back her head to laugh; Levitt saying, "So what does poor George do? I ask you. I never knew, because his company was moved up to Forli soon afterwards." Hugh McLeod, unsmiling, leaned his elbows on the table. He said to Levitt with a deadly patience, "Listen. That story didn't happen to your chum George in Italy. That story was going the rounds in the Western Desert; it's one of the stock stories of the war."

"This," said Gerald crisply, "might be the moment when somebody has to get up very quickly and take off all their clothes. You or me?"

Celia was silent. Levitt shrugged his shoulders. "As you wish. It did in fact happen to my chum, George."

"It could *not* have happened to your chum, George."

Across the table Coral had heard him, with the extra ear that obtained, Celia thought, in and out of wedlock. She called, "Hugh, why can't you ever let anybody alone? Why *shouldn't* it have happened to his chum, George? I'm sure—whatever it was —it happened to hundreds of people called George."

And now Baron's attention was caught; Rosie Erndle's attention was caught; the absurd crackles of independent talk had died. There was Levitt in the middle of silence, his dark, hound's profile pointing up the table towards his host.

"Violette," Celia said, leaning beyond Gerald. "*I* know what I've been meaning to ask you. What's the news of Catherine de Lille?"

She saw Baron's eyes jump angrily towards her: Madame Frassin said, "*Ah, la chère melancolique Catherine!* She is as beautiful, as brilliant, as ever. I have read the new play—a masterpiece!" She turned to Baron. "*L'Enchanteresse! Elle fait des veritables esclaves encore,*" and now Baron's fury made him rigid. The danger to Levitt was past.

("But why do I trouble to save you a tricky passage? Why do I protect you? And now I find that I am hating Hugh; not hating less for my certainty that he is right, that the thing did not happen to your chum George.")

Here was the dessert carried in in triumph; the ice-cream crowned with iridescent swathes of spun sugar. Here was the flashlight photographer. She watched Baron lift his chin; watched all the faces changing carefully for the flash. "One ridiculous evening among many," she said to herself. "It need have no importance whatever. So long as I do not speak, it is not there. So long as he does not know, there is nobody who knows, and I am safe."

(xii)

It was late. It had been going on for hours, Levitt thought, the adjournment to Baron's suite, the drinks, the rise and fall of words. Now only Gerald Lynn and Violette Frassin de Vièl were left, flanking Baron on the sofa. And Celia, distant from him by many miles, though he lounged in the chair at her side. This moment of silence between them must end, he knew. It was unbearable. She said suddenly, making her mouth crooked:

"And what was the story?"

"Which story?"

"The thing that happened to an alleged George in Italy."

"He flew home illicitly in a bomber, met his wife in secret and got back undiscovered. Only to hear from her three months later that she was going to have a baby. Query, what would the neighbours say? Deadlock for George, who'd be court-martialled if he let on."

"Deadlock," she echoed indifferently.

Levitt said, "It did really happen to George—George Fox-Brett; nice sad guy, just the type who would knit his own halter."

"You do a little in that line yourself, don't you?"

At once he was afraid. "What line?"

"The knitting line," said Celia. She rose. He was the last to whom she said good-night.

Now the light was gone out of the room. He tried to thrust himself into the talk, but her image went on recurring until he found that he had risen and left them like an automaton, that this was the only thing to do. I need not telephone, I think, said the automaton Levitt, taking its destined walk to the door.

She called, "Come in," and did not look up from the writing-table until he said, "Hello," shutting the door behind him. Then she gave him a long, puzzled look. She leaned back under the lamplight, pen in hand. "Recording Angel Department," said a little alarmed smart-alec somewhere inside Levitt's head.

"What is it?" Celia asked, more gently than he had expected. "Did J. G. send you?"

"No. Nobody sent me."

"Why, then?"

"I couldn't——" he began and stopped.

"Couldn't what?" The voice was still gentle, the look still puzzled.

"It's too difficult," said Levitt, "I can't say it."

When he took a step towards her, she rose; he saw the tremor of her hands.

"Shouldn't be difficult," she said. "What's on your mind?"

The words came, cracked; rough, too few words. "Telling you lies."

"Yes. I know," she said gently.

"You don't know it all.

"None of the things I've told you were true—I never changed my name. I never had a child who died; my wife didn't kill herself; I'm still married. None of the things were true," he repeated. "I'm a born liar; a pathological liar. I've always done it. It comes easier than telling the truth." He stopped speaking. There was a moment of stunning peace; he had not known that it would feel like this to tell.

Celia was still looking at him gently.

"Why do you say this to me now?" she asked.

He looked about him; at the flowers, at the gold-topped bottles, the line of photographs in their leather frames; at the lamp that was lit above the table and the strewn sheets of paper in the lamplight. Here there were clues to her, more easily un-riddled, perhaps, when she was not in the room.

("I don't know, I don't know you. Shall I ever know you? Why do you make me feel defeated, held-off, hated? What makes me come to you and tell you the things that will make you hate me more?")

He found that he had said, "Because I think you hate me," and there was no answer, until the shaking hands came up and caught his head between them. Then it was ended. There was only the tiger and the Dark Tower.

(xiii)

He woke, out of the dead-quiet sleep into the strange
familiarity. He stretched out his hand and at once her hand
clasped it.

"Hello," he said.

"Put the light on; I want to see you."

He leaned on one elbow, looking down at her. There was
something disturbing in the gaiety of this Nordic and pagan face
looking up at him from the pillow. It was an untroubled face.
He followed its curling lines with his finger.

"Couldn't draw you now," he said.

"Why not?"

"Can't draw beautiful things. Only ugly things."

"I'm not beautiful. You could make me ugly quite easily.
I've no bones. You have bones . . ." she said, holding his chin
too tightly, so that she hurt him. "And this I like . . . and
this——"

She made him shy. He turned off the light and laid his head
in the hollow of her shoulder.

"Are we being silly? I suppose we are," she said into the dark.

"I'm happy," said Levitt.

"Me too."

"I wanted you when I looked at you in New York; when you
were quarrelling with Van."

"I've never wanted anybody like that; without knowing, or
loving. How does it feel?"

"Oh, well," he said, "it's just saying to yourself, 'That would
be nice.'"

"I've never done it."

"Perhaps women don't do it."

"What are you saying in your head now?"

"Much the same thing, my beautiful."

Presently she said, "You are gentler than I thought you would
be; kinder, thank you," and the "thank you" made him laugh.
Then she said, "The illusion of peace."

"Only the illusion?"

"Oh—sure." It came out on a sigh.

"I'm not," she said, "a peaceful person. I can't be."

"Why not?"

"Just born restless; I get savage inside."

"With Van?"

"Not only Van. With J. G.; with myself; with anything that threatens what I love. And what one loves always looks threatened."

"Could you love me?" he asked lightly.

She grasped the hair at the back of his head. "I don't know. I don't love people very often. And I don't think I want anybody to love me. It complicates."

"It's security," Levitt said, "to be loved."

"Very American of you, darling."

"I'm not very American. I never want to go back. I only want to live in England. I even know the house. It's in Shropshire; not far from Shrewsbury. I saw it when I was on leave."

"What sort of house?"

"Georgian, I guess . . . solid red-brick; beautiful proportions, with grassland, and trees growing out of the grass, and halfway across the grassland a white fence like the rails around race tracks. I kept walking back up the road to look at it again.

"One of the reasons I can't go on living with my wife," he said, "is her hate for England."

"What is she like?"

"I don't honestly know. Just the sort of girl you marry when you're going to war."

"Any divorce likely?"

"No. She's holding out for too much dough. I left her the apartment, and all our things."

"Perhaps you'll find another girl in England, and have your fine house."

"I want this girl."

"No," she said, "or you won't for very long. This is fun and kicking up heels, and the result of having thoughts below the waist at the Pavillon." She pushed his head away, then drew him back and kissed him. "Besides, we are in a ship, where these things happen. Once I'm embedded in Carlington, I turn into everybody's aunt."

"Not my aunt, you won't. Whose aunt?"

"Liz; Tobias; Anthony." She laughed suddenly. "It was Anthony who first told me that story of yours tonight."

"*You'd* heard it before?"

"Well, yes. But unlike Hugh McLeod I don't shoot them down in public."

"Didn't what's-his-name, Anthony, tell it to you as having happened to a chum?"

"Lord, no. I do see," she said, "that there is a certain convention about making good stories better. Only Anthony's the last person who could do that."

"Truthful fellow?" Levitt asked, lifting an eyebrow.

"Completely. Almost boringly so, bless him. What's the matter?"

"Just making up my mind to hate Anthony. Hate them all; be jealous of them all."

"Oh, nonsense—you aren't serious? Put on the light. I have to see if you're serious."

"Well, of course if you make me do that I have to grin," he said—"just as—if you'd told me to laugh, I couldn't."

"But why should you want to hate them?"

"Perhaps because you love them."

"That's childish," she snapped. "D'you hate Terry?"

"I daresay I could be jealous of Terry, in time. . . . Shall I meet them all, d'you suppose?" he said. "Shall I come to Carlington? I've got to go on seeing you."

"But of course you'll come there; bidden by J. G."

"Not by you?"

"By me, if you like. He usually does the bidding."

"He's against me now, I think . . . since I fought him."

"No," she said. "Take my word for it. You trust nobody, do you?"

"I've trusted you."

"Will you go on telling lies?"

"Not to you."

"I don't believe you will to anybody," she said, "I think you're growing out of it. I think that's why you could tell. You must go home."

"No."

"Yes. I'll hate it when you've gone, but you must. It will be light in a little while and Terry'll come bounding in."

He stared at her. "Promise to hate it when I've gone?"

"Promise," she said lazily. Levitt looked away from her eyes to the shadow on the wall. Made by his head, his curved shoulder and the pillow, it had contrived a sudden monstrous likeness of Baron's profile.

"Look," he said, beginning to laugh; he moved and it was gone.

BOOK II

BRIG O' DREAD

(April–May–June, 1949)

BRIG O' DREAD

1

(i)

ALONE on the terrace, Liz looked at the day; she saw it from various angles of agony. She felt like a sentinel on the watch, up here. Down on the marsh, the trees were powdery green; all the colours of the marsh stretching to the sea were clear and flat, with the shadows of the clouds racing over them. It was a morning of sunlight and hurrying wind, a disturber of the peace. It was no ordinary day.

One of the worst signs of growing up, she thought, was that ordinary days came less and less often. She valued the look of the landscape; this at least did not change. The steep fields that sloped to the marsh, the line of willows where the stream bordered the wood, the white fence dividing Baron's property from the Carey farmland, these had been there always. She walked to the end of the terrace. Here was the mossy path that ran under the high red wall; here the dark clumps of rhododendron, and at the end of the path the white gate. Prince, the fat Labrador the colour of treacle pudding, bounced out of the bushes. He panted and smiled, waiting for her to open the gate. Liz hesitated. She needed Carey acutely. On an ordinary day (where had they gone?) she would have opened the gate and rushed across the cobbled yard to the studio. She could, of course, do it now. But the woman was there, the enemy, working with Carey. One did not expose family terrors and troubles to the enemy.

Liz turned back, arguing mutinously with Prince and God and spring. "*Nothing* stays the same, not even Carey; and one is supposed to be pleased. Look at this week . . . look at it.

I ask you. It begins with Tobias' awful secret; it goes on with Carey's father's funeral. It ends today with Celia and Nanny and Terry coming home, which was what we were looking forward to, so *that* has to be changed. More than changed, *ruined*, by J. G. coming too.

"*Why* couldn't he go straight to London instead of staying the night here? Then it wouldn't matter where Tobias has got to; Celia wouldn't care if he wasn't back in time to greet from the doorstep. (And he won't be; mark my words.)

"And on top of all that, Carey has to have the woman in the house. For two solid days, immediately after the funeral (as though he had only been waiting for that). Mixing her damned plaster and casting her stupid statue all day and sitting around in her awful eager arty-crafty attitudes all the evening so I can't talk to Carey for a *minute*. He never had her in the house while Randolph was alive. Next thing," she said to Prince, "he'll marry her. You just wait. And if Carey marries Jane Ireland, I shall die."

She tramped off the terrace; she strode between the high walls of clipped yew and across velvety turf to the grass steps. She liked this place. The steps led up to a tiny platform of a lawn, with a marble bench and a row of cypresses behind. Here, on three sides, cypress and yew hid all but the sky; you sat on the bench, with your back to the cypresses, looking down across tiers of lawn and terrace to the misty horizon of marsh and sea. You felt secure, in a part of the garden that was hidden and old. There ought to be a statue here, J. G. said. He wanted Carey to make one. He wanted the bench taken away. Why did people always want to change things—and like them when they changed of their own accord?

Liz glowered upon her grievance. It came out in tangled terms; of people saying, "*Hasn't* she grown?" Of the two old cottages on the corner being pulled down to make room for a new petrol station (and the worst of it, somehow, was forgetting what the cottages had looked like, becoming used to the grey asphalt, the red and green pumps). It came in terms of the grown-up consolations. "You'll like it when you get there",

"You'll soon get used to it", "You'll feel better tomorrow."
"As though one wanted to feel better tomorrow."

Idle to rage at it, idle to want to die loyal to a mood, idle to curse God for turning moods into memories. "Time, the Great Stinker, makes all their most loathèd prophecies come true," Liz thought, "and in a little while I shall have settled for this changed Tobias, with his lies and his lady in France. I shall have accepted the fact that Jane Ireland, with her shiny black hair and her blue shirt and her red trousers will always be haunting Carey's studio. I shall forget this morning.

"But I will never stop loving Carey," she said, "this I know." Even the new infliction of Jane could not make him dangerously different. Carey was a rock and a rock he would remain; golden and imperturbable, the nearest thing to God that she could imagine. Her childhood nightmare all through the war had been that Carey would be killed; or worse, come back horribly wounded and shell-shocked, an invalid parody of himself. But Carey had taken the wound, when it came, for granted. The stiff leg did not worry him; and the limp now seemed to be part of him, a characteristic rather than a handicap. In talk, he made the hideous experience at Anzio sound like a cricket game. "Carey," J. G. had said once, "is fortunate in being born without a nervous system." Would that there were more such births, Liz thought, my own included.

"He is the embodiment of reassurance. He is always right about everything. And he is the only person I shall ever love, in the truly *abominable* meaning of the word, not in the sense that I love Celia and Tobias, and——" she added guiltily, after a pause, "J. G. But *does* one love J. G.?"

Threshing for the truth, feeling the prickle of the hair shirt, she replied, "One must; or one would not be sorry for him," and got off the bench. Now she stood at the gap in the yews, looking across the gravel courtyard at the house.

The house, the red bulk with its ornate white frieze, awaited J. G. Inside it was turbulent with the preparations for him. Foliot, the secretary-housekeeper, Bolland, the valet, the Austrian cook and the Austrian maids were on tiptoe for J. G.

"He has been away six weeks . . . and now, in spite of old Randolph's death, and Toby's tricks, and the horrible funeral, and awful Jane Ireland, they seem like peaceful weeks. . . . And indeed they were, compared with what will be," she decided, stepping sorrowfully through the front door.

On the left of the hall, the door of the little green library stood half open; this room belonged especially to J. G. The door had been shut for six weeks. Now Liz could see the fresh daffodils and narcissi, the silver cigar-cutter lying ready on the small table, a slice of J. G.'s portrait above the mantelpiece. Here he dictated letters, here he liked to sit after dinner; one or two of the august week-end visitors were always led away here for private talks.

Passing the door with an anticipatory shiver, Liz halted at the foot of the wide staircase; she looked up to the landing where her mother's portrait hung; slick oil painting of the unfamiliar red-headed beauty. No memory of her mother remained to her. Baron would pause before the portrait on his way to bed, pause and sigh.

She could see him doing this now, could conjure the compact little shape in the plum-coloured dinner-jacket, with the slim black legs set apart, the grey curled head tilting wistfully; she could hear the rattle of the sigh.

All his ritual was coming back, storming the house ahead of him. As she came into the long room whose windows looked out over the terrace, she saw it fill with the pageant of the week-end. J. G.'s Sunday made it a mad ballroom from morning till midnight; the voices roared, the cigarette smoke thickened the air and he was a king in the middle of his courtiers.

But now the room was empty; a shell; with its golden-tawny hues, its bookshelves, its flowers and its comfortable furniture, it might, Liz thought, be any large room in a country house, harmless and welcoming. It was always less haunted than the green library or the dark-panelled dining-room across the hall.

He was on his way here. Nothing could stop that. "And even if Tobias weren't making an agony out of this arrival," Liz thought, "I *still* wouldn't want him to come back. Oh, grief, why not . . . ? It's so unkind.

"And, to those outside, so incomprehensible. Everybody thinks that it must be delicious to be the children of J. G. Baron —still rich and safe and spoiled and living in a sort of palace in the middle of the post-war world; we are archaic; we have servants and chauffeurs and gardeners. We are to be envied. Besides," she mocked, "we Meet So Many Interesting People. That is how it looks. . . . Well, we could tell them a thing or two, Toby and I," she thought darkly, and was then pulled up short by wondering what the devil the thing was that she and Toby could tell them.

She flung herself on to the sofa; Prince sank to the floor with a puffing thump.

"Honestly, I don't hate him. He frightens me and I am sorry for him, but those two halves don't make a hate, this I do swear.

"Celia hates him; she does not admit to hating him, but Tobias and I know it. And Celia isn't frightened of him, nor sorry for him, which proves my point. Celia's different. Celia, J. G. says, is her Mother All Over Again.

"Lucky Celia. Except it must be hellish to be coming home here to live, with the marriage all over; like coming back to school. Or that's how it would be for me." But her words ran out for Celia; who went by her mind always in a flash of king-fisher-blue and gold, most dazzlingly and enviably grown-up. "She'll get out again, somehow. One must get out, or die. I shall get out one day, I suppose. Escape him; not be in thrall any more.

"In thrall to *what*, for heaven's sake?" she shouted at herself impatiently. "Try to describe, for the benefit of a stranger who has never met him, the agony of J. G. Come on, now, try. What's the worst of him?" She stared at it in her mind.

"I suppose, truly the worst is the unpredictable mood; change. (Here we are at Change again; it begins to look like my King Charles's Head.) He's worse than weather.

"One can never guess if it's going to be rage, or roses, roses all the way. If it's going to be straight mean snubs or rolling Gothic phrases that bring a blush to the cheek. If it's going to be roistering dirty jokes or Victorian-father bullying, or that awful cold silent umbrage and the mouth going thin and the voice small. If it's going to be Citation of Family Characteristics In Front of Strangers (my worst) or ego-maniac outpourings to the Yes-Men." (Toby's worst; Toby called it His Early Struggles In the Collieries.)

"Then," she lectured the imaginary stranger, "you have further the muffled sigh, the Terribly Tired, Terribly Sorry-for-Himself mood. (Toby's 'Portrait of a Nobleman Grieving, Possibly In Search of Lost Pedigree.') Aimed at us. A series of accusations without a word spoken. Till we feel so guilty for having let him father us that we could cut off our right hands.

"Why—seeing so clearly—should one care, placate, dodge, feel uneasy, want to get out of the room, heave a sigh of relief when *he* goes out of the room? Why do one's nerve-ends tighten and one's powers of natural talk harden and dry like old people's arteries? Ah, that's the mystery, the doom, the Baron fever, the ague that makes us all have shaky hands and heart-thumps before our time. And Celia falls in love with a stinker of a different sort, and look where that gets her—and Toby makes great gestures of defiance, and I—I cower and groan and get sorry and feel sick and run to Carey.

"Only I can't run to Carey with that harpy chipping her bloody plaster all over the place."

Foliot, the dark, spectrally-smiling shape, who had been in the household for ever, opened the door. "There you are, Liz; I was chasing you. I have just telephoned Cunard at Southampton. They docked ahead of time; at—let me see, it must have been seven minutes to twelve. So—allowing about twenty-five minutes to get off the boat, get organised and away— well . . . they ought to be here soon after three o'clock, not later than a quarter-past, I'd say; certainly between a quarter-past and half-past three."

Solemnly diverted, Liz was unable to resist the temptation of asking, "And what time is it now, Foliot?" Foliot was haunted by time. She had a passion for accurate renderings of it. Her life might have depended upon the precision of "Eleven minutes past"—or "Say, four minutes to——" Tobias believed that she had a hand in the editing of *Bradshaw*, and he had once bet Liz that if Foliot's clothes were removed, they would find a clock set in her stomach, as in the American statuettes of the Venus de Milo.

"It's just seventeen minutes past twelve," Foliot said. "Is Anthony lunching here? Marya wanted to know."

"Couldn't say. He's got that Ireland daisy (. . . . for daisy read bitch . . .) working on a cast. I'll go and find out."

She had at least an excuse for going to the studio. She uncurled from the corner of the sofa.

"And Tobias?" Foliot asked, smiling the more, arching her painted eyebrows. ("Cross between a Modigliani and a benign vampire-bat," Tobias said.)

"Well, I don't know that either," Liz stalled. "He said early afternoon, so probably not lunch . . . He'll be here before they are," she added in defiance of her own doubts. She called to Prince and went out by the garden door. She went along the path under the wall and opened the white gate. She crossed the cobblestones. She came to the converted coach house, the studio with the wrought-iron sign hanging above. Anthony had made the sign. It was a spread-eagle of his initials around the wheat-sheaf that was the Carey crest; it was effective enough, so long as you did not look too closely.

(ii)

Anthony Carey was balanced at the top of a fourteen-foot ladder, cleaning the north skylight. In spite of his size and his stiff leg, he had no trouble with the acrobatics sometimes required of his trade. He liked to work on scaffolding; and this morning he liked this God's-eye view of his studio. He was without ideas for work, and this would have made him feel guilty if he had not set about the cleaning.

It was as near the perfect studio as man could get. His father had built it for him, and J. G. Baron had added to it over the years. Not a piece of heavy equipment, not a variety of tool was missing. Sometimes he felt overwhelmed with the space and size of it; it was really two studios, divided by a section with lower ceiling and extra skylight. He used the front studio for modelling, the back studio for marble- and stone-carving. He did his plaster-casting and kept his stores in the cellar below.

Anthony whistled, drove the wet duster across the glass, felt the drops of water fall on his face and glanced at the perspective lying below; at the orderly racks of tools above the work-bench, at the stands and the drawing-table, at the skeleton, at the careful anatomical sketches pinned to the walls. The finished pieces that he kept here were few: a black marble puma, a plaster head of Liz that had never been pointed up in stone, a pair of carved wood wrestlers and a clumsy granite horse. He gave pride of place to the cast of J. G. Baron's head and shoulders. Most of the other Carey products were discreetly hidden in the store-room.

He was not satisfied. He thought that he never would be. It was an old passion; he had begun to model in clay at the age of eight. At twenty-two, when the war came, he was halfway through his training. He was wounded at Anzio. In Rome, still convalescent, he had found a teacher. Invalided out of the army in '45, he had hurled himself back into his profession with enormous energy. Four years of intensive study and grinding labour had made him a good technician. But if you wanted to be a mixture of Michelangelo and Mestrovic—with a dash of Benvenuto Cellini—you had to have something more than energy.

You might, as Anthony did, despise the softness of the present-day sculptor, whose work stopped with the clay, who handed over to the professional enlarger and the compressed-air tools of the stone-shed; who waved his model a comfortable good-bye as it was trucked to the foundry. You might pride yourself because you could cast and carve and work over stone with a co-ordinated hand and eye; but if all your desperate efforts came out competently dull, miles short of your dream, what were you fit for? "Probably a nice quiet future as a monumental mason," said Anthony, these thoughts accelerated by the strivings of Jane Ireland down below. He went on whistling. She appeared at the top of the cellar steps and stood looking up. Her face was shiny, her trim, sleek hair ruffled; she looked like a harassed and effeminate young man.

"Want me?" he called down to her.

"I oughtn't to, but I do."

He swung himself down the ladder. He stood with her in the débris that strewed the wide cool cellar; he examined the cast critically. One side was free; on this side all the blue coat was visible; she had such a little way to go.

"Carry your chisel, lady?"

"It's cheating," Jane said, "but I wish to heaven you would." She sat down on the bench and mopped her face while he took up the chisel. It was the tricky stage demanding complete control, every stroke of the chisel gentle and watchful lest he cut the surface inside the coat. He was so much master of it that he could show off, saying lazily, "Give you a shilling a scratch." She took over from him when he was halfway round.

"There you are," he said. "You're doing fine. . . . Almost home. Don't hold the tool so tightly, there's a good girl." He stood over her for a little while, then sat on the edge of a clay-bin and lit his pipe. Staring around the cellar, he saw symbols of Carey failure: a featureless life-mask, a hand that looked like a stuffed glove, a stocky marble nude. "You ought to be heartened, chum," he said, "when you look at this junk."

"Your early stuff," she reminded him, still chipping, quietly concentrated. If, Anthony thought, I could get that pose, the lines and strains of that head and shoulder and arm, the braced body. . . . He knew Jane's body by heart, but it didn't help.

"I cut too deep there, damn it; that's gone through."

It was the smallest scratch; he mended it for her with thin wet plaster. "Won't show when it dries, Jane. I've done that dozens of times."

Presently he stood looking down at her enviously as she un-
covered the last of it. They paced around it together.

"Perfect," said Anthony. "Best you've done." Staring at the
cast he tried to see what Jane had that he had not. It was the
simplest of models: a boy's head, whose curling hair and parted
lips kept, he could swear, the liveliness of her first vision. It
needed no work at all that he could see, before it dried. But now,
like him, she sighed and frowned, saying at last, "By Jane
Ireland and Anthony Carey, no?"

"Certainly not."

Jane sneered. "No? Apart from mixing the plaster, bending
the irons and setting them, taking half the last coat off, and
mending the cut, you didn't do much, did you?"

"Your baby; I'm just an efficient *accoucheur*," Anthony said.

"My God, I wish I had your hands."

"And, my God, I wish I had your——" he paused, fumbling.
"What is it? Well, look at it, Jane. It's true; it's alive. One's
eyes stay on it. I can't make anything come alive—or compel,
like that. I'm an adequate craftsman and nothing else."

She said, "Hell to that," but she could not say more, he
thought, because she knew that he was right. She glanced at her
watch. "*Will* you look at the time? I've got exactly half an hour
before the train goes. What about all this mess?"

"Don't worry; Liz will see to it."

"Liz?" Jane's thin black eyebrows lifted. "How'll she like
that?"

"She loves it," said Anthony. "Loves messing around here.
Come on, now. Kiss him good-bye. He really is a beauty; and
I'll cherish him. When do you come back and fetch?"

"Not this week," Jane said. "Can't be this week."

"Come any time you like."

Now he saw upon her the mood of hankering regret; as they
went up the cellar steps, she put her arm about his waist.

"If you weren't so honest, I'd hate your guts," said Jane.

They faced each other under the dazzle of the north light.
The calm, waiting hush of the studio seemed to Anthony to
demand an important phrase; he had none.

"Okay," she said. "Okay. Don't try to think up polite lies, darling; they don't suit you. I'll get washed and tidy. Did you order the taxi?"

"I did."

They went out of the studio, up the courtyard and under the archway that touched the house. It was a small Queen Anne house, with a pocket garden before it; a grove of oak and ash hid the road. A rose-red wall hid the lawns, the clipped yews, the formal terraces of Carlington. Anthony had lived here all his life, until the interruption of war. And it still felt like his father's house, not his.

Waiting for Jane in the white-panelled sitting-room, it was hard for him to realise that this was over; it had been going on for so long. He felt as though upon the bed in the upstairs room the quiet figure were still lying; that he should go up and sit beside the bed and wait.

"He wouldn't want to be dead on this sort of spring morning," Anthony thought, looking out of the window.

Jane came downstairs; enamelled and different, already on her way to London; to the studio of the sullen, inspired De Fries, whose assistant she was; to the self-consciously Bohemian life that Anthony found a bore.

"I feel a pig for not seeing you off," he said.

"Don't apologise. With coveys of your precious Barons arriving any minute, you couldn't." She always retreated into acidity when leaving him. Her kiss was a cool touch on his cheek. She did not look back and wave, though he stood at the gate, faithfully watching the taxi go out of sight down the Ashford road.

"Women . . ." thought Anthony, lazily, without rancour, but with a feeling of guilt that was unnecessary. His was not the only bed into which Jane invited herself. She was as honest about that as he about his failure in love. But it did not make him feel any better. He turned from the gate in dejection.

Always, in his romantic head, there had been *La Princesse Lointaine*; surviving his early passion for Celia, surviving tea-shop girls, the Paris adventures of his student's days, and the

A.T.S. officer in Italy; Carey's dream of a woman far-off. He had never met the likeness of her in the flesh, nor did he expect to. She had the haunted beauty of the child Liz and the tenderness of a mother; she had Celia's wit and courage; she was equipped with intellectual lightning, all the domestic virtues and a temper as even as his own.

He stopped feeling guilty about Jane when he came back to the cellar under the studio. He looked at the head from every angle. "Anybody who can do *that* is all right," said Anthony; he gave the poor life-mask a good-humoured slap and went upstairs. He was on top of the ladder again when Liz came in.

"Hullo," she said, halting just inside the door. "Do I disturb?"

"No. I'll be through in a minute."

"Where is your lady?" she asked distrustfully.

"On her way back to London."

"Praise God," said Liz and threw herself down on the edge of the model stand. She sprawled.

"Poor Jane. Why do you hate her?"

"I do not," came on a mournful sigh from below. "But I am a fermenting compost heap of conversation and we have had none since Wednesday."

"I'm listening."

"I can't talk up a ladder. Are you coming to lunch? That is the first thing."

"Delighted," Anthony said. "Toby back?"

"*No.* Do come down."

"In a minute."

Liz groaned. Leaning over and down, he saw her head tilted back, the hair dropping away from the face; it was brown hair with a long, natural wave; the skin was pale, the eyes enormous, grey eyes that were black from here. Below him, in this perspective, she looked like a doomed ballet dancer, with the narrow grace of the body, the feet pressed together, the skirt fallen in a circle.

"You've no idea," she said, "of the awfulness of Tobias."

"I assume," said Anthony, dropping the wet duster with a plop beside her, "that he's over the Channel and far away. How does his chum Falchon get so much leave? All the commercial pilots of my acquaintance work to a punishing time-table."

"I can't explain," said Liz in a muffled voice.

Anthony came down the ladder.

"What's the secret?"

She was silent.

"You're the worst dissembler," he said.

"Still I have to dissemble. I promised Toby."

"All right, darling."

He put the ladder away and returned to her. She sat hugging her knees. "They'll be here by three," she said. "And the chances are that he won't. The message said Early Afternoon. Oh, *why* can't Toby learn to placate? Or *why* can't J. G. go straight to London instead of coming here? And why is nothing ever ordinary any more? And there are a thousand things I've been saving to discuss with you, and now we're here I can't think of any of them. Except asking about lunch, as I promised Foliot."

"Lunch," said Anthony, "will be more than welcome."

"Speak for yourself; I feel rather sick."

He said, "You've got jitters, chum." For utter beauty, he thought, looking at her, there is nothing to beat it. (Is it your beauty that turns all your tragedy into farce, as though—because they live inside that face and that body—your sorrows cannot be taken seriously?) She did not move. She sighed heavily and said, "I'll tell you something awful."

"Please do," said Anthony, trying not to laugh.

"Well, the person I look forward to seeing most is Nanny."

"Why is that awful?"

"It ought to be J. G. or Celia. But Nanny will be exactly the same, because she always is, and they won't."

"Celia's all of a piece," Anthony said. "She doesn't change."

"She's American now. You said so, last time."

"That's only top stuff. And it suits her to be American. It just makes more dazzle."

"Would J. G.'s quality be dazzle, d'you think?" She sounded excessively mournful about it.

"Well, not the same sort. He's another breed of fascinator."

Liz scowled. "No," he thought, "you can't see it. You belong to the tribe of foreign and remarkable Barons; to the Kingdom on the other side of the wall. And if I were one of you, I wouldn't see it either."

All his life they had possessed a mad, magical quality. The riches, the rush, the complications, the visitors with names, the huge cars departing and arriving, even the family tragedies, had endowed them, since he could remember, with the dazzle. Now that he was in his thirties he could take it for granted. And indeed be glad not to be a part of it; be grateful that he and his father had lived always independently, a solid peaceful unit in the Queen Anne house. Since the war, he had learned to notice Baron's hangers-on; the yes-men whom Tobias scorned. Although it was J. G.'s habit to refer to him as "one of the family", although his devotion to Baron never varied, he liked the facts of his own roof, his own money, his own work the more for contemplating the yes-men.

"Perhaps," he thought, "it is just because we've never been under any obligation to him that I get on with him so well. How right Daddy was. If he'd done what J. G. wanted, run the farm and taken the salary, we'd have been serfs."

Baron had bought the farm buildings and the farm land from his father in the 'thirties. Randolph had insisted on taking the lowest, fairest price. It had been a gesture of charity for Baron to offer him the management; the old man had refused. ("We're solvent, Anthony. So long as we keep solvent, we don't need to be rich, and we don't need to take a penny from anybody.")

After war broke out, when the agricultural programme and the subsidies made the farm a paying concern, Baron had tried again, and failed again. This time he was offering, not a salary, but solid profits. Anthony remembered the talk; Baron saying, "It's your land. It's been Carey land for centuries. I've regarded myself, for these few years, as an affectionate and privileged custodian." He remembered his father's courteous shake of the head. Talk between the two had never come easily. It was for ever formal. They were queer friends. "I've always thought it odd that Daddy could never get on back-slapping terms with him. Just as I wonder," Anthony said to himself, looking at Liz, "why his children can't get along with him better."

"*Fascinator*," Liz echoed. "He's going to be about as fascinating as a tarantula if Toby isn't here to make welcome."

"Well, who'd blame him? Toby ought to be here."

"I *know* he ought; damn his eyes."

"Don't worry; he will," said Anthony. Life was never as complex as the Barons made it.

"D'you want to sit there and brood, Liz? Or would you like to give me a hand down in the cellar?"

"Clearing up after Jane Ireland," said Liz darkly. "Anyway, it's lunch time." She rose and stretched her arms above her head. "I am in the process of knitting a delicious fantasy wherein J. G. has married again. That could happen, couldn't it? A beautiful American widow. He's keeping her as a surprise."

Anthony could not follow this one.

"Why d'you want him to marry again?"

"It would take his mind off," said Liz.

Anthony watched her spying upon the prospect of an imported stepmother. He could only dimly remember Baron's first wife. She had looked as Celia looked now. She had run away from him, taking Celia with her, and she had died in 1923 when Celia was nine years old. Celia had come back to Carlington. Baron had married again a year after that, the tricky, redheaded girl called Kit, so soon to die and leave Baron with the three children. A snapshot in Anthony's memory showed Baron in a state of collapse, Celia at fifteen, carrying all of it; running the house with Nanny and Foliot.

"I think he ought to marry Foliot, if you ask me," Anthony said, dusting the top of a turn-table. "She's madly in love with him. And he's stolen her youth, or whatever it is they call it in magazine stories. How old *is* she?"

"Ageless," said Liz. "Tobias believes that she subjected herself to some preservative process the time she went to Egypt on a

Cook's Tour. I never know why you don't sculpt her. All those bones."

"I had a shot once. She wriggled. And oh, Liz, it is borne in upon me today that I'm not a sculptor."

"*What?*" She jumped back from him in the doorway as though she had stepped on a spike.

"Well, I know she's not your favourite character in fact or fiction, but just run down the steps and look at that head of Jane's, now it's in plaster."

"What the devil has that got to do with your being a sculptor?" Liz flung at him. Her eyes were blazing.

He shrugged his shoulders. Her fury astonished him. "You're *not* to say that; you're not. I love everything you've done. I love them all." She rushed at the black marble puma. "I love this more than anything in the world except the red stone rabbit you did for me." She flung her arms around its neck.

"Do you?" he said, touched and remorseful. She went on hugging it. "What's the matter with you, Anthony?" she shouted over the top of its head. "Here." She rushed to the drawing-table and flung open the leather album that lay there, his book of press-cuttings. "A YOUNG MAN'S ADMIRABLE ONE-MAN SHOW!" she thrust at him, still shouting.

"That's a Baron headline," said Anthony lazily. "And I wasn't all that young. . . . Two years ago . . . I was thirty."

"Your-career-was-interrupted-by-the war," said Liz, making every syllable passionate and distinct—"If you deduct six years, you're only twenty-six." She slammed the book shut.

"What funny arithmetic. Why should I deduct six years for the war?"

"Because it wasn't fair."

"It didn't make a personal selection of Anthony Carey, darling. I'm lucky to be alive with only a stiff knee to show for it. *And* it handed me my chance of training with old Branca in Rome."

"All the same," she said offendedly, "you are entitled to take six years from your *sculptor's* age." She was scarlet. She snapped, "And if that's the kind of idea that Jane Ireland puts in your head, the sooner you terminate the liaison the better."

Anthony leaned against the door, overcome with giggles. The more he laughed, the redder and angrier Liz grew. She stood looking down at the table, tapping her fingers on it, a gesture of J. G.'s when irritated.

"I'm sorry . . . I really am sorry. . . . You're so sweet."

"Sweet as a stinging nettle now," she snarled.

"It was 'terminate the liaison'. You sounded like J. G."

"Well, it *is* a liaison, isn't it?"

"You shouldn't bother your head with such. Dear Liz . . . darling Liz, don't be cross. I think I'm a magnificent sculptor, really . . ." He tried to take her in his arms but she struggled and hit him on the nose. It hurt. He was chasing her round the studio in fury when Foliot's voice said archly:

"Excuse me, Anthony. But Marya was wondering about lunch. It's just three minutes past one."

"Now," Liz whispered, as they crossed the courtyard in Foliot's neat, spectral wake, "she'll think you were trying to rape me."

"Murder," said Anthony, "is the more likely fate for those who hit noses."

(iii)

The airfield was three miles up the road, going east from Carlington. To Liz it was casual, alarming ground, with its haphazard string of low wooden buildings, its shabby hangars and its groups of long-legged, untidy young men who were all friends of Toby's. The mysteries of civil aviation interested her not at all; this was just a territory of flat grass and windy air, the place where you walked and blinked at the sky until you saw sparks, awaiting Toby.

Always there were small aircraft taking off and landing; one landed now, a fragile fortunate shape that circled and sailed in, rocking on the tarmac as it came to rest. A young man who wasn't Toby threw one leg over the fuselage and jumped out.

He snapped his fingers to Prince, smiling at Liz as he went past. Liz, who had a deep distrust of young men, did not smile. She went on spinning on her heels and staring at the sky. The golden light of afternoon was here; it lit the marsh and the far edge of the sea.

The time was five o'clock, but she had lost all count of time. The day had broken to pieces when the black Rolls-Royce swept into the courtyard. In her mind only certain vivid moments stayed.

There was the look of Celia recaptured, the fairness and the laugh and the scent; the arms that hugged you closely. It was as though you turned on, in that moment, a love that you had turned off for fear of missing her too much. And after that heavenly impact of friendliness, greeting J. G. was no trouble; J. G. ducking out of the car with his characteristic movements, half pompous, half prancing. She could still see his image, his straddled stance in the camel-hair greatcoat, the grey curled hair and the bulgy forehead, the eyes that did not rest; the set, determined little smile that became a true smile only when he saw Anthony. There was the first sight of Terry; Terry was any small fair boy, faultlessly dressed and solemn, holding Nanny's hand. There was Nanny in the middle of the luggage; looking exactly the same, as though she had never been to America at all, perfectly composed and square and smiling. "It's your Aunt Liz, Terry. Shake hands with your Aunt Liz."

"But, oh God, Tobias, my lad, if you don't think there's murder waiting." She wrung her hands, gazing at the sky. Meanly she had left Anthony to face Baron's questions. She had escaped to the nursery wing where Celia was installed with Nanny and Terry; here she had taken refuge, frenziedly showing off the newly-decorated rooms, frenziedly helping Nanny settle Terry to his rest, then chattering and unpacking, coming at last to a dead, despairing halt in the middle of the bedroom floor as Celia called her bluff from the depths of a hot bath. "Liz, you'd better come clean. Where *is* the Bloody Child?"

Here was the Bloody Child now. The tiny aircraft whipped over the field, banked and tore so low past the hangar roofs that

Liz hid her eyes. It banked again and skimmed down straight; it touched the runway. The bright red head and the chestnut leather jacket hauled themselves out of the cockpit, followed by the interminable length of Toby's legs in pale grey corduroys. He did not see Liz yet. One of the young men came running and Toby was shouting to him, thumbing over his shoulder at the machine. Presumably the young man was to take charge of it. Toby began to run, halted, stripped off his flying-jacket and tossed it to the young man, who caught it; ran on again, still calling instructions back.

Liz barred his way silently. He pulled up on his heels. He grinned down at her.

"I met a lion in the Capitol," said Tobias, "it glozed upon me and went surly by."

He looked carefree and adult; the blurred look of youth that she remembered had left him for ever. He had neat features, Baron's small definite nose, a well-modelled jaw, a radiant, girlish complexion.

"You stinker," Liz said, "stinker; stinker; stinker."

"These are crude words. Not guilty am I. I had engine trouble—I've been sitting at Poix—are they here?"

"They've been here for hours."

"Is my absence noticed?"

"Noticed . . . words fail me," said Liz.

"I thought that the tenants might still be greeting Ould Maister——"

"Not for two hours, they don't go on greeting. I could bear it no longer. Don't think I came to meet you out of love."

Tobias said in cockney, "Well, ever s' nice of you, just the same. And Thank-God-for-Anthony's car to boot." He stroked its battered nose. "This poor Bentley; it has a lean and hungry look. Now, should we knit a lie? What did you say?"

"I didn't say anything. What could I say? What *can* we say?"

He giggled. "I know, I got stung by a wasp."

"Not in April, you didn't."

"Well, I barked my shin; barking up the wrong shin, as it might be." He started the engine.

"Don't," Liz said, "we can't move till we've thought of it."

Toby switched off the engine. "Say, say, what shall we say? Say I'm weary, say I'm old; say Jenny kissed me. . . . ('Where I *sat*', I always think so rude, don't you?) But why say anything at all? I went for a long, long walk and forgot the time."

"Just try it," Liz muttered.

"We'll try it."

He switched on again and raced the old car off the field; he drove with one hand on the wheel; he was happy; he was singing his song:

> "And I thought about the all-in-all, oh more
> > than I can tell!
> But I caught a horse to ride upon and I
> > rode him very well.
> He had flame behind the eyes of him and
> > wings upon his side,
> *And I ride!*"

"You don't give a damn, do you?" Liz said.

"About what, pretty creature?"

"About anything; I hate you."

"Tut. For you I cherish love."

"No; or you wouldn't do this."

"Engine trouble was what I had; I didn't do it on purpose. Beneath this harsh exterior there beats a heart of gold. My beloved Celia will forgive. How is she? And the brat? What type is this brat?"

"*Don't* drive so fast."

"The condemned man speeds to his doom," said Tobias; he returned to his song:

> "Inkpen and Hackpen and Southward and
> > away,
> High through the middle airs in the
> > strengthening of the day

And there I saw the Channel glint and
                              England in her pride
And I *ride!*"

"Toby."

"Yes."

"One thing I must know. Are you going to keep your hideous machine a secret for ever?"

"No, sweet rabbit, only until I have paid for it."

Now they were at the high red wall with the archway above the gate. Tobias roared into the courtyard, grazed the wing of the black Rolls, said, "That's all we needed," and jumped out, pulling down his waistcoat. "No reason," he said, "for you to witness the slaughter. You look green, poor Liz. I'm sorry." He bent and kissed her. "Wait for me."

"I'll go down to the willows."

"All right. Now for a frolic, now for a leap." He rushed into the hall. "He has no conscience, therefore no tremors," Liz said to herself. She crossed the terrace and went down the lower lawn into the field; Prince, the comfort of whose presence, she reflected, was akin to that of Nanny, trotted heavily beside her.

She had only just reached the stream and the willows when she saw him come; vaulting the terrace wall, racing across the lawn, galloping down the field.

"God tempers the wind to the shorn Tobias!" he shouted as she came to meet him.

"What happened?"

"He's closeted with the recording machine. Then he's going to rest. Dinner's at seven-forty-five. By the time he's dressed and standing under his portrait, the wrath will have shifted to Celia for being late. You see." He took out a packet of French cigarettes. "Here, have one." She was only half-consoled.

"But, Tobias, you won't get away with it. . . . Why do you do these things?"

"Couldn't say, couldn't say."

She looked at him doubtfully. "I'm so afraid," she began.

"Afraid?"

"Afraid you're in love with her."

"And who is 'her', may I ask?"

"Catherine de Lille."

"Certainly I'm in love with her," said Tobias briskly. "Could you imagine that these exploits are compelled by my admiration for Falchon or my passion for flying his second-hand machine?"

"Well, for flying it could be. But I *knew* it wasn't," she said despairingly. Now he walked as though in a trance, staring at the water.

"Why should you mind?" he asked, his voice hushed and cloudy.

"Love spoils everything. It makes the most awful things happen."

"What sort of awful things?"

She was thinking of Carey and Jane Ireland. She stalled; she said, "Like Celia marrying Van. You don't want to marry Catherine de Lille, do you, Toby, dear?" That was an echo from childhood. "Good-night, Toby, dear." Now he hated to be called Toby.

"Apart from the fact that she's married, pipe down," said Tobias. "You live in a vortex of unfounded fears. A lot of people my age form their first attachments for older women. It's quite natural, and utterly spiffing, according to the book of rules."

"But what can come of it? Other than the wrath of J. G."

"Of J. G., I spit me. Listen, Liz." He halted, stood before her, placed both hands on her shoulders. "You're getting worse about J. G."

"How?"

"More frightened. Nothing to do with my being late back, either. I've seen it coming upon you for months. The only way to do J. G. is to shrug; go out on your own line."

"Alas, I have no line."

"Then you'd better make one, and quick," said Tobias. "Honestly . . ."

"What sort?"

"Any sort. You're seventeen, you're grown-up. You can't

just sit here for ever and blush with delight when he gives you a smile and tremble with fear at his frown."

"Shut-bloody-up," Liz growled.

"Don't be cross. I love you very much, as you know. I want you to get away and have fun."

"All very well for you," she said. "You're brave."

"*Am* I?" said Tobias. Under the sunshot pattern of the willows, she saw his face turn shadowy, uncertain, alone. He was staring at a secret in his own mind. She had seen this look before. Another spring afternoon; the long relentless light and another shadowed face looking down with its secret. Nearly five years ago, and Celia saying, "I'm going back to Van." ("Love only makes unhappiness, this I know. And I see you alone with it now and I cannot tell you.")

"I don't think I'm brave," Tobias said at last.

"You are. You always were. None of the awful things frighten you; like flying or diving, and you *liked* the buzz-bombs."

"Physical bravado. This is not courage. This is a matter of gestures."

"*How* does one make gestures?"

" 'Struth——" said Tobias. "Of you I do despair. You ask and ask . . ."

"Well, if only people would say what they mean, instead of just telling one that one is wrong and not explaining. Nobody *ever* explains." She saw him look at her now with glimmers of sympathy.

"It wouldn't be any good if they did, sweet rabbit. You wouldn't listen—*or* believe, unless it was a person you loved very much."

"Yes," she thought, "that is true. I listen to Carey. I believe Carey. But Carey sees no reason for making gestures, against J. G. nor against my own cowardice; he is immune from the Baron fever." She clutched at Tobias.

"If I married the first person who asked me, would that be a gesture?"

"Half-witted are you. Come along, now the sun sinks and I

must bath me. We must change our clothes and make like nice
for Ould M. Hurry up. No time to play with the giraffe." It was
a phrase from long ago. "Come *along*; hurry *up*; no time to play
with the giraffe." Liz thought that Celia had invented it and she
could remember being sorry for the phantom giraffe.

"We needn't go in yet, surely?"

"What are you *frightened* of?"

"Of everything, damn it," Liz said and stood still. Tobias
began to walk away, then looked back exasperatedly. "You are
proposing to stay there and brood? And then fling headlong—
as for Ophelia?"

She began to giggle. "No," she said. "Wait for me."

2

(i)

THE unreality of return persisted. Standing at her bedroom
window, looking out at the shadowy trees, Celia felt as though
the scents of the garden, the knowledge of wood and marsh and
sea down there in the darkness, were made by a trick; the trick
of nostalgia conjuring them back to memory. Even when she
faced the room, its loved walls were thin; they might dissolve,
the white walls, the glowing fire, the bookshelves of the old day
nursery, and let America through. After the ship, the floor still
played the game of tilting under her feet; the slight dizziness
encouraged the sense of a dream.

So, as she looked about her, did the changes here. These
rooms in the east wing, the oldest part of the house, were the
nurseries and schoolrooms of the past. J. G., making them into
a suite of convenient pattern for herself, Nanny and Terry, had
divided the large L-shaped day nursery so that one half of it was
her bedroom and the other a sitting-room, with an extra bathroom for her own use. Across the passage Nanny and Terry had
the old night nursery, the old bathroom made modern, and the
schoolroom for day nursery. Curiously typical of J. G., she

thought, to set about these alterations and to say nothing of them. He must have ordered their beginning months ago, while his letters still pleaded with her not to leave Van.

He had gone to much trouble and expense. He had brought treasures out of hiding; the Empire bed that had been her mother's, all the Empire furniture, long stored away in the attics. The white fur rugs were new and the red and white curtains; in the other room he had seen to it that somebody made a selection of the colours and fabrics that she liked; had matched the furniture as far as possible with modern reproductions of the genuine stuff that was here.

"Carlington's your home . . . could you ask for a better?" the rich voice echoed. She thought of Terry's nursery, the bright paint and the splendid toys. Her gratitude was bounded by the sense of a noose tightening. Yet it was home. It was still the nursery, despite the imperious adult possessions. After any American room, she thought, one was doubly aware of its solid tranquillity. The only tranquil place there, the only valid place in her mind, was the house on the Vineyard. She thought of it now, the wooden ark on the rough grass, with the sea behind. It seemed very far and small. "But it is still mine," she said and blew it a kiss in thought and returned to the steady, peaceful contemplation of this room, this quiet, this knowledge of England. She bent her head to sniff the narcissi in the green glass bowl. She began to undress beside the fire, knowing that when she put out the light the fire would make patterns on the ceiling. "And where are you?" she asked Levitt. She was not yet uncomfortable with the memories of him. She felt as though he were here and she were showing him the room. It had been like this since the moment of stepping over the threshold. ("There is sharper edge to all of it, to everything that I see and feel, because of you.")

Nanny came from the sitting-room. "I haven't touched the big trunk yet, m'm. Will you want anything out of it tonight?"

"The presents are in it. Somehow I think I'll pend the presents till tomorrow, when the floor's settled."

Nanny said, "You look pale. Better get into bed quick."

"It's cold, isn't it? Or is it just England after America?"

"Must say I welcome it; that ship was stuffy too. Enough to make anybody feel queer. Get in, now. I put your hot-water bottle in and Miss Foliot thought you'd better have another, so there's two. Better sleep in your bed-jacket; there's nothing of these nightgowns of yours I always say. Here are your pills. Water. Got a book to read? Or don't you want to read; would you like me to take away the extra pillow?" Being put to bed by Nanny still had the finality of the last rites, Celia thought. She said, "I'm not going to sleep for hours yet. They'll all come up and talk. Lord, this is comfortable." Suddenly sorry for anybody who was not stretched out among clean sheets, she said, "Do go to bed, Nanny."

"I'm in no hurry." She put another log on the fire, then set out on a last tidying voyage about the room. "I must say, he's made it all very nice. Where *was* that naughty boy this afternoon, m'm? Sir James seemed really upset, Miss Foliot said."

"Tobias? Heaven knows."

"He's handsome, isn't he? And Miss Liz has turned into a real beauty; I never thought she would, bless her, such a scraggy little girl." She gave one of her sudden unexplained sighs. "Nice to be home, in spite of everything. Would you like me to bring you a cup of tea?"

"No, thank you, darling. Good-night."

("Where are you, Harry? Loping into the bar at the Savoy, I shouldn't wonder. But I will not follow you around; you are over; you belong to the voyage and the voyage is over. You are all the things that have hurt and confused me before and I will not go that way again. It will hurt me for a time; it is beginning to hurt a little now because I am tired. But I am not afraid of this hurt, I can be alone with it until it stops. And you will come here at week-ends, one of J. G.'s young men, and we shall smile at each other in a civilised way across a room full of people.")

Now she heard the first of the footsteps in the passage, the urgent knocking on the door.

Liz came in as though the devil were after her. She leaned against the door and laughed and panted. The dress was too old for her; Baron's present from New York, obediently worn tonight, a dark blue chiffon dress with a silver pattern from shoulder to waist. To Nanny, after a four-year interval, she was spectacular in beauty. To Celia, after only one year, she was too fragile and too tense; her cheeks were hollowing; this made the eyes look larger, the neck longer.

"Oh, I say, how quick and clever," Celia greeted her.

"J. G.'s wildly amenable; comes of being in an anti-Tobias mood. How tired are you? Too tired to talk?"

"Talk all night," Celia said. "Just so's I can do it lying down; the floor tilts."

"Horrible?"

"Not really. And it doesn't last. Come here. Let me look at you."

"Hug first," Liz said, scrambling into her arms. "Oh God, I'm so glad you're home."

"Stop shivering."

"Well, you're shivering."

"No, it's you."

"It's both of us," said Liz.

"Sure. The Baron shivers. Toby's hands are worse than yours or mine, I observe," Celia said.

"The family curse," said Liz.

"Just one of them. Sit on the bed. Cigarette? D'you mind not having your serious presents till tomorrow? They're in the big trunk."

"What are they? No, don't tell me. Talk is for now." She curled against the footboard of the bed. "Can you bear to tell about Van?"

"Not much to tell. It's finished. For good, this time. He's stalling on the divorce, blast him. Nothing to tell, darling," she repeated, "I just couldn't take it any more. For me or for Terry."

Liz said in a voice of doom, "Are you in love with anybody else?"

"No, certainly not."

Liz drooped with relief. "I thought you were, at dinner."

"Good God, why?"

"You looked private. It's in the air, I suppose. Do you know about Tobias or *not*?" she asked, frowning and lowering her chin.

"I think I do; some of it, anyway. Fill in. Where was he?"

"He went to France for the week-end."

"To Senlis?"

Liz nodded. "And he was supposed to be back yesterday; then a message came saying not till today. He keeps doing it. It began before J.G. left, and now he's got his own aeroplane— Oh God, now I've let that out."

Celia said, "His own aeroplane; well, well, that's all we needed. Who paid for it?"

"It isn't paid for yet. It belonged to Lionel Falchon—that's where everything started, because Lionel Falchon is Catherine de Lille's son by her first marriage."

"I know," Celia said, "I remember him."

"He's a commercial pilot; and he's taking ten pounds a month. But J. G. mustn't know, and I could kill Toby for doing that today, although I don't suppose he could foresee engine trouble, could he? But for doom and grief—d'you *know* Catherine de Lille?"

"Yes, I do. I don't mind that aspect of it at all."

"You *don't*?" Liz sat up with a start. "It's the *worst* aspect, isn't it?"

"No, darling. She's a peculiar person, but she'll do him no harm. In fact, I think it's probably very good for him."

Liz leaned back in despair. "You mean, it's true, what Toby says—that the books are all in favour of attachments to older women?"

Celia shouted with laughter. "*What* books? Those ones with the really fancy cases printed in Latin? I wouldn't know about books. I do know Catherine, and the château, and her life and her friends. It is exactly the sort of rainbow I'd be chasing, if I were Toby. But I don't approve of secret aeroplanes bought on the instalment system; and I despise his not being back today, because that's bad manners."

"But tell, tell. He never utters. What is she like?"

"Gentle. Comical. Kind. Goes around like somebody under a spell. She has, most unfairly, the reputation of eating people alive; in fact they eat her; she lets them; she's more a saint *manquée* than a courtesan. And for talent, in two languages, I'd put her next to Colette. Oh, there are a million stories about Catherine, most of them untrue. Don't worry, Liz. But he's got to make more sense with J. G. There's a kind of truculent silliness about the aeroplane that I hate."

"I hate it all."

"Why, sweetheart?"

"Because love spoils everything," said Liz. "Not that I can believe Toby *is* in love. He came back all pleased and singing 'The Winged Horse'; but perhaps," she added sorrowfully, "he was just putting a brave face on it . . ."

"No pleasure in love, in your view?" Celia asked, watching the drooped head, the fall of the hair on the firelit shoulder.

"Oh, *no*."

"Expound."

"Love," Liz said, "is wanting to *be* the person; wanting to be inside their skin and under their ribs and in their heads, to be hurt as much as they're hurt *when* they're hurt and be as ill as they are *when* they're ill and know everything that they're thinking—and being in agony all the time because you can't."

"Oh, dear."

"I mean it."

"Do you know, or are you just theorising?"

"I'm theorising, of course," Liz said. "And you are trying not to laugh; your mouth's gone crooked."

"I was just thinking—Liz, you're on my feet—what consoles me about you is that, like the tragic philosophers, you must be so deliciously surprised when things go right."

"Oh, I *am*," Liz said. "But isn't everybody? No; Anthony never expects anything to go wrong."

"Ah well, thank God for Anthony," Celia intoned, doing Baron.

"He *was* so good at the funeral; I simply hated the funeral.

I had to keep reminding myself that it wasn't really Randolph any more. So lonely, going down into all that cold yellow clay; and the planks and the ropes and dust-to-dust. Tobias wore J. G.'s cravat, you know; the puffy grey silk one. He spilt something on it. And afterwards Jane Ireland came to stay in Carey's house and make a beastly statue. I suppose she's his mistress, as though we had not enough troubles already."

(ii)

Downstairs in the green library, Tobias glanced at his watch; it was worn on the right wrist, face inwards, so that he could look at it unobserved. Many people, he reflected, wore their watches this way; there was no need to feel that it was a special anti-J. G. device.

The time was half-past ten. He looked at his father, seated once again in the corner of the sofa beside the fire. Now it felt as though he had never been away; as though the big grey head, the small shape in plum-coloured dinner-jacket and narrow black trousers had filled that corner of the sofa every night for the past six weeks. Above the mantelpiece the oil painting of J. G. seemed to smirk; saying—"We're both here now, and don't you forget it."

Here again were Baron's special things brought out of their brief retirement; the humidor, the port decanter, the silver cigar-cutter. Here was Mather again, shooting in with a little typed telephone message, J. G. glancing at it, shaking his head, handing it back, continuing to talk to Anthony, who faced him on the other side of the fire.

"Not a look my way; not a word," Tobias thought: "and his eyes slide off when I come into their range. All that is odious tonight am I; and I don't care."

He blinked at the fire; his mind was chasing back to Senlis; to the straight avenue between the poplars, the lake and the green lawns and the towers at the end of the avenue, the magic place.

He was walking into the room with the tall windows and finding
her there. She sat as still as a waxwork, at her desk, by the
window. He saw the small dark head, the lighted look of the
skin, the dreamy smile. Now the words spoken this morning
sounded again.

"But haven't you gone yet, Tobias? Raoul and the car have
been waiting ages. You'll be late."

"I couldn't go without saying good-bye."

"You have said good-bye three times. And your father will
envouler me more than ever if you're not back."

"Catherine."

"I said run along. Why do you stand there like a question
mark?"

"You haven't said if I may come next week-end. This gnaws
me as for worm."

"It must gnaw. I have specifically said don't come next week-
end. The company will be tiresome and you're wanted at
home."

"Pooh to home. All right. Desolated am I. I shan't see you
for ages."

"I'll be in London the week after."

"This, like Polonius' beard, is too long."

"Listen, Tobias, do I need to say it again? I love to have you
here. The last thing I want to do is to become a point of issue
with J. G. Baron, who finds me unsympathetic enough as it is.
Please be good. And please tell him about the aeroplane. And
please go. And when you get there, please be nice."

He remembered the feeling of her hand as he kissed it, and he
remembered her eyes as he went, looking back. He tried to see
through distances to her now. There would be people there;
always people; people to be entertained; people who wanted to
be listened to, fools, as though listening to Catherine were not
the only course of wisdom; people who wanted to borrow money
—and these would get it; and after they were gone she would go
back to the room with the high windows and sit at her desk and
write.

"Oh God," he thought, "I am just one of the people. And I

love you. And I have come too late. I want all the things from which time has shut me out: your memories, your youth, the whole fabric of your life." (The torment of references to these things; she had but to say 'Once when I was in Venice' for him to start awake and hanker to have shared Venice. She had but to say 'I'd been ill, I remember,' for him to feel resentful, sad that she could ever have been ill and he not know it.)

He said to her image, "And the least of it is knowing that you are no kinder to me than to any of the others who love you, men, women, servants, dogs. You love the whole world, my beloved; you do not like people often (at least you like me, one small feather placed in cap of this poor Tobias) but you love on a scale that's ludicrous."

His father's voice cut loudly into the dream. "When Glane's rebuilt, Anthony, I'll feel like saying '*Nunc dimittis*'." It was the word Glane that drew Tobias; he had loved Glane; five years ago, awed and angry, he had watched it burn from the hill. He walked through the shell of it sometimes; where the grass and the willowherb softened the shattered stones. But now it belonged to J. G. It was a project, sweaty with newspaper headlines; it was the strenuous child of the *Evening Flash* and *Sunday Sun*.

He was talking about a memorial statue for the village green. "I'd like you to have a shot at it, Anthony."

("How J. G. exaggerates his sweetness towards him, because he is enraged with me. And Carey remains undeceived. Carey is a bulwark. Anthony Bulwark Carey Esquire. The time has come, I think, to obtrude the unwelcome fact of my existence and see the eyes slide off.")

He rose. "Will you excuse me, please, J. G.?"

"What? . . . Yes," said his father, the eyes sliding off— "Going out again?" The lips were thin and the voice a thread.

"No. I wanted to go up and say good-night to Celia."

"All right. Don't stay with her too long; she's very tired."

He turned back to Anthony. Outside the door there was freedom. Tobias went into the dining-room, grabbed a quart bottle of beer from the sideboard and ran up the staircase; as he reached the passage to the nursery wing, gaiety returned.

He came to the door.

"Is it that I interrupt desperate female talk?" he asked, standing halfway inside.

"It is that you don't," said Celia from the pillows. He advanced, carrying the quart bottle as an amphora. "You look like all the most elaborate women in bed on stage or screen," he said. "Move up, Liz."

"*No*," Celia said, "you take the sofa. I won't have you drinking beer on my bedspread. What's the weather like below?"

"Fair over Carey and the home counties. A *deep* depression moving towards Tobias. Outlook for tomorrow, unsettled."

"Yeah; well, you bought it, darling."

"I know I did."

"I've told about the aeroplane," said Liz abruptly; "I didn't mean to." She looked so tragic that his momentary flicker of annoyance perished. "Don't mind Celia knowing—you must see his pretty aeroplane. Why do you look like that? Floor still tilting?"

"Not at the moment. I'm about to give you fierce advice." Tobias watched her, certain as ever that her judgment was to be respected, not wanting the judgment now.

"You must stop playing Little-Master-Thumb-His-Nose with J. G., darling. It isn't worthy of you. That's all."

Tobias said, "I know I must. But he buys it, too. Today was un-pretty, this I admit. May I use that glass?"

"No, love. Take one from the other room. I want it for my sleeping pills and after you've gone it will be all I have in its soapy repulsion."

"*Sleeping pills?*" Tobias posed as J. G. straddling. "Why not arsenic and be done with it? *That's* why you're a nervous wreck, Celia. If I played the tricks with my body that you play with yours——" He stooped over her and kissed her before he went to fetch the glass. "I'll be good to Ould Maister. I'll confess about the aeroplane as for love-child. . . . It is a matter of marked satisfaction to us to have you in residence, is it not, Liz? . . . You'll have to do some work on Liz, too. She's got moult or something. I think she ought to have a job." As he went into the further room he heard Liz wailing, "A *job*; as though that would help."

"What to do, then?" he called through the alcove, "just stay here and play with the giraffe?"

"I have my music," she said haughtily.

"Sure, sure. And I have my stage career, and J. G. looks as kindly upon one as upon the other."

"Still fighting that one, Toby?" Celia asked.

"No fight. It is what I am going to do. And if I thought Liz was equally determined to out-Hess Myra Hess, I would have no worry about the child." He seated himself on the sofa and poured the beer.

"Here's Thank-God-for-Anthony," said Liz.

Anthony knocked, opened the door a little way and put his head round it. "Too late? Dying?" he asked Celia.

"No. Heartily alive. How come you got out so soon?"

"He's on the telephone to Downing Street or God or somebody," Carey said. He came to sit beside Tobias, balancing a gramophone record on his knees. "Here's your record, Liz."

"Oh, lovely to remember. I wanted it for you, Celia."

"What is it?"

" 'The Lykewake Dirge'."

"It would be a dirge," said Tobias. "I have no urge to hear this dirge."

"Oh, pearls and swine," said Liz, "it's delicious."

"Cut the talk," said Celia, "and put it on."

"What, now?" said Tobias. "J. G. will think we're indulging in low carousal."

"He can't hear from this distance."

Tobias leaned in the alcove, watching Carey skirt the luggage and adjust the gramophone. Always it diverted him to see Carey emerge blithe and untroubled from any session with his father. ("What's your secret, Carey, *mon preux chevalier*? I wish I knew.") "J. G. do any more digging about my activities?" he asked, low-voiced.

"A little, old boy. Don't think he credits the car-break-down."

"No, well; I wouldn't myself."

"Shut up, Toby, don't talk now," Liz called.

Still leaning in the alcove, Tobias studied the plaintive voice, the warning notes. Shrill as the bagpipes, he thought, tall pointed notes, lunging at death.

> *"When thou from hence—away art past*
> *Every nighte and alle . . ."*

The thought of death was all terror, more than it had ever been. ("In death I shall lose you, Catherine; please God let us die together.")

> *"If ever thou gavest hosen and shoon,*
> *Every nighte and alle,*
> *Sit thee down and put them on,*
> *And Christe receive thy saule."*

He looked back at the firelit room, at Celia's fair head on the pillows, at the figure of Liz, crouched and dedicated.

> *"From whinny-muir when thou art past,*
> *Every nighte and alle,*
> *To Brig O' Dread thou comest at last."*

It was purgatory fire, now, the leaping flames; and still the message, *"If ever thou gavest"*. Giving was all. If you gave, it said, *"The fire shall never make thee shrink"*, and he saluted this, because of Catherine, the arch-giver.

He was still leaning there when the music ended. He woke. "Yes—all right, Liz. I really do like it." He came back to the bed and stroked her hair.

"Want any more, anybody?" Carey called.

"Something orderly," Celia said. "Make it the Double Concerto. You look bemused, Tobias."

"I want to talk to you, some time."

("At least," he thought, "now that she is home, we have a grown-up person with us. I cannot talk to the sweet rabbit, and Thank-God-for-Anthony's too much the congenital Guardsman.") He pushed Liz off the end of the bed, saying, "My turn"—and lay there with his long legs dangling, his head on his arm.

J. G. walked lightly. The first that Tobias knew of him was the door opening just beyond the footboard of the bed and the voice jarring into the neat, cool values of the music.

"Giving a party, Celia?"

Tobias sat up, seeing them: the lithe little figure of Baron, the thrusting head, the crooked smile; Anthony golden and unperturbed beside the mantelpiece; Liz tense; and Celia, lying back, sunnily glacial, "No party; just us."

"I thought you were tired. D'you realise what time it is?"

"Please, J. G., don't talk until this is over. We're listening." She waved a courteous hand to the sofa. After a moment he sat down, patting the space beside him and inviting Liz with his eyebrows and a smile. She sat down, taut and uneasy. "And now," Tobias thought, "I cannot listen at all. He makes the room quite different." He put his chin on his knuckles and stared at his father, observing happily that since they faced each other, J. G. had some trouble in not looking his way.

J. G. said, "Pretty stuff, what is it?"

"Finlandia, by Monteverdi," said Tobias, and was rewarded by a giggle from Liz. Celia did not laugh. J. G. turned towards Anthony; he was suddenly sprightly. "What's next on the programme?"

"Sleep for me, if I'm not driving you out," said Celia; "the room is now moving through an angle of ninety degrees."

J. G. gave her an exasperated glance, rose stiffly and made a herding gesture. Tobias uncurled himself at leisure. "Give up these boats," he said to Celia. "The aeroplane is the more civilised method of travel. Never a bump today; on a bat's back, from coast to coast." He winked at her and leaned above her pillow, conscious of J. G. frozen behind his shoulder, of Liz and Anthony calling "Good-night" and going; of Celia's comical grimace, that might be praise or blame.

"Come along, Tobias," said the thread of a voice at his back.

"One moment, sir; I wish to kiss my sister. Good-night, my beautiful. Shall I administer your sleeping pills one by one, or two by two? And spread a little liquefying cream over that calm mask?"

"Out, freshie," Celia said.

"*Aut* freshie *aut nullus*?"

"Get on, stupid," said Celia, "I love you. Bliss to be home. Good-night."

He was surprised to see his father stride ahead with Anthony, taking no more notice of him. He expected thunder. They went downstairs. Liz waited.

"*Why* did you do it? Say it? Like that? Then?"

"It swept upon me with uncontrollable impulse, as for sneeze. Good-night, pretty rabbit. Have no fear."

(iii)

Baron tied the cord of the black brocade dressing-gown about his waist. Quietly he left his room, came to the landing and mounted the stairs to the next floor.

His soft knock went unanswered; he walked in. He turned up the lights. Tobias slept as straight as a knight on a grave, the bedclothes neatly draped over the long body. The room was neat also. He took care of his possessions. Each, as Baron looked about him, seemed a defiant statement of Toby's passion: the old playbills; the toy theatre; the bust of Henry Irving; along the bookshelves, the plays of every dramatist from Aristophanes to Fry. There was a panel of signed photographs, all stage photographs; Jay Brookfield, Caroline Seward and, prominent now in the theatre, a dark, cloudy portrait, the work of a foreign camera—a nunlike head with wide eyes, Catherine de Lille. As he stepped closer to look at this, he heard Tobias' hushed voice from the bed.

"Anything I can do for you, J. G.?"

"Oh, you're awake, are you?"

"Within limits," said Tobias, sitting up on one elbow. "What time is it?"

"After one. I couldn't sleep. I wanted a talk with you." He tramped to the side of the bed. "Better have it out now, I think."

Tobias stretched a hand to the cigarette-box beside him, and lit a cigarette with fingers that jumped. "How all their hands shake," Baron thought resentfully. "What *is* it about my children that makes my life so impossible? Why can't they be like other men's children? Why can't I have a son like Anthony?" He did not want to let these thoughts go on; he had decided upon his rôle for now; it was the man-of-the-world, easy and ironic, the sophisticate with the masterful touch.

Toby's sleepy, drooping elegance in *crêpe de Chine* pyjamas did not make the going easy. "So you were flying today, were you?" Baron began. "Came out a little late, didn't it?"

"Better late than never, to coin a phrase," said Tobias. "And I apologise. It was part carelessness and part engine trouble. I did mean to be back."

"And I understood you to say 'coast to coast'; did I not?"

"Yes; fair stood the wind for France."

Baron seated himself on the side of the bed. He thought that Tobias was doing his best to be agreeable, but this did not help because he had never yet reached a true line of communication with his son. It shocked him to realise how little he liked Toby; the affected speech and the romantic air were irritating always, even when the boy was not indulging impertinent gestures.

"And, let me see, when do you go up to Oxford?"

"Ten days from now," said Toby, looking puzzled.

"Would it be too much to ask of you not to make foreign visits between now and then?"

He saw laughter in Toby's eyes. "No, as it happens, it would not."

"What do you mean 'as it happens'?"

"I wasn't planning to go."

"Ah—and if you had been, you would not have let your plan be disarranged by my request?"

Tobias cocked his head on one side, tapping the ash from his cigarette. His smile came and went.

"May I ask you something, J. G., before I answer that?"

"What? . . . Yes, of course—go ahead."

"Why the veto?"

"Because, my dear boy, I don't like to see you making a fool of yourself. I have asked you before, remember."

"Fool of myself?" Tobias turned pale. "Explain, please."

"Certainly. Running around in circles after Catherine de Lille, of all people."

Tobias was now so white that it made Baron feel ill to look at him. He looked away.

"I'm not unsympathetic to adventures, Toby. You're growing up; you must have your fun. I was the same. I was a lot younger than you when I had my first woman. And I can say honestly that I'd rather pay the upkeep of six London tarts for you than have Catherine de Lille make your rain and your fine weather." He had thought out the last phrase carefully. It surprised him to see that there was sweat on Toby's forehead; his hand shook so much that he dropped the cigarette on the sheet when he tried to take a puff at it.

"Relax," Baron said. "I'm not suggesting that you sleep with her."

"Quiet, please," said Tobias, at last, his voice muffled.

"Do I shock you?"

"N-no." The voice was unsteady, far away.

"You ought to be grateful for a broadminded father, you know."

Tobias said, "Well, possibly," and put out his cigarette. "Catherine of course hazarded that you might take this attitude."

Baron tapped his knee. "So she discusses me with you, does she?"

"Now and again, now and again. Sympathetically, I promise.

I understand that she once put you below the salt at a dinner party in Paris and you've gone on remembering. She was sorry she did that: she knows you cared."

It was true. It made Baron so angry for Tobias to know it that he did not trust himself to speak. Now they had changed rôles; Tobias was steady and sunny.

"Thank you kindly for the offer of the tarts. These I do not use. But if you'd like to pay for something, I'd be grateful for the first instalment on a second-hand aeroplane."

Baron jumped off the bed. "Are you losing your mind?"

"Not yet," said Tobias, "but then, I'm taking trouble."

"An aeroplane?" Hardest to forgive was the ludicrous shape that the interview was taking. "Lionel Falchon's machine?"

"Yes. He's sold it to me."

"May I ask how you fuel it?"

"In France. Plenty petrol."

"Is an aeroplane—may I ask—a necessary adjunct to a stage career?"

"Oho," said Tobias, "do we begin to admit to my stage career? Then these little words will not have been wasted."

The man of the world with his easy irony vanished in thunder. The authentic fury that only Tobias could provoke was here. He whirled to the door. He looked back.

"You've had your chance, Toby," he said, not sure what he meant by this. "And now it's over. You're still under age, remember. The aeroplane goes back to Falchon tomorrow. I'll write him a note explaining matters. And if you attempt to see Madame de Lille again without first asking my permission, I shall take you away from Oxford at once and put you into some kind of work that'll bring you to your senses."

He heard Tobias say, "You're not serious?" as he shut the door. Then he was striding away with the words, "Madame de Lille" still in his head. "Could have called her 'Catherine', couldn't I? Common, somehow, to say 'Madame'; suburban; why didn't I say Catherine?" But it was only one example of ineptitude in a talk that had taken inept turns throughout. And he had seen it so clearly, planned it so well. The quiet ultimatum, the whip-hand in the velvet glove. In Fleet Street he could put it over without effort, half a dozen times a week. Why not with Tobias?

He had come to the head of the stairs. He went down, the black brocade rustling stiffly about his ankles, past the first floor and the way to his own room: down to the landing. He stood below the portrait of Kit in her green dress. He stared at the mother of Tobias and Liz.

The awful thing was that he could not remember her very well. It horrified him. The punctual halt before this picture on the way to bed, the little sigh, were empty tributes. The one who survived in memory was Celia's mother, the first Celia.

Now he grumbled sadly, "Nobody can say I didn't do well. Both times. I married women of good family, married Above Me, they call that. . . . And meant to."

He recalled the determined apprenticeship to the world where he did not belong; the years of training, until at thirty-two, when he married Celia Hazelten, the polish was good enough. It had taken marriage to teach him that polish cracked. Now he could make all those torments return. And he could bring back, softened by time, separate from the torment, the good things of that marriage; his pleasure in the cool head and the hot blood, in her wit and her dignity.

Yes, he could restore the runaway. But Kit he could not restore. The flat, gay portrait smiled. In his mind she was equally two-dimensional; a character from a dated novel that he had read a long time ago.

She was a brilliant little creature, travelled and restless, her brain at odds with her pedigree. She had come to him for a job. She had something of his own buccaneering quality; she had got the job. She was one of his special correspondents when he married her. And after that? He could remember incidents, not feelings. She had suited him admirably. She had produced the two children (God knows how she had found the time, with her social programme, her travels abroad, the lovers that she took on the side). She was a lady, always a lady, a lady who was a tough and no trouble, a decorative adjunct, a piece of wayward but satisfactory property; no trouble until her death, as stupid a death as any woman could invite, six years after their marriage. Whose the child would have been he did not know nor care. Kit, being Kit, had decided against having the child and had died for this. And left him alone again.

And now he could hardly see her at all. Well, she had been dead for sixteen years; he might be excused this feeling of guilt. Yet she was the mother of Toby and Liz; her damnable breeding (the graven image that the young Baron had made to himself) went on in them. That was half the battle; the wrong half.

"I can't be such a bloody little snob as to feel that they're socially superior to me. Yes, I can; I do. That's why they get the better of me every time. What have I done to deserve *that*? To deserve Tobias and tonight—my first night home, too . . . ? And that bitch de Lille telling him about the time in Paris. . . . What have I done to deserve any of it? God, with his inhuman lack of consideration, only knows."

3

(i)

HAVING explored every first-class carriage on the train without finding Baron, Levitt took his seat just before the whistle blew. This was useful; this was what he wanted. "If you don't see me on the four-ten," Baron had said, "you'll know I've been kept and I'll be driving down later. You'll be met at Ashford, Celia or Anthony'll meet you."

As the train moved, Levitt was conscious of the old tune playing, the "Can't-Catch-Me" tune. It brought peace. Peace had been missing from the programme of the last ten days.

There was a city oddly unlike the war-time London that he remembered; there were the harassing series of strangers, editors, sub-editors, feature-editors and art-editors in the great grimy building north of Fleet Street; there were late meetings with Baron at the Savoy, and walking back alone to the flat because he hoped that the walk would help him to sleep, and not sleeping.

The flat was an alleged luxury flat in Curzon Street. It had as much character as an empty trash-basket and the look of the lighted hall through the glass panel of the lift depressed him; every floor was a duplicate of the last, with a mirror, a gilded table holding a vase of flowers and the perspective of identical doorways. He pressed the button and rose up, through tiers of honeycomb, until he came to his own floor, his own hall with the mirror, the gilded table and the vase of flowers. Then he walked along the perspective of identical doors until he found the one where his key fitted the lock, and then there were the two neat, anonymous rooms and bathroom, the cupboard-kitchen whose refrigerator was on the blink.

"I'll find somewhere else to live," he told himself every morning, "as soon as all this has quieted down."

All this would, must quiet down. He was taking himself, the newness of his life and work, too seriously. He was taking his phase of shadow-boxing with Celia too seriously. It was baffling to have been left alone so soon. To have had one telephone conversation of arid brevity and then no more words. He had needed her in this beginning. She would have helped to control the symptoms of the nervous disease that he had once heard her refer to lightly as "The Baron fever". He knew all about it now.

"It's odd," Levitt thought, staring out of the window at the blossom, gaily flowering in front of the small, sooty houses near the track. "It's damned odd. None of my bosses, from my first top-sergeant to my last colonel, from my art teachers to Grant Parker, ever did this to me. I took them as they came. Why can't I take J. G. Baron as he comes? Maybe because I never know how he's going to come, which Baron it is that's coming . . . and why should I care?

"What in hell does it matter if he's putting on his Winston Churchill and water act, or his country gentleman act, or his smutty-good-fellow act? What's it to me? Do I have to draw that face on the telephone-pad, dream of it in nightmare, take half his talk to bed with me, hear the voice go on and on? Am I scared or hypnotised? It won't do, whichever. It's got to stop."

He shut his eyes; they were hot and sore from lack of sleep. "But it'll be better tonight. Tonight I'll sleep. In the country; in her bed." He thought of it until his body hurt him. He opened his eyes.

He was aware of England now; of the bones of the land beyond the window; a field, a chalk hill, and a line of trees in green leaf; the landscape more understandable, more to be understood, than the fields of home. Being so tired, he was made melancholy in his affection for it. It belonged to him, and did not belong.

(ii)

For Celia, J. G.'s week-end loomed. "But I welcome it, in my restlessness," she thought. "It will do." She was flying the kite with Terry. The kite was up; it soared in its little box-shape against the sun. She gave the string to Terry; he said, "Take-it-for-a-walk," and staggered along backwards, looking up. She guided him through the gap in the yew hedges, on to the lawn. Here he ran to and fro. She climbed the grass steps and sat on the pompous marble bench below the line of cypresses.

Restlessness; the oldest demon. Ten days had been enough to bring him out. He brought a sense of suffocation, of being owned and caught, ensconced by J. G.; of being back at the beginning again, with time on her hands. "I have no serenity," Celia thought, "can't sit still. Never could sit still."

Work was the answer. She envied Liz at the piano, Anthony in his studio, Tobias on the eve of Oxford. She must, she knew, get a job in London—go hunting the contacts made in the war. Remembering those days, the days of writing scenarios for documentary movies, in an office underground, she looked at the only time when she had known peace. Yes, she had been at peace with the confusion and the red tape, the cancelled instructions, the punishing hours; at peace with the huge machine, with the improbable colleagues, with the black-out and the bombs and the eternal tiredness; at peace with war. "Because," she said to herself, "the war was one of the few opportunities for the adult to look ahead as confidently as a child at school looks to the holidays, saying *When this is over*.

"There would be an end, we knew. There was a date on a calendar somewhere, not known, but ahead, and if one lived, one would come out of the tunnel into the daylight; all private hopes and happiness were waiting on that date. Meanwhile, one accepted the tunnel. One never thought 'I must get away, get out'—because one knew first that one couldn't get away or get out, and equally, that one's escape was certain once the date came on the calendar."

It seemed wicked to look back nostalgically at war. "Be honest," Celia said to herself, "your trouble is Levitt, and only Levitt; and you have put paid to that one. What you have left now is not only time, but an excess of emotion on your hands; to be banked down, burnt out alone. But—not to smile inside because he will be here today, not to feel this quickening, this dazzle in the mind, that's a tough one. Hell, you know how to handle tough ones."

She was suddenly consoled by the thought of Anthony; she had met him yesterday afternoon limping through the white gate, wearing his working overalls, pipe in mouth. "I've run out of beer," said Anthony, "I want some of J. G.'s nice beer." He had stood looking at her with the Carey tranquillity radiating from him, the immense good-humoured calm.

"Beer? It's tea-time; I was coming to see if you and Jane would like to have tea with us."

"Jane just went out of my life," said Carey, "in a huff and a taxi." He laughed.

"Oh no."

"Oh, yes. Better so. Terribly difficult," he said, not sounding as though anything had ever been difficult, "to make that sort of person happy. I ain't the man for the job. I never was. Come on; beer. I got thirsty trying to say the right things."

"Tell. No, of course you won't tell. You're too much of a gentleman. Liz will be pleased."

"I know, Liz could never stand her, could she?" said Carey indifferently. "Can't think why. Jane's awfully *nice*, really."

"I'd like," Celia thought, "to have some of that boy's benign common sense. And I'd like to think that Toby or Liz would ever acquire it; which is as constructive as to wish that we were all three born with an extra leg."

Tobias, in riding clothes, came through the yews on to the lawn. Terry rushed at him, losing the kite. Celia watched them, mixed up together and rolling. "I will *not* be called Uncle Toby, d'you hear?" Tobias shouted, lying on his back, holding the child above his face.

"Why?"

"When you grow to man's estate, you will read *Tristram Shandy*; then you'll see."

"Why?" He began to wriggle and kick. Tobias put him down, lay still. Terry copied him, lying flat.

"Get up. Both of you," Celia said, "the grass is wet." ("At Carlington I turn into everybody's aunt.")

"I cool me. I am hot from horse," said Tobias.

"So am I," said Terry. Nanny came to call him for his tea. Tobias joined Celia on the bench. "Why are you brooding under sad cypress, darling, as for Feste?"

"Just sitting," she said. She took her lighter from her pocket and began to dismantle it. Tobias said, "What time will J. G. be with us? Already I feel the shadow of his monstrous wing. Do you imagine he'll declare a truce as it's my last week-end?"

"Who can say? Yes, probably."

Tobias wrinkled his nose. "I despise the silent war; the umbrage and the thin lips, the uneasy eye, don't you?" He stretched his long legs in front of him, thrust his hands into the pockets of his breeches, stared towards the sea.

"'Struth," said Tobias, "when I think with what angelic humility I surrendered the aeroplane. This poor aeroplane."

"Where is it now?"

"Falchon flew it back to France. I can picture it, waiting for me hopelessly, night after night, sleepless; haggard with great black circles under its cowling." He turned to her suddenly. "Have you a minute to solve me and absolve me? This of J. G. and umbrage——"

"Go on."

"Well, I could not in delicacy repeat the talk we had—the night he got home. But it ended up with a governessy ultimatum about Catherine de Lille." His voice scraped a little and she saw the colour deepen on his cheek; he had not spoken to her yet of Catherine de Lille. "Consummate rubbish. . . . If I saw her again without asking his permission first, he'd whip me out of Oxenford and put me in the collieries."

"Collieries?"

"Well, in effect only. Work, he said, that would bring me to my senses."

"Well, well, well . . ." It was so silly that she kept her comments back, trying to choose a diplomatic line; fixing the lighter.

Tobias said, "I'm coming down next week. Just for that. She'll be in London. Her play's opening, you know."

"All right; why shouldn't you?"

"Do I have to tell him? I've not the slightest intention of asking his permission, but do I have to tell him?"

"I don't know, Toby. Only you know the answer to that one," she said. "If you feel all right not telling, don't tell."

He said, "What do *you* think?"

"Darling, it doesn't matter what I think. That one, I repeat, is with you. It's dictated by the thing inside."

"The conscience that beats behind this pretty waistcoat? I fear you are right; you always are; look, here's Foliot. Bet you sixpence she says something about the time."

"I'm sorry to disturb you," Foliot said, "but Sir James called just two minutes ago."

Tobias held out his hand, palm upward. Celia said, "Does he want me?"

"No; it was just a message; he's been kept in London; won't be down until late; he's driving down. There's a Mr. Levitt arriving on the five-fifty-five and Sir James would like somebody to meet him; one of the family," she added lightly. "He didn't say which." She looked from one to the other.

"All right," Celia said, "thank you, Foliot. One of us will go." As she watched the neat black shape departing, she was angry with herself for this disturbance at the heart. She flicked the lighter, saw her hand shake, and put it back in her pocket. "Sixpence, please," Tobias was saying. "Is that the new cartoonist? J. G. was selling him to Carey. All the signs, as they fell on my pointed and inattentive ears, of becoming one of the regulars."

"He was on the boat with us. Will you meet him, darling?" She had to readjust her mind to the prospect of Levitt alone; she had imagined that he would arrive with Baron and the others in Baron's train: Gerald Lynn, Hugh McLeod and old Micklethwait, the veteran yes-man.

"How shall I know him, I ask myself?"

"He looks—to quote J. G.—like the Knave of Spades."

Tobias said, "Liz is going in, anyway, with Thank-God-for-Anthony. I might go too. You not?"

"Me not," she said steadily.

(iii)

This was better, Levitt thought; he looked at the oast houses, at the orchards, at the small fields in the afternoon sun. He was excited now. The train drew in to Ashford Station. He prowled, carrying his bags, looking for Celia. As the crowd thinned, he thought that he saw her, but when she came near she was not Celia at all; she was an older woman, a caricature, frozen, striding, with lined skin and peroxide hair. He was angry with himself for having seen the likeness. He stood still, looking both ways, irked by those who were being met, uncertain what to do. She was late, he remembered, by habit. Or perhaps she was waiting outside with the car. He was still quite sure that she would come. He went towards the barrier.

The large golden-headed man standing on the other side of the barrier looked at him questioningly. Levitt knew the face; it was the face out of Baron's photograph, the perfect Englishman with the pipe. He even remembered the shadow beneath the lip and looked to see if it were there before he said, "You're Carey, aren't you?"

"Yes. Hullo," the smile was friendly. "Give me one of those." He took the suitcase. Perhaps Celia was in the car; she was not; here was the car, a battered old Bentley, with a strap round the bonnet.

"Liz and Toby stopped for cigarettes," Carey was saying, "I think we'll drive slowly and find them." After a series of violent explosions the car started. "Sorry about that," said Carey. "She's on her last legs; and I take her out so little these days, not enough petrol."

Levitt said, "I thought the trade in black market coupons was wide open."

"So it is," said Carey with a grin. "I don't play, but I think I'm a fool not to."

Now they threaded a narrow street, and war memories came back, of loving the look of a country town, of catching his breath because it was not a shiny photograph in an English calendar nor a carefully-built movie set, but the different truth.

"There they are," said Carey. They were a tall red-headed boy and a girl with brown hair, looking in a shop window. Carey blew the horn and they turned and came towards the car. Each, he reflected, was a haunting of Celia, each a property of Baron.

Liz was more alive than the hackneyed nymph upon the lawn, more alive and more afraid. He saw the fear first, the beauty afterwards. Tobias he disliked at once without knowing why; he had one of those hushed, haughty voices that were an irritating possession of British boys; he was affectedly pleased with himself, Levitt thought, looking at the radiant colouring, the check suit and the yellow waistcoat.

They climbed into the back seat and hung forward, chattering in his ears.

"Drive slowly; our American visitor must see Ye Old Wool-worthey."

"And now, unwinding before you, some of the more spiffing council houses, each authentically stamped by the hand of the maker."

"Row on loveless row."

"This car must seem antique enough to him, no? It suffers from griping gas pains, Mr. Levitt. It gets no vitamins; alas, this poor car."

"Poor Carey has his name down for a new Bentley."

"And this he will not receive until he is too old to drive; this poor Carey."

"While J. G. fleets the time carelessly in his black Rolls; black is the market, blacker the Rolls. We expected you to arrive in this Rolls. What happened to J. G.?"

Levitt said, "He was kept, I guess."

"Kept by a woman? Tut," said Tobias.

"He won't be down till after dinner," said Carey.

"And nice as that is for us," said Tobias, "(Liz, the prudent kick on the ankle went out with Pinero) I call it highly discourteous to our American visitor. Now see the pretty marsh, the skipping lambs, only these lambs no longer skip, they are at the podgy, adolescent stage, meriting mint sauce. The horizon which you cannot see, there being a haze upon it, is the sea."

"And now," said Liz, "the great towers come in sight, the drawbridge swings. The rosy-cheeked children of the lodge-keeper drop curtseys."

They drove in through the arched gate. Here was the big sudden house from the photograph, the lawns and terraces and clipped yews.

"Ain't it awful?" said Tobias, standing in the gravel court-yard, looking up.

"The East Wing is nice," Liz said, pointing. "That's the only old bit left. The rest was burned."

Now there was the anticlimax of having arrived, the man-servant carrying in the luggage, a glimpse of a pale green room with bookshelves on one side of the hall, a dark gloomy dining-room on the other side; too many open doors; another at the back of the hall showed him a long, panelled room with windows looking out on to the terrace and the marsh. A fat, yellow dog switched his legs with a tail like a whiplash.

"Excuse, please. I wish to float my nephew in his bath," said Tobias and vanished. Levitt felt better now that he was gone. Liz and Carey escorted him.

"J. G.'s territory," Liz said, "you are two away from him." She hopped and pointed like a sprite. "His *bed*room; his *bath*room. *You.*"

It was large and full of comfortable things: a four-poster bed; a writing-table; fat arm-chairs; flowers; cigarette-boxes.

"We dine at seven-forty-five and it's six-thirty now. I don't know if you'd rather have a bath and change right away." Carey gave the impression of being master here, the eldest son; there was something a little irritating about his authority, his placid air. Levitt expected one of them to mention Celia and they did not. Carey said, "Come on, Liz. Leave the nice gentleman in peace. Ask for anything you want, won't you, Levitt?" He took Liz by the back of the neck. Levitt heard them begin to talk and laugh on the other side of the door.

"Changing for dinner," he thought. "Well, well." He stood at the window while the valet unpacked his clothes, watching the gold light in the garden. At the end of the terrace there was a path running under a high red wall; there were clumps of rhododendron and then a white gate.

Where was Celia?

(iv)

It was too long a dining-table for the five of them.

Carey sat at the head with Celia on his right, Liz on his left. Levitt was next to Liz, Tobias next to Celia. Dark and solemn as a dining-room in a British movie, Levitt thought, looking at the swollen silver on the sideboard, the oil portraits on the walls, the candlelight and the flowers. Celia's face in the candlelight baffled him. She had come down too late for the drinks. There had been the sight of her walking in at last, the dazzle and the flying look, the friendliness, the cool trembling hand in his, the little words.

"But you look exhausted. Has J. G. been putting you through it?"

"As a start, it has been pretty tough sledding." (Hedged about by the elegant, tiresome Tobias, by Carey playing host and Liz handing a dish of hot *hors d'œuvres*: what use was that? What use was this?) He talked to Celia in his mind, "I see your hair, the hair like a child's, I see your eyes and your skin and the black dress that makes the skin whiter and I want my hands on all of it. And you give me no clue." He forced himself not to look at her. He looked at Tobias, whose high collar and wide black tie gave him a Regency air. "How should I draw you? As a stag perhaps, a limpid and superior stag." But the gentleness of the face, its utter lack of guile, put him off. He glanced at Carey; the queer shadow beneath the lip was exaggerated now; it made an unexpected qualification in that fair strength. "If I drew you, it would be there, that dubious shadow, distortedly significant. Levitt's-eye view. And if I drew Liz," he thought, "I should widen those eyes to a horrified stare and bring out the cheek-bones and the length of the neck until all that I'd made of that beauty would be a mad child. Celia, you're lucky; you're immune; I can never draw you now. Damn it, are you going to let me sleep with you tonight?"

The servant refilled the glass at his elbow; he should be liking all this; luxury; rich men's goods. But he was not. He was shut out; even without the cryptic quality of Celia; there would be the sense of the family, ranged together, not needing him.

"An olive?" Liz said; he looked at her fingers on the silver dish. "Are you watching my shaky hand?"

"It's the Baron dipsomania," Tobias supplemented. "Don't let it worry you."

"High-strung types," said Anthony. "I always want to know what happens when the time comes for them to shake with fear."

"Our bones snap."

"No; we differ from the rest and go rigid."

"I really *do* go rigid," said Liz. "It isn't funny. I did when the buzz-bomb came down on Slater's farm. I couldn't move."

"Oddest effect of fear I ever saw," said Carey, "was a bloke in my company; he couldn't stop laughing."

"In the Anzio landing?" Liz said. "That's where this poor Carey won his pretty medal," she added to Levitt.

"Quiet, please," said Carey. Now, Levitt thought, he was caricaturing the modest hero; silencing Liz; saying, "Fear didn't turn me rigid; my face twitched; I winked and winked and couldn't stop. It went on for days. Looked a perfect fool."

"You've never told me that," said Liz, sounding startled sounding as though it were important for her to know.

"I'd forgotten," said Carey mildly.

"But you *weren't* afraid; you stayed under fire for *hours*, digging them out."

"Pipe down. I was scared pink, all the time; weren't you, Levitt?"

"Sure." His thoughts ranged back, over the things not to be said here, the things that he and Carey knew.

His eyes sought Celia's, and she met the look, still dispassionate and friendly; it was like seeing her shut away behind a glass screen.

When they rose, he tried to detach her from the rest, but she ignored the secret gesture of his hand, went on ahead of him with Liz.

"When J. G.'s not here," Carey said, "we have coffee upstairs in Celia's sitting-room."

"And indulge our vicious passion for music," said Tobias, stalking beside him. "J. G. has a healthy dread of music, other than 'God Save the King' and 'Land of Hope and Glory'."

At least he knew something of her now; could see from this chair the shape of her bedroom, with the Empire furniture, the red and white curtains. This room bore her traces; the smell of her scent, the books in American jackets, the photographs; she sat on the sofa with Tobias. Liz and Anthony took out the records. He was just beyond the circle again; he should have chosen another chair.

He stared at her fair head leaning back, at the line of the throat. He drew the listening faces while Bri*ten's "Earl of Moray" sang at his ears:

> "He was a braw gallant
> And he rid at the ring,
> And the bonny Earl o' Moray
> O he might have been a King."

"I *weep* for him," Liz said, "and I don't know why they sent that bloody Huntly to fetch him away. They might have known it would go wrong."

"This Huntly was without doubt a Puritan," said Tobias, "objecting to the Earl of M.'s relations with the Queen."

They went on arguing. Curious, Levitt thought, to become so passionate about a Scots ballad. He felt tired again, peevish with tiredness and impatience.

"Do I——" Tobias asked sitting up, "hear hideous echoes below? J. G. and his rude rout."

"Could be," said Celia lazily.

"Who's below? Art there, Truepenny? Who'll he have? Micklethwait, champing like a rocking-horse. McLeod, oh, Lord, let it not be McLeod. Every week he grows commoner and commoner; and McLeod-er and McLeod-er."

"He's no commoner than Micklethwait, after all," said Liz, "but Micky's a nice old silly."

"Anybody'd prefer Micky," Celia said.

"Poor McLeod," said Carey. "I dislike him, but I'm sorry for him."

"*Sorry* for him? Pale, fleeting, perjured Carey. Why? Because he's common?"

Levitt had no warning that his peevishness would turn to exasperation; he heard himself laugh, and the laugh was harsh and sudden. The heads turned.

"Funny, are we?" Tobias asked amiably.

"It was the word 'common'; the snob word."

"What would you say for 'common' if you didn't say 'common'?" asked Liz.

"Guess I wouldn't be bothered to say it. It's a sort of dowager's adjective," he said, conscious of Celia's speculative look, of Anthony halted with a record in his hand, of Tobias' lifted eyebrows. Danger, his mind said, danger, you're letting them get on top of you.

"Pooh to dowagers," said Tobias. He added, "Aren't there any common Americans? Or do you have a special word for them, Class-receded or Breeding-deficient?"

Celia's twitch of the lips, fighting her smile, was more irritating than the words. Levitt said, "I find the word 'common' archaic, that's all."

"Do you mean we're snobs?" Liz asked sadly. "I suppose we are."

"Word 'snob' itself's a little archaic, while we're at it," said Carey.

"Come off it," said Celia. "It's silly talk anyway." She rose. Tobias said in a sobbing voice, "Wiser, wiser. We forget that Americans are all born equal, with huge honest grins and a Cadillac in every cooking-pot. You must forgive our ancient and uncomfortable ways. Where are you off to, Celia?"

"Going down to spy out the land. Coming?" she said to Levitt. He heard himself say, "No, thanks; I'll stay here," and now he could not see how this had happened, the black rage that kept him still. She went out; the three of them were looking at him perplexedly.

"I don't like class snobs," said Anthony thoughtfully. "But I rather think that, in order to be a snob, you have to care. I don't care, for example, if McLeod is common or not, I happen to dislike him; not *because* he's common. People can be nice, and common. He just doesn't happen to be."

"Some of my best friends are common people," Levitt sneered in quotes.

"Well, yes," said Carey; he lounged against the mantelpiece. "Happens to be true."

Tobias leaned back, crossing his knees. "The voice is the trouble," he said. "No equality can ever obtain in this country as long as there are McLeod vowel sounds. In the United States, I imagine, a variety of nasal notes creates less impression of difference."

"Toby, that's rude," said Liz.

"I assure you," said Levitt, "that I can be infinitely ruder if I want to be."

"But why do you want to be?" she asked, wide-eyed and unhappy.

"Because," said Tobias, "he is irked by our patrician attitudes. If you care, my father started life in a Rochester slum; he was the son of a stevedore."

Levitt snapped, "Makes your attitude all the funnier, doesn't it?"

"This I do not see. Am I obliged to swear solidarity with all who pronounce Brown Cow 'Braown Caow'? J. G. educated himself, so's not to. Would you rather he hadn't?"

"I don't care either way," said Levitt; he rose. "Excuse me if I go down now."

"*Wot*—no time to play with the giraffe?" said Tobias. "Is it that we've ruffled your democratic feathers? Say, neighbour, I certainly am sorry."

"Oh, go to hell," Levitt said. As he shut the door he heard Carey say, "Democracy's manners appear to be slipping," and a laugh from Tobias. Raging, he went down the passage. The black, mincing housekeeper-secretary met him at the top of the stairs. She beamed on him.

"There you are, Mr. Levitt. Sir James has arrived; he got here just about twelve minutes ago. . . . Would you like to join them all for a nightcap? They're in the little library."

Already, as he went down the stairs, he could hear Baron's voice. And now his tiredness seemed like a separate person arguing with him, "Oh, look, you really can't do this to me." The tiredness was too numbing to let him care what he had said to them upstairs. He stood in the doorway of the little green library; Baron's welcome tunnelled into his ears. McLeod was there, Gerald Lynn was there and old Micklethwait, who managed the contracts; voices, glasses, all of it beginning again; as though one wanted another drink or another word. J. G. beneath his own portrait made a double menace, two little menaces, four cold eyes looking at him. Celia was still here. "It's going to be all right," he told himself, swallowing down the whisky, seeing the black dress that made the skin more white; answering Baron.

"Ought to have waited and driven down with us, Levitt. We've had a lot of good talk. Give him your theory on . . ."

"It wasn't so much a *theory*."

"*Beautiful* house, isn't it? Your first time here?" Old Micklethwait's false teeth clashed and shook.

("Celia, you're not going—you can't be going. Oh, wait . . . please wait.")

"How's that for a start, Levitt? Damn' good, eh?"

"What's the American point of view?"

("Not good-night. I don't mean good-night. Can't you see what I mean? I've got to talk to you now. Wait for me.")

"Only woman *I* ever met who really——"

"Remember those girls we took to the 400, Hugh?" "Ha-ha-ha . . ." "Give yourself another drink." "Night yet young, what?" "Heard a story this week, J. G.—just up your street." "I'm *sure* it's not fit for me, is it, Micky dear?" And looking at the door and knowing that he must go, as the automaton Levitt had once gone seeking her in the ship. He knew this, until his tiredness took over, the separate entity, rising, drawing him away, caring nothing for the cold search in Baron's eyes, the look that meant a bad mark. It was his tiredness that walked, that led him.

Outside her door he listened for a moment; he heard no sound. He knocked.

"Who is that?" she called.

"Harry. Can I come in?"

"Oh—yes." She opened the door. "Want some tea?" she asked. "Liz will be back in a minute. And Nanny. We usually have tea around now." She was in her dressing-gown, the thin foulard robe that he remembered.

"I've got to talk to you. Alone. Can I come back later?" he asked, swaying on his feet.

The square eyes narrowed at the corners. She said gently, "No, my dear, I'm afraid you can't."

"Oh, please."

"No, of course you can't. Don't be foolish." Her voice was now hurried, impatient.

"I want to sleep in your arms. I'm so damned tired."

She said, "You'll sleep better alone."

He swayed on his feet. "Is it because of their not liking me—because of the spat?"

"Are you crazy? Of course it isn't."

"Then what?"

"All that's over, between you and me."

"No, it isn't. It can't be."

"I told you—it must be."

"Why?"

She shrugged her shoulders. "Don't please stand here arguing. You're dead tired and you're not making sense. Please go."

"I won't go till you tell me why."

She looked at him steadily. She said, "Because that—for me—is a danger that I can't explain. You don't need me and I don't need you. When you're less tired you'll see that I'm right. And now——" he saw that she was trembling violently "—will you please go—stop making a fool of yourself and a fool of me? You knew it couldn't happen again."

4

(i)

"AND here," Baron said, as they strolled through the garden door, "is the place where peace begins. First thing I do, every Sunday morning, stand here and praise God." He was by no means certain that this was true, whether it had ever been true;

if pressed, he would, he thought, have difficulty in explaining exactly how one set about praising God. He added, "Here's where I can laugh at the spectres of trouble left behind; say to myself, 'Boy, you've given them the slip. Boy, you're home.' "

"Wonderful morning," said Micklethwait heartily, "wonderful to be here, sir."

Baron glanced at him; at the thin anxious head, the popping blue eyes, the puffed, rocking-horse nostrils. It was not a wonderful morning; the grey clouds and uneasy wind promised rain. Micky grinned, champed his teeth, threshed his arms, said to Levitt, "Did you ever see a better view?" Micky didn't mean that; it was just a convention; assenting rhapsody was the poor old bastard's line, after all. It was many years since Baron had proved Micky's spinelessness and gone on using him. He was an efficient doormat, not much higher up the scale than poor flat-faced Mather the secretary.

Was there the trace of a sneer on Levitt's face? Or was it only the new thinness of that face making the angles more pointed? "Don't know what's the matter with the fellow, I really don't," Baron said to himself. "Looked bad last night; looks worse this morning." He found the pallor and the thinness, the tired eyes, disturbing, somehow a reflection on himself as an employer.

"We've got the Prime Minister coming to luncheon," he said. "Damn' bore, but there it is."

Still Levitt looked detached, haunted, strolling beside him towards the formal gardens. When Baron looked at Micky, or Mather, or any of the assenting chorus, he could feel in his mind the movement that was like the twitch on a multiple leash, bringing them all to heel; each the dog with the slave's collar. He could not feel this with Levitt. And the listless, polite air was not what he wanted from a new man, for whom all Carlington waited, to be shown, flourished, dangled as week-end bait for good boys.

Certain ghosts always came to meet him by the walls of clipped yew. There was Celia's mother walking as, from the windows, he had watched her walk alone, an hour or more, on the last day. She had been a ghost here long before she died.

And Kit was here, dimly (he fought to make himself remember this picture), on a sunny afternoon with the two tiny children. Now he could make old Randolph Carey walk stiffly from the terrace and his eyes filled with tears.

They crossed the lawn. Micklethwait took out his camera. Always he brought his painstaking camera and he was a bore with it, but since photographs were of enormous importance in Baron's life, he suffered the camera. He posed with Levitt at the top of the grass steps, his chin lifted, his hands in his pockets. "Charming little grove, this, isn't it? Italian cypresses, those. I want a statue here; young Anthony thought a faun would be right." Levitt made the double grunt that Americans so frequently substituted for 'Yes' and continued to look ravaged. Micky called, "Just one more, sir. Can I have you by yourself, sitting on the bench?"

"All right, old boy, but make it snappy. I want Levitt to see Anthony's studio before we leave for Glane."

He led them by the mossy path under the wall, opened the gate and said to Levitt, "Now you're going to see the perfect studio. And a boy who really works, not just a fellow with a dilettante hobby. . . . That's the farm down there; my farm, in fact, but it's all Carey land. Hi, Prince!" The yellow dog bounding to meet them was a signal that Liz was there already. Not Tobias, Baron trusted. He had only this day left in which to make his peace with Toby and for the life of him he couldn't see how he was going to do it.

His plan had been to give the boy a rousing lunch in London tomorrow, the right kind of send-off to Oxford. But of course Tobias' behaviour had made the issuing of the invitation impossible. Or was it his own behaviour? The angry little sigh escaped in spite of him as they reached the studio door. He saw Levitt glance at him inquiringly.

"Attractive, this sign, eh?" Baron said, pointing upwards with his stick. "The wheatsheaf's the Carey crest—see the wheatsheaf? That was the first wrought-iron work that Anthony ever tackled."

Levitt made the double grunt again. Micky said, "Clever,

isn't it—*awfully* clever?" leaning back his head and champing.

Baron opened the door, calling, "Morning, Anthony—mind an invasion?" before he saw Carey. There was a moment of pure pleasure in standing here, looking down the long light perspective of the studio, picking up with his eyes the fittings and details that had been his gifts to Anthony. He knew them all—could catalogue them all, from the overhead travelling crane to the elaborate four-piece set of proportional compasses, French aluminium, with engraved calibrations, in the velvet-lined case. Anthony kept the place in beautiful order, too. And Anthony looked the part, in his blue overall, rising from the work-bench, limping towards them. His handshake and his honestly welcoming smile did much to console Baron for the instant freezing process that appeared to come over Liz. She was standing at the top of the cellar steps, carrying a pail of chipped plaster. She set the pail down, and came to meet him. His dream of a father-daughter relationship was one of passionate friendliness. Not with Celia nor with Liz had it ever shown the smallest sign of coming true. Deliberately he bent towards her to kiss her good-morning. She was at her most beautiful; her hands as he captured them were like soft thin birds, struggling to be free.

"Liz is Anthony's Number One assistant in the studio," he said to Levitt. "Don't let us disturb you, Anthony."

"Love to be disturbed," said Carey. "I was only cleaning tools, anyway. Like to look around? Do anything in this line yourself?" He made, Baron thought, a violent contrast to Levitt; Levitt in his expensive tweeds, with the carefully-chosen tie, slick and weary, his smile forced, his praise slow in coming; commenting more freely on the technical things here than on the examples of Carey's work. Liz had retreated down the cellar steps. Micky was champing and whistling.

Baron halted deliberately at the black marble puma, which Levitt had accorded only thirty seconds of scrutiny. "Magnificent animal, isn't he?" It was Micky who said, "Superb." Levitt, walking on with Carey towards the back studio, stopped before the granite horse.

"He's a sad failure," Carey said, laughing. "Meant to be

Toby's winged horse, but I gave up. You can't put wings on a percheron, and that fellow, for all my efforts, remained a hundred per cent carthorse. I want to put him out, but Liz won't let me."

"Toby's winged horse?" Levitt questioned; he had found something to say, and it was irritating to Baron that it should be this.

"Not precisely Toby's property, eh, Anthony? The Belloc poem——" he said to Levitt, "we're all very fond of it." This was not true; he was somehow afraid of it, embarrassed by it; the children's song. When they were younger they had roared it round the fire at Christmas and it was still Toby's face that he could see, lifted and shouting. It was, despite his denial, Toby's song especially. It was a shout of defiance; it had a kind of pirate happiness. The words galloped through his head:

> "He had flame behind the eyes of him
> > and wings upon his side
> *And I ride!*"

He said quickly, "That wooden group of yours was always one of my favourites, Anthony. Great vitality, hasn't it, Levitt?"

Still there was the look that might be a sneer, the foxy look. Then Levitt glanced away from the wooden wrestlers to a photograph on the wall. "I like that a lot. Yours?"

"No," said Anthony twinkling. "Done by rather a clever school friend of mine called Rodin."

Baron roared with laughter. The hot little flush on Levitt's cheekbones was payment for earlier sins.

But he had to keep returning to it in his thoughts, for consolation on the drive to Glane. Levitt now showed a spiky tendency.

"How d'you cope with the attacks on this rebuilding project from your own boys?" he needled McLeod. "Pretty savage, aren't they? I read 'em. 'Why not homes for the workers?' and all that crap." There was some point in the question. Over Glane, McLeod was caught between two fires, and though Baron could chuckle on the side of the Socialist reactions and Hugh's uneasiness, it was not Levitt's function to share in the chuckle.

Now he was after Gerald Lynn. "That was a sobbing little piece of yours about the crippled Boy Scout—you damn' nearly broke my heart."

"Darling, I was in floods of tears myself; had to *bale* out the typewriter."

Baron's fingers tapped his knee. Gerald had the hide of an alligator, but that didn't excuse Levitt.

"If you got this chap's fan mail, you'd have something to boast about," he said.

"Give me time," Levitt drawled insolently.

He need not, of course, be invited here again, but this would make Baron uneasy. He had Levitt catalogued as one of the regulars. His method with the men who outboxed him, as Levitt had in the ship, was always the same. He gave them a grudging good mark in his mind, shelved the possibility of rolling them under, and set about wooing them. All this week Levitt had shown every sign of letting himself be wooed. What the devil had gone wrong today?

When they got to Glane, the small dramatic network of ruins on its hunch of hill between the marsh and the sea, Levitt suddenly cheated him. He walked apart, his face stricken by what he saw. As they reached the heart of the broken village, he groaned an oath. That he should be so deeply touched made an awkward demand on Baron's forgiveness. But it wasn't enough, yet. He had introduced, into the ever-precarious fabric of Sunday, a disturbing note.

Sunday at Carlington, Baron told himself as they drove back under the rain, was an institution. It raged till nightfall, each sequence liable to overlap the last, with the afternoon visitors arriving before the luncheon guests went, the distinguished mob who came for drinks staying on till dinner, the whole day punctuated by those who had been given no specific invitation but asked to drop in next time that they were near-by. An institution. A noisy, glittering, tiring institution.

At the back of his mind there was sometimes the vision of

another sort of Sunday; a country-gentleman, Carey-family Sunday; a quiet day, with matins, roast beef and leisured reading, just himself and the children. He felt, on occasion, vaguely guilty because his Sunday was not like that. This morning's memory of Anthony saying, as they left the studio, "Time I got ready for church," lingered to rebuke him. And now they came past the church itself, the Norman church set high among its grass knolls and gravestones, above the village street. And then on the right there was the long red wall, the archway gate and the visiting cars already in the courtyard.

Nobody of importance as yet; Foliot feathering across the hall to meet him. "The Prime Minister on the telephone; he called just ten seconds ago, and I saw the car coming in, wasn't that lucky? His secretary's holding on."

"I'll take the call in my room," Baron said. He did not hurry; if the P.M. wanted to cancel, he had no kick; he merely wished that he hadn't mentioned his arrival to Levitt. (Levitt again.) As he reached the landing, he glanced upward at Kit's picture and suffered a sudden panic lest he had let the anniversary of her death go by without remembering. It was this month, surely; this week? Surely not. He would have to check as soon as he had talked to the P.M.

"*All* right, sir—sorry not see you. We'll all miss you. Understand perfectly . . ." He hung up, resenting Levitt, then hurried to his writing-table and turned the pages of a thick leather diary. It was all right. The black 'K' was carefully marked. Next Saturday.

As he came downstairs, he saw Tobias standing alone in the hall. The boy looked dazed; he held a piece of paper in his hands, staring at it.

"Good-morning, Toby," Baron said. He was surprised by the radiance of the smile, by the gentle "Hullo." After a moment's hesitation, Tobias said, "Could I have a word with you, J. G.?"

"What? . . . Yes, if it doesn't take too long. Celia looking after them in there? All right, come into the library." He felt the impact of peace that came with this room, with the sight of his own portrait above the mantelpiece.

(ii)

Tobias, not sure now whether the spontaneous move had been wise, lit a cigarette with fingers that shook. His father stood quite still, below his portrait, waiting.

"What's on your mind, Toby?"

"This of asking permission," said Tobias; better to jump in, he thought. He saw J. G. remember, half-closing his eyes, always a bad sign.

"Permission? Permission for what?"

"You know what you said to me; the night you came home. In my room." J. G. moved to the table, took a cigar and cut it carefully. "Mm?" he said.

"You weren't serious, were you?"

"What? . . . As I recall, throughout most of our talk, I was entirely serious. Why?"

("The ultimate in umbrage. Oh dear; oh damn.")

"Serious, I mean," said Tobias, "in suggesting that I should ask your permission before I saw Catherine de Lille again."

J. G.'s face had settled into Chinese calm. "Why do you want to talk about it now?"

"Because," said Tobias, "I feel it necessary to tell you that I'm seeing her next week. And although I'm not asking your permission I think it more courteous and more honest to let you know my intentions."

He could not tell whether Baron were in any way softened by his elaborate formality. The Chinese calm persisted.

"Does she plan to visit you up at Oxford?"

"No. She'll be in London. Her play opens on Friday."

"Ah. And you have some seriously important reason for wishing to see her?"

"Well, no. At least it is seriously important to me. But I couldn't in reason tell you that it mattered *sub specie æternitatis*."

"Hm." J. G. looked him up and down. "You are becoming very affected in your speech; do you know?"

Tobias felt his skin prickle. Blast him, he thought, five

minutes ago I was so happy that I heard bells ringing; he glanced, for courage, at the paper in his hand, the words of the telegram from France, "Bless you and may Oxford be the best fun—C." He raised his eyes from it.

"Affected? Am I?" he wondered.

"You want to watch it," said J. G. sharply. "Too many affected young men in this day and age. Well, I presume you know the Oxford rules; you aren't proposing to infringe them in the first week?"

"Not at all," said Tobias, trying to sound sunny, "I'm coming down to lunch with her on Saturday."

The silence lasted long; the face did not change. Wreathed in smoke, its stillness held the familiar, hypnotic threat. ("If Catherine had not taught me to be sorry for him, I should still be afraid of him.")

"On *Saturday*." The voice had acquired its quality of a steel thread.

"Yes." ("Something has taken a turn for the worse and I don't know what or why.")

"This coming Saturday?"

"Yes."

J. G. said, "You do not recall the date?"

"Fourteenth, isn't it?" said Tobias, baffled.

"I should have thought," the voice continued, "that if you spent Saturday anywhere other than Oxford, it would be here, with us."

"But——" Tobias began: J. G. interrupted him. "However, since the anniversary of your mother's death appears to mean so little to you, I will not press the point. Yes, Foliot?" The dark spectre had put her head round the door.

"Excuse me, Sir James, I thought you'd wish to know that Lord Eppersley has just arrived."

"I would indeed," said Baron in an entirely different voice, heartily genial. "The old rascal. Only wants to plague the pants off me about the steel industry. Just coming. All right, Toby." The smile of dismissal was a fake, put on for Foliot. He went.

"Of this hypocrisy I spit me, do you hear?" Tobias shouted at the portrait over the mantelpiece.

(iii)

It was a long time since Levitt had hated so much. He had not thought that this would come again: the mood of hating himself with the world that was against him; of standing still alone in a black corner of his own mind while the voices dwindled and the faces dimmed. It was like the return of a nightmare after an interval of grateful waking.

He looked down the long room, with its panoply of hostile, comfortable strangers; the great and the incidental, all were equally at home, equally far from him; the room was a hot tunnel of blue smoke and the scent of flowers and women; a roaring band clustered about Baron; smaller, no less loudly-roaring bands set apart in their own molecular groups. Servants carrying trays and glasses moved on a punctual relay race.

He could draw it; English Sunday evening in hell, Baron as the Devil, he thought, and on the thought he turned and left it. There was a sneaking hope at the back of his mind that some-body would come after him; one of the bigger fish; the politically-minded Marquis or the Ambassador, or the Grand Old Man of the Novel, or the Great Lady of the London stage; any one of them would do, just one to single him out and demand his company.

He shut the door; nobody had come after him. He was outside the room. It wasn't enough. He had to be outside the house. He went through the hall. It was a hundred years ago since he had entered by this front door with Liz and Tobias and Anthony; hoping and hungry, knowing that when he saw Celia everything would be all right.

He opened the front door. The rain fell softly; all was grey and quiet; he skirted the inimical cars in the gravel courtyard and turned to his left; he was on the terrace now and the roaring came out of the windows; he ran down a flight of steps on to the lower lawn, on towards the fields and the marsh. The misty rain was stronger than he had thought; he would be soaked through (the new suit, the Bronzini tie, the London shirt—the hell with it). There was something soothing about the rain and the field, the wet swathes of low cloud, the dark woods and the hidden sea. He came on, to the white fence that marked the beginning of Carey's land.

He looked back and up, at the bulk of Carlington, at the trees that hid Carey's house. He was remembering the house that he had loved, on the Shrewsbury road, with its trees growing from grass and its fence like this one. He stood shivering, holding on to the fence, breathing in the cool wet air.

"They're even taking this away," he said, "this that I loved. I'll hate England now," and knew that this was a lie, that he could not hate it except in the cryptic double-mind that hated and loved with one mood.

He knew that he had stood alone before, as bereft as this, hating and loving like this; on a Californian ranch, where the great and careless people after whom he strove treated him like a dog. He had hidden that memory deep, until he could bring it out and laugh at it and fool himself that it had been a salutary lesson. Now it came back in its furious original shape; the nightmare that was only a prelude to today's nightmare. Because then, at least, he had not been given the gate.

"Did I think she loved me? No; I didn't even ask her to love me; we were having a good time, that was all. It was fun. And now, damn her, she's turned it into something more important than fun." He called her names in his mind, "Spoiled, conceited bitch. 'A danger that I can't explain.' 'I don't need you any more than you need me.' 'Sleep better alone.' Damn her. I'll never see her again."

He let go of the fence and plunged on down the field; there was a stream here and a line of willows, then the little dark wood. He followed the stream, his feet squelching in the muddy grass at the brink.

"If it hadn't been for that I'd have made out all right; if she hadn't kept me guessing, I could have got off on the right foot with them all. Even with that smug bastard Carey; I can get his number; I can get anybody's number. Could have joined in their Goddamned cute family jokes, played it pretty, made them like me. Now they hate my guts.

"Baron, too. Doesn't seem to see I'm there. Last thing I ever expected to care about; but in this place it's Anthony, Anthony, Anthony—and the children, and the Goddamned house and the Goddamned garden and Carey's Goddamned studio. Feeling deserted by Baron, eh? That's a honey; that's a peach. Celia certainly did a thorough job when she told me I could sleep alone."

He kept coming back to the silly little quarrel about snobs; the words were still sticking under his skin like a bunch of thistles, making him squirm; his own words most of all. "Why did I ever start it up? I was tired; they got on top of me. All her fault. Waiting for her; wondering. Get anybody down.

"Damn them, as if I care." He was in the wood now, pushing through low branches that sprang back, flinging showers on his face. "Conceited, snobbish tedious family, crazy for them-selves; no time for anybody else. *No time to play with the giraffe*; hell, why remember what they say? They can keep their corny private jargon and stuff it."

Today was nearly over, the day through which he had lived shut out and raging; there was just the evening ahead, it would be like the day. "And tomorrow, though I certainly can't wait to get out of here, there'll be London again. (The lift, the honeycomb, the passages all alike, and the empty apartment, and remembering how it felt when you walked out of it on Saturday)."

"Hell," he said again, scrambling out of the last trees into another field. "I'm me. I'm Levitt. I could have gone over big with those people today. If I'd not been cheated, if I'd slept. If I'd not been too damn' tired to talk. Couldn't even tell the pretty stories. That's her fault, too. Drives me crazy, thinking back. Humiliating myself that night on the ship, confessing to lies, being sorry I'd lied to her. She isn't worth it; she isn't worth this. And I've let her wreck me, wreck me with myself, wreck me with Baron, maybe.

"Yeah. . . . Maybe Baron'll fire me when he knows I'm in

Dutch with his family. (See warning by Grant Parker.) Yeah, he'd care. S—— to him and to them."

He stood still, betrayed. He saw that his carefully-acquired idiom had slipped, his polish was gone. Even his thoughts talked in the plain peevish language of any little nobody brought up against the wider world. This made him hate Levitt still more.

He was on the other side of the white fence now, on Carey's ground. The mist had drifted lower; it hid the shape of Carlington; it hid Carey's trees.

The yellow dog came leaping out of the mist and behind him was Liz, walking alone. She wore a mackintosh trench coat and her hair was all tucked away under a black beret.

"Hullo," he said curtly.

"I thought it was you," said Liz, "I saw you go down *hours* ago. Do you like walking in the rain with no coat?"

"I don't care, really."

"But you're soaked to the skin."

"Never mind. Rather soothing."

"Oh, well, if you like it——" she said. "But I was worried. So I got Prince and came to look for you."

He stared at her unbelievingly. "You were worried? About me?"

She nodded.

"But why? I'm old enough," he said, "to come in out of the rain."

"It wasn't that. I just thought we'd all been rather mean to you last night, and you looked as if you were having a horrid day, and I know about going for walks alone when there are a lot of people having a good time. Only I'm not really sure," she added, "whether people at parties *are* having a good time, or just looking as though they are. But that may be prejudice because I never have a good time myself. I think you ought to come in and change your clothes. Not just stand still in it."

He could not speak.

"Why are you looking at me as though I were a headless ghost on a blasted heath?"

He said, "You'll never know."

5

(i)

ON Saturday morning Baron awoke in his suite at the Savoy Hotel and breakfasted early, doing his best meanwhile to think about Kit. He found more than usual difficulty. Today, the fourteenth, assumed another, unforgivable importance; today Tobias was coming to London to lunch with Catherine de Lille. In every paper that he opened now he found a solidly enthusiastic review of her new comedy. He avoided them with his eyes. Drinking his third cup of coffee, he paced before the windows, staring out at the Embankment gardens and the grey, shining river.

He was still angry with Tobias. But it was not only anger that kept him pacing. He was at odds with his own behaviour, and that was worse. Letting the boy go off to his first Oxford term without the planned celebration, without more than a forcedly amiable good-bye, this was not the conduct of the father who Baron believed himself to be. My only son, Kit's son, he went on thinking, until he was so wretched that his own shortcomings wholly obscured the irritating image of Tobias. Just as Mather appeared for instructions Baron had his idea. It came in sacrificial shape. It would, he thought, make some atonement to Kit as well as to the boy. He would drive up to Oxford tomorrow and spend the day with Toby.

Touched as he was by the magnificence of the gesture, he still knew that his resolution would weaken if he did not act at once. Carlington was where he wanted to be; the Rolls was ordered for the late afternoon.

"Mather, get through to Miss Foliot at once, will you? I've changed my plans." He heard her gay, arch voice. "Hullo, Sir James, good-morning; it's a beautiful day down here. Shall we see you before dinner?"

He explained why not; he made her read the list of guests, sent the appropriate messages to the ones who mattered and was cutting short her professions of disappointment when she gave a frightened hiss, "Oh, and I forgot—Mr. Levitt. He's due this afternoon. Would you like me to cancel him, or will you be seeing him in town?"

"I shan't be seeing him. Better cancel; no, wait. Mather can talk to him from here." He had almost forgiven Levitt last Sunday; Levitt's heartbreak over Glane had begun it ("though that little runt McLeod had to sneer; said it took an American to sob over a bit of bomb damage that was five years old"), and on Sunday evening Levitt had mysteriously recovered his manners and his entertainment value. ("Extraordinary how he seemed to get on with Liz, too; she's by far the trickiest of them. Thought he was making a pass at Celia on board ship. I was wrong.") Levitt had made further appeals to sympathy since Monday, by producing four brilliant cartoons in a row when he was almost speechless with a sore throat and a feverish cold.

"Tell you what, Mather," Baron said, "get on to Harry Levitt, give him my love and say I'm running up to Oxford to see Toby; but if it would amuse him to be at Carlington with the family I'm sure it would do him good. Tell him to do just as he likes, stay in bed if he wants to, get a good rest; they'll look after him. And you let Foliot know, whichever. And remind me— send a telegram to Mr. Tobias at Corpus Christi, saying I'll be up to take him to lunch tomorrow. No hurry for that. He won't be there till this evening. I'm going out now. Back in—er—say fifteen minutes." ("I sound like Foliot, myself.") Crossing the Strand, he gave self-conscious glances to left and right. He had done this before on Kit's anniversary. He would not like to be seen doing it. He walked up Southampton Street, turned left into Maiden Lane and went down the steps, through the dark doorway into the church. It was a Roman church; Kit, who was superstitious, had made a habit of coming here to light candles. He was a little offended to discover a service in progress ("on a Saturday, too; their trouble is that they overdo things.") He knelt at the back. Presently he found that his prayers which, like many prayers, were a more than usually severe exercise in thinking about himself, proceeded; unhampered by the high colours, the lights, the junky statues and the murmurings of the priest at the altar.

"I really think I'm behaving rather well in going to Oxford, don't you? He has been extraordinarily tiresome and insolent, and this *is* a gesture that I'm making, it's a sacrifice for me not to get to Carlington—as of course you know—and it's the sort of thing you like people to do, isn't it? If it is, I do—er—wish that you could signify your approval—not by a miracle or anything like that—don't mean to take up your time in any way—just by making me feel I'm doing the right thing.

"I'm sure it is the right thing. After all, I know what's right and I know what's wrong, just as you do, if you'll excuse my saying so, but I should like to *feel* right, for once.

"Oh, and please, if you're not too busy, will you ask Kit to forgive me for not thinking about her more often? I really do try, but with time going on—and so many commitments and worries . . . I hope it doesn't make her angry. I hope it doesn't make you angry. I hope I don't make you angry, anyway.

"I don't think I do, because if I did you wouldn't have let me get so far, would you? You'd have kept me down, kept me as a little twerp in Rochester, wouldn't you? Don't object to the word twerp, I hope?

"You have shown me a great many favours, please don't think I'm not grateful, I'm damned grateful (beg your pardon). And I don't want to pester you, because I know only too well what it's like to be pestered; I mean, take Eppersley and those steel-production figures; not that I'm trying to suggest I've got anything like your amount of responsibility. But could you, er, besides giving my love to Kit, just see to it that tomorrow goes off all right? Tobias is such a difficult customer; could you, if it doesn't shock you to be asked such a thing, make me *like* him a little better? I really don't like him much, it's no good hiding that from you, is it? And, oh, could you see to it that I don't run into him anywhere today, with that woman? Well, I think that's about all. If you could arrange things comfortably, I'd be in your debt for ever. Excuse me, of course I'm in your debt already, that goes without saying. Amen."

(ii)

The message from Baron put Levitt in two minds.

It was anti-climax. He had been poised to take a hurdle.

Some of last week's nightmare was exorcised; by Liz; by the easier evening; by Baron's pleasure in his work, Baron's matter-of-fact assumption that he would come again and come regularly. But there was still Celia to make a hurdle of today; Celia and certain memories that died hard. "But you have to do it, you know that," he had told himself. "Get your nerve back; it's the only way. Besides, he'll think it too damned queer if you don't."

And now he need not.

His mind was already accustomed to figuring Baron's re-actions before he figured anything else. "He might be flattered to think I'd rather not be there when he isn't there. *Or* he may feel insulted on behalf of the house and the family. The message said to do as I liked, but I guess the most apparent facet of working for J. G. is that you don't do that.

"I can call up one of them at the house and take soundings. Not Celia; not Carey; Liz; I'll call Liz, see if she thinks he's just being polite; if they want me. *She* won't just be polite; I'll know from her voice right away." When Miss Foliot answered, he was infuriated to find that he had said absentmindedly, "May I speak to Mrs. West?"

"She's in London for a few days, I'm afraid. She may be back tomorrow."

("Relieved or disappointed? You can't be sure.") He asked for Liz.

"Hullo," said Liz. "You're coming down today, aren't you? . . . Oh, please do. Darkness falls from the air; Tobias at Oxford—and Celia's away. There's only Anthony and me, grieving. Don't you *want* to come?"

"Sure; I was just checking. I'll be on the four-ten," he said.

"Oh, lovely; we'll meet you." He hung up, thinking, "I believe that child *did* like me suddenly. Maybe she likes anybody she gets sorry for. . . . Tobias at Oxford, says she. Do I keep my mouth shut about last night? Guess so. To all of them. Guess that's what he meant."

He lit a cigarette and cocked his head on one side. Still miserable with his cold, he had gone to Gerald Lynn's supper party; he could not, he thought, afford to pass up an invitation from Lynn; and he had been flattered, after the débâcle of Sunday, to be invited. Lynn might well have refurbished his memories of the Californian ranch. He never mentioned it, but there was sometimes now in his eyes the look that said, "Got something on you."

Gerald Lynn lived in Victoria Square; it was an after-theatre party and Levitt had idled his time away at a movie, going home to change, making a respectably late appearance at the canopied door with the brass dolphin for knocker. The mob, impressive enough, had parted suddenly to disclose Tobias. He was sitting on a beaded footstool (Lynn's house was furnished in the exaggeratedly Victorian manner; it was a riot of looped curtains, antimacassars, shell boxes, red velvet, and papier mâché.) Tobias wore tails and a white tie; he was at the feet of the woman for whom the party was given, the legendary Catherine de Lille.

Perhaps, Levitt thought, he had been too busy hating Tobias last week to acknowledge his grace, his good looks, the odd radiance that separated him. At least now in memory, these were all that he could see, the look of Tobias seated there, and the look of the woman. Her appearance of youth was remarkable; her stillness was strange when he compared it with the wriggles of vivacious persons all about her. It was like seeing Helen of Troy at close range; he had to take the features one by one; the dark hair parted low on one side, the rounded forehead, the wide, charitable eyes, the straight nose and delicate cheekbones, the surprisingly perfect mouth; these went to make up the face that had, said Celia, launched a thousand lies. It was a beauty that might have been stilted without the warmth in the eyes, the lighted look of the skin.

Still it stayed with him, the picture of those two. Tobias had

bowed to him, turned back to Catherine de Lille. They had had
no words until, waiting for a taxi on the doorstep, he had heard
the hushed, haughty voice in his ear.

"Is it that you are going to Carlington tomorrow?"

"Yes, I am," he said, turning.

"Well, cover my well-shaped and flying tracks, I beseech,"
Tobias said with a smile whose dazzle was reminiscent of
Celia's smile; he ran down the steps; he leaped into a long car
drawn up and waiting. Catherine de Lille was in the car; Levitt
saw her profile and a man's profile leaning towards her from the
front seat. Tobias ducked in under the shiny roof; his face
became one with the little lighted group of faces behind the
window, moved and was gone.

"From what Celia told me in the ship," Levitt thought,
"he's sticking his neck out. None of my business."

All the way down in the train he shut his mind to last week's
journey. It was not easy. He remembered how sure he had been
that Celia would meet him. When the train drew in to Ashford,
he saw Liz, standing a yard from the carriage door. She was
alone, holding the yellow dog on a leash. As she turned, he
realised that his eyes were glad to find again that endearing and
vulnerable face.

She said, "Thank-God-for-Anthony's being prim about
petrol, so I had to order this." It was an old car driven by an old
man; the inside smelt of stables. "You were very sweet to come,"
said Levitt. "You could just have sent the taxi."

"But so depressing not to be met. And no trouble, I'm sure,"
said Liz. "I like meeting people. Are you *reeling* from the shock
of J. G., like us?" Her eyes were even larger than he remembered.

"Shock? What sort of shock?"

"His going to Oxford to see Toby. We are not sure what it
bodes. Carey thinks white garment of repentance; I am bereft
of thoughts. Ominous, because different, I'd say. You should
have heard Foliot cancelling the Sunday visitors; it took an hour
and a half—say an hour and thirty-three minutes."

"Why the three minutes?"

Liz giggled. "Aren't you on to Foliot yet? She can't speak without saying that sort. You listen; we usually bet on it. What do you think J. G.'s up to?"

"Search me," said Levitt.

"He hasn't missed a week-end here since the Ice Age, except for being abroad. Prince, get off the gentleman's poor feet. And the anniversary too. It is, not to put too fine a point upon it, the anniversary of my mother's death, but you needn't say things, because we don't remember her. But we always have to behave as though we did. And J. G. spends the day looking bereaved. I do not mean to sneer," Liz added. "It is just that we cannot join in. So today is really a relief. I hope you won't be bored, with just Carey and me. Celia ought to be back tomorrow."

"I won't be bored, I promise," he said, cutting off the thought of tomorrow in his mind, watching the marsh come, the slope of land down from the crest to the flats, the colours made by the sun. He could see the white fence where he had stood alone in the rain. Now the marsh was hidden, by the trees in Carey's garden; here was the long red wall and the archway gate.

Here was the house again, and he felt that he had known it a long time.

(iii)

Carey was the only one who went regularly to the village church on Sunday morning. He knelt in the family pew that still bore his father's faded visiting card in a little bronze frame. From here there was the familiar view, the Norman arch, the flat velvety shapes of the brasses, the stone tablet with the urn above. He heard the vicar's mournful sing-song:

"O God the Son, Redeemer of the world,
    Have mercy upon us *miserable* sinnahs."

Carey thought the Litany something of an exaggeration. He did not feel like a miserable sinner, and he was sure that no one else in the church did, with the possible exception of Miss Penfold the postmistress, who had religious mania. But the Litany was part of the drill; you accepted it and were polite to it; your thoughts strayed.

They strayed to love. God is Love, said the Book. Carey had no doubts about God. God was there, and that was that. But love, the kind of love that he had in mind, was a more precarious matter. He searched, trying to find the explanation for the small, desolate pang at his heart.

Liz was a child; Liz was like a younger sister. Liz hero-worshipped him in the way that a sister would hero-worship an elder brother; he could not, for all his simplicity, have failed to be aware of it in the last few years. Had he taken it for granted, perhaps? Been scornful of it? No. It just hadn't mattered to him very much. He had even—in the early stages of Jane Ireland—found it a little pathetic, a little irritating.

Well, and now? Why this sense of sudden deprivation? Just because Liz appeared to find Harry Levitt good fun? "Levitt's a far nicer person than I thought at first," Carey admitted, going back over last evening, over the peaceful trio that they had made at dinner, and the session in Celia's room with the gramophone. "I like him now. Perfectly natural for Liz to want to go riding with him instead of coming to church with me. She doesn't come to church every Sunday. Why do I feel like this?"

He thought of *La Princesse Lointaine*, his dream of a woman far-off. Her image looked a little pale this morning. Instead he saw Liz sweeping the studio floor, in a pale green overall, Cinderella with her broom.

"It is time that Liz had a boy friend, really it is. Usually she reacts to young men as she reacts to spiders; we've all deplored it. But—need it be this one?"

He thought that he saw why he minded Levitt. Because of the other slick dark stranger with the American voice, the stranger who had taken Celia away. He had been twenty when that happened, and it had hurt him. The Levitt pattern was the Valentine West pattern. Why must they come here, these strangers, to disrupt and snatch?

The perplexity was still with him when the long service ended and he stood in the square shadow of the Norman tower, greeting the faces that he knew. It was still with him as he strolled back to Carlington. When he came in under the archway gate, he saw Liz and Levitt. They were still in their riding clothes; holding a conference beside the yew hedge. Liz rushed at him. She clutched his arms.

"It's the end," she said. "The *end*."

"Let's hear the beginning," said Anthony; it was the first time that he had welcomed one of her wild despairs.

"Tobias is at Senlis," Liz said and fell upon his chest with a groan.

"Who told you?"

"He telephoned, while we were out riding; he spoke to Foliot. This is the message. Could you meet him at the airfield with the car at four sharp—because he has to get a connection for Oxford, and won't," she slowed up—"have—much—time. Can you beat it? For utter arrogance, inconsideration, goat-like imbecility— and J. G. stepping out of the Rolls at Corpus Christi even as we stand here?"

Anthony patted her; as a rule the Baron crises aroused in him a strong temptation to giggle. This one did not; perhaps because it was a worse deadlock than usual, or perhaps because Liz was taking it on the chin. He said:

"Is it possible that J. G. changed his mind, and let Toby know?"

"Of *course* it isn't. First thing he asked Foliot was whether J. G. was here. As soon as she said No, he said he'd be flying over. Foliot's eyes were popping. She didn't know anything about the aeroplane. Now she's all set to go up and meet him at the field herself."

"Did she tell him J. G. had gone to Oxford?"

Liz groaned again. "Never occurred to her. For a really happy disposition, you can't beat Foliot. When I asked her that, she said—with every tooth flashing like a heliograph— 'Why no, of course not. I knew Tobias would have let Sir James know that he wouldn't be there.' . . ."

Levitt, lounging with his hands in the pockets of his breeches, grinned at Carey and flickered his eyebrows. "I'm trying to console Liz this way: J. G. wouldn't pay a surprise visit to Toby, surely. He'd call up first and say he was coming. Not finding Toby, he wouldn't go."

"In that case," Liz snapped, "why isn't J. G. here?"

"Give him time," said Levitt still grinning. "He may turn up any minute."

"That," said Liz faintly—"is hardly my idea of a consolation."

Carey thought it over. "Darling, it's one of those things that nobody can do anything about, which makes it easy. We'll meet him with the car and give him hell and put him on his train. As for J. G., well, all we can do is wait and see what happens. Don't you agree, Levitt? Now let's have a sherry."

Liz said mournfully, "The consolations of the bottle are not for me, as you know. Anthony, *what* makes the Bloody Child do this?" She added, walking between them to the house, "and what is more, Harry says that on Friday night——"

"No," Levitt interrupted her, his hand grabbing hers. "Please not. That was just for you. And I doubt I ought even to have told you."

Before Carey had time to digest his unreasonable indignation, Liz was saying, "But we have no secrets from this poor Carey; all secrets are shared and all go with us to a joint grave. And the sooner I get to my section of the said grave, the better I shall feel. Now tell."

Levitt's dark face was still troubled.

"He meant cover his tracks to J. G., not to us," Liz urged. They came into the long panelled room; Anthony poured the sherry.

"Don't make him tell if he thinks he shouldn't, darling. That's not fair."

She scowled, "Oh, all right," she said, "but I'll make Toby tell you. No, I don't want any disgusting sherry. Oh God, the wrath to come. . . . And this was being the only nice Sunday we've had since he came back."

(iv)

Tobias walked in the garden with Catherine. The garden broke through to the lake, the great stretch of formal water with the grey stone statues on the bridge, reflected. The trees were in full leaf, the sun was strong, the light more clear than the light over English fields.

"It is where I belong," he thought; "when I am old and distinguished, I shall live in France. ('What good to be old when you will not be there?')"

"Thank you for not stopping me," he said abruptly.

"I couldn't stop you."

"Oh, yes. No," he said, frowning, "perhaps not, this time. It was one of those minutes of acquiring a sense of proportion; suddenly seeing what was of true importance and the ridiculous pygmy-size of the obstacles in the way. And of course J. G. began it. He always invites one to kick up heels."

"You cannot," she said, laughing, "blame J. G. for everything."

"At least, *grace à toi*, I am not afraid of him any more."

"I expect you always will be, a little."

"God forbid. Why do you say that?"

"I've told you . . . the only people who can make one afraid are the people whom one can hurt and those who do not speak one's language."

They had come to the stone fountain; its basin and statue green with moss. Here they had posed for the photograph that he loved; the photograph would tell time for ever that he had been here with her.

Catherine lingered, taking a cigarette from her case; Tobias lit the cigarette.

"Certainly J. G. and I do not speak the same language. But I doubt I could hurt him. I believe Anthony could. I believe he prays every night, 'Please God, make Tobias more like Anthony.'"

"There, poor darling," said Catherine with a chuckle, "he might as well rise from his knees."

He thought, "But you have never met Anthony. How clamorously I talk to you of all of them and you listen and seem to know them and to care. Does everybody do this to you? Bring you their people? Yes, I think so. How many mirrored people do you know—reflected people—second-hand phantoms?"

She was watching him. "What are you brooding upon, Tobias?"

"How I talk," he said inadequately, "and you've never met them, except J. G.—and you always listen." His syntax, he realised, frequently failed him in her presence; he had no pretty speeches here.

She said, "I know Celia."

"Yes, I had forgotten. I must talk to her about you. I keep meaning to."

"Why?"

He could not say why. Catherine said musingly, "They're the kind who find happiness late."

"Celia's kind?"

She said, "Yes. Self-disciplinarians."

"Unlike T. Baron, these. Is Celia so disciplined? How do you know?"

"I saw it once; when she was feeling ill and behaving beautifully."

"Yes; typical Celia. . . . I see what you mean. And they find happiness late?"

She did not answer; she had gone away into absentmindedness, looking across the lake. "There go the ducklings," she said; "difficult to realise that they aren't made of tin and run by clockwork." He looked at the arrow-head ripple, the tiny jerking bodies; then, looking at his watch, he saw that time was short.

"Oh, tell me more things," he clamoured at her. "You don't tell half enough. You let us all go on and on. You don't talk about your own things ever. . . . Do you care about them? Even the play . . . you watched it as though it were somebody else's; I was looking at you all the time."

"That was uncivil to the actors." She gazed at him thought-fully. "I don't believe there is much that I can tell you. You have at the moment a most *rusé* and knowledgeable look; why?"

"I am counting my assets; as for bankrupt business man," said Tobias. "All of it, from the moment that I ran out of Oxford into London, with wings on my heels . . . as far as this; as far as the ducklings." He wanted to touch her hand; he made a groping gesture, then drew his own hand back. He stood there, re-playing the scenes in his mind. He thought, "And today I shall fly alone. And I like that. But I shall remember flying with you and Rene and Lionel in the civilised Air France, drinking champagne. And arriving in the dark; and the onion soup; and waking up in the room with the tapestries.

"I had a dream. I forget exactly what it was, but it was good. You were there and somebody was telling me that I needn't go back, that this would go on for ever. I should remember this dream."

He wondered for how long he had been silent. "It is a silence I must keep. I must not say what is in my mind; not to you, to whom I can say anything. I have said it to Liz, but that is to talk to rabbits. Must I be content to tell my love to Liz and not to you? I must. It is a matter of manners, and on these I pride myself."

He saw her slanted smile. "Come out of it, Tobias, whatever it is. Your time is running low." She stretched out her hand; he clutched it too quickly, in deliberate misunderstanding, clutched it and put it to his lips. He looked up from the hand. Formal, he thought, and mine, the fountain, the lake, the light, the humble salute; yes, I belong here; that was part of the dream.

He had kissed her hand before; she had not looked vulnerable nor afraid before; Catherine, who was afraid of nothing. He saw that he had to talk.

"Time is a mocker," said Tobias to the face of his consolation. They walked back under the trees. She was suddenly so quiet and sad that he felt himself, for the first time with her, obligated as a man to take over the moment and make the shadow less, whatever the shadow might be. He began to chatter.

"Extraordinary, this of Time," he said, "how when one was a child there was so much. I observe my nephew killing it by inches, rolling about in boredom between bouts of toys and eating. And I observe me, slave to a wrist-watch, calculating the number of things that I mean to do between now and the age of ninety; which would include getting my degree—and it must be a First, to spite the gloomy doubts of one Sir James Baron; perfecting my stage technique until I am knighted at twenty-five —but that would invoke Sir Toby . . . damn it, I will not be Sir Toby—any more than I will be Uncle Toby——" He looked at her to see whether the shadow were still there. "Or perhaps one could grow to love it," he said, "Sir Toby Belch; for Baron read Belch. By deed poll I could be Belch."

All that she said was, "Please fly carefully, won't you?" And now they were almost out of the shade of the trees. He could see the grey stone façade, the scatter of people on the terrace waiting for her. His heart beat towards his throat. He tried to think of an elaborate phrase and arrived at, "Oh dear, no time at all." Since she was still silent he searched for more words.

"There is a poem I just found, that I like," said Tobias.

"Say it." Her voice was quiet, desolate; she stood still.

Under what was to him a royal command, he became nervous; the silence hung. Then he began to speak, not giving it what it deserved.

> "The day was at first as a year
>   When children ran in the garden;
> The day shrank down to a month
>   When the boys played ball.
> The day was a week thereafter
>   When young men walked in the garden;
> The day was itself a day
>   When love grew tall . . ."

He paused; his throat dried. He thought, "Today is itself a day; I know this." He turned and stared into her face; he felt wild happiness and wild sorrow fighting. The sun and the noise of the birds and the face with the shadow upon it mixed with the verse. His voice shook on the last lines:

> "The day shrank down to an hour
> When old men limped in the garden.
> The day will last forever
> When it is nothing at all."

And now there was silence again. "We are in a different dimension," he thought, "from those people only fifty yards away, up the slope of sunny green lawn. I can see the colours of their clothes, their movements, the glasses that they hold in their hands. I can see René, your husband, the stiff elegant grey figure at the balustrade, watching us, waving to us. I can hear their voices. And in a moment we shall go up the lawn, out of the shade of the trees, and join them. And then there will be no more of me here; I'll be running, through the house, down the shallow stone steps to the car, leaving all of it behind; leaving you who are part of it.

"I am just an incident. Somebody may ask, 'Who was the boy with red hair who ought to have been at Oxford?' and you will tell him, say my name lightly and pass on to another subject, mix with the crowd who claim you and forget me at once. But just within the circle of the shadow of the trees, as we are, I feel that you know about the dream, that you want me to stay."

Suddenly courageous, he turned to her; he saw her as sharply true as though he would never see her again; an image of flesh and bone and liveliness that frightened him. It made him forget that he had recited the poem very badly.

"All I know is," he said, "that I love you with the whole of me. I'll do anything you want me to do; all my life. You have my heart. I'd die if you told me to; and if I live to be ninety I'll still love you."

He shut his shaking hands together and waited, staring into her face. He could not believe that there were tears in her eyes. Then he asked bewilderedly, "But why does it make you cry?"

She said, "I don't know, Toby."

(v)

Celia drove the last ten miles to Carlington in the early afternoon. The London tasks were done. The job awaited her; the nameless, shapeless and well-paid "advisory" post in the scenario department. Its prospect was not inspiring. All the war-time contacts had pointed to it; none of the war-time colleagues survived in their original shape. Was it only her memory that accorded them a light-hearted independence? Now they were chunky young men of the depressing seriousness to be found in British movie-directors; an agonised self-importance as though they carried the world's future on their shoulders and must be forgiven brusque manners. The chairman of the company exuded the stateliness to be expected from a cardinal. He had welcomed her; more accurately, he had welcomed the gloss of J. G.'s name and what he called her "Transatlantic awareness". She was saving this verbal horror for Tobias.

She had found a house; a house with a garden. Here she was not entirely decided. Nanny would be pleased. Terry liked Carlington, according to Terry, better than anywhere on earth, except Martha's Vineyard. And if J. G. reacted violently against the move to London, was it worth the battle? "That, in the next few hours, I shall discover. Who's in the mob this week-end? I ask myself." The name of Levitt came up in her mind, the danger signal. "No, not again. Not yet. He'll have the sense to stay away. I trust him that far . . ." She found herself obliged to stare at the unresolved doubt, the indecisive pain left by the act of decision.

"Do I regret it? Bitterly. Why have I done this to us both? If I go down deep enough for the answer, I know. It is still the old answer. He gives me the sense of insecurity—the Van terror—that I refuse to suffer again. I knew it on the first evening at sea when I knew he was a liar. Too much of Van in the lies. (Nothing of Van in the confession. On that night, I let him love me; not until that night; it could have happened before.

Was I touched by the confession? Did I fool myself that it made him an honest man?)"

She drove in under the archway gate. The only car in the courtyard was Carey's. No visitors. Puzzled, she climbed out of the car, lit a cigarette, strolled into the house. At the same moment Liz and Levitt came running down the stairs.

The shock of him hurt; she hoped that she was not changing colour. She was grateful for the tiger-leap that Liz made; she could hide her face on the shoulder before she greeted him. He said gaily, "Hello; good to see you." She saw him all the time, the dark equation, the intruder, while Liz told the story:

"And no word from J. G., so we imagine that he is razing Oxford to the ground, or alternatively storming back here; in which case he may arrive before Toby."

"That would be nice."

"Meanwhile—unconscious of their doom the little victims play."

"Meaning Tobias?"

"Well, no: though I suppose it would apply. I meant Foliot and Nanny and Terry. They've left in a body for the airfield; they all think it's the most spiffing fun."

"A welcome committee," Celia said. "Not precisely what he deserves."

"And this poor Carey has just discovered that he hasn't enough petrol to take him to Ashford."

"I suggested a taxi," said Levitt; still leaning against the newel-post, irritatingly at home.

Celia snapped, "I'll meet him. I've got petrol."

"Oh, wonderful," Liz said. "Then we'll come with you. Go and tell Anthony, Harry, will you?"

"Sure."

"Why are you cross?" Liz asked.

Celia said, "Why is he here?"

"J. G. invited him. You don't hate him, do you?"

"No. I just didn't expect to see him."

"He's much nicer than we thought," Liz said, looking troubled.

"That wouldn't be difficult."

"You do hate him."

Celia said impatiently, "Nothing to do with hating. But if J. G. and Toby are really likely to collide in the next half-hour, there's no need for Mr. Levitt to have himself a nice time watching."

Carey and Levitt came back together. It angered her to see that Anthony also had accepted him. She thought he knew that he had stolen a march on her and he looked pleased about it, grinning like a fox.

(vi)

Standing in the sun, staring upward at the empty sky, Levitt thought, "She hasn't spoiled it; hasn't broken the tune. When I first saw her I thought that she might; that the three of them would gang up on me together and I'd feel left out again. But I don't; I feel like part of it."

Was it, perhaps, a family that he had needed, all this time? The imperceptible 'They', whose outlines had changed so often, whose perspective was always the same, that of the remote group; were they identified at last by these people?

It might be so. He did not know, otherwise, why he should feel so greatly at ease. He looked at them one by one: at Liz with her profile lifted, her hair blown back, the undefended face watching the sky; at Carey, no longer a menace, merely a large blond Englishman talking to another large Englishman, the grizzled ex-flyer who was the boss here. He looked at Foliot standing a little part with Nanny; Foliot's cardboard-flat shape in the grey suit and the long aquiline shoes; Nanny's rounded shape in the grey suit and square black shoes; Terry's hopping abstractedly on one foot, and Celia adjusting a pair of dark glasses.

"You were right," he said to her in his heart, "and I was wrong. I don't think I'll be able to tell you so; I think we'll talk about it some time, years ahead. I'll not plague you again. My body will want it when I look at you; but my head will agree to settle and forget. I plunged at that meeting too soon. And I'm grateful to it, and to you. But I didn't deserve it. I was taking it for granted, along with J. G.'s contract and the whole English adventure, just another lucky break for Levitt. You slapped me hard enough across the jaw to cure me of that way of thinking. Maybe it's unfinished business, you and me, but it doesn't feel like that now. All I want, just for the moment, is the feeling that I've had since yesterday; of belonging here. It's easier to belong when J. G. isn't around; when there's just Liz and Carey and Nanny and the boy; and the house; I've got the hang of the house now; I liked waking up this morning, and knowing I was here. That's the tune I was afraid of your breaking; but it hasn't broken yet."

He watched the dragon-fly shape of a small aircraft coming in; saw it rock and run to a standstill, the dazzled flickering of the propeller turn into two slow-moving blades. He stared at it all; the drab hangars, the green flat grass, the asphalt runway. Below them, because they were higher than Carlington, a wider fan of marsh spread out, green, gold and brown, stretching to the lip of the sea. Against the sea at one point there was a water-tower, a mottle of roofs, a faint smoke. He heard the wind-sock flapping and the murmur of Carey's voice talking to the grizzled man. He heard the sudden, impatient sigh that Liz gave, just as the grizzled man said, "Here he is," and another man in grey flannels came out of the low wooden office building behind them and stood on the steps looking up.

Tobias, he thought, and found that he could not get back to his first impression of Toby; to the unreasonable irritation; it was gone; there was the radiant smile, the voice that said, "Cover my well-shaped and flying tracks," then the look of him running down the steps from Gerald Lynn's house, and the profile behind the little lighted window of the car, moving into the dark.

(vii)

In the pilot's seat, Tobias was singing loudly:

"Inkpen and Hackpen and Southward and away
  High through the middle airs in the strengthening of the day."

He was over the airfield now; it streamed away beneath him;
looking down, he could see the tiny group waiting; he waved to
it wildly; he roared over and out again toward the sun.

"And there I saw the channel glint
            and England in her pride,
      And I ride!"

He saw the sea come back, nearer now, bluer now, a dazzle
with the sideways-slanted roofs and fields at the edge.

He banked and turned. It was a tricky landing; you could
overshoot. (Once around again, and the whole sky to play with,
and the face before your eyes that kept the dream steady, the
dream wherein you need not leave her, ever any more.)

"For you that took the all-in-all,
            the things you left were three:
      A loud voice for singing and keen eyes
            to see."

The engine went rough.
"Pooh to you," said Tobias; and then it cut out.

(viii)

Liz was saying, "I never know why you have to bank; it feels
horrible, and I'd have thought that you could skim around and
come in flat."

The sudden cough of the engine was unbelievable; after it coughed, the sound seemed to be pinned inside Levitt's ears, just as the little slanted shape of the aeroplane coming down the sky was stuck to his eyes. He heard the second splutter, then a shout beside him and the ground grew men. Where did they come from, the men on their quick feet, the figures hurling themselves into the crash-truck so that its red shape moved at once? Was that the truck's engine starting up or the other engine still spluttering? Yes, one more cough and then silence. Oh no, he thought, no; no; no. It was all too slow to be possible, the shape of the aeroplane still coming down the sky.

"For God's sake keep her nose down!" he shouted, as if Tobias could hear. But the nose went up and it was happening.

As he grasped Liz she wrestled and tore at him; over her shoulder there was Carey running straight out to meet it; Carey would be killed too. Somebody was screaming, a high-whistling scream, "That's Foliot," he thought, but he could not see her; he could see Nanny, clutching Terry, stumbling with him, holding him close, bowed over, facing away from it; Celia just behind them, forcing Nanny down with stiff arms while her head twisted back to watch the aeroplane; her neck stretched, her profile paper-white. He got his hand across Liz's eyes; he had to keep looking; he saw the plunging shadow; he saw Carey pulled back, knocked aside to safety, and he turned his head away before there was the last of it, the crackle of thunder, the smoke rising, the oily flames.

6

(i)

"SIR JAMES will have to keep you waiting a few moments," Mather said, "his doctor is with him."

"How does he seem?" Levitt asked.

Mather's face flattened yet more discreetly. "He's very nervous this evening." The careful little cough indicated that he had another message to give: "If you'll excuse me, Mr. Levitt, please don't let him talk too long. He—er—gives so much of himself, and that's what causes the trouble. That's what brought on the attack. Of course we're all hoping that the cruise will put him right. He ought to have got away sooner, in my view."

He hovered a moment, as though he expected more of Levitt than the assenting nod; then he went out.

Levitt waited. He stood by the window, looking down on to the Embankment gardens, the gold river. It felt like a year since he had talked to Baron. It was less than three weeks. Three weeks, they seemed, of fanfare for Tobias. Tobias was public property now. Tobias belonged to the four million readers of the *Flash* and the *Sun*. He would live for them a little longer, in memories of the full-page photograph with the black rim, the romantic Rupert-Brooke profile above the single-line caption; in terms of Gerald Lynn's article, "I Knew This Boy"; in the sugar of an anonymous sonnet called simply "Toby". He would live for a while in the record of Glane; "Toby and Glane" had been the title of Gerald's second piece; a convenient flourish, the dovetailing of Tobias into the village history; Gerald's neatly moving paragraphs told how Toby had watched the bombing and how, long afterwards, he still took solitary walks to the place. Fanfare for Tobias, Levitt thought; and he didn't like it, but he could not blame Baron. It was the only sort of tribute that J. G. would know how to pay.

Restlessly he paced before the window. Was it the luggage, strapped and labelled, that turned the Savoy suite back into the suite on A deck, where all this began? He felt something of the same mood, the same flavour of the disquieting unknown; as though all that he had lived and discovered in the short time since belonged to a chapter closed by Tobias' death. It was a new Levitt who faced the new chapter.

Still on his eyes there stayed the image of the aeroplane slipping down the sky. There was still the echo of the moment that had left him tougher; that had opened his eyes and set up a sense of proportion in his head. Some of the things met in war had done that. No closely-personal tragedy ever could, he thought; it came when you saw other people's destiny operating. As at Monte Cassino, so on the airfield above the marsh.

The inner door of the suite opened and Baron was there. Levitt had not seen him since the memorial service, and then Baron had been a glimpse of set grey face under silk hat, hurried to the car by a bodyguard with the photographers training on him like a gun crew. The heart attack had come two days later.

He stood in the doorway; he looked shrunken and dubious; a tragic old dwarf with a sweet smile. His voice sounded weak as he said, "Hello, there," in careful American greeting. His clothes were frivolous; a checked blue suit and a shirt of the same limpid blue, a fat blue *crêpe de Chine* tie. The wide black band was more than usually noticeable on the sleeve of this jacket. He sank down in the corner of the sofa.

"How are you feeling, sir?"

"I'm all right, boy. So very happy to see you; been meaning to see you before, but these damned doctors. . . . You were there," he said; the corner of the mouth slanted. "You saw it happen."

Levitt nodded.

"Quick stuff," J. G. said. "The best for them. Not for those who are left behind." His heavy eyelids drooped. "On my way to meet him; but of course you know that."

He paused for a moment. The old, wary look returned.

It was a slip. It stunned Levitt. Around the office he had heard the inaccurate version, letting it pass unchallenged because he could not bring himself to disperse it with the first-hand truth. All that week-end was locked up inside him. And now he saw that J. G. was the author of the inaccurate version. He felt winded, bemused.

("When O'Rourke said, 'The chief was on his way to the air-field,' I could have answered, 'Like hell he was; he was raging around Oxford, waiting for Toby. Anthony didn't get him on the telephone till five o'clock, and he wasn't back at Carlington till nine.' But I didn't say it. If I had?")

Baron was saying something about Carey; the words "A

tower of strength" came through. They were illogically painful to Levitt, the memories of Carey in command. "He was magnificent," Levitt said, ranging back over the nightmare and the figure of the calm, efficient captain presiding. But the fact of J. G.'s self-deception returned to hit him and take the memories away. "You *can't* kid yourself that far," his thoughts argued with the little sunken face. Fanfare for Tobias.

"A wonderful boy. I feel myself blessed, even now. . . . If he'd grown up in the war. . . . Same thing . . . same loss. . . *Among the very brave, the very true.*"

("I'm stuck for words.")

"Unusual; his wit; his adult quality. He had, you know, a very great attraction for older people. That wonderful woman Catherine de Lille . . . she's coming to see me this afternoon. Almost a mother to him . . ."

Levitt said, "I'm very proud to have had the chance of knowing him," and the words in his mouth had an actual taste, a palpable sourness as though he ate something bad.

Baron gave a heavy, rattling sigh like the sigh of the yellow dog, Prince.

"But the trouble at my age is that one's body plays up to a shock like that. I wouldn't go if they didn't insist. Expect to be away about a month; cruising; Carol Baer's yacht; very decent of him. . . . Taking Liz and Anthony . . ." His eyes wandered. "Probably you knew that, too . . . you've seen them?"

"Well, no; I've kind of kept away. Thought they'd rather not have outsiders around. Told Carey I was there if I was wanted." His words still stuck.

"Very good of you," J. G. said with the sweet smile. "Beautiful wreath; hope you got the note of thanks. . . . Now I'd like to give you a few pointers on the job." He became sharper, more coherent. "As far as the *Flash* goes, just keep right on doing your same stuff. Cartoon's a great success, isn't it? You're satisfied, yourself?"

"Oh, sure, I'm having a wonderful time with it."

"That's good; that's good." His voice turned feeble again, then sharpened. "For the *Sun*, I want you to aim, between now and August, at the British summer-resources: seaside hotels; holiday camps; travel and so on. I don't care how you do it; so long as you point up the discomforts. O'Rourke has quite a few ideas; you'll get together with him. Don't find O'Rourke difficult at all, do you?"

"No, sir. He's nicely crazy."

"Good. Nicely crazy; that's true, that's good." He folded his small strong hands in his lap; he peered at Levitt. "You yourself? Not lonely here? Made some new friends? I'm glad. One needs friends . . . I thank God for my friends."

Levitt said, "Well, I won't keep you, sir. *Bon voyage*, and I hope the cruise'll do you a lot of good. Look forward to seeing you back."

"Thanks, boy," said Baron. He stretched out his hand; for the first time Levitt felt the same tremor that ran through the other hands. "If you want a quiet week-end or a night in the country, don't forget Carlington. The house will be open and I want you all to go there when you feel like it. Micky and some of the others'll be going. Don't hesitate. Take a friend along any time . . . plenty of room. Good-bye, Levitt. God bless you. And——" he paused, with the tears welling up, "I'm terribly glad you knew Toby."

Outside the door Levitt stood still, shook his head, found himself asking urgently, "But how do *they* take this act? Liz? Celia? Carey? Above all, Liz . . ." During these haunted weeks he had wanted most of all to comfort Liz. But that was Carey's job.

"God's truth," he said to himself, waiting for the lift, "I didn't have time to see much, but I saw enough and heard enough to know his attitude towards Toby. Is this restitution? Or is it——" Celia's words came back, "one of the hundred and one masks in his repertoire?"

As he stepped out of the lift, he saw Celia coming through the lobby. Off guard, not seeing him, walking alone, she was greatly changed; haggard and pale, arousing his tenderness. He barred her way and took her hand.

"Oh, Harry. Hullo. Have you been with him?"

"Yes; he sent for me."

"I was just going up to say good-bye." She rested her hand on his arm as though she needed support. "Isn't anywhere we can get a drink first, is there? I need one awfully badly."

"I'd say come to my flat, but if he's waiting for you——"

"He isn't; he's not expecting me."

"Fine; I'll whisk you there in a taxi and bring you back. Take it easy, now." She said, "I'm all right," and still let him hold her arm. "Fifty-eight Curzon Street, and make it extremely snappy," Levitt said to the driver. "I'm all right," Celia repeated, "just plain tired. How did you find him?"

"I don't know yet. Quite different. Soft—kind."

"Tobias the most wonderful boy in the world?"

"Roughly."

"Such ——" she said. It was unlike her to swear. He laid his hand on hers. "It seems years since I saw any of you. How's Liz?"

Celia said, "Variable. I'd like to keep her with me, better all round. J. G. won't hear of it. And she, poor darling, has developed it into a kind of martyrdom crusade. Go she must; I've been arguing that one for two days . . ." She leaned back and shut her eyes. "Pay no attention; sorry to be a sissy."

"Nearly there," Levitt said.

The taxi stopped and it surprised him to remember that she had not been here; her image was as much a part of its furniture as the gold tables, the mirrors, the vases of flowers. He kept his arm around her in the lift; there was, in the sudden wish to cradle and comfort her, the beginning of desire, the tiger pacing.

"Now," he said, "I'll fix you the biggest drink in the game."

"Not too big, for heaven's sake, with J. G. ahead." Her hands shook so much when he gave her the glass that he had to hold it for her.

"That'll do it," said Celia, grimacing over the first swallow. "Thank you. Very present help in trouble, Mr. Levitt."

"Wish to God there were something I could do. You're not going on the yacht?"

She shook her head. "I'd only make it worse. I can't take these sky-rockets of public mourning, you see. They just enrage me. The whole act is such a farce that it makes me sick."

He said gently, "And Liz?"

Celia's smile slanted. "One half of Liz feels the way I do. But she threshes; she's deeply sorry for J. G. So'm I, come to that. But I won't string along with the act, because I can't. Liz thinks I ought to; and she's beginning to get angry with me. Which is just as well. . . . Only thing that worries me about that is her fight with herself. She's not strong enough to fight yet. But she'll be all right with Carey, let's face it; she's always all right with Carey."

He was aware of the twist of jealousy, knifing him. He felt insane, his heart crying suddenly after Liz and his body wanting Celia. He looked again at the fair head resting on the hand that trembled.

"One can kid oneself so far that one believes, after a bit, I guess," he said.

"Meaning J. G.?" The weary eyelids lifted; the square, brilliant eyes took him in as though, he thought, she identified him, on that count, with Baron.

"Yes."

"I wonder. Did he try to sell you the story that he was on his way to meet Toby?"

Levitt inclined his head. "He pulled himself up halfway—remembering I was there."

"And you said?"

"What could one say, Celia?"

She murmured, "Such damnable nonsense. He didn't even *like* Toby."

"Remorse must be a stinker, just the same."

"So you cover it with orchids, like a gangster's wreath? Sorry," she said. "I know I sound tough, as usual. No reason, I guess, why he shouldn't play it this way. . . . Just so's I don't have to watch." She put down her glass. "Well, bless you for the drink."

"Aren't you going to finish it?"

"I mustn't. Sorry you had to have all this, chum," she said wistfully.

"Oh, please . . ." he kissed her hand. "May I see you sometimes while they're away? I won't be tiresome."

She smiled; it was almost the old smile. "Thank you, Harry. Yes, call me. But I shan't be at Carlington. I've taken a house in London; St. John's Wood." She gave him the number and he wrote it carefully with his gold pencil. "Terry?" he said. "How's Terry?"

"All right, really. He didn't get it entirely; it was too quick; and we've fooled him that it wasn't Tobias. But I want him away from Carlington for a bit; he asks all the time when Toby's coming back, and he keeps wanting to write to him at Oxford. I think once we're in the new house he'll lose the association; he's awfully young, after all, and he'd known Toby such a little time." The matter-of-fact note in her voice, the absolute control, shamed him for wanting to weep.

(ii)

Baron looked at the clock. She would be here in a few minutes now. One of the symptoms of this state of mind was the tremendous eagerness for a new person, a new target for words and attitudes. They were all stimulants; if one could assure their regular supply, one would not need to think. But after a while one grew tired and had to rest and then the thoughts came walking. He wanted a cigar. They had said not to smoke cigars. Fretfully as a child wanting a sweet, he stretched out his hand to the humidor and drew it back.

"Scared of the doctor, eh?" he remarked to himself with a pleasant chuckle. It was easier to think this than to admit the larger shadow that scared him.

Mather said, "Madame de Lille is downstairs, sir."

"Ask her to come up." He rose and stood before the mantel-piece. He went down deliberately into the wistful fatherly dream. It helped, to think of old Randolph Carey, to murmur afterwards, "Randolph'll look after him; Randolph will see to it that he's all right. Must be a bit strange, just at first."

When she came in, he saw her through the mirror of his tears. He remembered her peaceful walk, her straight shoulders, the motionless beauty of the face. "Really, a most remarkable-looking woman for her age; and those legs," said the satyr Baron, shocking the Baron who mourned. He kissed her hand.

"It's extraordinarily good of you to come," he said, "knowing how seldom you visit London; I'm most touched."

"Please. It's nothing," said Catherine de Lille.

"Do sit down. Let me offer you a drink?"

"No, thank you very much." She sat down and was at once motionless; most women wriggle, Baron thought, take a long time to get comfortable, fuss with their skirt, don't know where to put the handbag; restful, this sort. He said, "As I told you in my reply to your letter, I really only wanted to say thank you—for all you were to Toby; and to ask you not to feel badly because it happened like that."

She hesitated. The trace of a smile came and went. "On those things of course," she said at last, "it is impossible to have a point of view."

"What? . . . You mean—don't quite understand you, I'm sorry."

"I mean the death of the young. I lost a son in the war," she said, "so I know this a little at first-hand."

("Good God, whose son was that now? Blake's, I suppose; she only had the one boy by Falchon.") The fact of her loss made a small irritation in his mind; he felt robbed of privilege.

"Don't want you to think that it was in any way your responsibility," he reminded her. "Sort of thing that keeps one awake at night."

"It hasn't," she said gently. "Not, I think, because I'm lacking in conscience. But from something that Tobias said to me just before he flew. I know that I couldn't have stopped him. And I do believe, though to say so now to you may seem an intrusion, an offensive assumption of philosophy, in God's design."

"What? Yes, yes, *yes*; so do I," said Baron. God had been all over the place in these last weeks; extraordinarily useful, God; almost felt like a friend, one had mentioned him so often.

"But I want you to understand," she said, "how deeply sorry I am. If I feel like this, what must you feel?" She moved her hand palm upwards. "Out of the microscopic compass of my right to mourn him, I can just sight yours—and that is all. I loved him dearly."

She was making him uncomfortable.

"If there is anything more I can tell you," she said, "about those last two days—it may be that details are comforting, I don't know: I wrote them in my letter because I thought they might be." ("No movie-star's eyes can compare with them, still; the smallest lines, of course, showing now; just little lines; I'd give her thirty-five, if I didn't know.")

He said, "I've read them more than once. Half a dozen times, in fact." (Not true, but courteous; she had, after all, taken trouble. . . .)

"He was—more grown-up than I had seen him before," she said musingly. "A moment of maturity that was very palpable. The poem——"

Baron remembered that her letter had contained a poem, recited by Tobias on the last morning. It was not the kind of poetry that he liked.

"I had never heard it until that day," Catherine said. "After his death I found that he'd copied it out for Lionel. I'm having it cut on stone; there's a fountain in my garden that he was fond of. The stone will be there. No name or other legend; only the words. I thought I should like to have them there."

Baron stared at her; the idea of a memorial to Tobias had not occurred to him until this moment; there would be a head-stone, of course, in the churchyard. But now, by her words, he was embarked. ("There should be a memorial. A statue in the garden at Carlington; of course there should. There will; what's more Anthony must do it. I know the place. Up on the little lawn under the cypresses, where the marble bench is now. Toby's memorial. By Anthony. It's right. It's magnificent.")

The new stimulant made him forget Catherine altogether. He woke to hear her saying gently, "You're tired, aren't you? Would you like me to go?"

"No, no, stay a little longer. Talk of the boy. . . . I'm a bit feeble, I'm afraid. Ah, time for those damned drops," he said as the nurse came in.

"I am sure," said Catherine de Lille, "that I should go," and she rose, holding out her hand to him.

"We're friends, aren't we?" said Baron. "He's made us friends. When I'm stronger I'd like to see you again. Like to see the—memorial stone when you get it up. We're putting up a statue, as a matter of fact, ourselves, in the garden at Carlington. Bless you, my dear. Thank you for loving my boy."

Her face did not change. He could not tell what she was thinking. As she reached the door he said abruptly, "He loved you, too."

She turned. Now there was a look of pain, a curious darkness upon her; as though he had said something outrageous. After a moment she said, "To be loved is the one thing that one never learns to take for granted. Good-bye, J. G. Take care of yourself."

"Should have thought," Baron said to himself, "that you'd had enough of it in your lifetime to take it for granted, my girl." He swallowed the drops. He felt weak, but triumphant.

"You ought to rest now, Sir James. Remember we've a journey tomorrow." He was to motor to Carlington, pick up Liz and Anthony, catch the *Golden Arrow* boat at Dover. He wanted to talk to somebody about the statue at once. Old Micky, drifting in apologetically, would do. The nurse tried to put Micky out. "Stop nagging," Baron said; "when I'm tired, I'll tell you."

"Care for a game of chess, J. G.?"

"No, thanks, old boy. Rather want to talk to you. I've got a project I'm pleased with." But it was really no fun telling Micky anything; he was always rapturous and champing; Anthony was the boy; Anthony and he would work out the idea together; Anthony could make the preliminary drawings on the yacht.

"Hullo, J. G.," Celia said. He was not expecting her. He had thought, and hoped, that their last good-bye was said. She offended him with her elegance, her self-control, her friendly, assured greeting to Micklethwait.

"How are you feeling?" she asked him gently.

"Not too bad. Bit tired. I didn't know you were coming to town."

"I'll be pushing off, sir," said Micklethwait. His hand-shake was hearty; he said all the usual things. Celia waited equably, seating herself opposite to him, removing her gloves.

"I met Catherine de Lille downstairs," she said, narrowing her eyes at the corners, a habit of hers that he mistrusted.

"What? . . . Oh, Catherine de Lille; yes. Nice of her to come."

"Very nice," the cool voice echoed. He stared uneasily. "You sound as if it were more than I could have expected."

"I think it was," said Celia, still gentle.

He sighed. "No, no . . . at these times . . . but you've got a hard streak in you; you always had. Just like your mother." He shielded his eyes with his hand, slipped down lower among the sofa cushions. "I'm very tired, Celia."

"So am I. I won't keep you long. I just wanted to say good-bye."

"You're still set on taking this London house, eh?"

"Yes. We'll move next week. It's right for Terry."

He said, "I don't like it."

"I'm sorry, J. G."

He tapped his knee restlessly. He wanted to talk about the memorial to Toby. Wisdom held him back. Celia's attitude in the last weeks was unforgivable; her mother could not have improved upon the cold reserve, the listless disdain of all that he had done to pay tribute to Tobias. She looked ill too, and he felt the familiar exasperation.

"Are you all right? Better give yourself a drink or something."

"I'm all right. I don't want a drink, thank you."

"You'd be far better to come with us, leave Nanny and the boy comfortably at Carlington. Easily arranged."

Again there was the quiet, "I'm sorry, J. G."

"I don't know why you always have to be different," he grumbled.

She shrugged her shoulders.

"It's selfish. Liz would like to have you."

"No, my dear, she wouldn't. And I still wish that you'd persuade her to stay with me. You could, so easily."

"Would you mind telling me why I should do such a thing?"

"Oh, J. G. Look, I don't want to tire you, it is just that you'd probably have a much more placid time alone with Anthony. Liz will only be seasick and miserable; and a boat—any boat— is the worst possible site for brooding. It isn't good for her."

"Allow me to know, please."

"Well, that's all. I can't stop you," she said on a sigh.

"Certainly, you can't. I don't know why you trouble to make the point. I should have thought your lack of consideration had already gone far enough."

He saw the flash of anger before she hid it. He had to go on:

"I know your absurd belief that one shouldn't show one's feelings. But anyone would think from your behaviour that the death of your brother meant nothing to you."

He regretted it as soon as he had said it. Her pallor came with the same frightening suddenness that he remembered on Toby's cheek a month ago, when he had spoken of Catherine de Lille. She touched her forehead with her finger-tips, shut her eyes, made a gesture with her hand for him not to speak. He waited; he was worried now, and it was bad for him to be worried, he thought peevishly.

When she looked at him again, she was still white; her voice was quiet and menacing as she said, making her mouth crooked, "Toby's death means a different thing to each of us. Do you know, for certain, what it means to you, J. G.?"

He was silent; outraged. "If I spoke the truth," he thought, "it would be to say, 'Yes, it means everything. It means that—at last—he belongs to me.' This Tobias, the face in the photograph, the boy in the sonnet, the figure on Gerald's pages, is mine. And I can love him. I can make gestures towards him, as I never could while he lived. I can be at peace with him, and with all his affections; I can be friends with Catherine de Lille. I can make Tobias anything that I wish to make him now. This is what you guess, damn you; sitting there, with your crooked mouth.

"Do you guess the rest? That there is still the other Tobias at the back of my mind? The one who has escaped. The one who stays set for ever in his damned defiance, his cool hostility, his remoteness from me. That Tobias I hate. I shall always hate him. For some hideously unfair reason, anybody who is dead looks as though he were in the right. He does. Always I shall feel that I was in the wrong, and I'll never forgive him that. I have forgiven God, because I am afraid of him. But I'll never forgive the other Toby, the real Toby, the one who got away.

"Do you guess it? Keep your guesses. It will never be told. Because I'm myself, because I'm Baron and no weakling, I'll carry the truth alone."

BOOK III

THE ALL-IN-ALL

(December, 1949)

THE ALL-IN-ALL

1

(i)

THE London house stood in a garden, halfway up a long avenue planted with trees; one of the avenues in St. John's Wood, that had declined from a rich residential past. Despite the blackened façades, the windows left blank by bombing and the gaps grown over with willowherb, the marks of London, there was a country feeling here; it lurked palpably under the town. At each end of the backwater avenue there was London; a wide main artery street, a bus route. In the middle of the avenue one was safe from London, or so Carey thought.

He came now to the house, Celia's house; it was of late Georgian architecture, a solid red cake of a house, with newly-painted window-frames and a tended garden; its lawn set it back from the road and a flagged path led to the door; it made a suddenly prosperous interruption to the dingy, forgotten façades.

Anthony opened the gate. This was a freakish day of December sunshine, and there were colours still in the garden; a late, absurd red leaf fluttering from the wall, a yellowish winter rose. Nanny opened the door to him.

"Isn't it a lovely day; we really *are* having a mild winter. The boy's quite ready for you. I hope he'll sit still."

Anthony followed her through the hall. It was palpably Celia's house, he thought; it suited her; he looked at the curve of the staircase, the huge flowers on the landing; her scent clung here. He looked at it differently today, because there were things that he did not understand.

"What's this about your coming back to Carlington?" he

asked Nanny. She said, "I don't know, sir, for certain. Mrs. West'll tell you about all it, I expect." Her mouth was set, prim, hiding a secret. He remembered this look from childhood; Liz was right; Nanny never changed.

Her small, busy shape went ahead of him, down the passage that ran from the front hall to the long room at the back of the house. This room was a converted studio, wide and lofty. Its effect, as you opened the door from the passage, was magically surprising. There were three steps leading down to a parquet floor; a gallery at the far end; an open brick fireplace. The windows looked on to the back garden, on neat grass, leafless rose trees, a red wall.

"Here's your Uncle Anthony, Terry. Now you'll be a good boy, won't you?"

Terry said, "Try," without hope or enthusiasm. Anthony said, "Just sit on the stool, old boy; as you were; you can keep the aeroplane."

He found his drawing-blocks and pencils on the table where he had left them. He looked over the rough sketches. Yesterday he had been satisfied; today they were nothing. That set him thinking about Toby's statue. He moved his chair until the light fell as he needed it and began to make another sketch of the child's head.

Why did Celia want this, suddenly? He did not know. It had been almost a command, full of urgency and unexplained, "Could you get something on paper this week? I don't mind if you never model it; I'd like to have some sketches." And after that she had made the hint about moving, "Maybe I shan't have the house much longer." "Coming back to Carlington?" "Probably, yes." But there had been a brief hesitation before she said it.

"Can I talk?" Terry asked.

"Yes, rather."

"Well, when's Christmas?"

"Just about three weeks off."

"Ages."

"Yes."

"We *are* having a mild winter, aren't we?" said Terry, putting down the toy aeroplane and hugging his knees.

"Very mild," said Anthony courteously. The echo of Nanny made him grin; the thought pleased him; it crystallised the feeling in his heart. Mild winter . . . yes; at last, and unbelievably, peace was coming back.

Seven months and more since Toby died. Looking back across the time, he could see them all working their way through. Routine, order, a shape to every day, had become their imperative need. He saw himself going blindly ahead with his labours, drawing, modelling, remodelling, casting, discarding; he was not satisfied yet, though the stone would be ready for his final touches this week. ("Not satisfied; my epitaph; but at least it is done, and at least I went at it so hard I had no time to think.") He saw Celia striving for the same immunity; working a nine-hour day at the movie job; bringing home scripts to read after dinner. He saw Liz at the Academy of Music, turning into a student and seeming to grow younger before his eyes, ever more quiet and elusive; Liz was a hatless hurrying figure with a leather case in her hand; Liz was a bowed head and quick fingers above the keyboard; he heard himself sigh without having thought that he was sad about Liz.

Terry said, "Have you got a pain?"

"No, thanks, old boy. Keep your chin up, just for a minute. Then you can rest."

He saw Levitt, capriciously a part of the family fabric now, burying himself in work, taking on a commissioned book that gave him no spare time at all. He saw J. G., whose restlessness took a different form, inventing journeys; flying to India and New York; defying doctors; making political speeches all over the map of the British Isles.

So much for the summer and the early autumn. And he could see the pattern that they had followed, only because it was past. Even this house was losing its significance.

It had been a refuge during the months when they found themselves avoiding Carlington. Obliged to work in his studio, he had still run here for week-ends or odd nights when he could not bear his own company. Liz had stayed here; Levitt had caught their habit of calling it "the house" without further identification. J. G. alone stayed away from it; though he too was avoiding Carlington. The Baron Sunday had lapsed for a long time.

But since autumn the pattern had begun to change. Carlington was there again, gradually reinstating itself, turning back into home. Now Liz came to London only on two days a week for lessons. This was his, Anthony's, first visit in several weeks, at Celia's sudden request. The week-end was back; the Baron Sunday was back; Levitt took a Friday afternoon train and drove up with Baron on Monday morning.

And Celia? Just as J. G. had kept away from this house, so now Celia rejected Carlington. Anthony welcomed the thought of her hinted return to it. When he looked back at the old days, it seemed impossibly cruel to lose Celia as well as Tobias from the new order. But there was a widening of the rift between her and J. G. Ever since Toby's death he had been aware of it.

Just what had widened the rift, he did not know. He knew only that she had hated the newspaper fanfare more than any of them had hated it. He recalled her barbed comments on the memorial statue.

"Charming. An urn? A broken column? Or a sundial telling us He Counted Only the Happy Hours? Why do we have to have a memorial to Toby in the garden? As for dogs. 'Rover. A Faithful Friend'."

Naturally she would not say this to J. G. And J. G. never spoke of the rift. But perhaps it was ending now. Perhaps they would be four again; a different four: Anthony, Celia, Liz and Levitt.

He frowned, with his pencil in mid-air, forgetting to tell Terry to come back to the stool. Terry was making a two-note tune on the piano behind his head. For Anthony, the two notes chirped "Lev-itt—— Lev-itt."

Levitt was there always; in the likeness of a new, adopted brother; as though, by his presence on the airfield, he had qualified to be one of them. It was queer, Carey thought, their acceptance of Levitt. "Or do I mean it is queer that I should accept him, seeing how much he means to Liz? When I am alone it feels as though I'm living over a volcano; then I see him again on Friday and remember that I like him; and I watch the two of them together, and I dare to believe that he means no more to her than I do. (Oh, Liz, Liz; where have you gone? There was a time, I think, when you could have loved me.)" Often he could be certain that she loved nobody, that she would never love at all; then he would see a look pass between them and the glinting menace of Levitt would return; the Knave of Spades; the slick dark stranger.

"Come back now, Terry; only twenty minutes more."

"What happens after the twenty minutes?"

"You have your lunch and I catch a train."

"Why?"

"Because that's the way it goes."

"Which way does it go?"

"What go?"

"The train."

"Oh, I see. It goes to Carlington."

"I'd like to go. Soon we will. But not Uncle Tobias," said Terry matter-of-factly.

Anthony was silent. The child expected no answer; he forced himself to sit still. This sketch was a little better. Presently he said:

"I'm going to leave these for your mother, Terry; will you ask her if she likes any of them? If she doesn't, I'll have another shot next week."

"Are they all me?"

"Supposed to be."

"Well, thank-you-very-much-for-having-me-I've-had-a-very-nice-time," said Terry in rapid recitative; he yawned widely.

At the door he said, "Don't you want to take your blocks and pencils?"

"No; I'll leave them here. Plenty more at home."

"May I use them?"

"I'd rather you didn't, chum. Look, you can have this pencil, if you like."

"Thank you very much."

Anthony opened the front door; a telegraph boy was coming up the flagged path. "Mrs. Valentine West live here?"

"Yes; I'll take it. Nanny!" he called from the hall, "telegram for Celia. I've left it on the table." He heard the faint echo of her answer and went on his way, wishing that Celia were coming too. Idle to ask her. He looked back at the house, caught himself wondering if she were lonely. No, not Celia; a person who needed nobody, at ease alike with her sophisticated movie job, her international chums and her widow's household.

Strolling towards the Pullman car at Cannon Street, he saw Levitt waiting, looking for him, and this was odd because Levitt never caught the one-twenty.

Carey waved, walking faster. Levitt grinned and waited. "He has changed in looks," Anthony thought, remembering the time when he had first met Levitt at Ashford station. His face had filled in. With the English hair-cut, the bulky English overcoat and dark silk scarf, he was different; he looked not only more prosperous, more settled, but gayer and somehow more wise.

"Nice to find you," Carey said. "Shut up shop early?"

Levitt said, "Had to. Ould Maister just landed me one in the solar plexus."

"What sort?"

"Tell you," Levitt said as they climbed into the Pullman. "I took us a table. Here. Want a drink?"

"Bottle of beer," said Carey.

"Make mine a double pink gin," Levitt said to the steward.

"Wot? In the middle of the day?" said Carey. "Breaking with tradition, aren't you?"

"Sure," said Levitt. He looked grim.

"What's happened?"

"I'm going back to America."

"Good God! When?"

"Next week."

Carey blinked. "You don't mean for good? He hasn't *sacked* you? He couldn't——"

"Not yet. It's for two months. I'm still under contract. I'm to send my stuff from there." He wore a look like that of a hound on a strong scent. "J. G. didn't suggest for a minute that he wasn't satisfied; said he wanted some new angles from me; thought a 'Levitt's America Revisited' would be amusing. But I'm uneasy, I'm tellin' ya," he said with an exaggerated accent. He drained his drink. "Call it ominous, don't you?"

"I don't know that I do," said Carey slowly; he was seeing the gap that Levitt would leave at Carlington. "A two-months' assignment, that's all."

Levitt still frowned. "I got an overtone. The air's been a little cloudy lately. He wasn't pleased when I took on the book; and I know I've been overworking. Seems to me that the bite has gone out of the stuff lately, and I can't help feeling that J. G. shares the view."

Carey said, "I'm sure he doesn't. . . . Come to think of it, I like the cartoon much better now than I did at first. If I don't sound impertinent, it seems to have more—more humanity, more weight. I thought that mine-worker one on Tuesday was a beauty."

Levitt looked pleased. "Did you? Bless you. J. G. liked it at first; then, when the reactions weren't so hot, he pulled out. Told me we must remember that people don't want to be *moved* by the *Flash* cartoon, just shocked." He left his soup unfinished, leaned back impatiently and lit a cigarette.

"Lord, we're going to miss you," Carey said.

"*Hell*, I'll miss you . . . all of you. First thing I thought. Couldn't make like nice when the old boy said he knew I'd be ripe and ready for my native land again. All the time he seemed to be hurling it at me as a glittering prize; gift-wrapped; with love and kisses from kind Ould M." He peered gloomily at the meat and vegetables, stubbed out his cigarette, began to eat. He held his knife now, Carey observed, instead of laying it at the side of the plate as he used to do.

"Won't you be glad at all to see America again?"

Levitt shook his head. "I've no life over there; nobody much I want to visit." He frowned again. "Got my roots down here, I guess," he said and abandoned the meat course. Carey could see

it; Levitt never talked of his home nor of his beginnings. For
Carey he had no context other than London and Carlington.
Apart from his war memories, he might have been born at the
age of thirty-three on the railway platform at Ashford.

"Yes," Carey said. "I think you have."

"J. G. doesn't know it, though," Levitt added, lighting another
cigarette. "Said he was sure I'd like to be home for Christmas.
Christmas in U.S. is poison ivy to me. If you've never seen it,
you can't imagine it."

"What's it like?"

"A commercial whoop-de-do starting early in November. A
million department-store Santas, booming at terrified tots.
Canned Carols blasting out of loudspeakers. By the time it's
through, you never want to see a wreath or a tree or a bell or a
ribbon, or a piece of gift wrapping-paper again. And the
poinsettias—Holy God, the poinsettias . . . I'd forgotten the
poinsettias." He put his head in his hands. "Red flowers," said
Carey vaguely; he could not see what they had to do with
Christmas. "Why didn't you ask J. G. to pend it till New Year?"

Levitt raised his hand. His expression was indulgent. "Carey
—dear Carey—my most revered and estimated Carey; because
Baron happens to be Baron. With any other boss, I'd not only
have asked to pend it, I'd have come straight out with my
questions. I'd have said, 'Isn't this the prelude to firing me?'
made him talk."

"Well, but I can't see why you didn't," said Carey patiently.

"You lead a sheltered life. . . . You happen to be immune
from the Baron fever. You're probably the only person who is."

"It's a bogey; a myth," Carey protested. "Liz and you just
encourage each other to believe in it." Levitt shook his head
tolerantly.

"You're immune," he repeated, "it's as though you're a good
sailor and we get seasick." He stared at Anthony for a minute
and then began to draw on the menu: when the steward served
their coffee, he handed it over. "First time I ever got you right,"
he said.

Anthony studied the sketch carefully. In common with many

people, he thought, he was not really sure about his own appearance, could not say for certain what his looks were, and was not altogether convinced that he would recognise Anthony Carey if he met him in the street. But Levitt's conception was surely an odd one. The face had a private, doubting look.

"What's this bloody great line under my lower lip? As if I were pouting or pursing?"

"It's there," said Levitt, "that shadow."

Carey looked a moment longer. "Well, if you want to know, I think you've made me look like a pansy who's about to rob a bank."

Levitt laughed and tore the menu across.

(ii)

"And here," Baron said, as they strolled through the garden door, "is the place where peace begins. First thing I do, every Sunday morning; stand here and praise God." He remembered that this was Saturday; he had brought the new young man down a day ahead, the better to sound him out. He decided to leave the 'Sunday' slip uncorrected. It made perfect sense, after all.

The new young man made appreciative noises. It was another morning of wintry sunshine; the colours were sharp. The leafless trees were delicately outlined; there was a dazzle of mist between the marsh and the sea.

"Here's where I can laugh at the spectres of trouble left behind; say to myself, 'Boy, you've given them the slip. Boy, you're home.'"

"I like the winter," said the young man. "I like to be able to see the shape of the trees." He was Lawrence Peet, the new political correspondent for the *Sun*; the latest acquisition bought from a rival. He had good clothes, a public school tie, adequate looks. Too much of a gentleman in appearance, Baron thought, for one to suspect the pungency of his mind.

He strolled with Peet towards the formal gardens. The punctual ghosts were waiting, by the walls of clipped yew:

Celia's mother and the hardly-recaptured wraith of Kit; old Randolph Carey hobbling stiffly; and with these the new ghost, Tobias; flaming hair and head tilted back, a laughing sceptical mouth; always Tobias came as himself; never as the dead son so tenderly, expertly mourned.

"There," Baron said, pointing with his stick towards the row of cypresses—"is where the statue's going; Anthony Carey's memorial to my son. A beautiful thing. You'll see it; not yet. I can show you the drawings. Anthony always works over the larger stuff at the stone shed. . . . Beautiful figure," he repeated uneasily. "Ought to be up in a week or two. I wanted him to submit the cast for the Glane Memorial Prize, but, as the honest old fellow says, it isn't exactly right. It's exactly right for Tobias though; the figure of a boy with a fawn. There'll be no name, or other legend. (*Who had put it that way? Oh yes, Catherine de Lille.*) We shall just know—all of us—that it's for Toby." He felt the tears rise. He stood still. Peet watched him sympathetically.

"Well, if I'm going to run you over to Glane and be back in time for lunch, we mustn't linger. Just take a quick look at the studio first." As they went through the cut between the yews, he heard the red-haired ghost shouting gaily, "*Wot?* No time to play with the giraffe?"

He led Peet along the mossy path under the wall, towards the white gate; and paused to point out the glories of the view again.

"Pity you have to see it for the first time in December. These rhododendrons for instance, as magnificent a show as you can imagine." He unlatched Carey's gate. "Now for a sight of the perfect studio; and a lad who really works; I expect we'll find Levitt there too; know Levitt?"

"I know his work," Peet said, "I haven't met him."

Baron halted, his hand still on the gate, studying Peet's careful profile.

"What d'you think of the Levitt cartoon, Lawrence?"

Peet hesitated. "Want me to be frank, sir? On the understanding that when people say 'frank', they inevitably mean critical and not complimentary?"

"What?—oh, surely," Baron grinned. "Go ahead."

Peet said, "Well, when you first got him, I thought he was impressive. Thought he might turn into a second David Low. But he seems to have fizzled out. Perhaps I'm just tired of his line. He hasn't got the savagery of Low, nor the chaotic comedy of Giles. That's only my view, for what it's worth."

"I wanted your view," Baron said. He filed the comment in his mind as he led Peet over the cobblestones to the studio. Faithfully he pointed out the Carey wheatsheaf in wrought iron. Faithfully he said as he poked his head round the door, "Mind an invasion, Anthony?"

His pleasure in the studio, at the sight of Carey in his blue overall, limping to meet them, was mitigated. Levitt, as he had expected, was using the drawing-table; he had strewn it with proof sheets and pulls; blue ink and black, pens and erasers; all the paraphernalia of his damned book.

Baron saw that it took him a moment to snap out of his concentration; that he rose with an air of abstracted politeness. His assurance was irritating now, as it had been irritating months ago; even his clothes were irritating; he wore a duffle coat and corduroys; it was cold in the studio. To make matters worse, Liz was helping him with the proofs. There was ink on her fingers and she too rose slowly; she came to kiss him; once again he was conscious of the change in Liz, the quiet dignity that shut him out, just as the childish sorrows of the earlier Liz had shut him out, making him feel that she would run to anybody with her grief before she ran to him. Now the impression was different. She would, he thought, run to nobody; unless—and he could not help giving Levitt an uneasy glance over her shoulder. He shifted his eyes quickly to the stand where Carey was working.

"Off on something new, eh? I told you, Lawrence, this boy never stops. What is it this time?"

"Nothing yet," said Carey with a grin. "Celia wants a head of Terry; I've been making sketches of him up at the London house. Then I found an old sketch I did here last summer and it seemed a bit better than I thought; I was just seeing if I could set up from it." Baron catalogued his own gift, the proportional compasses, before he asked: "Did Celia commission it?" and heard the rasp in his voice.

"Don't be crude, J. G."

Anthony contrived to say this without sounding offensive, whereas—Baron thought—one of the children would have made it an insult.

"Money, money, money; all you magnates ever think of," Carey went on, grinning broadly.

"Well, I'm damned if I'll have you treated as the family sculptor; 'doing' us all for nothing. If Celia wants a head of Terry, she can afford to pay for it."

"Cut rate, though; only fair," called Levitt; he had returned to the table and was obviously pining to get back to work. Liz added, "Anthony's doing Foliot for you as a Christmas present; a bronze nude; *cire-perdu* process; with a clock in her stomach that really goes."

"Repulsive children, mine," Baron said to Peet. "Come and look around, now. I can conduct the tour, Anthony boy, if you want to go on working." Liz and Levitt had returned too promptly to the proofs. Carey said with his eternal good-humour, "Delighted to be interrupted. You know that."

Looking at the book of drawings for the memorial statue, Baron felt uneasiness return. He watched Peet and could not tell whether his enthusiasm were true or a good fake. Somehow, though he would admit it to nobody, Carey had disappointed him. The earliest of these drawings dated from the Mediterranean cruise last summer. It was Baron who had insisted upon the album, it was bound in morocco; it was handsomely fit to hold every sketch made in Anthony's endeavour. He tried to tell himself, as Carey turned the last pages, the three separate views of the boy with the fawn from which he had set up the plasticine model, that the endeavour had ended in triumph.

"Of course you can't really judge from these," he said to Peet. "The cast's magnificent. And when we see it in marble——"

Just what was wrong with it? He could not identify his disappointment. This was competent, like all Anthony's work; nobody could find fault with the grace or proportion of these drawings; nobody, he was certain, would be able to find a technical shortcoming in cast or stone. "Anthony's a damned good craftsman," he said to himself, "and that's better than any fireworks. We're going to love the statue, all of us." Peet seemed to know something about sculpture; he was questioning Carey on the rivalry of the lost-wax and sand processes, the subject obviously set in motion by Liz's idiotic remark about Foliot. Here Baron glanced over his shoulder, down the length of the studio; saw the two bent over the drawing-table, Levitt's swaddled shoulders and gleaming dark head; the profile of Liz, the long wave of brown hair falling beside her cheek, the scarlet sweater.

"Don't mind their chasing you off your own table, eh?" he said to Carey.

"Lord no. I'm not using it."

"Well," said Baron to Peet—"we should be making tracks for Glane."

(iii)

"No," Levitt thought, "it isn't possible that this is going; that this time next week I'll be three thousand miles away from them . . . I just don't believe it."

At the piano Liz was playing; he could see only the top of her head from here. Because Baron had wanted Liz to play to them, they were sitting in the panelled room instead of the library.

"He looks old tonight," Levitt thought. "Old and malevolent. Wish to God I could work up nerve enough to ask him what really goes on in his mind about me."

He shifted unhappily, rose on the pretext of pouring himself a glass of water and sat down in a chair that gave him an uninterrupted view of Liz. She wore the look of peace that came to her when she played, the look of the dreamer forever quiet with her dream.

She was the cherished companion of this adventure and by next week she would be gone. He went on worrying about her.

She would have Carey, but Carey did not know it all. Nobody but he, Levitt, knew it all.

"I ought to talk to Carey, but I've given her my word that I won't. Maybe I'll talk to Celia." He saw little of Celia in these days; he went to the house sometimes, but only when Anthony or Liz was there. They were friendly and far, each with the other. He would catch sight of her in a restaurant, across a crowded floor, and look at her and remember, staring with his secret that was no longer bitter or sorrowful. "Funny," Levitt thought, while Liz swung over from revue tunes to classical solemnity, "that one went through to the age of thirty-three without growing up. And it was Celia, though she'll never know it, who began the process of chastening H. Levitt into some likeness of an adult. . . . Yes, since I can't talk to Carey, I'll talk to Celia.

"Oh, England," he thought, "oh, Liz . . . I *can't* leave you alone to keep up this act—and you do it so well—with nobody to share the truth behind the act. I can't leave you in your dark."

He had had few words alone with her since yesterday. When he broke the news of his going, Carey had been there; after dinner the three of them had played cards and to his whispered question Liz had said, "No; promise; I'm going straight to bed."

("Did you, though? Did you lie to me? No; you can't lie; you can act but you can't lie. And the only lie I've told in ages was to say I'd be away six weeks instead of two months; and then when dear innocent Anthony corrected me, I told him he'd got it wrong. But your quiet, my sweet, is the bad sign, and we must talk.

"Maybe I'm worrying too much. It's always the same. In the train yesterday with Anthony, I was fussing about me and my future. The moment I see your face—most beloved and defence-less face—I lose sight of me. All that matters is you.")

Coming to the end of the fugue, Liz shut the piano. "Will you excuse me, please, J. G., if I go to bed now? I'm tired." The still, detached dignity reminded Levitt of Celia.

Baron's eyes went worried. He said, "You look pale, child. Aren't you well?"

"Perfectly well. Only tired, thank you. I got up early.

Good-night, Mr. Peet. Good-night, Anthony." She looked at Prince, asleep on the hearthrug. "Will somebody see that he goes out?" She kissed Baron's cheek and moved to the door. Levitt rose to open it for her. He said, "Good-night, Liz," and she smiled as though from behind a cloud.

"She plays beautifully," Peet was saying.

"And she's really working at it," Baron said. "Nothing wrong with her, is there, Anthony?"

"Don't think so. She did get up early; we all rode before breakfast."

"And she's had a hideous time with my proofs," Levitt said, because Baron's eyes were saying it for him.

He waited impatiently, through the diplomatic fifteen minutes, observing, without disquiet or distaste, the wooing of Peet by Baron. Carey was doing a crossword puzzle. The hand of the sunburst clock on the panel above Carey's head moved intolerably slow. ("Make it sixteen minutes for luck. Well, here we go.")

He rose. "Will you forgive me, sir? I've got work to do."

"Work, at this hour—good God! He's showing off," Baron gurgled to Peet.

"It's the truth," said Levitt; "got to re-write six captions and put another five hundred words into the preface."

"That book of yours—more trouble than it's worth, if you ask me," said Baron. "Still, we'll give it a glorious boost when the time comes, sell a million copies. Good-night, Harry." The malevolence was gone; he was all benignity in upward-curling lines. His wave of dismissal was a sweeping arc; ample enough for dockside or airport.

Having shut the door, Levitt ran; darting up the stairs and along the passage to the nursery wing. He could just hear the music; she stuffed a duster into the gramophone lest it should be heard below.

> "Ye Hielands and ye Lowlands,
> O whaur hae ye been?
> They ha' slain the Earl o' Moray
> And laid him on the green."

Never did ballad sing more piercing sorrow. She lay on the sofa with a rug across her feet. The fire was unlit. Only one lamp shone in Celia's deserted room. It was different now, with Toby's possessions here, the toy theatre, the grim eagle bust of Irving, the playbills; cold and shadowy, the memorial room.

"Hullo," she said quietly.

"Liz, it's freezing in here."

"Never mind; get the fur rug from the other room; that's best."

He fetched it and sat beside her, nursing her feet.

> *"O, lang may his ladye*
> *Look frae her castle doun,*
> *E'er she see the Earl o' Moray*
> *Come sounding thro' the toun."*

and the threnody and the last sad, unexpected chord and silence.

She lay quite still, her chin pointed at the ceiling, her hair fallen back.

"So pretty," she said. She made no sound when she wept; she never did; there were just the tears running out of her eyes on to the cushion. He stroked her hand, watched her, said nothing.

"I had the nightmare again," she said presently. "That's why I got up early."

"Yes, I thought you might have."

"Will it ever stop?"

"Sure."

"When?"

"Well, it comes less often now doesn't it? You haven't had one for nearly three weeks."

She sighed. "Why do I keep on feeling that we're being mean to him?"

They were nearly always the same questions. He said, "I've told you, that's normal. I had it about my buddies who were killed in the war. One feels privileged for being alive. It goes, after a time. Just keep saying to yourself, I love him; there was never a thing wrong between us; and I know he's happy."

"But *is* he? He must be so lonely. He must miss us. . . . There's nobody there he knows and likes."

"Darling Liz; it can't be that sort; you know it can't. Heaven is straight happiness for ever."

"You do believe it? You swear you believe it?"

"I swear." ("And curiously," he thought, "I've told that lie so often that I've made it true; I've begun to believe in it, this amateur's sketch of heaven that I've made for you; first shot I ever made at it; something like the toy theatre.")

"But we're betraying him with J. G. That's what Celia won't do; I know that's why she stays away."

"Tobias wouldn't want you to fight with J. G. just because poor old J. G. goes to town about him in the Press, and puts up a memorial. Toby didn't just fight him for fun; he fought him over an issue."

"And now," Liz said, "there are no more issues." But she did not look appeased; her tears were over; there were only the little dark smudges on the cushion.

"Put on 'Lykewake,' will you, Harry, please?"

"Not for a moment, darling. Listen; would you try to promise me something?"

She shivered and looked wary.

"While I'm away," he said, "will you not come up here alone? It's going to worry me so much."

"Why is it going to worry you?" she asked, after a pause wherein the frown came and went on her forehead, the thread-thin, nervous lines.

"Because—hell, because I can't bear to think of it. I don't mean never come into this room; I mean—not alone, in the dark, and play the tunes. Have Carey here."

She said quickly, "I couldn't," and stared past him.

"Why not?"

"It wouldn't be fair. I have hideous remorse for loading it on you. I ought to be able to do it alone."

"Carey would help, though, wouldn't he?"

She shook her head violently. "No and no and no. I wouldn't

do that to him. He loved Toby as much as I did. It would
only make him miserable. I can't, Harry, please."

For the first time in many months, he felt the thrust of
jealousy towards Carey. He had counted himself privileged to
share this; he still did. But the value that she set on Carey's
feelings hurt a little.

"No," she said. "I'll be all right. *Not* to worry, please. It's
only six weeks," and on that he heard her voice shake and saw
her eyes set. He thought, "It isn't good, tonight." He knew
every symptom now; he had watched and watched.

"It's things *stopping*——" she muttered. "It was always the
worst." She began to shiver violently and he pulled the fur rug
up to her chin.

She said, "And we never went back to Glane. Things like that
are awful; now you can't go again and you wanted to; you liked
it."

He rested his chin on the top of her head. "This one at least
we can exorcise. We'll go tomorrow. Take the Bentley. First of
the month, and Carey's awash with petrol. Now you're going to
bed."

As always, they lingered a moment on the landing, looking
down, under Kit's portrait, at the empty hall, listening, lest the
others come. It was a queer conspiracy; he had learned to take
the innocence of it for granted, but tonight, because change
shadowed the face of his world, he found it newly remarkable.

After they had listened, he went up the second flight of stairs
with her and sat on the top step, hugging his knees, waiting for
her to call. He waited a long time, and tonight there came the
images that he had to fight in his mind. He fought them.

Presently she opened her door. "I am sorry. I had a bath;
most inconsiderately, but I was so cold. You were sweet to
wait."

He followed her in. Absurdity of absurdities, he thought, and
yet I shall miss the moment as much as I've missed what I used
to believe were the only real moments, the tiger and the Dark
Tower.

The things in the room were all familiar: the toy animals

ranged along the chest of drawers; the triple mirror with the
beaded gilt frame; the painted Italian furniture; Toby's picture
with the statuette of the Virgin beside it; the photographs of
Anthony and Celia. On the bedside table he saw the red stone
rabbit, and the poetry books.

Liz threw off her dressing-gown and climbed into bed.
She sat up straight against the pillows; her hair hung down
on each side of her face. More than once he had asked himself
how she could be so childish still, so untroubled by her own
beauty; unconscious of the line of her neck, her bare shoulders,
the small breasts showing under her nightgown. But it was so;
and it was only tonight that made the thoughts hard to hide.

"*One* cigarette?" she asked, her eyes enormous and pleading.

"No; you're sleepy, you're fighting it."

"How can you tell?"

"By the corners of your eyelids. The cigarette'll wake you up.
I'll give you a drag and that's all."

She gave it back to him.

"Okay?" He put it out. "Prayers?"

She nodded. It was weeks ago, when she had been in far
worse case than this, that she had asked him. She had said,
"Will you do something for me? Say your prayers in your head
while I say mine. Toby and I used to do it sometimes." Touched
and bewildered, he had stood like a ramrod, forcing fake
prayers. But it was easy to pray tonight.

"Look after her while I'm away; don't let her be hurt or
lonely or have the nightmare. Make her go on getting better."

She never kneeled, nor bowed her head, only clasped her
hands and stared through the wall at God. "Amen," she said
aloud, before the confused clamour of his prayer was ended.

"Good-night, Liz."

"Good-night, Harry, dear."

This was the worst of it, and he had to be gentle.

"Are you cold?" she asked, "or have you caught the Baron
shivers?"

"I'm cold as all hell. Now, sleep, will you, please? And
tomorrow we'll go to Glane."

Outside the door he walked softly, looked over the banister rail and went tiptoeing down to the next floor. Tonight especially, it seemed a grotesque parody of all the surreptitious walks that another Levitt in another life had taken, away from bedroom doors.

2

(i)

"*Why* does it please you so much?" Liz asked and added, "But of course I am no judge, because it will be new and I hate new things."

Levitt hesitated upon his answer. They had been late in their escape from Baron's afternoon, and a red sun was sinking. They stood at the centre of Glane, on the high green knoll that was like a boss in a cruciform shield; the bones of the village were laid bare in the rebuilding; you saw the original shape and plan. Whole corners had gone down since he was here last. The view was unobstructed from east to west. Where the machines had cleared the broken stumps of house and wall, there were wide flat spaces.

The sunset fired the slim tentative scaffolding and the first low bricks; in this light, as they walked, all the plain practical signs, even the nothingness of the frozen mud spaces, had a meaning. It was an overtone that he could not catch; some proud reminder, just beyond earshot. He could only identify his satisfaction in the thought that on this small hill, facing the sea, there would be another Glane; he could think of it, with the old vanished Glane making a ghost fortress in his mind.

"It pleases me, I suppose, as a symbol," he said at last. Liz gave him a flying, sceptical look. "As for J. G.'s leaders?"

"Oh, kid away. I like it, and with that you must be content." He took her arm. She said, "Well, you won't when you see the finished job, mark my words. It will be sudden and antiseptic with a huge hideous monument just *there*. If only this poor Carey could get the prize."

"He can't; and he knows he can't," said Levitt.

She looked up at him. "What do you think of the boy with the faun? Truthfully?"

"I guess I like it; nothing wrong with it, and that's all."

"You know what it ought to have been, don't you?" she said after a moment, heavily, as though she were breaking silence upon a profound secret.

"No; I just know he scrapped dozens of ideas first. Liz, you're cold; we must go."

"It ought to have been the horse; the winged horse," she said in a half-whisper.

The memory came back to him; of standing sullenly in Carey's studio, looking at a clumsy half-modelled horse in granite. He had come across the verses later in a volume of Belloc, that belonged to Carlington. He could not remember them.

"It was Toby's song when he was happy; it was all our song when we were happy; ages ago."

("Odd that you have told me so much, and not that. You haven't spoken of the Winged Horse before.") He said, "Sing it to me."

"I couldn't. I doubt I'll ever sing it again. And I quite see why Carey couldn't sculpt it. I suppose I sound affected, but those things are always hard to explain."

"Darling, the sound of your teeth chattering makes conversation difficult. Come along. I'm going to drive you into the town and give you a cup of tea."

"I'm still full of lunch," Liz protested. "It went on so long."

"Even so, tea will warm you."

It was Liz and not he who halted beside the car to look back. "Like a ship, beached on its hill," she said, "I suppose that is because the scaffolding in this light has the look of masts and rigging." He looked back again as they drove, saw the white mist rising to meet the red glow, the little frieze of Glane still clear of the mist; then the mist grew watery and Glane went as though drowned.

"Last time," he said to himself and thought superstitiously—
"I'll never see it again; never see it finished." He drove out by
the straight road to the forlorn seaside town.

Funny, to think that one would miss this sort of hotel, with
its uninspired front room, its plated teapot and tasteless cakes,
the sagging brown chairs and the dying fire. There was nobody
else here. They took a chair on each side of the fire. Liz sat on
her feet while she poured out the tea. She had pulled off her
beret. He watched the shadow on temple, cheek and throat.
"What a nonsense Carey made of that head," he thought.
"Even I could make a better job of it, I think. God knows I
know it by heart."

"Got a photograph I could have?" he asked abruptly, the
words contradicting the thought.

She looked puzzled. "Of what?"

"Of you."

"Yes, I think so," she said too brightly after a pause. "There
are hundreds of depressing duplicates in the archives. Those in
tulle on a cushion, with soft-rounded curves, can be found by
the gross. Only I never know which is Celia and which is Tobias
and which me. Will one's own baby look exactly like all other
babies, d'you think? I'm sure I shall put mine down in shops
and lose it and get somebody else's unrewarding baby. More
tea?"

"No, thank you."

"Don't you like it?"

He put down his cup. "It's either the tea or the thought of
flying on Wednesday; I feel peculiar inside."

"Oh, poor Harry. Does the aeroplane frighten you?"

"No, not a bit. That's just plain dull."

"Celia said so. I *can't* believe it; don't you see the stars
enormous and the mountains of the moon?"

"No; you just see the inside of an old motor-coach."

Liz frowned. "I'd like to think I'd done it. To be able to
stand in New York and say, 'There, my pretty creature, you
have flown the Atlantic—just like anybody else.' Oh, but
never."

"Never? Couldn't you do it with me?" The note of his voice was more solemn than he had meant; and he thought that the note of her voice matched it when she gazed at him and said, "I might. I think I could."

"I shall pretend you're with me, all the time," he said on a sigh. It was different, talking here; the drab anonymous room loosed his tongue as Carlington could not. "I'll carry you around in my pocket and take you out and show you things."

"Yes, please." He saw her lips tremble. "Everybody I love goes away; it is a doom; and generally they go to America." He mused on the words 'I love' and discarded them; in the idiom of Liz their meaning was childish, unmysterious. "America is doom," she said. "It was doom to Celia."

He stared into the fire, lighting a cigarette. "Celia got out; she'll always get out. She'll never compromise. That one will never be tied."

"No. Is that because she's brave?"

Levitt blew smoke rings. "Yes. But, for all her defiance, she hasn't met trouble head-on yet. When she does, she'll do it beautifully."

"How do you know? Because you loved her?"

He looked up, startled. The face of Liz was solemn and candid. He was silent before its certainty.

"Do you still?" she asked gently.

He said, "Where did you get that idea from?"

She said, "It was true, wasn't it?"

"Sort of. It isn't any more. Who told you?"

"Nobody. It was in the air. At that time," she said, speaking as though it were twenty years ago, "I was in a vulnerable state myself. Now I am old and resigned and nothing hurts—nor shall again. Which is nice in a way, according to Rupert Brooke:

'I thought when love for you was dead, I'd die.
 It's dead. Alone, most strangely, I live on . . .' "

He looked at her in profound curiosity.

"May I ask who it was?" he said at last.

"But don't you know? I wore it on my sleeve; on all my sleeves, as for mourning band."

"Well, then, Carey. But——"

"Well, then, Carey—but what's the 'but'? And please give me a light."

Levitt rose to give it to her and stayed standing, his hands plunged in his pockets, trying to analyse the 'but'. He arrived at:

"But why doesn't he love you?"

Liz stretched her arms above her head. "This question, as I recall, is the one that cannot be asked or answered. I have tried to console myself with the theory that he would think it incestuous but the plain answer is he just didn't love me. And doesn't. And won't. When Anthony likes girls, they are the Jane Ireland sort who can be gone to bed with at will. I've nothing against that, have you?"

"Nothing at all," said Levitt heartily.

"For Carey, I mean."

"Nor for anybody else."

"Oh, well," Liz said, "perhaps I shall acquire the habit some day," and rose from her chair. He said urgently:

"You don't still love him, do you?"

She shook her head; he was not reassured; she said, "This was a fruitless errand; and since——" She stood still under the ugly central lampshade; the white light showered on her face. Plaster cast for Carey, he thought; my love, my little love. . . . He said, "Since?"

"I was going to say something of the kind that Foliot would call Not-Backward-In-Coming-Forward. Why do common people always have expressions for things when we don't? Oh, I forgot, you don't like the word Common."

"How you chatter," he said. "Say your thing. Doesn't matter what Foliot would call it."

"All right. I was going to say that since you, I haven't needed Carey so much." She looked suddenly desolate. "Oh, God, why must you go?"

"Ask J. G.," he said bitterly.

"Of J. G. . . ." she hesitated. "*There* you and I share what Carey can't . . ."

"The Baron fever. Yes, we're both scared of him."

"Shall I ever not be?" she asked humbly.

"Once you've got out, like Celia, I think you won't be scared any more. Once you're free."

She clutched his arm. "But when shall I be free? . . . Don't you see how abominable it is? No, you can't, can you? You're going to be free this week."

"Oh, Liz, d'you think I want to be?"

Now her face became mutinous, accusing, charged with truth.

"How could you *not*? Oh, I know you're sad to leave England, to leave us . . . but inside, it *must* be bliss, that bit. I know it is. Not to have to see him for weeks and weeks and weeks. Can you imagine how it will feel? Not Saturday any more, with the car coming in at the gate and all fun killed stone deaf? Not that shadow, that string-pulling, that jitter in the air? That eternal uneasiness. Have you thought how good it'll be? The blessed peace. Not to hear his voice; the jokes with the yes-men or the stories or the awful lies about Toby? Not to have those eyes looking at you, digging at you, blaming and searching and asking all the time? You stinker, you're getting out. And I'm not. Will you write to me, will you tell me how it feels to be three thousand miles away from J. G.?"

Levitt said in feeble comfort, "We make too much of it, you and I."

"No, we don't," she said passionately, "damned if we do."

"He's been awfully sweet, these last few weeks."

"Why should *that* be so important?" Liz snapped. "Should we be bound by that, wiping the sweat off our foreheads for that, mopping and mowing with pleasure because He's Been So Good-Tempered? What tyranny *is* this? Who cares? Don't tell me; I know; we care. But why should we?" She began to pace like Celia. "The hell with him. He wins every time."

"No, Liz, he doesn't."

"He does. Look." She came to a halt, pointing her finger at

Levitt. "I loved Toby. Anthony loved Toby; Celia loved Toby. Somehow J. G. has managed to put it across that he was the only person who really loved Toby. It's a bloody lie."

She let her hand fall to her side. "And the awful thing is that when I'm with him I come near believing it. And that's betrayal.

"Don't you see? Sooner or later, I'll betray anybody to him; even you. I can talk big like this now, and then I'll go back and suck up and be sorry for him and I'll never get away, never, never, never. Except to the nursery at night." Her voice went up into hysteria. "That's mine; mine and Toby's; he can't take that away, can he? Nobody can."

Levitt grasped her arm. "Cut," he said, "cut, will you? You've had enough."

"Enough of what, pray?"

"Enough of Carlington."

"Well, that needn't trouble you, my pretty lad; you're going." She drooped suddenly. "Oh, Harry, I am sorry. Rain blows upon me; I don't mean to be mean to you." She made a face at him. "Go hang yourself, brave Crillon," she said gaily, "and have fun. And come back."

Now there was the marsh again, for the last time. The head-lamps chased its mystery; low trees and white rising mist; the shadow of a church tower; an owl in shuffling flight. It was fairy ground, smuggler's ground, jack-o'-lantern country.

"Low down, low down where the little green lanterns shine."

He glanced at the childish head beside his shoulder. He thought of the other Levitt in other cars with girls, and he despaired.

"Take me with you, Harry. Don't leave me here."

"What did you say?"

"I said take me with you."

"I can't," said a queer abrupt voice coming out of him.

"I know you can't," said Liz sadly.

"Wait," said Levitt. There was a lane that twisted off here towards the sea; the left fork was the road for Carlington; he took the right. There was a thorn bush and a broken fence, white in the range of the headlamps, with the sighing dark of the marsh beyond. He switched off the engine.

"What is happening?" she asked.

"Mustn't fool about things like that. They're important."

"Why are they important? You must say." And now, he thought, she knew; the long innocence was ended. He felt stunned and small.

"Because I love you, darling."

"Really love me?"

"Yes."

She put her hand on his, quickly; and once their hands were clutching, he could talk.

"I love you as I never loved anybody. I'm yours. For what I'm worth. For ever. I want to marry you and look after you and live for you and die for you. It's all I'll ever want."

"Me . . ." she said in a whisper. Then he had no more words; he had let the prisoner escape at last, and it was the escaped prisoner who held her, trying at first to be gentle, then finding that she did not want him to be gentle. After a while he dared not hold her close any more.

They sat in drained silence.

"Can I have it in words, Liz?"

"Yes. I love you."

"Sure?"

"I think I have for ages."

"Not this way—did you?" His voice was again curt, inquisitorial.

"I don't think I know much about this way. Nobody ever made love to me before. You're the first person I ever kissed."

"Would you be frightened of—all of it, with me, married to me?"

"I don't know. I don't think so, now. But you can't marry me."

"By God, I can. I can get my divorce and come back to you."

She leaned her head on his shoulder. "It is like an express

train thundering through a station when you're standing at the edge of the platform."

"You're too young," he said; "that's what they'll say. Oh, Liz, don't let them say it. Wait for me."

"Must I wait? Can't I come too? I like your face when it goes crooked," she said, "but I can't see it very well."

"Wouldn't mind seeing more of yours; there's a flashlight somewhere." He was drowning in peace; he groped with lazy hands for the flashlight.

"Please, Harry . . ."

"Please what?"

"Take me with you. We can be married in Salt Lake City or wherever it is they get the divorces with speed. Why are you laughing? Isn't it Salt Lake City?" She played the flashlight full on his face. "To be married," she said. "How improbable; the sort of thing that other people do," and kissed his nose and flung herself into his arms. "Oh, take me, take me. You cannot leave me here to pine and peak; not if you love me, you can't."

"Sweetheart, what else can I do?"

"Make a gesture," Liz said, "Tobias was very positive about gestures. . . . We can't tell him, anyway."

"Tell who?" he said, knowing the answer.

"J. G. The Hooded Monster. We must run. That's all we can do—run."

He held her close again. "But of course we'll tell him. Tell him tonight."

"My God, no," Liz said. Her hands became frantic, pulling at the lapels of his coat. "We can't do that; you can't do that, swear you won't make us do that."

"Beloved stupid."

"I mean it. You've got to swear on sacred bones. He'd wreck everything. You know he would; how could you *not* know? I don't believe," she said after a minute, "that you're scared of him at all." She made it sound as though she were accusing him of treason.

"I don't believe I am, any more," Levitt said. "Not now. You've done that."

"Monstrous. But *swear*," she said. "You've got to swear Not tonight."

"All right. I'll swear. Not tonight. And now swear you love me, please. Quickly. Yes; like that." ("But all this has such a devilish dreamlike quality. I'm afraid. Afraid you'll turn into mist and drift away over the marsh and I'll wake up, walking here; wandering; cold and alone.

"Low down, low down, where the little green lanterns shine
O maids, I've done with you, all but one
                    —and she can never be mine.")

(ii)

The house had changed; the house was conquered; it was his own place, humming with his secret. The face that looked at him out of the mirror while he brushed his hair was changed too. It gave back to him a sparkling serenity. He ran down the stairs alone, feeling as though he walked through a crowd that cheered him. He crossed the hall, opened the door upon the clamour inside, saw the crowd and felt that he was most splendidly alone. For a moment he thought, "How can they look at me and not know?" Then, as he greeted Carey, it became fun that they should not know.

"Car go all right?" Carey asked. "The starter's death, isn't it? Here, don't you want a drink?" He grabbed one for Levitt from the nearest tray. Carey was changed; he was sorry for Carey now. "This poor Carey, yes indeed. You great good-looking imbecile, she loved you once." The fair tranquil face smiled at him; the glass lifted.

"Happy landings," Carey said.

"Oh, hell, I'd forgotten," said Levitt; but he could blink away the prospect on the dazzle of Now.

He drank deep; then looked down the room towards the fire. The look was a luxury. There Baron stood, with his motley court about him. The newest courtier, Lawrence Peet, was at his elbow.

"I know that beginning, Mr. Lawrence Peet," thought Levitt; "I have fixed my face in that mould of attention; I have laughed that scrupulous laughter; I have hovered upon him with care. I wish you well of it, Mr. Lawrence Peet. For me it's over."

Baron's eyes met his; just for a second there was the cold chord of danger; then Levitt raised his glass to meet the eyes. The grey curly head inclined in a little bow; J. G. raised his own glass. "Here's to you," Levitt thought, "you've lost out on this one. You can't scare me again; and you won't scare her. It's the two of us together now; two against the world, and two against J. G. Drink it down."

He could imagine that J. G. lowered his eyes because he was abashed; that the quick turn of the head towards Peet and the rest, the thrust into animated talk, were the movements of a man taking cover. He went on staring, trying to draw J. G.'s eyes this way again, until Carey said:

"What d'you think you're doing? Hypnotising Ould Maister?"

He knew without looking over his shoulder when she came into the room. He watched her move up the floor towards the court and the courtiers. He had her secret smile and he treasured it but this moment hurt because with the sight of her he needed so urgently to ask: "Do you love me?" and be answered. He could not know peace again, he thought, until the words were said. The mood of humility followed the mood of triumph too fast.

(iii)

Across the table, between the candles, there was Carey's face. Liz wanted to look to her left, to find Levitt's profile, but he was separated from her by three; it was a crowded table tonight, uncomfortably crowded; there were young men at each side of her; one was Lawrence Peet. His enormous composure embarrassed her; she grew quieter and more quiet, gazing at Carey.

"Good-bye to you; that is how it feels . . . and it feels like good-bye to me as well. The me I used to know has gone; or at least is going; must be going; this is too new for her; too wild; she couldn't do it, not that one.

"She loved you, Anthony. And you didn't see it or care. You could have kissed her and held her as he did this afternoon. That was what she wanted; well, the hell with her, I say. She has vanished in a thunder-clap. But do not, I beg, smile and give me that half-wink; that caressing look of reassurance. It hurts, and you are wasting your time. This is not Liz who sits here; this is somebody who belongs to Levitt, who will go with Levitt; who will make the gesture that Tobias begged her to make; d'you see? No, you don't see. It is my secret, mine and his. My husband, he'll be. I cannot get it into my head. Except that I know it is the most grown-up thing I've ever done.

"And I love him, do you hear? I love the way he looks. I love that crooked laugh. I liked it when he made love to me. And I shall travel half across the world with him and laugh with him and have fun with him always. And forget you. I must forget you. I love him. It isn't the same love that I had for you. But why should it be?

("Oughtn't it to be? Can one person love two ways? No; what has happened is, as I have said, that I am another person now. The first Liz wanted refuge, reliance, the rock and the mountain, the god she made of you. She was a poor thing. She was a frigh ened little numbskull. I do not need the great God Anthony any more. I am headed another way. For adventure; with him. 'The bright eyes of danger'. I must repeat that line in my head a great deal; it is a spine-stiffener; it makes adventure possible; and lovely.)

"It feels so queer. Looking at your face in the candlelight and knowing that I've burned my boats, that I've thrown out the dream, that I belong to the dark one, the new one, the Knave of Spades. It's he who's going to set me free, poor Carey; not you; free from J. G. and free from all that's old. And I'm not afraid.

"Am I not? Yes, I am. But that is all right. You can be afraid without being a coward. Remember the talk about that, here at this table, the first night he ever came to Carlington? (That was the time you told us about your eye twitching after Anzio . . . no need to remember any of those things any more. They aren't going to matter any more. They mustn't matter, now.)

"I'm off, Carey; off with the raggle-taggle gypsies, O. You can't catch me. Going to be married, no less. Going to America; flying the Atlantic. How my hands shake; Mr. Peet is looking at my hands. Toby; I wish you were here. You would be on my side, wouldn't you, Toby? You'd say it was the right thing to do. But—is it the right thing to do?

"Toby, make it the right thing to do. Make me not be afraid."

(iv)

It was true; and no dream. Levitt told himself this all night; waking and not believing; drowsing and waking again to disbelief. He thought his way up the stairs to her room, wondering if she too lay awake.

He came back suddenly from a short interval of sleep and saw that it was almost six o'clock; somebody had gone past his door, he thought; and he opened the door and looked out into the passage. Nobody there. Now he was wide awake. He left the useless bed; he bathed and shaved.

He played back the scenes of last night; the trapped feeling at dinner, the trapped feeling afterwards; the moment of assurance when he stood beside her in the panelled room and the quick end of it when Baron's messenger haled him away to the bridge table. Playing bridge like an automaton; the cards had her face on them. ("How long, this avarice, this miserly rage at the minutes wasted?")

He was wasting them now. Did she sleep or wake? It was beginning to be light. The face in the glass as he tied his tie was no longer serene; it was haunted and anxious. He kept remembering things that he must say to her, things not yet said.

What had he said, when they met at last, by the unlit fire in the nursery-room? It was not clear; it had gone by too quickly, after the urgency of waiting. They had clung together, with the fur rug wrapped over them; they had whispered and played the tunes. She had given him the photograph; it would not be long, he thought, before his eyes wore out its consolations. He took it from the mirror's frame where he had stuck it; he held it, gazing at the face, remembering the lips. "Was I too fierce, too eager? Oh, please let me not have been . . . it was so difficult not to be."

With a pair of nail-scissors he trimmed the border off the photograph so that it would fit into his wallet.

"And all day," he thought, "all day alone. But I'll catch the earliest train I can. I'll be with you again tonight. Without J. G., without the mob. And we must talk; we must know what we are going to do."

It was not yet seven o'clock. He sat down at the writing-table.

"My love,

"My only love; only true love that I have ever had or known . . ."

He was still writing when Bolland brought the breakfast tray.

"Good-morning, sir. You're the early bird. May I pack for you?"

"No need. I'm coming back tonight. What's the time?"

"Eight-fifteen," Bolland said. "Sir James has ordered the car for nine."

Levitt looked about him in a daze; the lamp on the writing-table shone yellow; the pale, frosty sunshine was all over the room. He drank his coffee; he added the last lines to the letter.

Now he needed reassurance as badly as ever. "I must go up to her," he thought. "Can't not. Just so's J. G. isn't out and about."

He lit a cigarette, standing at the window. He remembered

the first time that he had stood here, a stranger spying out the land. He saw the end of the terrace, the lower lawn; the dark clumps of rhododendron, the mossy path that ran under the wall to Carey's gate. This morning it was a garden fragile and gleaming with frost; here the sun struck through a haze that hid the marsh beyond.

Now he heard the voice singing below; the singer was out of sight.

> "And once atop of Lambourne,
>   down toward the hill of Clere,
>   I saw the Host of Heaven in rank,
>   and Michael with his spear
>   And Turpin out of Gascony and Charlemagne the
>   Lord
>   And Roland of the Marches with his hand upon
>   his sword."

It was exultant, soaring; the song that she was never to sing again. All happiness was in it and all freedom; Toby's song.
He stood still, holding his breath.

> "For you that took the all-in-all, the
>   things you left were three;
>   A loud voice for singing and keen eyes to
>   see——"

He pressed his hands together. The image of the winged horse flashed across the sky. Triumph, triumph, triumph, he thought; you are happy; you are not afraid.

> "And spouting well of joy within that
>   never yet was dried!
>   *And I ride!*"

He leaned out over the window-sill, calling, "Liz! Liz!" But no answer came; she must have gone into the house.

He ran out into the corridor and met Baron coming from his room.

"Well, good morning," Baron said, barring his way comfortably. He was all malevolence, smoothly-shaven, brushed and brilliantined, the neat goblin wearing a dark blue suit; exuding a strong smell of eau de Cologne. Mather was behind him, carrying two brief-cases.

"Since you're so dynamically ahead of time, we might as well start," J. G. said. "That is, if young Lawrence is ready. Just knock on Mr. Peet's door, will you, Mather? Ah, Lawrence, over-punctual, just like us. Would you say that the eagerness with which we greet Monday morning is a little pathetic? All right, Mather. Tell Forrest to bring the car round."

"The car's there, Sir James."

"By which we can conclude that Forrest is also subject to the Monday anxiety-neurosis. What's the matter, Harry? Forgotten something?"

"Yes . . . no," said Levitt wildly. They were at the head of the stairs and Liz stood below them in the hall. Now it was just a jumble; her voice saying to Baron, "I got up early"; the extreme pallor of her skin and the light in her eyes; the feel of her hand trembling in his; then he went on past her and the letter was still in his pocket.

He gave the letter to Foliot; he climbed into the car.

"First stop, Cobbett's Wen," Baron was saying.

He looked back at the archway, in the faint hope that she might be standing there.

Then the brief agony settled, like the dust on a summer road. He had heard the song.

3

"HEAR you're off to U.S. How does that affect you?" O'Rourke's grin was skull-like.

"Variously," said Levitt. "That's a lousy block they've

made." He threw it out. It was hard to concentrate; everything was piling up inside his head. ("Would it be better to see Baron today—here? Get it over with? She'd probably settle for it, once it was done.")

Meanwhile the grin of O'Rourke, the continuing speculation.

"What's the chief's plan? You to castigate the American Way of Life? Or is it Big Brotherhood? Levitt the forger of lasting links?"

"Search me. My instructions are of the loosest."

"As it was in the beginning," said O'Rourke, "the cloud of unknowing, from which—inevitably—the sharp outlines of a diabolical and detailed plan emerge, just when he wants them to and not before. Shall we go up to the comps' room now?" The telephone on his desk chirruped and he answered it, "Yes, he's here. For you," he said to Levitt.

"She would not call me here," said Levitt to Levitt.

"Harry?" It was Anthony Carey's voice. "Sorry I couldn't catch you this morning. I'd like to see you today, old boy. Can you manage it?"

"Sure. I'm coming back tonight; earliest train I can get; I'm aiming on the four-ten."

"I'll be in town," Carey said. "I'm driving up. Let's meet there, can we?"

"I guess so. Where? When?"

"What about the house? Celia's house?"

Levitt frowned. "It's a hell of a long way out of my way."

"Please try," Carey said. "Quite urgent, really."

"Well, all right. But I couldn't do it before three; and I don't want to miss that train if I can help it. Must it be at the house? Are you working there today?"

"I thought I'd better," said Carey.

"Okay, then."

He hung up; it might perhaps be useful to talk to Carey. He hadn't promised Liz not to tell Carey.

"Or maybe she's told him; and he wants to give me a line on J. G.'s reactions. Helpful type, this poor Carey."

He liked Celia's house. Walking from the Underground

station, across the main artery street into the avenue, he found the words of the song in his head. He walked fast, under the black plane trees.

Though Carey said that this was not London, it was to Levitt essentially London; in its shabby monuments to the blitz, its jungles of deserted garden, its pale grimy façades. It had a peaceful and surviving dignity. "Cobbett's Wen—hell," he mocked Baron, "London is more mine than yours."

Now the red Georgian house in the tended garden; it made an echo of the house that he had seen from the Shrewsbury road; the solid lines of it gave the same peculiar comfort, an affirmation of peace.

Terry's nurse opened the door to him. "No, Mr. Carey's not here yet. I didn't know he was coming; he didn't telephone; what a pity. I've got the boy in bed with a cold." She led him through the hall; he could catch the trace of Celia's scent. He followed Nanny down the passage, into the studio-room; felt the magical impact of its size and space.

"Quite a nice fire," she said. "I don't expect Mr. Carey'll be long."

Levitt loitered before the windows, looking out into the misty garden. He remembered this morning's garden. The tune was fast and furious now. How did the words go? Something about Roland of the Marches. Another line came back:

"He had flame behind the eyes of him
and wings upon his side."

He strolled and hummed it; this was magic too. He could see it in his head, the horse with wings.

On the table under the window there lay drawing-blocks, neatly spaced; a rank of sharpened pencils; Carey's sketches of Terry; he did not look at these. Feeling his fingers twitch, he pulled a chair to the table.

"*He had flame behind the eyes of him
and wings upon his side.*"

He played with the pencils, testing them until he found the right lead. As he slashed the first line he felt the thinness of the paper; he would have liked a firmer surface, but his hand had taken over and it was impossible to stop.

He watched the head come, the curved neck, the exultant wings; yes, he said to himself, yes, yes, yes. As ever under his hand there were few lines, but when they flowed to a finish he saw the horse. He sat a long time staring at it.

What had happened? What was it that this had, this dictated drawing? Some grandeur that belonged to the winged lions of Egypt, a soaring quality that was not within his knowledge. It is the song, he thought; it is the image in the sky.

("And it is beautiful; and I made it; I who can't draw beautiful things, ever . . .") On that thought his hand moved again, scrawling "Levitt", the crested signature. After a moment he wrote the date. Then he sat there, grinning at his horse.

Not until he heard footsteps in the passage did he realise that it was secret; he had no time to think why. Perhaps because it was for Liz. Perhaps because he was half afraid of it, needing reassurance that it was as beautiful as his own eyes told him. But not Carey's reassurance; not now. He tore the thin sheet off the block, folded it across and slipped it into his breast pocket.

Carey opened the door and said from the top of the three steps, "Hullo; you beat me to it." Though he smiled, he looked less placid than usual; the smile went and a grimness took its place, the expression of a man who had a tough task ahead. Levitt gazed at him, aware of a fast falling shadow.

"Anything wrong, Anthony?"

"Yes, I'm afraid there is. That's why I wanted to talk to you here; somewhere we could be alone and quiet." He limped into the middle of the room.

"What goes?" Levitt said harshly.

"You'll hate me for this," Carey said, standing still, plunging his hands in his pockets. "But I can't help it. Only thing to do. And I don't want you to hate her."

"Get on," said Levitt.

"She'd rather you didn't come down tonight."

Levitt grunted; funny sort of grunt, he thought; like an animal. He saw Carey's blue eyes fixed and asking him for help.

"Get on," he said again.

"She—she can't do it," said Carey, "d'you see?"

"Can't . . ." He stopped. "She told you that?"

"Yes."

"You . . . why not me?"

Carey shook his head. "I suppose because she feels wretchedly ashamed of herself—having said she loved you and having to go back on it."

"Damn you," Levitt said.

"She's awfully young," said Carey. "She's only a kid, remember. And you've helped her so much."

"Cut."

"I mean," Carey said, "you know much more about her unhappiness since Toby's death than I've known."

"Sure, I do."

"Well——" Carey snapped his fingers. "I never liked a job less than I like having to do this to you. It's just that she's lost her nerve. Yesterday it was all true; it was a terrific adventure; she thought she could do it."

"And today?"

"She's frightened."

"Of me?"

"Of all of it."

"I see."

Carey took his pipe out of his pocket; he shook his head again. "I tried to persuade her to tell you herself, but she couldn't face it. She'd been awake all night. She was in an awfully bad way this morning."

"This morning . . ." That hit him. Carey was saying something and smiling ruefully, but the smile meant nothing, and he could not hear the words except as noises; the noises made a wall and they got in the way.

"This morning," he repeated stupidly.

"She came over to my house," Carey explained.

"*What time?*" The words had a futile urgency. Carey did not know how important that was. He saw the puzzled look in the blue eyes.

"Time? I'm not sure. Pretty early. It was still dark. . . . I was asleep. Look, Harry, don't feel too rotten about her coming to me; I've been part of the family all my life."

"Stop," Levitt said. (The footsteps going past his door, the empty passage; she had gone on, creeping down the stairs, flying through the darkened garden, by the path under the wall.) He looked at Anthony. Thank-God-for-Anthony; Anthony Bulwark Carey, Esquire.

"It's you she loves, eh?" he said.

Carey reddened a little. "I don't want you to think——" he began.

"I don't have to think. Don't stand there blushing and covering up and trying to be sympathetic. Damned smart, aren't you? How did you take it? What did you tell her? That you'd been blind all this time? Huh? Still blushing? That's what you said, I guess. Goddamned if you didn't. . . . And how did she take that? Not in such an 'awfully bad way', after that, was she? Doesn't matter what you say, you son-of-a-bitch —I know the answer."

He knew it. Already its echo sounded differently; with a mocking note; the voice in the garden, singing the song of freedom, the voice of the person who was happy and unafraid.

("And I thought I had given you that. I thought it was for me.")

He felt his dry lips drawing back from his teeth; he knew that the look of the fox was there, Levitt sneering at Levitt.

4

(i)

IT was six o'clock when Celia came back to the house. Fog had come down with the winter evening. She watched it change the avenue; here were the hazardous, shortened distances, the departing trees, the street lamps dimmed. It made sudden quiet, sudden risk. It gave importance to the warmth of a lighted room; the taxi-driver was a forlorn adventurer, lost as he turned. She felt the raw cold of it on her face, walking through the garden.

She stood in the hall. She looked up the staircase towards the flowers. Was it the fog that made the house feel different tonight? No, not the fog. The walls were thin, the floor hollow beneath her feet; the house was precarious, the house was coming down.

"Damn it, I will not feel like this," Celia said to herself. "Simply a matter of getting over there fast—and fixing. That's all it is. It's only Van. I can fight Van. I've always fought Van. Nothing to be scared of. Why do I shiver? Because I'm cold. I'll go up and take a bath; then I'll have a drink. This black tent dropping on the mind, this sense of doom—nerves. And I despise nerves."

A little of the fog had penetrated the indoor air; it was cold and threatening. It was too quiet here. And now she heard the door of the studio-room opening, far down the passage. Then there were slow footsteps, heavy footsteps, uneven footsteps, walking towards her. There was no light in the passage. Who, in the dark?

"Don't be an idiot," Celia said to herself. She was ashamed that her voice should sound urgent and abrupt, calling, "Who's that?"

"Celia?" It was Anthony's voice. Anthony came into the hall.

"Did I frighten you? I'm so sorry."

Her heart was still thumping. She said, "You did, a little. I'd no idea you were here."

"Didn't see the car outside? No, in this fog, you wouldn't. I parked on the other side of the road," he said. It was the reflection of her own mood, she thought, that made him look darkened and perplexed. He stood with his head lowered; what troubled him? Then the look was gone; it was the honest and reassuring face of Anthony, smiling at her as he held her hands.

"Something wrong, Celia?"

"Why do you ask?"

"What? . . . You look very white. I can only assume that you've been burning the candle at both ends, as usual," he said, doing J. G.

She laughed. "Bless you, I couldn't be more glad to see you, anyway."

"Looks as though you'll have me on your hands for the night, if this doesn't clear."

"Well, fine. I'm not doing anything. We'll have dinner here. Only for heaven's sake put that light on. Creeping in darkened corridors doesn't suit you at all."

He said, "Darling, you're jittery, aren't you?"

"Awfully, yes."

"Would a drink help?"

"It would. But I must go to Terry first. Help yourself and wait for me."

As she went up the stairs she thought that he could be told. Since he was caught here unexpectedly, she might take him for a sign. Still there was the reluctance to tell.

Nanny knew; one could tell Nanny things in shorthand. As they left the night nursery together Nanny said, "Excuse my asking, m'm, but is there any news?"

"Yes. I talked to New York on the telephone. Don't worry. I'll tell you all about it later. Anthony's staying the night here; can you fix us some dinner? We'll eat by the fire in the studio room." She patted Nanny's shoulder and said again, "Don't worry."

While she changed her clothes, she argued, "Why tell Anthony? Why tell anybody? All that needs to be told is the fact of your going; the half-truth will do. For J. G., for all of them."

In this room too the fog chilled the air; her own face in the glass was a haunted face, pale and afraid. "For once, but that is because I'm tired, I could haul down my flag. I want somebody else to advise, to take over, to fix . . . the thing that I have never wanted. Fool," she said to the reflection, "you got yourself into this mess and you'll do the salvage work. For people like you, there are no helping hands held out; you could have had them, I suppose, if you had thought them worth seeking; but it's always been the other way." She smiled crookedly upon the past. "Independence; gestures; refusal to compromise; calling the tune. . . . Look where it's got you. And when it's time to run for harbour—well, puzzle: find the harbour."

Oh, but it wasn't time to run for harbour yet. It was time for another fight, that was all. Alone. Why alone? "Pure habit, I think," she said to herself, "just the ingrained conviction that it's up to me to foot the bill. And not only on the cash side of the ledger, either. I've trained myself (consciously? unconsciously?) into the belief that I can, should, must take anything; that to put the burden down in any other place is weakness, that to be strong is to be alone."

She fastened the jewelled clips on the collar of her shirt; looked at the restored façade of Celia West and shook her head.

Baron's voice reached her ears now. "You've a hard streak in you; you always had." A comfortable analysis. When he spoke of ruthlessness, he saw you marching over the dead bodies of others; he did not see that the dead bodies were your own.

As she opened the door and stepped on to the landing, his image came to meet her. The goblin's image, smiling and sure. "You'd better come to me, my girl. Who else?"

She went down the stairs. In the studio-room Anthony waited, with his back to the fire and a glass in his hand.

"Don't you look pretty? Here's your drink."

"This I need. Thank you." She glanced at the drawing-blocks on the table. "Did you come here to work?"

"Partly . . ." He hesitated. "Had to come up, anyway; boring bit of business; Papa's will, as usual. When I found Terry was in bed, I had a shot at some sketches from memory. . . . No good."

"May I see?"

"Sorry, darling," he said. "I tore them up. Now, what's your trouble?"

"Must I have a trouble?"

"No must; but I think you have."

She sat down in the chair beside the fire. He remained standing; before his gentle look, his reassuring familiarity, she felt weakness win.

"All right, then. But you must remember that it's top secret, that the version I give you isn't the version I'll give J. G. or Liz . . ." She hesitated. "How much d'you know about me and money, Anthony?"

He frowned. "You and money. . . . Your money, you mean? All I know is that you inherited your mother's money—which is a lot, and that as an American resident you keep your capital over there. Why do you ask me?"

"Just didn't want to bore you with the details you knew already. That's correct," she said, "with the exception of one tense and one verb. My mother's money was—not is—a lot; and I've lost—not kept—my capital over there."

"*Lost* it?" Anthony put down his glass on the mantelpiece. His surprise was comical; she wanted to laugh.

"Oh, nonsense," he said. "You're being funny, aren't you?"

"No."

"Then why do you look as though you're going to laugh?"

"Partly your face," Celia said, "and partly because it does strike me as very odd not to have any money at all. I get the sort of laugh one gets when one breaks something irreplaceable in somebody else's house. Hysteria, possibly."

"But how the devil could you lose it?"

"To be accurate, I didn't lose it; Mr. Valentine West did."

The door opened; Nanny came in to set the table. "We can go on talking," Celia said. "Nanny knows all about it. She has to, bless her."

Anthony said, "You'd better have another drink. What happened?"

"He made some spectacularly good investments that went spectacularly wrong. And now it appears that the dear little fellow has helped himself to the residue. I transferred three thousand pounds over there last summer; on Baron's tip that devaluation was coming. I left it sitting in our joint account in New York, more fool me. I'd forgotten it *was* a joint account. So like me. So like Van to remember."

Carey said, "By God, that husband of yours deserves to get himself shot."

"He will, I trust, one day. Don't click, Nanny; I mean it."

Anthony said, "Don't blame you. But look here, who's handling this for you? What does J. G. say?"

"My lawyer's handling it over there. Terry's trust is safe, the capital's here. Thank God I moved it. J. G. doesn't know and I'm damned if he's going to know. I'm off this week; heavily in the red for the fare and the general pay-up all round." She felt better now for having told. "I'll fix it, Anthony. And if I can't, I know Grant Parker can. He's married to Van's aunt; and he likes me, and he's the only person I'd dream of going to if Van got really tough."

Anthony paced in front of the fire. "How can he get tough?"

"He's got letters. I don't know what sort. 'Ambiguous' is my lawyer's word for them. I suppose I wrote something silly. I'm an ass over money, as you know." She laughed. "What adds charm is that Van has now turned limpid about the divorce. He's been refusing to accept the papers for nearly a year. Now he'll take them—if I renounce my claims to the cash. He's a sweetheart, isn't he? Let us eat. What is this, Nanny?"

"The Irish stew, m'm. If I may so, Mr. Anthony, I wish you'd persuade her to tell Sir James all this. He's the one to tell." She went out, and Anthony said, "He is, y'know."

"He's not, y'know. Don't let's talk about it any more. Eat the Irish stew; if you can. When Nanny says 'The Irish stew' she sounds like a restaurant menu, doesn't she? She means that we had it for lunch. The little less and what a world away."

Anthony giggled, cut the giggle short, said, "Don't change the subject. I love Irish stew. What do you say to J. G.?"

"Just that there are snags coming up over the divorce, that I have to go for a few weeks. He'll be pleased to have Nanny and Terry back at Carlington. I'll kid him that I'll be coming back there too."

Anthony said, "I see it's a tough one, telling him."

"Too tough." She met his eyes. "I've been independent of J. G. since I grew up. And I thought I'd made that independence by fighting him. Now I see that it was largely made possible by the fact that I had my own money. Sordid truth; the last argument of the stinker: 'I pay, don't I?' And it holds good."

"Darling, you're all mixed up," said Carey. "Money doesn't make stinkers."

"Doesn't it, though?"

"No, it doesn't. What about Daddy?"

"Agreed. But odd, I always thought, for an army type to turn into a good business man."

"It didn't change him," Anthony said. "Look, let me lend you five hundred—drop in the bucket?"

"You are very sweet. But I mustn't take on obligations now."

"Hell," said Anthony. "What's the matter with obligations? How can one be part of the human race and *not* have obligations? Everybody owes something to somebody." She saw the shadowed look on his face suddenly, the troubled shadow that she had seen when she first came into the house. Then it went.

"What is it, Anthony?"

"Nothing."

She said, "You've got a worry; or a secret; and it does not suit this poor Carey."

He looked up with a grin. "This poor Carey's very well-suited today. I'm now going to talk to your sister on the telephone. I talked to her while you were changing, by the way. She sent much love."

"Why this chatter?"

He hesitated, looking suddenly shy.

"Out with it," she said.

"Well, you see, Liz and I," said Anthony, now pompous and mumbling, "came to the same conclusion this morning. As a brother-in-law, I hope to give satisfaction."

(ii)

They came through the cut in the yews and crossed the turf. "Too sad," Liz said, "that you'll be gone before the statue's up. I know you're still desperately anti-memorial, but you'd have liked to see it, wouldn't you?"

"I'll be seeing it in a little while," Celia said; no need for any memorial, she thought; this part of the garden was for ever haunted by Tobias. She saw him lying on his back on the lawn, holding Terry above his head.

"How long *do* you think, really?" Liz persisted. "A month?"

"Not much more."

They stood looking at the three marble steps that had replaced the grass steps; the bench was gone; a marble floor awaited the statue. She remembered sitting here on the bench with Tobias; Foliot crossing the lawn: "A Mr. Levitt is arriving on the five-fifty-five."

"You won't linger," Liz said. "Promise not to linger? I couldn't be married without you."

"Why should I linger?" ("Liz is the only one who guesses; nothing psychic about that; her habit of expecting the worst. Perhaps I have caught it; never did I feel so doomed.") The look of the marsh, the look of the garden, the waddling, golden shape of Prince, made her want to cry. She said, "Got a cigarette, rabbit?"

"Yes; here. You aren't really worried, are you? Was J. G. nice?"

"*What . . . ? It's up to that lawyer of yours, isn't it? . . . Oh, well, if you want to go rushing off again, I can't stop you, I suppose*," said Celia in painstaking imitation.

"He'll melt," said Liz. "Towards the end of lunch. Good-byes always melt him."

"Believe it or not, I prefer him frozen solid. As to which, I'm cold. Let's go to the studio and badger your gentleman-friend for a cup of tea."

Liz said, "We can't do that; he's working on something that isn't for the public eye."

"How very odd. What is it? Something rude?"

"I hadn't thought of that," said Liz delightedly. "What do you think it is? A phallic symbol? Shall we ambush it? We could get a ladder and look down through the skylight . . ." She drooped. "Oh, God, I can't believe you're going; that this evening you won't be here."

"Nor me," Celia said slowly; she leaned on the terrace wall, staring down across the marsh.

"What are you concentrating on, so hard?"

("Saying to my eyes 'I beseech you to remember'.") She said, "Just looking."

"America doesn't look like this at all? Not any of it?"

"Not really. But it has consolations. The Vineyard, for example. You and Mr. Carey must come to the Vineyard, sometime. What's on your mind?"

Liz tugged at Prince's ears. "I was wondering. Will you see Harry Levitt in New York?"

"I don't know. I might; why?"

"Could you give him a message? I keep trying to write, and I can't. Just say I'm sorry and it was all my fault and I shall bear the scars of remorse until I die."

"Good God, what's that about?"

Liz said sadly, "Alas, I cannot explain." They went into the panelled room. "What did you do to Levitt, for heaven's sake? . . ." Celia asked. "Not talking?"

Liz hesitated. "Look; I think I *could* tell you . . ."

"Ah," said Baron at the door. "I was just thinking that a glass of sherry was indicated. I saw you out of the window; taking a farewell look at Carlington, eh?" Liz was right; he had decided to melt; he was arriving at a pink mood. He said, "I'll drive you up this afternoon, Celia. Then, if I'm stuck, you can take the Rolls to the airport. But I hope I'll be able to see you off; just depends on that bastard Eppersley. Well, happy landings; where's your young man, Liz?"

"He's working. He'll be over for lunch."

Nothing had ever made J. G. happier, she thought, than the betrothal of Liz and Anthony. "And I need have no more fears for Liz. That is the best thing that has come out of this year." She said, "Excuse me if I go and collect my son."

Now the nursery wing, for the last time; and the feeling that nobody but Nanny understood it all; the familiar busy figure bending over a half-packed suitcase, the briskness and the smile and the anxious eyes.

"J. G.'s driving me in. Directly after lunch. So I'll hug you now," Celia said. "Take care of you both. I'll be back faster than light."

"I wish you'd let us come to the airport."

"No, darling, sorry; but better like this."

"Don't get too tired, now. You'll have a rest before the aeroplane goes, won't you?"

"Oh, sure. Bless you, darling. Thank you for everything; till very soon." She had to look away from Nanny; she clutched the square hand, calling, "Terry; come on; lunch-time."

"Why am I having my lunch downstairs?"

"For a treat, chum."

"Are you glad you're going to America?" he said on the stairs.

"Well, I don't like leaving you. But it's only for a very little time."

"Nanny says that you'll come back at once if not sooner," Terry said, halting on the lowest step.

"Probably sooner. What a delicious smell of lunch, don't you think?"

He sniffed doubtfully. "Onions. Will you bring me an aeroplane?"

"Yes, I will." She picked him up and kissed him and put him down again; he said, "We always have to hug very tight, don't we?"

The last that she saw of him was at the archway gate, standing with Nanny and Anthony and Liz; the four arms waved until the car turned the corner.

BOOK IV

THE RED PAVILION

(March, 1950—June, 1951)

THE RED PAVILION

March, 1950

(i)

THE fact of waking in a new room was not new; your mind catalogued the latest successor in a line of guest-rooms and hotel bedrooms. Already, after only four months, you could not, Celia thought, remember them all. And it was dangerous to lie too long because the room that was furthest away in time returned; its detail was complete, where the detail of the rooms between was not; if you kept your eyes shut you were fooled into believing that you would open them upon the Carlington nursery; see the bookshelves, the white fur rug, the wide fireplace.

She, who had once loved to lie in bed, had now the habit of rising quickly. The morning mood was full of traps. From the living-room Pat called, "Hello, want your coffee now?" Pat was already dressed; her enamelled executive look equipped her for a day of skilful wrestling with imponderables. You could hear the President saying, "Meet Mrs. Friedlander, she takes care of our Public Relations." Everything about Pat, including the apartment in the East Fifties, was neat, smooth, streamlined. Every gesture, including the offer of the apartment, was calculated. She had some of the qualities of Becky Sharp and she rated Celia high enough in the imponderable scale to offset a nominal rent.

"I'll be back at five for the bags," Pat said. She was flying to California tonight.

At the door she remembered to ask, "What's your day? Lawyers again?"

"Lawyers again."

"Well, spit in his eye," Pat said, and went.

Restlessness made it impossible to sit still.

As Celia turned left into Park Avenue, New York lunged at her. No other city, she thought, dealt the high cards and the low cards more dispassionately; there never seemed to be a middle run. Today, the low. The city turned a cold, stone face upon her. The sky and the towers alike assumed a flat hostility. She could tell, without a clue, that today would be no good.

She crossed Park Avenue and walked, avoiding with her eyes the shop-windows on Madison. The shop-windows were disconcerting; she began to notice their effect only after a few months, the effect of too many things; too many material needs were urged here, needs called 'Musts'; products of too many busy brains devising aids to beauty, hygiene and home management. They made her feel slightly seasick by now; particularly when they exhibited food, clothes, or books.

Here was a bookshop. In panic salvoes the paper jackets told how to acquire maturity, serenity and freedom from most of the normal human emotions; urgently they offered new light on atomic warfare, child-psychology, cancer and the Home Beautiful. Here best-selling novels, huge with self-pity, explained in four-letter words that American soldiers did not like war. Here new mental diseases were advertised as triumphantly as cures, and religion took many shapes. In the last window the religious display collided with the arts of cookery. Celia went on her way under the impression that she had been invited to buy the Catholic Cook Book of the month with 2,000 recipes A.D. and a foreword by the Cardinal.

The anti-American irritation was unpredictable; America was her adopted country; she had loved it since youth, but when only its top layers were visible the irritation came. She was already feeling it threaten when she entered the post office.

American city post offices, she thought, displayed only too clearly America's contempt for the postal system. Nobody, asked on the street, could ever tell you where they were. When sighted, they wore a protective colouring almost as dingy as that of the State liquor stores in Philadelphia; their aim, you would say, was to lurk modestly forgotten. They were few, and widely spaced, so that you could not buy stamps.

There were other devices, Celia reflected, to stop people from buying stamps, particularly from buying the right amount of stamps to put on a letter. It was in the nature of a social gaffe to try to buy stamps across a counter. Even in hotels you now met the obstacle of the stamp-machine, with its demands for change, its three little levers and the nine-cents' worth of stamps in sanitary cardboard folders that you could buy for a dime. The designer of the little cardboard folders had somehow made it much easier to keep the folders and drop the stamps on the floor.

"The foreigner," Celia said to herself, "might be forgiven for concluding that letters come under the heading of un-American activities. Now, will there be one in the box?"

A box number was the only solution to the changes of address; she could see the front of her box from the door, set in the shimmering honeycomb; the hopeful façade. No, there was nothing; yes, there was. One letter. She found her key and opened the box. The letter was from Liz; she stood looking at the blue Air Mail sticker, the Carlington postmark, the flying scrawl. She put it in her bag and went out.

The drugstore was two blocks down. She liked the drugstore. It was clinically white and silver; it gave her a sense of anonymity and freedom and she didn't know why. The counter was empty; the curly-haired boy in the white coat whistled and polished the urns. She sat there, drinking black coffee from the thick white cup and reading the letter.

"DARLING,

"God help us, but you tarry and we pray and pray. Your last letter sounded as though you were worried. You don't tell much, do you? Why don't you?

"Please make speed. The garden is going to be utterly spiffing. Somebody brought J. G. a lot of new little flowering trees from South Africa and apart from having to have the giver here at week-ends (*another* young man, with an iron-bound moustache and an endless stock of uninteresting information about the colonies) we are pleased. The lambs are about; blunt in profile and weak as to legs.

"I went to London last week; I don't in the least mind buying the clothes provided that nobody refers to them as a trousseau which I find embarrassing, like nearly all French words. But without your coldly accurate judgment I know I have made some hideous blunders and you will be particularly cross about the hats. I gave up and let the woman decide. I *cannot* see why marriage necessitates hats, but J. G. and Nanny are against me.

"Wedding now set for June 3rd, J. G. banned May, though I'm sure Tobias wouldn't mind in the least. I dread the anniversary; *could* you be back in time, please? I only dread it, I mean, because J. G. will make a thing of it. I dreamed about Toby quite differently last week; he was very happy and offhand and had only gone to live somewhere else. I didn't even wonder why we hadn't met for so long. But it left a sad echo when I woke up.

"You should see what's going on in the studio. Or rather you shouldn't; it has become a factory of noises and fixtures and wood shavings and shellac and strange men and cans of beer. What appears to be in process of building is a kind of basket-work monster. But oh my God how beautiful when done, I make no doubt. We have had the plaster cast photographed and I will send you one when ready—oh but please cable and say Don't—I'm On My Way. . . .

"Terry really *is* happy; when I asked him if he missed you he said 'Yes; but then I know where she is,' which struck me as showing far more philosophy than any of my remarks or thoughts show. He pays only the politest, most distant attention to J. G. and likes the farm-boys and Anthony's assistants much better than he likes us, though we suck up like crazy.

"Darling, I must stop. *No* time to play with the giraffe. *Make speed.* I love you so. Enclosed is Terry with Joe from the farm, and a *Times* crossword."

Celia stared at the snapshot; he looked longer and thinner;

she could see the corner of the farm building behind the figures, and a slice of Carey's field. She turned the crossword over and read the house agents' advertisements on the back. "Cotswold cottage for sale" assumed an importance. But it should not, yet. It was too early for homesickness. Reading the backs of English press-cuttings was symptom of a much longer exile than four months.

"The moment I know that all is fixed, these will stop. It is fear, O little hunter, it is fear." She put the letter back in her bag. The New York scene clashed oddly upon it for a moment. As she hailed a taxi, she reminded herself that the subway downtown was not only cheaper, but quicker. "No use; people are divided into two groups: those who can contemplate public transport and those who cannot. But soon I must change my type; except that I think I never shall. My standard of values is set for ever; one day I think I shall drop dead of starvation while hailing a taxi."

The taxi took her across town, then by the East Side highway, along a short stone canyon, to the cliff face of the building that housed the lawyer. She walked through a high cavern of brass and marble to the elevator. This building had begun to wear the aspect of the corner provision store when one had lived on the same street for years. Tim Cronin was a constant, a chum, waiting in his room on the twenty-sixth floor; a round-faced chum with horn-rimmed glasses and a bow tie.

"Hello, Celia, come on in."

The familiar sights were here; the files ready on the side-table; some new letters spread out on Tim's desk; the chair set ready for her, the drab weapons for the endless battle; Cronin taking his seat, offering her cigarettes.

"Well, I've got very little that's new, I'm afraid. Van's latest and most offensive suggestion is that you've still one solid asset: the house on the Vineyard. I told his shield and buckler that when we wanted assessments of your property we'd ask for them. But honestly, Celia, I believe you ought to think about selling that house. We've got a long and expensive court case ahead of us."

She said, "No. I'm not selling it. That's for Terry, that house. What was the result of your conference?"

"Fifty-fifty. Henry puts the chances no higher than that. He doesn't think that they can help finding for you on the bank transaction. Legally, Van was entitled to the money; morally he wasn't; we can count on that. But as far as the investments go, Henry agrees with me that it's only an even chance. Just depends on which way the court takes those letters of yours." His swivel chair squeaked as he fidgeted; he played a tattoo on the desk with a ruler. "It's a gamble. We hold one strong card; that is, Van's offer to accept divorce papers on the withdrawal of your claim. We haven't got it in writing; my secretary would go on the stand as witness to the telephone conversation. But of course he'll flatly deny having made it.

"They'll pull out every stop, Celia: the deserted husband; the wife who took the child away. Van will swear he'd take you back tomorrow. *And* you're the daughter of a rich man. We can't say that he's put you and Terry in lasting trouble. We shall say that, of course; but it won't go. They'll bring up the fact of the trust-money in England. We can counter with the answer that you can't move that capital now, thanks to British Treasury regulations. We can show that it's a comparatively small sum, just enough for his keep and part of his education. That doesn't get us far."

Celia frowned.

"And the next point to think about is what we get out of him if we *do* win. My guess is that he'll go into bankruptcy. I've been doing my level best to get a line on his affairs; they aren't promising."

She said, "He lives pretty, they tell me. But that's no indication. So do I, by ordinary standards. Will his lawyer bring the Vineyard house in as further evidence of my immense riches?"

"Sure."

She gazed out of the window, at the stone cliff on the other side of the canyon; its relentless wall hid the sky. She had stared at it many times since December. Depressing to recall that they were still at the preliminary stage; it was itself divided into so many stages that it felt like a long journey.

There had been the stage when Van pressed for a friendly talk, without legal barriers; the stage when it looked as though he would make an offer; the stage when he retired to a sanatorium with a nervous breakdown; now the stage of preparation for action. She liked this the least.

There was, about the processes of the law, a sense of shifting ground, of untruth; the false defences; the doubts that Tim threw upon the result of the case compared with the opposite sureness, the big threatening words in the letters that he wrote. The planned stages, the jockeying for position, went against the grain.

Tim kept her busy with old facts and old figures until half-past twelve. "Now come and have lunch. Automat?"

"Certainly."

"Why do you like it? Not in character."

"It makes me laugh."

At the table he took a press-clipping out of his wallet. "You knew this, I guess. It was in Sunday's *Times*."

"No; I didn't," Celia said, having read that Sir James Baron was expected to arrive in New York shortly. "He wouldn't let me know long in advance, anyway. More likely a cable the day he sailed. What of it, Tim?"

"In spite of all you've said, he's the answer to Van. He could scare him pink."

"No."

"Then it's got to be Grant Parker. Tell him the story and get *him* to put the heat on Van. Parker and J. G. are your two hopes; I'm serious; out of the office I can tell you flat that in my view the case is a hopeless proposition."

She was silent, choosing words, playing with the food on her plate.

"Tim, look. Leaving out J. G. for a moment; what can I say to Parker? 'Your wife's nephew swindled me; it's up to you to do something about it.' Van's not his responsibility. Besides, Van's got himself in with the Parkers now; I told you that.

He's at their house every week-end. One of my reasons for
avoiding them."

"That's just pride again. Pride won't get you anywhere in
this. You've got to check on your assets and use them. Doesn't
matter how you get the thing fixed; the point is the fixing. You
can't go on this way, my dear. Just what, if I may be brash, *are*
you using for money?"

Celia said, "Debts, naturally. Don't mix with pride, do they?"
Now she lost Tim's words, because she was seeing the meeting of
the Titans, Baron and Grant Parker; two millstones to crush
Van between them. It did not look right; nothing looked right,
neither the powerful short-cut nor the longest way around the
law; not her own pride and not the debts. Not Van's evasion nor
Tim's prescription of means-to-an-end. It was a sudden tangle of
darkness from which you emerged saying, "Find me one honest
man."

(ii)

She went into the shop and the steady-voiced young woman
strolled to meet her, saying, "Hello, Celia—where have you been
hiding? You look wonderful."

"Your suit," Celia said. "Ripe rare old vintage by now."

"Let's look at new vintages, shall we? I'd no idea you were in
New York. Mariette! I want you to put on the black and white
Dior for Mrs. West. Sit down and have a cigarette and tell me
about Europe."

No need to mention that your credit was not what it was; in
the view of the steady-voiced young woman, it still was. No need,
on the other hand, to buy the clothes; just a sudden crossness
with everything, a crossness that picked on your own appearance.

It was too neat a coincidence to meet Sandra Parker coming in
through the door as she went out. Blue foxes, blue hair, black
velvet suit and velvet-black eyes, a sugar-almond skin and jewels
flashing like masthead lights.

"Hello, Celia." It was a fake smile; the eyes were doing
addition sums.

"How long are you here for this time? . . . Do call me; come and lunch. You look fine." Sandra went past her, towards the steady-voiced young woman.

"As though," Celia thought, "Van doesn't tell her all that goes on. Why pretend? Why pay lip-service with 'Come and lunch'?"

Alone in Pat's apartment she saw that the time was six o'clock and that she had nothing to do till tomorrow morning. She loitered, unpacking, taking possession, aware all the time of intense melancholy standing only a yard away; the black mood ready to move in. She had the habit of other people's houses by now; this was a two-room apartment, entirely comfortable, perfectly equipped, unimaginative; the bedroom had no door; seated before the living-room fire, she looked through the alcove, saw her own things on the dressing-table. Better, a little. She took down a suspiciously clean and new-looking anthology of verse from the shelves. When all else failed in familiarity, you stretched yourself out on the lines of poetry that had been there always.

But the restless noises of New York beneath the windows soon took peace away. She shut the book and said aloud, "Well, chum, we appear to be hungry." The apartment annoyed her now; it had a brittle, phony look, a cellophane feel. She put on her coat. She took from the writing-desk a roll of unread *Tatlers*, with which Nanny had faithfully included a copy of the *Flash*. The apartment was on the second floor and she walked down the stairs, she turned towards Lexington, went past the corner drugstore, up the next street in the direction of Park. ("Oh, really, where do you think you're going? You cannot dine here and sign the bill; here where seventy-five dollars' worth of signatures sit clamouring for your attention. But I suppose it is in character; at least it appears to be what I am doing.")

She went through the lighted doorway, into the world that still remained to her, the headwaiter's kingdom, as familiar as a nursery. Somebody called "Hello, Celia." She waved and went on, pretending a rendezvous. She chose a table at the back of the room, beside the window. Here there was the illusion of privacy, and from the bow, the beaming smile, of the proprietor you would not think that you owed him a nickel.

So you increased your obligations by smoked salmon, half a bottle of Meursault and Eggs Benedict.

She read devotedly, not looking up. At first this was consoling. But even the *Flash* delivered the lethal message of homesickness. She put it aside and made a list of the things that depressed her. She wrote neatly; it was a game that she had played with Liz and Tobias, always halted by Liz becoming sorry for inanimate objects. She wrote tea-leaves; Kansas; the Industrial Revolution; dried figs; Hawaiian dancing; ferns; Unmade Beds; Benjamin Franklin.

"You would like some more coffee, Madame?"

"No, I don't think so." She asked for the bill; one more signature, one more overtip to make up for it. She rose and went. The two who had waved to her had left their table. One person was sitting there now. It was Harry Levitt, reading a book.

For an instant she did not believe in the sight of him. She had to stare at the dark head, at the profile, at the hand that held the book. He looked up. With a rush, the fact of him came to confound his image in memory; darker, livelier, broader, with brighter eyes and a kinder smile.

"Not possible," he said, getting to his feet. His embrace was the hug of a brother; he might have been Anthony. "Sit down, for heaven's sake. Drink with me; indulge me; I'm pathos. Alone in New York. I only flew in from Chicago just now. What'll you have?"

"I don't know, yet." It was ridiculous to be so glad to see him. ("As a change of toothache?" her mind mocked.) She sat down. "Aren't you considerably behind schedule for your return to England?"

"Well, no," said Levitt, beckoning the waiter, "and I'm getting damned homesick for it. But you're a remarkably good substitute."

"I warn you," she said, "I'm in hideous humour; tired, cranky; the worst possible substitute."

"Stay you with flagons," said Levitt, looking down the wine

list; he gave the order. He blew her a kiss. "What are you doing on this side, anyway?"

"It's a long story. I'd rather hear yours."

"Mine's simple. J. G.'s kept me running around on this assignment far longer than he said. He's due here ten days from now, as I guess you know. I'm hoping that's the end of it." Now he looked wary. "Or maybe I'm not hoping."

The waiter brought the bottle. "It's the Krug you liked in the ship," Levitt said, his eyes still watchful. He tasted it; they raised their glasses silently.

"You haven't been in New York all this time, though," she said. "I'd have seen you."

"I've covered the country. It s larger than I'd remembered."

"All work? No play?"

"Very little play," he said, "ur less Reno qualifies."

"Reno?"

"It was time," he said, "to put an end to that bit of unfinished business."

"How does it feel to be free?"

For a moment he looked at her disbelievingly. "What?" she said to the lifted eyebrows. "Just," he said after a pause, "just, somebody else asked me that; in another context; something I'd forgotten; doesn't matter." The eyes were still wary; it was the look of insecurity that he had worn at the beginning; it was the way that he used to look in the glass, anxiously keeping an eye on himself. "Tell me how they are; all of them," he said abruptly.

"All fine, I think. You know that Liz and Anthony are going to be married?"

"Yes."

She remembered the message from Liz; while she hesitated, Levitt said, "And Terry? Is he here with you?"

(iii)

"I see what you mean," said Levitt, standing in the middle of the living-room floor. "It's just a New York apartment; they come off the conveyor belt by the gross." Beside his memories of her, the pictures wherein she moved, dazzling, assured and far-off, this person seemed quietly stricken, aloof with a secret that must be sad.

"How do you find it now, over here, Harry?"

While he talked she was attentive. He met again the quick response of the mind that understood his slant. She was, as before, diverted by anything outside herself; she was, as before, the last person to dig the deeper thoughts out of you. She was one of the few women who could talk impersonally for ever.

He had forgotten her; that was the truth; so great a slice of knowledge had been cut between; a whole cliff of experience had fallen into the sea. She was, of all people, the one he would have asked for tonight, had he remembered enough. It was important that she was not a stranger to the things that had hurt him, nor so closely linked with them that she could revive the hurt. He felt that her context was still the ship, the voyage of discovery begun a year ago.

"It isn't that I don't like this country," he said, "it's mine, and in many ways I love it. But I don't feel equipped for its future. What people of your age and mine, who saw the war through in Europe, are asked to do here is difficult. We're asked to straddle a whole gulf in history; to take a full stop as though it were a comma.

"It isn't that I'm sympathetic to Russia, I think that Russian communism is the current misfortune of a barbarous, immature and bone-stupid bunch. But I'll never get myself into a state of mind where I can see the German war as a harmless little stage on the way to war with Russia. It left me short of energy, short of moral indignation; I used up most of my stock between '40 and '45. I'm not quick enough on the draw to jump around in a *volte-face*, hug the Germans and the Japanese and start all over again.

"I'm out of touch. I can't get steamed-up about communist infiltration, or air-raid drill or the newest perfection of atomic horrors. This is a new page of history; I see people living it, believing it, working towards the next page. And they're foreigners.

"The more I've travelled here, this time, the less I've known. From the war talk to the T.V. sets, it's all an enigma to me. I find myself unreasonably irritated by details; by the noise, by the radio commercials, by the juke-boxes. Wouldn't it be possible to put a nickel in a slot marked SILENCE and buy five minutes of that?

"I don't know my own people any more. You can see that by the stuff that I've been turning out for J. G. Those aren't caricatures. You've got to see a thing straight before you can draw it crooked. And I can't see this America straight.

"And I'll have to learn.

"Because it looks as though I'll have to stay here. It's up to J. G., of course. But this is a precarious little interval."

"When does your contract end?"

"In three weeks' time."

"I don't like that," she said abruptly. She frowned, the frown that he remembered on the other forehead, the thin, nervous lines. Then she narrowed her eyes at the corners, challenging him. "Do you, Harry?"

"No. Nor the fact that I'm now told by cable to take a holiday till he gets here. I wanted to take it in England; then I thought I'd better play it his way, wait for him. I'll go right afterwards, if I've still got the fare."

"Go back? Even if——"

"Even if he fires me—and he will—yes," said Levitt to the light, brilliant eyes. "I'll have to; just for a little time. If I don't, there'll be a poison blowing from England always; and I can't risk that; I love it too much. And that's all I can explain."

She nodded. She said, "Liz gave me a message for you."

"No, please; I don't want it. I can guess it. A 'sorry' message, wasn't it?"

She nodded again.

"Mind if we never talk about that, Celia? Not bitterness; merely a thing I had to bury pretty deep."

"I should think," she murmured, "that you'll want to bury the whole Baron family pretty deep, any minute now."

"No, bless you. It's all all right."

He expected the crooked smile of mockery; instead she looked sad.

"Because of Liz?"

"No. . . . Lord, no. Just because of Baron."

"Do you hate him so much?"

Levitt shook his head. "I can't hate Baron; because I don't really know who he is. Sometimes I don't think he knows, either. I hate certain things that he does, but that's not all of it, I just know that if I had to go back and fit into the set-up again, resume my rôle as one of his young men, have that eternal shadow-boxing with a mind I can't follow and don't want to follow, make like nice when I feel nasty and step down into subservience every time he waves one of his moods at me, well the answer's No. I couldn't do it again; and I wouldn't. Not for a million on a plate. It's over."

She did not speak; the heavy-lidded eyes watched him tranquilly. But now, and this was odd, the tears came to them.

"One finds those things out, I guess," he said. "You asked me how it felt to be free. I'm not free yet. Not till I've cut loose from him. It isn't susceptible of explanation; it's the thing that says 'No' inside. I'd sooner starve than settle with J. G. again."

The lines smoothed off her forehead; he saw her relax as though a long anxiety were ended.

"Find me one honest man," she murmured, looking past him. Then she made a gesture with her hand; he leaned across to take the hand in his, knowing now that he could come to sit on the floor at her feet, leaning back his head against her knee; above his head the light, haunting voice dropped to its deeper note, saying quietly, "Curious, that it should be you."

April, 1950

(i)

Levitt paid the taxi and stood with his suitcase in his hand, looking up at the second-floor windows. "Home, for the moment," he thought. "Temporary refuge; just one of the unrealities in this interval that's all unreal." He pushed open the main door, carried his suitcase up the stairs. He put the key into the lock. Inside the apartment there was the same unreality, made sharper because she was not here.

He felt that he was looking at the shell of Celia. He carried his suitcase in under the arch of the alcove and unpacked it. He stowed his possessions neatly; there was plenty of room. He put down his pigskin toilet-case gingerly on the corner of the dressing-table, then moved it into the bathroom. He came back through the arch, carrying cigarette cartons and sketch books. From his pocket he took a small white package, turned it over in his hands, placed it in the middle of the mantelpiece to wait for her. While he was doing these things, peace of mind made him almost sleepy.

"Better check on the dinner," Levitt thought. He squatted in front of the ice-box. It was all there; not the kind of dinner to be eaten by people whose funds were running low (any more than the white package on the mantelpiece was a recognisable gift from a man whose fortunes were falling); there was even a bottle of champagne. He could not accustom himself to the idea of Celia's being broke; he could not feel the precarious state of his own finances. "We are alike," Levitt thought. "We always were."

He went back into the bedroom, took off his jacket and shoes, put on dressing-gown and slippers, returned to the living-room. There was more than an hour to wait for her, more than an hour in which to muse on the word Now; it had a shrinking quality.

"All that I can feel is peace. And no sense of infidelity to——"
He performed the mental twist that was like locking the door in his mind, the twist that he had schooled his thoughts to make when they came to the dream that had crashed, to the December days. All of that must, for the sake of sanity, remain hidden; like the drawing of the horse, folded in his wallet, never looked at now; just a piece of paper whose edge at the crease of the wallet was turning dark.

"Peace. . . . Not for long, though. Two more days. J. G.

will be here in forty-eight hours' time. What's the old bastard's line, I wonder? Who can tell? We'll have to watch our step when he gets here. Celia doesn't care; says on a six-day visit he'll be easy to dodge. Must think of a cover address. Don't want to have to lie to him. Funny, how I used to enjoy telling lies; prettying them up till they were as good as I could make them. Nowadays the truth seems so much less trouble.

"She wanted me here; that's sure. And I wanted it. I'll come back to her when I've done my bit of exorcism in England. Good to have her to come back to. Not so good when she goes." He looked ahead to his life over here as it would be after that; to a scaling-down of standards; to a walk-up apartment on the West side, and a third-rate contract for a strip cartoon. It seemed improbable; he blinked at it.

He was on the point of falling asleep when the door-bell rang. It wasn't Celia; Celia had her own key. He went into the bedroom, peeled off the dressing-gown, kicked off the slippers, put on his jacket and shoes. The bell rang a second time while he was doing this. As he went to the door he heard light footsteps walking away.

Baron turned from the head of the stairs. They stood looking at each other.

(ii)

It took Baron a moment to recognise the man who opened the door. The hall was unlit and he saw only a dark head, a grin, a tall, well-built body. Then Levitt said, "Hello, J. G.; won't you come in?" quietly, as though he had been expecting the visit.

"Well, Harry," he said. "Well, well . . ." This was exasperating. He had Levitt catalogued for tomorrow and he wanted to be word-perfect for the interview. He shook hands, while Harry said easily, "Did Celia get your schedule wrong? She wasn't expecting you till Thursday."

"I had to fly two days earlier than I meant. Got in at midday. Yes; very good trip. Thanks, Harry." He followed Levitt in; he did not like the look of the apartment at all.

Levitt's smiling assurance had not diminished; gained, if anything. "Can I offer you a drink, J. G.?"

"Thanks, boy; I am a little tired; I'll take a Scotch and soda. How are you, after all this time? You're looking very fit."

He would avoid the talk if he could. If he couldn't, and something in Levitt's look suggested that it might be difficult to avoid, the military rôle would be the best; the Randolph Carey rôle; always safe; no moment, really, for wit, for arabesques nor deep emotional thunder; just the Carey-type colonel with the tough job before him, in the shape of the junior officer who hadn't made good.

Clipping his cigar, he watched Levitt sit down and wait, at ease and with a disturbingly apparent question in his eyes.

Thinking rapidly back over Levitt from the beginning, he remembered most clearly the moments of mistrust, from the ship to those last winter months. True, there had been long intervals when he was pleased with Harry, but they were not easy to recall. Mistrust predominated. Mistrust of the stranger; mistrust of the friend; mistrust of the growing humanity and lessening bite in Levitt's work; mistrust of Levitt and Liz. All those moments had added up to the decision that Levitt must go.

"I've been looking forward to a talk with you," he said.

"Farewell talk?" Levitt asked, with a lift of his eyebrows.

"What? . . . I hope not," said Baron.

"Well, the contract's at an end; or nearly. Expires on the fifteenth," Levitt said; his nonchalance was offensive.

"Indeed? I didn't know it was so soon."

"Come, come," said Levitt, genially.

"Really. I let Micky keep the tabs on those things for me, you know," said Baron, matching the geniality. "Can you lunch with me tomorrow? I'm at the St. Regis. Say twelve-forty-five?"

"I'm afraid I've got a date for lunch. What's wrong with now?"

"I'm pretty tired, Harry. Comfortable as the flight is, it still takes it out of one, I find. Besides, Celia'll be here any minute."

"No, she won't, I'm afraid. Not before six." He smiled and looked at his watch. "Only five-ten now."

"I was talking to her lawyer; he said she'd just left his office."

"She was going to her hairdresser after that," said Levitt; still he smiled, stretching a hand to a cigarette-box. "Surely it isn't so difficult?" he asked gently. "You've only got to tell me that you aren't going to renew my contract. I promise not to argue. I don't want to come back."

No time now for the military rôle. This demanded terrorism. Baron stared at him, lowering his eyelids. Then he made his voice thin: "I beg your pardon?" The look and the voice had seldom achieved less result.

"I said I didn't want to work for the *Flash* again," said Levitt sunnily. "I've nothing against the *Flash*. I just know I can't go on. Sorry."

Another change of front was indicated; Baron made it. "There you interest me. I've guessed it myself, mind you . . . not such a fool as I look, they tell me; but I'd like to hear why you're not satisfied."

"Oh no," said Levitt. "I couldn't tell you. It wouldn't be fair, even if I could put it into words, which I doubt."

"Nonsense, Harry. You and I have always been able to talk turkey."

Levitt's grin widened. His eyebrows lifted higher, as though Baron had said something too outrageous to be borne. Massively, Baron ignored the look. "Come along now, boy; I want to hear." He inhaled cigar-smoke; Levitt inhaled cigarette-smoke; the gesture was impudently timed.

"Be simpler, wouldn't it, J. G., if you told me why you didn't want to renew? But I don't need to hear; I just need the fact, so I can fix my future. Save you a lunch, too."

Baron paused. Then he crossed his knees, tapped the ash from his cigar and wooed Levitt with his tenderest smile. "Let's go into this. Did you find perhaps that the American scene was your natural target after all? Some of your American stuff has been magnificent, you know."

He had the sensation that he had known before in an interview of this sort; that he was paying the victim an unnecessary compliment; playing a difficult fish with neat manipulations of the line while all that needed to be done was to swat a fly with one stroke. Levitt shrugged his shoulders: "Glad you liked it."

"But perhaps," Baron said, "the gap has widened."

"Gap?"

"The gap that's represented by three thousand miles of water and a dollar-deficit; the gap between your country and mine." He made a mental note of the phrase for future use.

"I'm beginning to realise," he went on, "that it's getting more difficult, not easier, for the two sides to understand each other." He broke off; he was staring through the alcove into Celia's bedroom; at this angle he could not see the whole of the room; he could see the end of the bed, half the dressing-table and a chair. On the carpet, just below the chair, there were two red morocco slippers; a man's bedroom-slippers. "What do you think?" he heard himself asking smoothly. "What's your view, after your survey on this side?"

He heard Levitt's voice, "I don't believe there's much point in giving you my views. They're not relevant. All I know is that I can't work for the *Flash* any more."

"Then I accept your resignation."

The fly was swatted.

"Might have held off a little longer," Baron thought in the sudden quiet, "if it hadn't been for seeing what—come to think of it—was obvious when you opened the door to me. I've always been right about you, Harry Levitt. Sleeping with my daughter, eh? Am I going too fast, perhaps? May not be your slippers after all; she may have a dozen lovers here, for all I know." The prurient thrust of curiosity was sharp; his tongue touched his lips. "No . . . I don't go too fast, ever. I know it all before it happens; just my hunch—the thing that has made me Baron.

"I knew damn' well when you were making love to Liz. But you didn't sleep with Liz, you prowling little swine; I saw to that; Celia's the best you can get for yourself."

Righteous and sickened, he rose from his chair. "And I've come here to offer her help," he thought.

Levitt also had risen. He still wore the look of mocking serenity as he said, "I'd just like to remind you that I haven't resigned. There was never any need. You made up your mind to fire me last December and you took the gentlest way of easing me out. I guess you'll want to wait for Celia, so I'll take a walk."

"Good-bye," Baron said; he was prepared to ignore an outstretched hand; the hand was not stretched out. Levitt gave him a little bow. Baron turned on his heel, marched to the window. He stood there, looking down on to the tops of yellow taxis, hearing the hooters blare a long mad chorus; he tried to assemble his thoughts.

The door shut. He heard Levitt go down the stairs.

As he had suspected, the slippers were now gone from the bedroom floor. He opened cupboard doors until he came to one that was locked; he stood there, feeling the smile turn his mouth sideways at the corner. He opened the drawer of the dressing-table; no clue there. He went into the bathroom.

"H'm. Forgot that, didn't you?" he said, looking at the initials on the pigskin toilet-case. "You're not so damn' smart, Harry Levitt."

He made with his hands the brushing gesture that swept away the dead fly. He went back to the living-room.

"No need to worry about fixing him. I've fixed him."

("Have you, Baron?")

"What? . . . Yes, of course I have. He can't afford to lose that sort of job."

("He didn't care, though. Why didn't he care?")

"Just goddamned bravado. He cared all right."

("Said he didn't want to come back.")

"Protecting himself . . . saw it coming."

("Looked happy, though; all the time.")

"Why not? He's shacked up with Celia, so he's crazy for himself. But you can't dine out on —, my boy."

He picked up his unfinished drink; no need to waste time

on Levitt; that was the last of Levitt. "He can rot. But Celia——"

He sat down heavily to wait for her. While he waited, melancholy came in waves; he felt old, weak; baffled.

"Why couldn't she tell me she was in trouble? Pride, her damned, foolish, ungrateful pride. Running away over here without a word to me. If I hadn't got it out of Anthony, I'd never have known. I really think she must be losing her mind. Jumping into bed with this gangster . . . Celia—I always thought she had dignity," he mourned. "Whatever one could say about her mother, there was real dignity there. And her money—her mother's money; dropping it down a drain; I warned her." He sat with slumped shoulders. "Tired," he thought, "really it seems as though I were never to have any peace. Having to rush over here like this."

("Celia didn't bring you over; you had to come, anyway.")

"What? . . . Rubbish; the business could have waited. I'm here because I'm worried. Worried again. Just as Anthony had made me so happy with that beautiful work of his, too. And the wedding; so much to think of . . ."

The room filled with a gold sunset and still he sat there grieving. When he heard her latchkey in the lock, he hardly moved.

(iii)

From the sidewalk Celia looked up at the windows, knowing that Levitt was there. Oddly, this interval of shining peace brought back again and again the first night at sea, a year ago; the rippling, deceptive calm before the storm of loving; but this calm was not deceptive. She could see no storm ahead; only that a quiet place had been reached at last. It was a harbour of the mind that prevailed against the harassing external weather; against the debts; against the slow marshalling of weapons in Tim Cronin's office; against black fear. For the moment, because he was there and waiting for her, she could believe that all the troubles were about to end; that

Grant Parker would end them by magic, three days from now.

She crossed the hall, playing the talk back in her head; past the secretarial barriers of voice to Grant's own voice, the slow friendly speech, "I'm glad you called me. I've been wondering. . . . Off to Europe next week and a sadly tight schedule till then. Can you lunch Friday?"

It was partly with Levitt in mind that she had pushed down her prejudice against ringing up Grant. It was just possible that he would employ Levitt again. "At least, from now till Friday, we can hope on all of it."

She opened the door. She knew at once that he was not here; she looked at the black hat on the table in the little hall; the hat was unmistakable; you could not say why this was so; there was nothing to distinguish it from any other soft black felt hat, but it was J. G.'s and nobody else's. "So he got here early," she thought and went in. He was sitting in the arm-chair beside the window, hunched like an owl. As he rose she saw the flattened grey curls, the downward lines of grief, the puffiness under the eyes; it was the faintest of smiles, though he held out both hands to her and his legs stamped their little dance.

"My dear—I was almost asleep."

"When did you get in? If I'd known . . ."

"It was a last-minute change. I called Tim Cronin's office to find you." That shook her, as though he must now know all that went on; and indeed he looked as though he knew. "I can't say I care for this place of yours very much," he said. "It's like one of those rooms you see behind shop windows."

"It is, a little. I don't like it, either. It's only a stopgap. Let me give you a drink."

"I mean," he said peevishly, "I don't want to talk to you here; I don't feel I can. Will you come back to my suite? Change first, if you like. I've got some dinner guests; quite amusing people; but not until eight-thirty; plenty of time to talk."

"Certainly I'll come to the St. Regis. But I mustn't dine, J.G. I'm sorry. I've got a guest coming up here."

The eyes were cold and sad. "I should have thought you could put him off. Your father's first night in New York; we haven't met for mônths."

"Sorry, darling; it's too late to do that. If I'd known earlier, I could have cancelled him."

He looked as though he would ask whom she expected; then he said, "Oh, all right. Come along, then."

Outside the door, he revived; he was brisk and ominous now; she recalled childhood walks with J. G. when he was in a bad temper. This was like that, striding to keep up with him. "No point in looking for a taxi," he said, every fifty yards. When the lights were against them, he stood still, looking thunderously, majestically at the sweeping traffic; then plunged on again; his breath was short; he panted. In the hotel foyer she saw the agonised, familiar glance to left and right, the search of Baron, hoping to be seen and known; if you dropped dead beside him at this moment, he would not notice. The search was all. It persisted in the elevator; he talked loudly and his eyes were busy at every floor.

Here was his kingdom again; here was the recording-machine; the typewriter; the flowers and telegrams; Mather feathering to and fro.

"All right," Baron said when Mather was gone. "Now you'll tell me everything. Don't stall, please."

"It is Van who's doing the stalling." She was still in the mood of peace, finding it hard to concentrate or care.

"What's happened to your money? That's what I want to know."

She said, "Oh, the money . . ." and wondered who had told him. "Well, that's something else again."

"Don't talk in that sloppy, bored way, please. Listen to me. I want complete frankness. I'm tired of deceptions. If you can't make a clean breast of the whole thing to your father, it's a sad pity. Let's know exactly where we stand, eh? See what the issue is, and face up to it."

She said, "J. G., you throw me when you take this line. I can't think straight because I keep waiting for you to say Brass Tacks and Cards on the Table."

"Please don't be silly. I want a clear statement of the facts that you told Anthony."

"Anthony?" Now she was shocked. "If I told Anthony anything, I told him in confidence." She could not imagine how Carey could have forgotten that.

"You did indeed." Baron snapped his fingers. "And why trouble? I can put two and two together. Naturally I asked dear old Anthony if he knew anything."

"And naturally," she said, "dear old Anthony broke his word and told you. No, not naturally at all. Most unlike him."

"It was his duty to tell me, Celia."

She frowned, trying to keep her temper.

He said, "Just what I told you would happen. Isn't it?"

"Yes, it is. And nothing to do about it now but sue Van."

There was the beginning of satisfaction in his face; the musing light in the eye, the crinkles at the corners of the mouth. "Next thing you'll tell me is you didn't take my tip last September; left your dollars in London and let devaluation catch them."

Celia said, "On the contrary; that's how I lost three thousand pounds odd. I shipped it over and Van helped himself."

"Why the devil didn't you put it in a separate account?"

"Didn't occur to me."

Good-humour was dawning over Baron with the magic speed of a sunrise at sea. "Didn't occur to you; typical. All these years I've been telling you. . . . How many times have I said money doesn't take care of itself?"

"About four hundred and thirty-seven, in my hearing."

Baron said, "Well, the first thing for me to do is to talk to Tim Cronin; then I'll tackle Van. No point in bringing a court case. These things can be fixed. Seen Grant Parker?"

"I'm lunching with him Friday. I see what's in your mind. But Van's dug himself in very well there; if Sandra weren't his aunt, he'd be in her bed every Saturday."

J. G. said, "What? . . . rather an unpleasant thing to say, isn't it?"

"Yes, and deservedly."

"Tell you one thing, young woman; you're flying back with me next week."

This she hadn't expected. She said gently, "Thank you, J. G., but I think not."

"Think not, eh?" The Chinese look chased the smile away.

"Kind of you," she said, "but this is all a little too rapid."

"When I move, I move fast. You ought to know that by now."

"I don't want to sound ungrateful; but the answer is no, thank you."

"Would you mind telling me why not?"

"Because, darling, I can't be bossed around."

Baron stamped his feet in a gay little shuffle. "I'm afraid that what you can or cannot do is no longer your decision. You're my daughter, and it's my direct concern to get you out of trouble. What do you suppose people would think of me if I didn't?"

"Dear J. G.; I've never been worried by what people would think, or say."

"You're my daughter," he repeated. "And that's all that matters to me."

She was silent, seeing the word 'My' as if it were written in the air above his head. 'My' daughter; 'my' son . . . the spiral of possession winding back to Baron. She saw again why he himself was not to be treated as a grown-up person; he had never reached the moment of maturity; the moment of handing over; the knowledge that somebody else mattered more than Baron mattered. He saw his responsibilities as his rights; he believed in the illusion, 'This is mine', as children believed in Father Christmas; not knowing yet that nobody was yours, that your loves, flawed by belief in ownership, were not loves at all.

"Please, J. G. I repeat I'm grateful, but I'm not coming back with you. And I know you mean it kindly; but please don't go buying air tickets and commandeering Tim Cronin and running the whole situation without me. I don't want that. Please not." He stood looking at her.

"I do need," she said, "to preserve some remains of independence. I've been working on this for months alone. It is my life, after all."

The light left the eyes again; the curling lines straightened.

"Got this lover of yours in mind, eh?"

"What did you say, J. G.?"

He was frightened now, she thought; so he barked the louder, "Any idea of keeping on with him, staying here, that's out. I won't have that, d'you see?"

(Keep quiet, she told herself; say nothing; let him run to the end of the rope, if he will.)

"I'm talking about Harry Levitt."

She was silent.

"Not very nice, for your father to have to know these things."

She took a cigarette-lighter from her bag and began to dismantle it in her lap.

"I should have thought you'd have more pride."

She shook the flint out of the lighter and examined it; then put it back again.

"I suppose you know I've fired him? I'll tell you why. Not only because he's no good at his job; because I don't like him. He's bad news, Levitt; he's a nasty piece of work; has he told you he was making love to Liz all last winter? H'm?"

"Quiet, please, J. G."

"I'll not be quiet."

"Then," she saw her hand tremble as she lit the cigarette, "you'll have to forgive me if my manners don't hold out."

"Manners? Breeding, eh?" He snorted and pranced like an angry little bull. "Your hypocrisy makes me quite sick. Listen, I don't care who you sleep with; it's no concern of mine as long as you show some discretion about it. But I won't have my daughter living like a tart."

She thought, "There he'll stop." Her anger had become a separate personality, to whom she was saying, "Take it easy; take your time."

She stared at him. The contrast between the fleeting eyes and the confident mouth reminded her, for a solitary, detached minute, of certain things that happened in Tim Cronin's office.

She waited and watched the mouth quiver, twist, re-shape itself
for the ultimatum.

"You'll break with Levitt now—or I'll not raise a finger to
help you."

"And why?" Her own voice had become, without conscious
effort, a lazy drawl. No use to strive for pity nor for common
ground. Somebody else was playing this scene, she thought; her
mother, perhaps. The antagonism felt old, rehearsed. The dis-
tortion of the little strong face under the flat grey curls was
familiar, a mask of hatred. The voice shook.

"I should have thought one decent instinct would have told
you why; one thought of your son; your family, your sister;
your dead brother's memory——"

"That's fixed it," she thought, in the last red flurry where
the two people joined as one, herself and her separate anger;
there was no more wisdom, nor kindliness, only a cruelty
keener than his.

"In the matter of Tobias——" it was remarkable that the
words still drawled themselves lazily. "You and I stand on
opposite sides. We always shall. I loved him; and you didn't.
You hated him. Please remember that I know that; and I don't
forget it; not for all the sonnets in the *Flash* or statues in the
garden. You have a very effective substitute now; the son you
always wanted. I sympathise and I understand; you couldn't
get him any other way. And you had to get him somehow,
because you can't rest when they escape; and they always will
escape, d'you see—you clutch too tightly . . ." She spoke to
the pallor and the creases and the ice-cold eyes; thinking
suddenly that this was the last talk they would ever have, he and
she. "But you'll leave me, if you please, my own version of
Toby; my own memories. Never mention him to me again;
there's no language in which we can talk of him."

Now it was like the moment in the ship when he got the news
of Randolph Carey; only it was far worse; it was looking at
ivory and dead grey eyes. And hearing her own voice, that
snapped the thread: "I have to escape you too, J. G. I'm sorry,
but that's the answer."

September, 1950

(i)

The man behind the counter was charming, as always, and as always he took a long time to come to the point. There were the preliminaries: weather, health, war. Then there was the examination of the jewel through the small black microscope held to his eye; with a running commentary on the decline in values; ending on the question, "What sum had you in mind, Mrs. West?" Meanwhile a boy came in, handed over his watch without a word, was given a ticket and a ten-dollar bill in equal silence and went out.

"Four hundred dollars," Celia said.

"I'm sorry—*very* sorry; two hundred would be the most I could——"

"All right; two hundred." It was a formal exchange, but she was left wondering, as she had wondered before, whether her own relief had let her down; whether she should have tried to extract another fifty. Two hundred dollars today had the power to dazzle. She saw her hand shake as she signed the contract; it was still shaking when she took the bills.

"This means we can get out, anyway; with a pretty margin." Guessing at the hotel bill, she lost some of the affable talk.

She stood on the sidewalk in Eighth Avenue, searching in her bag. The leather note-case when found held two snapshots and an English twopenny stamp, still surviving inexplicably. After she had folded the bills into the note-case it bulged. "I feel," Celia thought, "as though I had just fed a starving dog." She hailed a taxi.

She recognised the difference in mood, the forgiving state of mind that allowed the afternoon its wet warmth, the Avenue its roaring commercial ugliness, the traffic its snarls. She went on being comforted, thoughtless, until the taxi drew up at the hotel door. The desk and the cashier had looked quite different this morning; now they held no menace.

"You're checking out today, Mrs. Levitt?" She despised the need for 'Mrs. Levitt'. She said, "Yes, we are. Around five, earlier, if my husband gets back."

She looked at the bill. Other people studied the figures carefully; she had not yet learned to do more than glance at the total, register surprise and pay. Seventy-four dollars for five days was, inevitably, a little more than she had anticipated.

She opened the door of the room. The luggage was half-packed. She took off the jacket of her suit. It was too hot for a suit, but the suit was better-looking than any of the worn summer clothes.

She finished the packing, neatly and swiftly; it was habit, routine; it demanded no thought. Now there was a paradoxical sense of homecoming and peace about moving on. Luggage, tissue-paper, clothes whisked from hangers, and cupboards left empty, these had acquired the gift of reassurance that should belong to the static. It amused her to know this, to see all the small aspects of disorientation adding up to home. She set Levitt's pigskin toilet-case in its right corner, shut the lid. There it was again, the pattern of neat luggage, ready to be moved. It had a rich look; most of their possessions had that look; both of them still shimmered a little to the casual eye. But the possessions shrank, and the shimmer, Celia admitted, staring at her hand without the last ring, wasn't what it was.

Self-consciousness was still new; an inheritance of this time. You could no longer, she thought, take you for granted; you were for ever, in Tim Cronin's phrase, checking on your assets, ponderable and imponderable. You were too often called upon to measure chances, to assess you as a risk before somebody else made the assessment and chose or refused the risk. It was not a lone fight. In the word 'you' she included Levitt. " 'You is us,' the two of us, thank God." (The two of them, living in chamois-leaps over trouble and, so far, landing. But the precipices grew steeper, the footholds smaller, more precarious.)

She had left the key on the outside of the door. She heard him turn it now. There was the pulse of the heart, the knowledge of safety.

"Hello, there."

"Hello, sweetheart."

He was too thin; his best suit hung on him; but he had the raffish, starry-eyed air that meant good luck. It did not vary. The embrace did not vary, the bones of his body pressed close to hers, the lips set upon hers, then the hand coming up to caress her head.

"All right," he said. "Home and dry."

"Which job?"

"Neither yet. That's what I've got to decide. But Dwight's paid a thousand into the bank. He'll take a chance on whichever I choose. And he doesn't care if he waits a year," Levitt said; "God knows he can afford to." He hugged her tightly. "We can relax, just a little, no?"

It was good; she blinked upon it. Levitt's friend Dwight Estofen, met only once, was a baby-faced bore. Now he grew wings and a halo.

"Off we go," Levitt was saying. "Darling, you could have waited for me to help you pack. Come to think of it, you showed commendable faith in packing at all, didn't you? I'll call down for the bill; just put my head under the cold tap, first; on account I think a thousand bucks has gone to it. The head, I mean, not the tap." He flung off his jacket.

"The bill's paid."

"The bill's what?"

"I said paid."

"Who paid it?"

"The last of the Baron diamonds. Sorry, love; I panicked."

"Damn it, Celia, you promised me you wouldn't."

"I know."

"You swore."

"I know. But I got worried in case one of the awful things happened, at the last minute. And I thought silly, with the Sylvesters' house just sitting there waiting for us. Sorry, darling. It was well meant. And I got two hundred bucks and the bill was only seventy-four."

"How did it come to seventy-four?"

She said, "I never do know how it comes to what it does. It just always does."

"Yeah, doesn't it?" They began to giggle. "Oh, but honestly," he said, "what's the good of my extracting promises from you if you never keep them? It's the one thing I hate you to do. And you're always doing it."

"Well, but I can't do it any more; the jewel case is now an empty husk."

"We'll get them out tomorrow." He came from the bathroom, rubbing his hair with a towel.

"Tonight it's champagne," he said. "And caviar. We'll dine at 21. And the bed at the Sylvesters'—if you'll forgive my looking into the future—is the biggest and best double bed I ever slept in."

"With whom—if you'll forgive my looking into the past?"

"I was alone," said Levitt, "so help me."

Now it was routine again; the luggage carried out, the two of them deserting another room; the elevator, the foyer, the taxi.

"Nice hotel, really," she said.

"Nice now it's over," said Levitt.

"Whichever comes through," said Celia, "let's try and get up to the Vineyard for two weeks, next month. We can open up the house and picnic."

"Sure; we need a holiday," Levitt said. "I was thinking, wouldn't we like to live in the country? Dwight knows a house for rent, little house; Bedford. Better than New York; I could take commuting with a car. And we've got to have a car."

"I'd like the country," she said. It was familiar, hopeful fantasy, his hand resting on hers, the luggage crowding their knees, the moving taxi, the golden blink of the future. No use persuading this mood that a thousand dollars was not a million; this mood knew that it was. This mood discounted each of the bright prospects that had shown their faces and gone. This mood did not believe that 'one of the awful things' ever happened.

"Terry'd rather be in the country; wouldn't he?"

"Supposing—" she said, "you decide that the Boston job's the safer bet."

"Well, then we can live on the Vineyard," said Levitt; but from the note in his voice she knew that he wasn't taking the Boston job seriously.

As they passed Seventieth Street, he leaned towards the window, looking east. "Always I can see myself scudding out of that door; on my way to England; on my way to you; just an ego with its nose down on the scent."

"Do you wish it hadn't happened?"

"Only good thing that ever happened."

"Promise?"

"Promise."

Five blocks higher, they came to the house.

Inside the hall it felt cool; it was more like a London house than a house in New York; they walked up a short flight of stairs and found a living-room that was walled with books, a faded, panelled bedroom; Celia went from one room to another, pulling up the blinds. She looked at a green tree beneath the window, at the afternoon light coming into the room with the books. This was familiar also, the quiet invasion of a new refuge and Levitt setting down the luggage on the floor.

They made their usual rapid exploration, measuring cupboard space, bureau drawers left empty, bottles left full. She took in the details haphazardly, as she unpacked and wandered between the two rooms: a bedspread of French tapestry, red and white and green; some Piranesi prints, duplicates of those at Carlington; curtains of tawny velvet and a faint, shabby scent of dried rose petals; in the living-room the same curtains, a large fat sofa, uniform cigarette-boxes of gold and white china; a writing-table under the window. It was soothing, the hour of late afternoon, the hour of having arrived. Money was here again and freedom waved its hat.

"Think I'll take a bath," she said, "and change."

"Are you tired? Yes, you are." He came to her and stood, holding her face between his hands. "God, I do put you through it, don't I? And you're so good; you never let the strain show till it's over." His finger traced the circles under her eyes. "Those," he said, "only come up when everything's all right again. I love you so."

"And I love you. And your resistance and mine are cut to much the same pattern; you look pretty beat yourself."

"We'll sleep tonight," Levitt said. "Don't take too long, darling; let's dine early."

She had not yet learned to hurry; she had learned new tricks, but not that one. Meticulous neatness and method had always come naturally; speed had not. Sometimes she felt that her progress was haunted by the ghost of Nanny, saying regularly, "I don't want to hurry you, m'm, but. . . ." She lay in the bath a long time. She idled from the bath to the looking-glass; she fixed her face. Still in her dressing-gown and slippers she returned to the living-room. Levitt was at the writing-table with their account book and a box file; a list of figures grew beneath his hand.

"How much do we owe Tim Cronin? This is only the bill for the fees up to June." The case against Van was in the lists, a month ahead now.

She said, "It's very little more than that. He paid himself out of the Vineyard rent cheque. Remember? And I'm seeing him tomorrow; I'll get the account. But it's one that can ride."

"I've got plenty riders in the file," said Levitt. "This time next month—no more riders." He rose from the table and poured the drinks. He began to thrust their future ahead in rapid stages of prosperity. He talked only of *Searchlight*, the more precarious of the two alternatives. Celia did not trust in *Searchlight*; a small magazine, expensively produced, strenuous alike in its good taste and its sophistication. It was not yet popular. The lure for Levitt was obvious. It meant New York. Its survival was in the hands of three civilised young men. Its offices were as elegantly brittle as itself. He would have a pale green room and a pickled wood desk and the title of Art Director. The only hazard was the salary. Levitt's agent had hinted that the three young men were looking for somebody who could bring money with him, buy a partnership in the company.

When compared with *Searchlight*, the Boston future looked small and dull. A second-rate daily paper wanted a strip cartoon; this should centre round the fortunes of a child, and Levitt had spent the last gloomy weeks in Hollywood devising children; nasty little boys; nasty little girls. It was the nastiest of the little girls who had attracted the offer.

While he talked, she thought that he might have forgotten the last five months; the uneasy term of free-lance peddling, the debacle of the movie cartoon whose beckoning chance had taken them to Hollywood, whose collapse had left them stranded. He had the bounce of a terrier; and, by heaven, he needed it.

"Here's to *Searchlight*," she said. "I must dress. Have these Sylvesters a gramophone? If you play a record to me, I'll make more speed."

"That's your story," said Levitt.

Presently she heard the tune, '49 vintage Cole Porter. The music helped the inquiring mood of the first drink. She stared at herself in the mirror, conscious of the same reflection halted in yet another glass; a thinner, paler version of the face that she had once known, the curling lines of laughter more visible, the little lines on the forehead now permanent. "I am beginning to know what I will be like when I am old," she thought, undismayed. Before the glass she had set the rank of photographs in the thin leather frames: Terry in the sun at the Vineyard; Tobias astride the terrace wall; Liz on the lawn; Anthony with his statue.

It never occurred to her to replace these with newer photographs. There were wedding pictures of Liz and Anthony, honeymoon pictures, endless snapshots of Terry. These lived in the scrapbooks; the scrapbooks held England: photographs, postcards, press-cuttings, pictures of Glane, of Carlington. She worked on them faithfully, keeping them up to date; she worked on them alone; she looked at them alone. They were the secret part of her life, not shared with Levitt.

Why not, after these months together? She did not know.

His silence put a virtual ban upon talk of Carlington, upon news of the family. It was not a bitter silence; it suggested a bereavement that she must respect. Only occasionally, it came to the top in a violence that was to her mysterious; a sudden burst of drinking that brought Carey's name to his lips; always Carey. Long ago, she thought, he had forgiven Liz; down below, he still hated Carey. She had taught herself not to speak of Carey, even in calm weather.

So there they were, each with a secret place of the heart. It should not be so. It must be vanquished, one day. There should, she thought, be no privacy between two who loved each other like this. Because this was love. She knew it and he knew it. For her the earlier, younger loves had been forecasts, rough sketches, hints at this truth. If this were ever taken away, there could be only later sketches made in retrospective imitation, shadowy feeble efforts to re-create what did not happen twice. And when he told his love for her, she knew that he was not lying. Only when the violence swept him did she feel insecure, remembering the first Levitt, the dangerous darkness, the Knave of Spades.

"You appear to have made no perceptible progress in the last twenty minutes, my love."

"No, do I? It's a gift."

"There's no talent to touch it," Levitt said. "What d'you figure would happen if we found ourselves in a burning house?"

"I don't figure. Except," she said, after due reflection, "that it would be somebody else's house and uninsured. All right, now; five minutes, but don't watch me."

(ii)

Levitt was in a King-of-the-Castle mood; persuading himself that to be back in the chips after the lean interval was better than being in the chips all the time. Celia was the only person with whom he could share every nuance of life on a financial roller-coaster. True, it made for fights; but it made for fun. It made for days like this when you lunched off a hot dog at Howard Johnson's (though he doubted whether Celia had lunched at all) and strolled at evening into the lighted tent of the rich, not caring if the bill came to thirty dollars.

Here you met the people whom you had not seen for a while; they were your friends, you would say, but they were zoned. They lived within the borders of a territory where you could not live all the time; you went from them into foreign parts whose geography included Howard Johnson's and the pawnshop on Eighth Avenue.

Some of them, no doubt, had their own summonses beyond the border. Eating in expensive restaurants was no gauge of solvency. It was merely, he thought, a sign of the credit that Celia and he could still command; personal credit, rather than financial.

Personal credit, the imponderable whose make-up included appearance, manners, name, the habit of public places and a circle of acquaintances whose assets, when examined, might yield nothing more solid than appearance, manners, name, the habit of public places and a circle of acquaintances . . . he saw the spiral; he saw the whole unsupported structure made by smooth agreement; the pattern of signed bills, large tips, easy words.

"Take a cheque? With pleasure, Madam."

"Perfectly all right, sir; leave it till next time," and the careful drill that taught saleswomen to say, "Is this a charge?" before daring to presume that you would pay cash.

He was still musing upon it when Celia returned from her voyage to another table. "I cadged these from Gerald," she said, holding up the yellow packet of English cigarettes.

"Did he just get here?"

"Yes; want to join him for coffee?" There was the slightest edge of anxiety on her now. He had no views, one way or another, about having coffee with Gerald Lynn. It might mean talk of Carlington, of Glane, but not the sort of talk that worried him.

"Yes, sure. All right with me, darling."

"Odd," she said, "how that sort always knows. I could see a 'so-they're-going-to-be-married' look in his eye before I got to table."

"So they are," said Levitt. He stretched his left hand across to hold hers, raised his glass in the other hand. "Married by Christmas; case won by Christmas; rich by Christmas; and we'll have Terry here by Christmas."

She said, "Certainly." She never pulled him down from fantasy to fact; he could leap ahead over all the obstacles and she would talk as though she too believed. Looking at the luminous fairness, the eyes, the flash of laughter, he could still wonder that all this belonged to him; that the heart was his, and the body, and the thoughts behind the forehead. No, not all the thoughts. He watched her light the English cigarette and asked,

"Transatlantic schizophrenia worrying you tonight?"

"Nothing's worrying me tonight."

"And if it were," he thought, "you wouldn't tell. Never did anyone take her anxieties so gaily for granted; they get the dignified brush-off every time."

"But England pulls," he said, "it must pull."

"Well, of course, it pulls. For you, too. You ought to have gone in the spring, as you meant to."

"Not without you, darling. Never regretted that decision."

"And yet——" she said and stopped. He knew what she remembered; his saying to her on the night of their re-meeting, "If I don't go now, there'll be a poison blowing from England always." He said quickly, "Gerald got any news of J. G.?" Oddly, his silence on Carlington never included J. G. Alone out of that past, J. G. could always intrude upon their talk.

"Oh, yes."

"How is the old boy?"

"Well, grieved; harassed by strikes at Glane; no message for me; just a pained sigh and a reference to people who won't see reason. Followed, Gerald said, by an anti-American sermon that ran twenty minutes."

"Target, Mr. H. Levitt, I shouldn't wonder." His eyes

wandered. "Who's in his party, Gerald's, I mean? The pillar gets in the way from here."

Celia hesitated, narrowed her eyes at the corners. "Gloria Coates," she said. "And Mr. and Mrs. Grant Parker."

"No kidding?"

"No kidding. Grant and Sandra in the flesh."

"And you're suggesting that we join them for coffee?"

"Why not?" said Celia tranquilly. "It's Gerald's invitation."

He crushed out his cigarette with violence. "I can't," he said. "And you can't, either."

"Certainly I can."

"All right," he said. "That's up to you. I'd have thought after the brush-off he gave you last spring . . ."

"Listen," said Celia, "when Grant cancelled that lunch, I decided not to try to see him again. You know that. He'd seen J. G. and my guess is still that J. G. sold me down the river. Have I made one step in Grant's direction since?"

"You're about to make one now."

She shrugged her shoulders. "Manners are manners, after all."

"I don't use mine when it comes to Grant Parker. I haven't seen him since I walked out on him. I'm not going to suck up to him over coffee."

He saw that he was making her angry. She said, "Nobody has asked you to suck up, stupid."

"Well, you go," said Levitt. "It's fine by me, just so's I needn't. Say I've got to make a long-distance call. I'll wait for you in the bar."

Their eyes fought it out for a moment; then she said, "Very well. I shan't be more than fifteen minutes."

"Take your time."

Sitting at the bar, he thought, "She must see why I can't do it. She doesn't. Damn it, why should I sit down with Grant, answer his Olympian questions, try to make it sound good?

"What does she expect me to say?—'Oh, I got tired of working for Baron; tired of the big money. Thought I'd try free-lancing for the hell of it. Went to Hollywood on a wild-goose chase for the hell of it; didn't really want the contract; delighted when it fell through.' 'Doing now? Oh, I'm on top of the world; making up my mind between a shaky future with *Searchlight* and a second-rate Boston job.' 'Ever regret having left *Point* and *Steer*? Jupiter, no; told you I got tired of the big money, didn't I?'

"Oh, come on, Levitt, don't sit here cooking up a rage on our first good evening. But it's always happening; once we get a break, it happens. If it wasn't this, it would be something else; we both behave so well when things are wrong that we always celebrate the moment when they're right with a five-star quarrel. Nerve-ends raw. Well, we won't do it tonight; we won't spoil it; by God, we won't. Though of all the unreasonable, insensitive, inconsiderate—I'll take another brandy, please.

"Fifteen minutes . . . I don't know why she troubles to tell such lies; she doesn't believe them herself; ostrich lies; just as she says, 'Ready now' when she's only got as far as her girdle. Fifteen minutes wouldn't take you past Gerald's first volume of gossip, my pretty; and then you'll have to stay for the Grant Parker headline edition of world events; and then it'll be Sandra's turn; you'll want to hear about Elsa Maxwell's party, or maybe the Pope's party, or an austerity romp at Buckingham Palace with Princess Margaret playing the flute, I wouldn't know. Your world, my love, my international, insensitive, myopic, skim-the-surface love.

"And England, of course. How stands the Old Lord Warden? The Old Lord Warden can stand me another brandy, and like it. You'll have your British accent when you come down, if you ever come down. . . . Ten minutes with Gerald and you'll have got it back; twice the speed and half the audibility; clip, clip, clip, chuff-chuff-chuff. Anybody'd think I don't love you. Keep me waiting another five minutes and I'll know I don't love you.

"And if you come now I'll still be mad. If you don't keep me waiting all of half an hour, you'll rob me of my grievance. Half an hour she'll take, I said to myself; that's what I want you to take. Oh, hallo, darling, have a brandy."

"No, thank you, love. Gerald just gave me one."

"Mind waiting a minute while I finish this?"

"Of course not." She spoke amiably enough, but some threats to peace were here; in the sunny, glacial look that she had decided to wear, in her low-voiced, punctilious request for a light.

"Lighters all on the blink?"

"No. I just forgot that the one in this bag wants a flint."

He lit her cigarette. "How were Grant and Sandra?"

"Much as usual. She did the talking: war and polio and communism; straightforward American jitter talk."

"Tempered, I trust, with solid British common sense from Mr. Lynn and Mrs. West."

"Oh, sure."

There was a silence.

"Let's go," he said. Only the threats to peace; they might still pass the dangerous corner. Once in the taxi, he had to invite it.

"Grant revive his invitation to lunch?"

"Yes."

"And you said?"

"What do you suppose I said? 'God, yes, I'm free any day between now and Christmas. And bring a cheque with you.'"

"Thought that might be the object of the coffee-drinking expedition."

"Sometimes," she said, "you exhibit a common little mind."

"At least I don't sit down at a table with him."

"No; and that was rather common of you, too," she said looking out of the window.

"That's not fair. Why should I meet him? The guy who's got the biggest laugh of a lifetime on me. Why should I put myself in his way?"

"Why keep out of his way? It's over now. You'll have to meet him sometime. It's merely a question of a few guts, Harry."

"I lack guts?"

"About that, yes."

He laughed. "Now I can feel Carey all over you."

"Carey?"

"Pompous, stiff upper-lip talk. All Carey."

"*Why* do you hate Carey?" she asked, her voice deeper, sounding friendly now.

"Hate him? I never think about him. He's just a stuffed shirt. What's there to think about? Thinking all there is to think about Carey wouldn't take a moth five minutes."

"All right, Harry. Let's cut, shall we? It isn't worth a row."

They were back at the house; he paid the taxi. They went upstairs in silence; there was a savage singing in his ears; he felt the red fury on its way.

He walked to the writing-table under the window. Digging at the wound, he had to sit there, opening his brown manila envelopes one by one, taking out the sketches, the rough schemes, the finished products of this year.

He strewed them on the table. He picked them up, examined them carefully, laid them down. It was the same nervous search that he made every few weeks. He looked for reassurance and he could not find it. Something had gone; the thing that had made him Levitt, Levitt of the U. S. Army, Levitt of the Book-of-the-Month-Club, Levitt of *Point* and *Steer*; Levitt who was bought by J. G. Baron in the spring of '49.

The bite was out of the stuff for ever; he still had an agile pencil, but the X-ray eye, the eye for flaws of character, was dulled. Only the crested eyebrow of a signature remained constant. "Tame," he said to himself. (That was what the English reviewers had said of his new book.) "They're tame; and they used to be wild. Tame as goddamned Carey's goddamned sculpture."

Still there was silence behind him. Celia was wandering around the bookshelves.

"Why did it have to go? The thing that I could do? The only thing . . ."

He glanced over his shoulder; she had taken a book from the shelves; she was lying on the sofa, reading. He went on with his obstinate agony, wanting her to notice it and to speak.

"Goddamn it," he said to himself, "I'll do it again." He pushed all the drawings back into the files, haphazard; he cleared a space, he took a block and a pencil and slashed; it came out as Carey; he had known that it would. He put Carey into an exaggerated check tweed, stuck an outsize pipe in Carey's mouth, fitted a chisel into Carey's hand. Then he drew a chunky, lop-sided marble figure of a naked woman. He added some vulgar detail to the statue. Then he tore the sheet across, despising himself.

His anger was dying; he felt heavy and lonely. "Here lies one whose name was writ in comic strips, and pretty punk comic strips at that."

He glanced over his shoulder again, saw the fair head quiet on the sofa cushion, heard the soft switch of the pages. He sighed.

"Hello," she said, not looking up.

"Hello. I love you. I'm sorry I was sore and rude."

"Bless you. I was rude too. Come here."

"It's just—oh God, I don't know what it is," he said with his head against her shoulder. "I've got you and that's the best thing in the world. And you've risked everything for me; and I'm not worth it."

She stroked his forehead. "None of that. We're all right."

"What are you reading?" he asked lazily.

"Poetry; they've got some nice poetry."

"You always read poetry in a new place."

"Just because it is a new place," she said. "Like putting one's feet up on familiar furniture, d'you see? This one," she said,

> " *'The long light shakes across the lakes*
> *And the wild cataract leaps in glory'*—

that's got school ink on it; and the smell of blackboard chalk and a playing-field outside the windows."

He watched her sorrowfully. "Where's home, Celia?" he asked on a sigh. She held his hand.

"Home's where you are, stupid."

"Mean it?"

"With all my heart."

"Promise?"

"Promise."

"Why do we always have to keep saying promise, I wonder? Is it that we don't trust each other to be happy with what we've got?"

"There's a man in here who'll tell you what we've got," she said, opening the book again:

> " *'Now while the dark about our loves is strewn,*
> *Light of my dark, blood of my heart, O come!*
> *And night will catch her breath up and be dumb.*
> *Leave thy father, leave thy mother,*
> *And thy brother;*
> *Leave the black tents of thy tribe apart.*
> *Am I not thy father and thy brother,*
> *And thy mother?*
> *And thou—what needest with thy tribe's black tents*
> *Who hast the red pavilion of my heart?'* "

Presently she lay awake and looked ahead to the morning. Would this quiet certainty prevail against the morning mood?

(iii)

It was another morning in New York, cut to the pattern of this year, but with a difference that would make it memorable.

There were no letters in the box at the post office; for once she was not disappointed. She walked the two blocks to the drugstore. It was a little cooler today, with the hint of autumn. Here was the clinical, white and silver refuge; the curly-headed boy who whistled; the black coffee in the thick white cup. Eleven o'clock. Her appointment with Cronin was for twelve.

"Think fast, think hard; there's an hour to go. In an hour will come the moment to burn your boats." Levitt's voice echoed: "Married by Christmas." It was a gesture of hope, an act of faith; it was what he wanted, just as *Searchlight* was what he wanted. He jumped the walls in the way, and said that it would happen.

"And you? Make up your mind; now, for the last time."

In one sense, it was made up. She could not live without him; if she left him, it would not be living; it would be a crippled walk, alone. Even to try to imagine it made her feel ill, after a little while. There was, she thought, no place for them in the same world if they could not be together; better for one to be dead.

But she was not free to choose Levitt for just that reason. Terry stood in the way. "Think hard; think fast; it is now. This is it. Are you right or wrong?"

It was almost impossible now to stand away; to look at him and sum him up. When she tried, she saw facets, some important, some irrelevant; facets that were separate, not making a whole portrait. She saw his physical toughness; the fact that he could sail a boat; his skill with his hands; the kindliness and competence with which he had nursed her when she was ill in Hollywood; his unexpected faith in God; the fact that he said his prayers.

She saw the dark thing; the secret and the hatred; the violence that came suddenly; and, more deadly perhaps, the weakness that she shared, the gambler's shiftlessness, the utter failure to take thought for tomorrow. This would stay. The dark thing must go. Not until the secret was out, and conquered, would he be at peace. She could not see how this would happen, but she knew that it must happen and that probably it would break him when it did happen, break and renew him again. She felt that she had watched him grow, and mature, through a series of trials, each of which had torn him down and built him up. The last trial was still ahead. Curious, to be so certain of that, without a clue to the secret.

"I, as I used to be, would have said 'No' this morning. I would have said that he was still too much of a risk, that for all his sweetness and his strength, I was giving Terry a risk for a stepfather.

"Who am I, now?

"I am stripped, I think, of all that I had; I have only the life that I share with him. The life of chamois-leaps and gambler's chances."

Certain aspects of this must go, too; the checking on the imponderable assets; the speculator's look that assessed a lunch with Grant Parker alike with the jewels for the pawn-shop.

"But can it be done, by either of us, with our fatal side-slips into debt, into don't-care, into extravagant fun? I only know that not until I can see our life in terms of security for Terry, can I take Terry into it. And not until I am married to Levitt must I have Terry here.

"So this morning the chips are down. I must stake on Levitt or I must pull out of the game.

"Do I stake on Levitt? Do I say to Tim Cronin, 'Withdraw the case; take Van's terms. I'll give up all claim to the money if he'll agree to the divorce'?

"Or do I say—'Go ahead with the case; shut the door on the divorce—shut the door on all chance of marriage to Levitt'? And when I have fought it, and lost, borrow the fare—go back to England alone?"

There would be no sign from heaven; no last-minute miracle; of that you could be sure.

She paid for her coffee, walked out on to the Avenue. She hailed a taxi.

"If you stake on Levitt, it may be months and months before you see Terry again. It may be years before you see England again." They were all there in her mind, Terry, Liz and Anthony, Nanny's bustling figure, the look of the land that you had besought your eyes to remember; the sense of safety.

And here? The bright eyes of danger.

J. G. bobbed up briskly now, on prancing legs. "I could still fix it for you, Celia. Give up this lover of yours and I'll fix it. You know that. I'm your father, after all. You're my daughter."

Levitt's voice cut in; a quiet echo, "It isn't susceptible of explanation; it's the thing that says 'No' inside. I'd sooner starve in the gutter than settle with J. G. again."

("*Find me one honest man.*")

Now there was the short stone canyon; the stone cliff rising above her; the brass and marble; the doors of the elevator; the twenty-sixth floor.

"The chips are down," she said to herself, "I stake on Levitt."

May, 1951

(i)

Celia carried the toy aeroplane out on to the rough lawn and pointed it into the wind. It was a fragile hollow thing of aluminium, attached to a rod and a reel; now the wings revolved frantically, with a spinning, humming noise; they turned into two blurred lines and she could let it fly. The wind took it; she reeled out the line and saw it go.

It became a silver hawk, high up, with a life of its own, the line running and running until it was far above the sea. The sun hurt her eyes, staring after it. But she could not stop staring. It had an oddly perfect beauty, the small silver bird up there in the blue sky.

She went on playing with it for a long time, though there was food to be bought and the mail to be fetched. The aeroplane was more than good fun; there was a shining pleasure in it, a winged-horse ecstasy.

She wondered if Terry would be able to manage the reel. She would, she thought, write him a supplementary note with the instructions in the box. Or perhaps, when the call from New York came through, she would know that there was no need—but one must not think. The target of today was to keep from thinking.

She could still hear, far up, the little throbbing noise of the wings. It was better than any kite. She watched a gull flap past within its range, wondered what the gull thought about it.

Reluctantly, with dazzled eyes, she began to wind in the line. The wind was steady and it came straight all the way; it was within a few feet of the rod when it fluttered and dived. She carried it carefully as she turned towards the house.

From here the house made the shape of an L; grey shingles with white window-frames. It still reminded her of a Noah's Ark. A porch ran in front of both arms of the L. The shorter arm had been built on three years ago; as a nursery wing for Nanny and Terry. Here now, in the room that used to be Terry's day nursery, she kept her own private things, the scrapbooks and the papers. There was a table and a chair, an electric heater. The back room, the night nursery, was still piled up with the porch furniture; they had stored it there for the winter.

She laid the toy aeroplane in its box on the table. She went across the porch to the main building; one large living-room, haphazardly but comfortably furnished; larger now that the oil-stove was taken away. Levitt's work-table, neat with his absence, ran half across the room.

She mounted by narrow wooden stairs, steep as the companion-way on a small boat, to the first floor. In the bedroom, whose windows looked on the lawn, the flag-pole and the sea, she searched her bag for money; she found seventy cents, more than enough for the stamp on Terry's letter. She thought that she had sixteen dollars in the bank, but the bank would be shut by now. When Levitt was away, she tried not to charge for food.

The afternoon sunlight, the promise of summer, made whispers in the house. She did not dare to listen to them. Instead, as she ran down the perilous stairs, she thought of the house itself. They had seen the winter through here, and the spring. They had chopped wood with fingers that froze against the axe (that was before Levitt sold two drawings to *Esquire*, and they bought the oil-heater.) They had burned the rubbish in a field of snow; they had lain awake in the north-easter and felt the house shake as though they were at sea. They had watched rain and sleet; they had seen the island shrouded and heard the fog-horns' lost cry. And now it was warm again; the double windows were off and the screens were up: tomorrow, when Levitt came back, they would put up the patched canopy over the porch, bring out the deck-chairs and basket tables from the night nursery. Soon it would be warm enough to swim.

She went out of the front door, down the rough steps to the gravel driveway, with the plot of turf and the thin pines that separated it from the road. From here, the house was more of an ark than ever; you could not see the short arm of the L; just a grey oblong ark with white paint, set among small trees and lilac bushes that had taken a battering from the wind.

It had a faithful quality; she loved it more now than she had ever loved it. Before this, it had been a house for holidays; marred by Van's dislike of it, marred by Van himself. Now it meant something. But still its calendar was the calendar of a time that must end. Today? "No; don't think."

She had a struggle to start the car. The car was acting up with monotonous regularity in these days. It was an atrocity, bought for thirty-five dollars from an advertisement in the *Vineyard Gazette*. It would not be long, she thought, before it fell to pieces.

In the village street you could see that summer was beginning; the square white ferry was in, and a stream of cars drove off, impeding her on Main Street. She went into the post office. The girl behind the stamp window took the letter for Terry, weighed it, said, "Thirty cents this time. How's the boy?"

"He's fine."

"Coming over soon now?"

"Very soon, I hope."

There was mail in the box; rolled-up English newspapers and magazines, a letter from Liz, the letter in Nanny's handwriting that would enclose one from Terry; in fact the jackpot; the only pleasure that she found in Levitt's absence was the freedom to rejoice in this. "And I will save it all until I get home." She went into the provision store. Her assembled needs in the wire basket never looked like anybody else's; a can of chili con carne, a melon, a carton of cigarettes and a pot of red caviar. Then she came to the series of "Oh—— and's" which were the things that other people remembered first, bread and milk and coffee.

The man behind the counter found her a source of entertainment.

"Charge, Mrs. Levitt?" The name had ceased to sound the echo from the days when they used it to placate hotel clerks. They had been married in November.

"Yes, please. No. I'll write a cheque." As ever, he had to supply her with a blank cheque and a pen. "It is curious," Celia reflected, "that whatever efficiency I may possess—and that is not so little after all—stops short at the provision store."

She had to loiter, looking down to the dock and the ferry. Always, at the sight of any boat on any water, there came the illogical hope. As she started up the car again, she was playing the game; the game of faith. "It will happen. However long I have to wait, it will happen." All the stages of it were planned in her head, from the moment when she saw them come down the gang-plank; Nanny giving Terry a push, because he was looking the other way, he hadn't seen her yet.

Then New York, buying clothes for him; and at last here, where she was now, driving along the West Chop Road to the house.

But there were moments when your faith dipped and you could not see it happening at all. All that you could see was life on this island, with Levitt going to Boston twice a week; the trail of debts gradually diminishing; not yet paid in full, no margin, ever. They could just do this, the two of them, on the strength of X. ('X' was the horrible little girl in Levitt's cartoon; they both hated her so much that they could not mention her by name.) They had talked of getting one room in Boston, of Celia's supplementing the funds with a job of her own. They had talked of selling the house.

But in the hope of reprieve, in the hope of Terry, they went on keeping the house. It was their one asset. Nanny wrote that she would take no wages, that she could pay thirty pounds towards the fares. After that there had been no more talk of bringing Terry here without Nanny.

Now there was still more than an hour to wait before the New York call came through. She lay on the sofa, for the orgy of letters and newspapers; she began, as ever with the letter from Liz:

"My love,

"At last the fate for which all from Foliot to the farmer's wife have been spying without mercy since our return from the honeymoon; to wit, baby. This is due in November. I should prefer another process, as for eggs. Need I say more? The unrewarding details of this stage must still be familiar to you. I've been keeping it under my hat (a quaint conceit) until certainty set in.

"Anthony is taking it much more calmly than J. G. who is carrying on in several categories. He rushed out and bought a book called *How To Have a Baby Easily*, and kept it on his desk at the office all day until O'Rourke asked him how come he hadn't found out long ago. I laughed at first, but it has now become The Joke of the Month for May and the palate wearies. To avoid J. G.'s ministerings and probably midwifery, I shall have it in London, in a nursing home.

"The lambs are long past being lambs now. The black one went. *Too* mean, as they swore they wouldn't, and I'll murder who did as soon as I find out. Terry doesn't care at all, as J. G. has given him an Alsatian puppy (treacherous, Nanny says, meaning the breed, not J. G.). Nor does he now address a word to Prince. When love is over, how little of love even the lover understands.

"You say in your last 'Does he ever make the smallest sense about me?' (Meaning J. G., not Prince.) This I find hard to answer. He has, I think, been a little more reasonable since your marriage, which, I was confidently expecting, would be the last straw. At least he's stopped saying 'She's only got to make a move and I'll bring her home and look after her.' (Since it would now include bringing H. L. with you, perhaps this does not argue greater understanding.) He still goes on for hours against America and all things American. He was asked to lecture next autumn over there and turned it down. H. L.'s name is still unspoken. But there *is* a glimmer somewhere.

When we were at Glane last week (plinth and steps in position; statue due from the foundry next week; official opening of Glane, by Royalty, no less—end of June . . . all prettily timed with the Festival of Britain) wish I could lose this bracket-habit. Start again.

"At Glane; a very pretty day and looking down from the knoll where the plinth is; and he was in his most 'one-spot-to-choose-beloved-over-all' mood and he said suddenly, 'Which of us, would you say, is the fondest of this countryside?'

"One of his *awful* family-preoccupation questions; but, determined not to suck up I said, 'In my view, Celia'; and he winded me by saying 'Yes, I agree'. So, thundering on, I asked why he didn't pull himself together and stop being injured and do a high-powered currency wangle and send you and Harry some money? Then, said I, they could come home, even if it were only for a little time; they could come and fetch Terry.

"That bitched it. First a 'What . . .?' Then the gradual withdrawal of the features, as though he were putting them into cold storage. Then 'Celia's future is in her own hands, not mine.' I said, 'Well, nice for Celia, but you could still send them some money, couldn't you?' and then it was umbrage for the rest of the afternoon.

"I think it amounts to this. He hasn't forgiven you or H. L. and he'll let you both sink or swim. Nothing short of a threat to Terry would make him change. But he sees that Terry is all right, protected by the English trust fund, able to stay here happily with Nanny (of course T. misses you, but children's missing isn't our non-stop ache of agony after a year; I doubt it hurts at all).

"Anyway J. G. can crow because he can give T. a home where you cannot. And he has a lovely time inside his head, I suspect, asking himself what you would do about T. now if there weren't Carlington?

"Deep down, I know that he honours you. Probably you're the only person beside Anthony whom he does honour.

"And God knows, darling, I honour you.

"Anthony is overworking. Two *more* commissions have

come in as a result of the prize. I wish he slept better; but he
says it's of no importance and that he was like this for a bit after
Anzio. I said that if marriage to me, and my impending mother-
hood, were co-equivalent with Anzio, it was high time for
divorce despite the unusual circumstances.

"I love him more and more. If it weren't for him I could bear
nothing (not even the baby, as I see you about to remark . . .)
particularly not J. G. It is the *utter* trust that one reposes, the
Rock thing, the pure gold thing. I chatter. . . . No more now,
except prayers, so long by this time that ladders between
Heaven and Charing Cross must look like runs in nylons by
comparison.

"Great love to both of you from both of us . . ."

(The message always unanswered . . . By habit, Celia prepared to call over her shoulder, "They both send love", and meet
the expected silence.)

Nanny's letter was set to pattern:

"Dearest Mrs. Celia,

"Thank you for yours of the 25th and to say that another
lovely food-parcel arrived safely. It is good to know that you
are both well and expect good news soon and that you are now
being so fortunate with your weather.

"The young man is very well, somewhat obstreperous since
the puppy. I have banned it on the bed.

"If it is possible to send some socks, drawing of foot enclosed,
we do need at least four pairs. They go so fast.

"Isn't it lovely about Mrs. Liz?

"Please remember me respectfully to Mr. Levitt.
                              "Your loving old

                                                    "NANNY.

"P.S. The American magazines were a great treat; how smart
all the clothes look, don't they?"

Celia glanced reflectively down the length of herself, at the
white shirt and faded blue jeans, the bare feet in old sandals.

A half-sheet with ruled lines contained Terry's usual observations about Nanny being very well, himself being very well, grandpapa and the puppy being very well. His writing was, if anything, worse. There was a tactful insertion by Nanny, "Please give my love to my stepfather." He ended, "When are we going to America, Your loving son, Terence."

She held the half-sheet of paper against her cheek. It was hard to remember now that she had ever known him except as these pieces of paper.

She began on the magazines. There were two prizes for the scrapbook; one a double-spread of Glane, above the caption, "A Great and Beautiful Achievement". The other was of Anthony Carey, a photograph taken at Carlington; he stood on the white step at the foot of Toby's memorial; just his head and shoulders, looking up, with the statue cutting a sharp, exquisite shadow on the white stone.

Each dull landscape, each ordinary house that she saw photographed here, was haloed with unreality, a sign of the England far off. It was a different homesickness now. It was patient and unafraid. Before Levitt it had nagged like toothache, because that country was more real than this. Levitt had made the point of reality; in loving, you put roots down into the foreign earth. But you were condemned for ever to the split heart, the double pain, the knowledge of having tasted truth in two places.

Presently she sat in the bare working-room and pasted the pictures into the scrapbook. It was in its third volume now. (A relief to do this today, without the head lifted to listen, the shutting of the book as his footsteps crossed the porch.)

She was back in the living-room by six o'clock; when the telephone rang, its sound was meaningless, too long expected. The telephone was on the window-ledge in the hall, between the living-room and the kitchen.

"It's all right," Levitt said. "Home and dry."

"No."

"Yes."

"Tell."

"Well, it was up to Dwight, really. They want me, but this

other guy can bring five thousand dollars capital in with him.
And, well as *Searchlight's* done this year, they could still use
that. David was extremely civilised about it; said if I could put
in two thousand, that'd cover them with the backers. So I talked
to Dwight. And it's in the bag. He's sent the cheque. I draw
director's fees first of the month. They've raised them, too,
since we talked. All set, darling."

She did not think that it would be so hard to understand.
When he said, "I'm going to Cunard first thing tomorrow.
What's the earliest date that they could sail, d'you think? There
may be a cancellation we could take up," she began to realise
that it was true.

After she had hung up, she remembered a dozen things that
she had forgotten to ask him. She stood in the middle of the
room. The room looked quite different.

(ii)

Levitt came out of the Cunard offices on Park and walked in
the direction of Fifth Avenue. He was heading for his bank.
After the bank, lunch with Dwight Estofen; then the *Searchlight*
offices and then La Guardia for the flight back home.

"They grin like a dog and run about the city," he said to
himself. "Certainly. And what makes me grin the wider is the
fact that it proves to be *Searchlight*, after all, that's done it. The
long-shot, the risk, the fifty-to-one-against. Nobody'd have
given ten cents for its chances last year, when I had to choose
Boston. Now, another six months and we'll put the *New
Yorker* out of business. That's what Dwight said. He's smart,
Mr. E. He's on a good thing and he knows it.

"And I'm back. I'm still worth something. They valued my
eye, my taste and my judgment enough to go on wanting me, to
try again, to get me. Poor old Boston; poor *sweet* little X . . .
guess I could keep on doing X as a sideline, but what the hell?
(Better to write them before I see them, if I've a moment; break
the news.)

"It's a real job again, an exciting job, a back-breaking job in August, when we start on the fifteen-page expansion. Have to be in New York all the time then. Celia and Terry must stay on the island till it's cool. After that—wonder if Dwight still has a line on the house in Bedford.

"It's been a long, long winter," he apostrophised Bronzini's window; "and I need a new tie. That's what I'll do; buy myself a fine new tie. No, I won't; not till I've bought Celia a lighter; time she had another funny lighter." He walked on.

"Oh, thank you, God. Sorry I keep forgetting to say thank you enough," he said at the corner of Fifth Avenue. "Thank you for all of it. We earned it, I guess, or you wouldn't have given it to us. Now all I ask is that you fix that cancellation so's they'll get here three weeks from now. That's not for me, that one; that one's for Celia. You will, won't you? She's been so good." He looked back at the spring and the winter, saw her in a parka and a fur cap, emptying the garbage; heard her swearing light-heartedly at the oven when the main fuse blew; saw her bending over his bed, still contriving to be *de luxe* in appearance, at five a.m., with the temperature at zero; saying, "The loathsome hour has struck; your coffee's ready." He saw her face at evening, quiet with her thoughts in the place where he could not follow them. There was the abandoned nursery room where she went to paste the cuttings in the scrapbooks, alone.

"You'll give her that," he said confidently to God.

The bank was on 49th Street. He remembered that when he had made his first deposit here, in the arrogant past, it had seemed to him a place as soothing and kind as the right sort of church would be if one were the right sort of Christian. It had, he thought, certain church attributes, brasswork and marble and rules.

He had loitered here occasionally, looking across the rail to the carpeted sanctuary where men of authority sat at shiny desks and refused to make loans (only he did not know that then). He had lingered, studying the uniforms of the benign gunmen on the doors, taking a mental snapshot of power; his own power also, the power based on solid earnings.

The bank had not looked like that in a long while, nor would again. It didn't scare him any more, but he knew that, for soothing and kindliness, a black panther might have been a better bet. The bank had become a tough opponent in a long boxing-bout. The square man with his name identifying him from a bronze tablet on the flat-topped desk was just one of the opponent's many fists. But today it was Levitt's round.

"Hello, Mr. Levitt. Sit down, won't you? I'll be with you in a moment." He conducted the last of his telephone conversation with the maximum of what Celia called authentic American delay: the repeated "Fines", "Sures", "Okays" and "I'll tell you's" strung out like beads on a necklace. Levitt's cigarette was finished before they were.

"We-ell," said the bronze tablet, "fine and dry today, isn't it? Can do with some more of these fine, dry mornings, commuting from the country the way I do. Pretty nice up in New England now? I'm very fond of Martha's Vineyard. Do you know——" Levitt lost it.

"Going back there tonight," he said. "But I'll be back permanently two months from now. I'm going in with *Searchlight*."

The bronze tablet showed signs of respect. Levitt talked airily, his eyes on the clock. Then he said, "Would you just mind checking for me; I'm expecting a credit from the Estofen office. Mr. Dwight Estofen was sending it over by hand yesterday afternoon; two thousand dollars."

Whether the bronze tablet knew or did not know, it would still go through the motions of finding out; which involved a long, leisurely walk to the other end of the public counters; a stroll back, with a pause (doubtless for talk of fine, dry mornings) at a solvent-looking person wearing pince-nez. He still wore his smile when he came back to the desk.

"Sorry, Mr. Levitt. Nothing's come in for you yet."

There was the familiar mixture in the mind; the feeling that you had hit an air-pocket; no floor; no stomach; the nod of assent from some steady, quiet onlooker who had never believed in any miracle. Then your voice, saying placidly, "Oh, well, I'm lunching with Mr. Estofen, anyway, so I can find out what goes."

(iii)

"What I'm up against," said Dwight, "is my partners. See how I'm placed, Harry?"

"Sure." The lunch had been going on for ever and the only thing that had emerged in clear focus was the way that Dwight Estofen was placed.

"It's not that it's such a large sum, it's just that they don't feel justified in sanctioning it just now. Times is tough, you know."

("About as tough as chiffon pie on your capital, chum, but let it pass.")

"I never figured on their taking this attitude, Harry—I'm sorry. It was different with that loan in the fall, of course; that was a private loan—out of my own pocket; easy to do it; glad to do it."

("Oh God, do you have to say it again? If my balance since I paid the deposit to Cunard wasn't standing at forty-eight dollars and twenty-five cents I'd stuff it down your throat—no, i wouldn't stuff it down your throat.")

He listened to the various tunes: "What I suggest you do— you're seeing the boys this afternoon. Tell them there's a ninety per cent chance we'll come in later on. . . .

"What I feel is that you're worth plenty to them, quite aside from any capital you can—or can't—put into the business.

"What I think is—you'll find they'll jump at you. Probably a bit of blarney, that asking for two thousand; what's two thousand to them, after all?"

("Just about what it is to your partners, baby-face; no more, no less.")

"What I know is that most intelligent people like straight talk. You go straight in and say to them 'Here's how things are.'

"What I believe is——"

("And what I say is, you could have said all this yesterday. But of course you couldn't. You were a great eager slab of butter and egg before you talked to your partners. Doesn't take much partner-talk to turn rich boys like you into the slip between the cup and the lip, does it?")

He said, "Well, thanks, Dwight. I'll have to be off there now. I'll let you know what works out."

"Do—do; be sure you do. Call me, won't you? Drop you anywhere? Sure?" The last of him was his fat bottom ducking into the sedan, with the chauffeur holding open the door.

Levitt walked slowly to the corner of Madison. Already the rushing up of reinforcements had begun inside his head. "It's possible that when I get to David's office I'll find they've decided for me after all, they've decided to waive the money; that's how it'll be. And if it isn't, well there'll be a way around; David will know somebody who can chip in."

("Yeah. David does. There's the guy with the flair and the five thousand only waiting for you to fall down on this.")

He stood still, facing the red lights; watching the consolations vanish; there went the future, the fun, the new job, the new money. He could not yet face the thought that there went, also, two passages on a Cunard liner from England; there went the assurance of Terry's future here.

He crossed the Avenue.

"Damn it, why did I have to tell Celia last night? Why couldn't I have waited till today. . . . She'll take it; she'll take anything; she's taken plenty." His thoughts went ahead to the airfield on the island; to the look of her waiting by the battered car. The fair head, the flash of laughter, the happiness that he must shoot down; she would know before he spoke; the question in the eyes would not last long.

"And I know what she'll say. 'Tough on you, having to tell me.' "

He turned in, through the doorway with the plate announcing *Searchlight Magazine, Inc.* beside it. He went up in the elevator; he said, "Hello" to the girl on the switchboard. She smiled at him and said, "Go right in, Mr. Levitt," thinking no doubt that everything was the same as it had been yesterday. He walked along the light-painted hall to David's room.

(iv)

It was only when he was at the door of the telephone booth that he thought of lying to Celia. He paused outside the booth to work on the lie.

It was like finding an old, unaccustomed weapon back in his hand; he was not sure that he could use it.

Whatever he said, it couldn't hold for long; it was, temporarily, the best present that he could give to her. Unless she saw through it. "Not the liar I used to be," he thought, and grinned at the rueful way of thinking; regret for a rusted talent.

"But we'll try; we'll do what we can; those who cannot bring home the bacon can at least avoid bringing home the bad news. I won't think it out in advance. I'll let it come." He opened the sliding door, dropped the coin, dialled Operator and asked for the Vineyard number.

"Hullo?" He could see the telephone on the window-ledge, Celia perched there, the sun coming through the window on to her hair.

"Hullo, darling. Look, I'm not catching that plane tonight." It was the first thing that came into his head; it came briskly and gaily. "Hate to be another night here, you know that."

"Nothing gone wrong, darling?"

"Nothing at all, no. Everything's fine. There's a hope of a cancellation for a sailing on the seventh; they're cabling London. Don't signal Nanny till they're sure; you haven't, have you?" He tried to keep the note of anxiety out of his voice.

"I cabled Nanny," she said, "couldn't not. Just telling her it was all right and that the date would follow."

"Oh, yes, of course. Fine."

"Harry, something has gone wrong, hasn't it?"

"I swear it hasn't."

"You sound . . ." the voice stopped.

"Listen, sweetheart. All that's happened is they want just one more meeting, tomorrow morning. With——" he named his agent, "to go over the final draft of the contract. Couldn't do it today because David had to go out of town early, his kid's not well; they're worried, think it may be polio, got a specialist coming to look at her; tough on David." Really remarkable, he said to himself, how it flows when you let it tell itself.

"Oh, I see." She sounded reassured. "Poor David. All right, darling. Same plane tomorrow, d'you think?"

"Maybe the earlier one. I'll call you. What have you been doing?"

The voice was gay. "Fixing like crazy; I've got all the stuff out of the nursery; chose some stuff for curtains; can we run to a sofa for that room? I found quite a nice one secondhand over at Oak Bluffs . . ." The words went in like small spikes. Presently she said, "And you, sweetheart? Nice day?"

"Nice day. Cunard: then lunch with Dwight, all very cosy; saw the bastards at the bank, astonishingly polite they were, too. Saw David. Oh, and I bought myself a tie," he said, "went into Bronzini's and got a fine new tie."

"Well deserved. Pretty, is it?"

"A dream of beauty; you'll see."

(Can always say I forgot to pack it.)

"I love you."

"I love you. Till tomorrow."

He stood there, dropping in the extra coins for overtime. He waited in a dream, wondering what to do. "That's fixed it," he kept saying in his head. "That's fixed it; she's cabled them. Now I'll have to find the money."

("But the door's shut. It's all over with *Searchlight*. You heard what David said.")

"If I called him back now—said I could get it by tomorrow."

("No, chum, you can't risk that. Anyway, he'll be on the line to the character with the flair and the five grand by now.")

"I've got to get the money. I can't let her down."

He came out of the box; an impatient, waiting figure slammed past him and went in.

He stood again on the corner of Park where he had walked blithely this morning on his way from the Cunard office; the sunlight and the sweeping traffic, the long perspective stretching away, were as different from this morning as though he stood in a new town.

"Four hours ago——" he thought. "Oh, leave that one alone. It's like the guy in the de Maupassant story who saw his lottery ticket posted as the winning number, and walked around the square being a millionaire inside his head, then came back and found the number changed. That's a consoling kind of story; shows it might happen to anybody. Was it de Maupassant? I guess it was; all those stories are, the way all epigrams are made by Dorothy Parker."

Parker; the name stayed with him. Grant Parker.

The lights changed.

"You're crazy," he said to himself.

"It's the last thing to do. Damn it, it's the last thing you can do. You, of all people. Parker, of all people."

He walked slowly, uncertainly, for half a block. "No, you couldn't do it. She wouldn't want you to do it. He wouldn't see you, anyway. Get the picture; get the picture of you walking into that building again.

"And what d'you say to him, if you force your way in (with a gun and a police badge?) past the front desk and the platinum blonde on the reception floor, past the secretary (barriers considerably more effective than barbed wire, those are) into the Presence? (Into the room where you cut your own throat so jauntily in '49.) What do you say? . . . 'Look, Mr. Parker, I know I'm your least favourite character in fact or fiction, but I want some dough badly.' . . . 'Hello, Mr. Parker; it's me again. I want a well-paid job, beginning as of tomorrow.' . . . 'Don't get up, Mr. Parker; I just came to borrow five thousand bucks for Celia.' Oh, stop. It's not only crazy, it's a nightmare. It's the one thing in the world you couldn't do."

He stood still. He turned back. He went into the hotel from whose lobby he had called Celia. There was a line in front of the telephone booth now. He had to wait. (Plenty of time to change your mind, to run away.)

He waited until his heart began to beat noticeably, thumping at the base of his throat, playing a quick tattoo. He felt his body shake. "But that's nerves; that's just thinking about it; anybody'd have jitters." He watched the busy profile of the woman in the booth; chatter, chatter, chatter; she stood up now; she opened the door. The booth was warm with her scent and her cigarette smoke. He had to make two stabs with his finger before he controlled it enough to dial the number correctly.

"Good afternoon. Parker Publications." The unvarying sing-song.

"Would you put me through to Mr. Grant Parker's secretary, please."

"Who shall I say, please?" (Barbed wire entanglement Number One.)

"Mr. Harry Levitt."

"One moment, Mr. Levitt."

Somebody had drawn a little picture of a rabbit on the wall above the telephone; he stared at the rabbit.

"Sorry, the line's busy . . ."

"I'll wait."

Really it was rather well done, the rabbit, it had a frisky liveliness. He took out his pencil, began to sketch a second rabbit, looking at the first.

"Still busy, I'm afraid . . ."

It was too hot in here; he opened the sliding door a little way.

"I'm connecting you now."

"How do you do, Mr. Levitt." Same secretary; he could see her ivory-white face and smooth black hair.

"Hello, there. Would you ask Mr. Grant Parker if he could see me for a few minutes; it's urgent and serious," he said, hearing his voice come out all wrong, first a light stammer, then a heavy, hopeless note; it was not in the least what he had meant to say.

"Just a moment, please."

The moment strung out; he lit a cigarette, kicked the door open a little wider. The line outside was forming again.

"Are you in town, Mr. Levitt? Could I have your number

and call you in a day or two? Mr. Parker's all full up this week."

"I'm afraid that won't do. I have to leave town tomorrow. It is very urgent."

"I'm sorry," she said.

"Look, if I came to the office around five and waited; he might be able to see me, mightn't he? Just for a few minutes; I know that's the easiest time, most days; I've done it before."

"That wouldn't help today, Mr. Levitt. Mr. Parker's got a meeting out of the office at four-thirty and it's four-ten now."

"May I speak to him, then?"

"I'm sorry, he's got somebody with him just now." The voice was like a bright glass wall, he thought; not barbed wire any more, worse than barbed wire. He said, "What about tomorrow morning? I could come as early as he liked."

"Just a moment, while I look in his book." She said, "Tomorrow morning's perfectly terrible," sounding as though this pleased her. "It's nothing you could *write* to him about, is it, Mr. Levitt?"

"No, it isn't. Any time in the afternoon?"

Another wait. Now she was bored and cross. "If you'd like to take a chance around two-thirty, that's the best I can suggest; it would be better to telephone first; or just look in, if you're passing; it's really not more than a chance."

"Thanks a lot," he said, and his voice betrayed him again by sounding a note of hearty enthusiasm as though she had done great things for him.

He looked at his watch, saw that the time was four-fifteen; there were twenty-two hours in which to be alone with it.

(v)

The doorway to the Parker Building was half a block west of Fifth Avenue. Looking up, you were made dizzy by its shimmering white wall; mountain sickness, Levitt said to himself with a sneer. From this angle you could not see the tower, the summit, the beacon whose neon rays shone all night. Beautiful building, the Parker Building, you heard people say. Fit cradle for the million-dollar triplets, *Point*, *Steer* and *Democrat*.

The doorman in the grey-blue uniform with the peacock-blue lapels recognised him, and there was a moment when it felt all right, talking to the doorman. Once inside the white and silver lobby, hate began. The reception room was on the third floor; he stepped from the elevator into its white, pillared oval. He looked on chromium; on white rawhide sofas and chairs; on a birchwood floor and white fur rugs. On birchwood tables, copies of the millionaire triplets were set out for reading; with white cigarette-boxes and white book-matches. A chromium ash-tray on a stem stood at every possible point where an ash-tray might be required.

At three white desks, the three young women whose hair was nearer white than gold might be the same girls who had been there in his day or different girls with the same faces.

The nearest girl was flashing at a privileged-looking man with a grey moustache. "He wants you to go right up. The messenger will take you." Levitt watched the grey-blue uniform leading him away. He took the privileged person's place.

"You have an appointment, Mr. Levitt?"

"Yes, I have." He glanced at the huge silver clock set in the panel above her head. "I'm a few minutes early. His secretary said two-thirty."

"Will you have a seat, please?"

He picked up a copy of *Point*, sat down in the rawhide chair and began to read desperately, trying not to hear her telephone conversation with the secretary. "Not Mr. Ruysheimer, no— was he expected for two-thirty? Mr. Harry Levitt . . ." She said nothing after that; she hung up and called to her neighbour at the next desk. "If Mr. Engel comes through on your line, please put him on to Mr. Parker right away; on extension One-Three." One-Three was Parker's private line. Who the hell was Mr. Engel? Levitt stared acrimoniously at a thin young man now emerging from the elevator with a portfolio under his arm. He was on obvious terms with the third of the platinum young women.

"Hi, Tim."

"Hello, peaches."

"Fresh," she said. "You'd better hurry, too. Jack Morgan's yelling for you."

Jack Morgan was the chief art editor. "Time was when he used to yell for me," Levitt thought, watching the thin young man depart; it was only one's state of mind that made everybody here look successful, secure, busy and wanted. He watched the hand of the clock move from the silver blob that meant two-twenty-five, past the two-thirty blob and on and up. He read another few pages, dropped *Point*, picked up *Steer*. Rotten bad cartoons in both, he thought; that new guy's no good; not so new now, he's been holding the job down since I went.

The three elevator doors opened and shut, the traffic in visitors was brisk and smooth. Nobody had long to wait; there would be the little buzzing noise at the elbow of one or another of the three young women, then the summons to the grey-blue uniform, then any person who was not Harry Levitt escorted away. One woman alone had been waiting longer than he. She was large and fat; her dress had a large fat pattern of black and pink. She sighed from time to time and helped herself to another cigarette from the white box. But even she was on gay terms with the nearest platinum head. They kept grinning at each other and shrugging, and the fat woman's lips would form the word 'S—t', and the girl would wrinkle her nose sympathetically.

The silver minute-hand was almost touching the three o'clock blob now. Hopeless, Levitt said to himself; might as well call it a day. She had said, "Just a chance around two-thirty." Three o'clock was Titan's time, big boys' time; big boys coming in their Cadillacs from leisured lunches to be announced on extension Thirteen and sent straight up.

He lit another of his own cigarettes, still stupidly determined not to smoke Parker's. He said to the platinum head, "How about it? Can you call through again?"

"No need," she said. "His secretary'll call me back."

Levitt sat down again; got up again. He was too dried with impatience and anger to make any sense of the interview now. It wouldn't have been any use, anyway, he said to himself. It had been going cold on him since half-past four yesterday.

"Don't think I'll wait," he said, not saying it quite loudly enough for the girl to hear; there was a buzz at his elbow; she answered, then threw a dazzling smile at the fat black and pink woman. "*At* last. Up you go. I'd give him hell if I were you."

"I'll be going," Levitt said, this time with intention to be heard. One of the elevator doors opened and Grant Parker loped across the white room. He went past Levitt to the reception desks.

His appearance was so unexpected as to be comical. Levitt found himself staring stupidly at the lanky figure, the domed skull and monkish face. ("Wants to see Mr. Grant Parker, I guess," he said to himself; "funny, aren't you, Levitt?") Parker wore no hat; he must have come down from his office. He said to the girl, "Did you keep that package for me?" The moment had for Levitt a supreme slowness; it strung out for hours, Parker standing with one hand on the desk, the words lingering on the air. "Did . . . you . . . keep . . . that . . . package . . . for . . . me?"

"Surely, Mr. Parker; here it is."

"Thanks," Parker said, and this moment also lengthened. The gift-wrapped package took an incredibly long time to travel from the girl's hand to Parker's hand. "I've been standing here for hours," Levitt thought, "wondering if he'll see me. I ought to have spoken ages ago."

Parker turned from the desk.

"Why, hello, Levitt. How are you? I heard you'd called up." The lean face, the hooded eyes were neither hostile nor friendly. "Did you want to see me?"

("If I had the strength to say 'No' I'd say it.")

He said, "Got time for me now?"

Parker looked at his watch. "Yes, I think so. Won't take too long, will it?" He held up the package. "Got to drop this off on the next floor down. You go on up."

Now that it was happening, it made no sense; neither the different smile on the face of the girl, nor the grey-blue uniform leading him; nor, at the twenty-eighth floor, the room that he remembered. Here was the woman with the ivory face; assembling her features quickly into welcome. "Mr. Parker sent you up? Oh, splendid. How lucky you waited."

("No thanks to you, bitchkin.")

"Since when," he said, grinning at her, "has Grant run his own errands?"

"I beg your pardon?"

"Carrying packages around the place," said Levitt. "Gift-wrapped too."

"Oh, yes. There's a birthday party going on. One of the news-room staff; that would be it. Mr. Parker always takes care of those things. Do go in and sit down, Mr. Levitt."

He stood in the middle of the floor. All that he saw was flat, two-dimensional; he might still have been remembering the room. He felt as tired as though this were ended, and it had not yet begun.

(vi)

When Grant Parker came back to his room, he saw Levitt standing by the window. The strong light gave Parker every line and detail of the new face; the new face interested him; it was weary and dull-eyed, but the look of Levitt that he remembered most clearly had gone; the watchful look of the man who trusted neither himself nor the world outside him. This Levitt might be ten, not two, years older. The sunlight showed some glittering grey hairs above each temple, lines on the brow, lines at the corners of the mouth. He was tired, shabby, strong.

"I'd forgotten," Grant thought, "the resemblance to Van. But it's Van without the lacquer; Van with a backbone; Van with a straight eye. In other words, not Van. And oddly enough, not Levitt."

But he had never liked Levitt and he was not prepared to like the new version. "Why did I ask him up? Curiosity. He's always been a thorn in my flesh, somehow."

Grant was not used to thorns in his flesh; when your legend was that of a battleship with armour-plating and big guns, you were surprised by such incisions.

He was saying, "Sit down. Tell me how things are going with you."

Levitt sat down. He said abruptly, "They're not going. I haven't come to talk about me. I haven't come to ask you for a job."

"No," said Parker, smiling at him, "I didn't imagine that you had."

"In fact," Levitt said, looking at him steadily, without a smile, "I really came here without much idea of what I was going to say to you." He frowned; Parker could see him thinking it out, whatever it was. The frowning silence was queer; it gave no impression of nervousness; it compelled attention as though he watched Levitt performing a tricky task with his hands, lashing a rope, or driving in a nail at a difficult angle.

"Where are you working now?" Parker asked, having waited.

"In Boston," said Levitt. "Doesn't matter. Look here, I married Celia West; you knew that?"

"Yes, I did." None of the conventional words came to Parker's lips. Against his will, he had to go on watching Levitt, waiting for Levitt.

"This is for Celia." The frown went. "I think it's the best thing to do," Levitt added, in a kind of aside that could, Parker thought, have been addressed to his own conscience.

"Will you help her to get the money back? The money Van took. That's stolen money."

Grant contented himself with a mild, "Why do you say so?"

Levitt appeared to misunderstand the question: he said, "Because she's got to have money now. I thought I'd fixed it. There was a job coming up and it went down. And she's been waiting all these months to bring her boy over; we couldn't afford it, do you see, on what I was earning, and now we still can't.

"But I told her that it was all right. She doesn't know it isn't. She cabled them; she's getting the house ready for them.

Perhaps you don't understand how important that is. When you've been waiting, the way she has; and she's been so good. It was tough sledding in that little house on the Vineyard this winter; she's done it all. We couldn't even afford a cleaning woman.

"The physical toughness isn't anything compared with the things you think; when you're stuck three thousand miles away from England and you haven't seen your son for a year and a half. And she never says one word; she behaves beautifully, always."

He had spoken slowly and quietly. He hardly moved. Grant found himself remembering the restlessness, the sparkle, the eyes that strayed towards the glass.

He said, "Yes, Harry. Yes, I see how things are." The story assorted oddly with his last sight of them both, drinking champagne at 21; but he believed it. "That wasn't quite what I meant. I meant, why do you say Van stole her money? It's something of an accusation and——" he paused, "it doesn't happen to be true."

"It is true," Levitt said.

"No."

"Yes."

Grant took his time, thinking back: "I've always been fond of Celia. Never known her well, but liked and admired her instinctively. I'm not surprised that she—ruffles well, as Meredith phrased it. But she's no idea of money; never has had any idea of it." He smiled. "You must have had a chance to find that out yourself."

Levitt did not smile. He said harshly, "She's like me. We aren't naturally wise. We do run into debt. But we pay our debts. Unlike Mr. Valentine West."

Grant held back the big guns. "Wait a minute, Harry. Celia told Van to speculate; not only gave him *carte blanche* to do it, but told him. He didn't want to. He knew he might lose it; and he did lose it; with her full permission."

Levitt said, "Van tell you that?"

"Not only Van."

Now Levitt smiled. "J. G. tell you too?" he asked, exuding the same light, remorseless patience.

Not yet time for the broadside, perhaps. "You mustn't cross-examine me, you know," said Parker gently. "I have my version of those facts, just as you have yours."

"Does your version include the money Celia sent to this country, to protect against devaluation? Van cashed in on that; it was in a joint account. He took the lot; he knew perfectly well that he wasn't entitled to it."

Grant was silent. This might be true or a lie. He had not heard it. But then he had shut his ears to many of the words, Sandra's words and Van's. He found it easier, where Van was concerned, to shut his ears and let his eyes slide off; to accept Van's weak, decorative presence on the fringe of his household. There were plenty of little men on the tacit payroll and Van was, after all, a relative; the only son of Sandra's dead brother, whom she had loved.

He let it go. No broadside was required; there was a flaw in Levitt's story.

"Answer me one question, Harry. Just one. If your accusations are true, why did Celia withdraw the case?"

It was unanswerable and he waited for the climb down.

"That's easy," Levitt said. "If she'd brought it, Van wouldn't have accepted divorce papers. It was a tricky case, but she was going to fight it with all she'd got. Only, those were his terms. And she took them. Because she wanted to marry me. Maybe it doesn't seem to you the best of reasons. But it was an honest one."

True, or a lie? Still holding himself in reserve, Grant was quiet; he tried to assess the man before him.

Curious now, he thought, that the most palpable presence in the room was neither Levitt nor himself, but J. G. Baron. It was J. G. who seemed to be here; arguing frantically against Levitt. Against Levitt's stony conviction, against the words, "She's been so good . . . she behaves beautifully always," the palpable J. G. was fighting; using the words that he had used in the spring of last year:

"Celia's chosen her way . . . washed her hands of her family . . . washed her hands of everything, money included . . . poured a fortune down the drain . . . shiftless and ruthless as well . . . broken my heart . . . broken Van's heart . . . made everybody wretchedly unhappy. . . . No good trying to help Celia, because she won't be helped."

("It's a serious thought," Grant said to the memory, to the palpable advocate, "that I could let you pervert my judgment, J. G. No. You couldn't. You didn't; not really. I cancelled the lunch with Celia because it was too quick, coming on top of all that. I wanted time. You're a strong personality; you've a way of tunnelling into my bloodstream and I wanted to get you out, before I saw her.

"Why not? I like to make up my own mind.")

My own mind. . . . For a moment it looked uncomfortably as though Van and J. G. between them had made it up for him. ("No, not Van. I've never been touched by a word Van said. Van's a cheapjack, a braggart, a liar. It was J. G.

"But surely I gave her another invitation, another chance? Yes, I did. More than one. And she refused. I could ask Levitt why she refused.

"Obvious, though, isn't it? She knew she couldn't justifiably ask me for help. And he has the damned impertinence to do it for her. What's important now is that I don't let him influence me one way or another. He's a slippery customer; he always was a slippery customer. I'm not giving him any more time.")

Let the guns bark, he thought. He wondered for how long he had been silent. Levitt's patience was still there, a monumental calm, challenging him. The figure in the shabby suit, with its still head and hands, waited wearily; the weariness did nothing to diminish the air of certainty.

"Why should I believe you?" Parker flung at him. It was the first thought that he had allowed to come spontaneously into words; suddenly it had become the only question to ask.

"Because I'm telling the truth," said Levitt.

And now Grant found that he was back at his mind's first comment:

"Like Van; only not like Van."

Silence strung out between them.

June, 1951

(i)

When Celia came out of the nursery room, Levitt was on the lawn, with the toy aeroplane. She stood watching him, from the porch. He paced backwards, looking up at the silver thing in the sky, wholly absorbed.

"Why doesn't he tell me what happened? What is this hold-up, this wait? If he doesn't tell me soon, I think I'll die." Behind his head she saw the dark blue sea, the white sails, the brazen sunlight.

She went out on to the lawn.

"Hello, darling. It's a menace," he said, still looking up. "After a bit, one wouldn't do any work at all."

She thought, "Terry could have had it by now; I could have packed it and sent it off."

"Harry——"

"Yes, love."

"Anything happened?"

He turned to look at her; his skin was already brown; he tanned quickly; she could see the light grey hairs above his temples.

"Not yet; no."

"You see——" she said unhappily, and stopped; how to explain, without accusing him, that your hope was down and dwindling; your trust shaken, and the glorious reprieve of two weeks ago turning into a dream? And this was easier to take than the letters that you had to write, the thought of Nanny and Terry waiting.

"I'd rather know," she said. "Always I'd rather know. I do realise how tough it is for you to have to tell me, but can't you tell me?"

He said, "No. Sorry." He began to reel in the line.

"If you did hear from David now that *Searchlight* was out, you'd tell me? You wouldn't keep stringing me along? Promise?"

"Promise."

"I've told you, I do understand how tricky these things are. If it did happen it wouldn't be your fault."

He went on reeling in the line. "Listen, darling, I swear that this is just a hold-up. It's driving me as crazy as it's driving you. It's just a question of waiting."

The wind was unsteady today. Now a down gust caught the aeroplane, rattled its wings and sent its silver beauty diving into the grass. Levitt walked after it, winding up the last spirals of line, stooping to set them free where they caught on plantain or thistle. When the toy lay on the lawn beside the rod, it reminded her of a flying-fish on the deck of a ship.

"Wish we hadn't played with it so much," she said. "It's dented. I'm going down to the village now."

"I'll come with you. Silly little X can wait."

"Got any money?"

He fished in the pocket of his shorts. "A dollar, thirty-five. I'll cash a cheque."

In the newspaper shop he said uneasily, "I want to buy you a lighter; it's time you had another funny lighter. Like this one?"

She accepted the gesture, but not the lighter. "Honestly, darling, we haven't got five dollars to fool with."

"Let's go get the mail. Maybe somebody's sent us five dollars to fool with." He swung her hand in his. He was at his most gentle, but the secret frowning look never left his face.

She did not like the post office any more; the girl at the stamp window would ask when Terry was coming. She did not like the shops on Main Street any more. Some of the things that she had chosen on that one bright day were waiting to be claimed and paid for; toys for Terry, cushions and a length of chintz for curtains. In the shops too there were those who would ask eagerly, "Is he on his way yet?"

"No," Levitt said, standing in front of their box with the mail. "Nothing at all. I'm irked to think of the number of people who sit down at their writing-tables every morning and say 'Well, I don't think I'll sent the Levitts any money today.'"

"All I have is an uncouth demand for a cash settlement," she said. "What do you want for your dinner?"

"Make your funny tomato-thing; and we can have the rest of the cold cuts."

"All right. But we're out of butter. Isn't it odd about butter?"

They bought the butter. Driving home, she said, "Would you like to drive over to Edgartown and dine at the Harbourside?"

"What with, my love, my love?"

"They'll take a cheque on the Vineyard bank."

"Yes, but will the bank?"

"I just thought it would be fun."

They could never tell which of them would next be seized with prudence, which with recklessness. They were always changing rôles. It was like being one person, not two, Celia thought, till you came to the locked door.

"Well, let's have a swim and a drink first; and then see how we feel."

The car chugged up the last of the driveway. "Must turn on the sprinkler," Levitt said and loped off.

She stood beside the lilac bushes, thinking, "I don't know that I can stand another evening of this. If he drank enough he'd tell me. He's being careful not to drink. What the devil went on in New York?" She went into the house, forgetting that the butter was in the back of the car. She got their swimming-suits. They went down the rickety wooden steps from the lawn to the white sand. There were tufts of grass growing in the sand; the empty shore stretched away on either side; the water lay against the hem of grey rocks without a wave. The tide was low; they walked a long way before they plunged.

"Cold," Levitt said, coming up beside her. "Want to go to the raft?"

"Yes, I think so. We ought to haul it in another twenty yards, for Terry."

He reached it ahead of her, gave her a hand to pull her up.

He squatted now, chin on knees; she watched the water trickling down his spine.

"You're too thin," she said.

He did not answer. She heard the small sigh.

She thought, "You are not fair to me. You are lying. When you sigh like that I know it isn't going to be any good. Why can't you say it?"

"That gull looks exactly like Baron," Levitt said. "See? Baron when he's going to quote. Smug. Butter wouldn't melt in its beak."

"Oh, my God. The butter. It will be a pool of oil on the back seat."

"We'll go in, anyway," Levitt said. "A drink would be nice."

When they passed the door of the nursery room, she turned her head away. It was beginning to be a hate, with its unfinished preparations.

"Couldn't you tell me?" she asked him just once more as they crossed the porch. He stood still, looking at her, in his towel robe.

"You've got to wait," he said sadly, "just like me."

He brought her the butter to the kitchen, where she was getting the ice for the drinks.

"Oh, dear."

"Yes. I know. Perhaps it will recover by and by." He grinned at her; his eyes were still vulnerable; he turned away quickly. She laid the limp, reproachful mess of butter in the freezing compartment of the ice-box. The telephone rang.

"I'll go," Levitt said.

There was one cube of ice stuck solidly in the tray. She was still digging at it, when she heard Levitt say, "Hold on, please. It's for you."

"Who?"

"I don't know. New York calling."

The telephone slipped in her cold fingers as she perched on the ledge. "Mrs. Levitt? Mr. Cronin's office . . . Mr. Cronin, I have Mrs. Levitt for you now."

Puzzled, she said, "Hullo, Tim." He had not called her for months.

"Celia. I tried to get you earlier. I guess you know all about this."

"All about what?"

"About——" he stopped. "I've a cheque here for you. Didn't you know?"

"No. I didn't know. A cheque is always nice. What sort of a cheque?" She was looking out of the window; she could see the lilac bush, the hood of the car, the thin pines.

"Mean to say," Tim said, "that this comes as a complete surprise?"

"Well, yes, it does. Whose cheque? How much?"

She heard him chuckle. "Quite a nice sum. Five thousand dollars; with a note saying that further repayments will be made regularly. The cheque's signed by Mr. Valentine West, but the note comes from Grant Parker's office. Of course I thought you——"

She lost the words. She was still staring at the lilac bush, at the hood of the car, at the pine trees.

It was over. That was all she knew, in a second of icy quiet, a second through which she heard time walk, from the past to the present, changing the world.

The cold quiet broke; into a sound like the noise of bells.

"Are you there, Celia?"

"I can't talk. D'you mind?"

She went past Levitt in a blind stride; she thought that she said, "It's over," but she was not sure. She was out on the grass, looking at the sea.

There was still the noise of bells; for a moment it was that; then the hurricane hoofs of the winged horse beating; the soaring rush that thundered you up to the throne of God to shout your thanks in his face; it was light that blazed.

Then she looked down at the grass and saw the toy aeroplane lying there beside its rod; the slight silver shape, dented where it had hit the rocks.

Levitt came towards her from the house. "I needn't pack it up," she said, "I thought I'd have to pack it up."

(ii)

Levitt added the last lines to the lay-out in front of him, rose,
stretched and wandered on to the porch. It was an afternoon of
sunshine and light wind; the canopy flapped over his head. The
four o'clock ferry went past, a blunt white shape on the blue.
He idled on the lawn, watching it. The boy who had been
putting up the shutters at the nursery windows appeared at the
newly-painted door.

"All through now, Mr. Levitt."

"Oh, fine. What do I owe you?"

"That'll be three dollars."

Levitt walked in to look at it; it was not yet in order. It was
all new chintz and new paint and new things. There was a
child's desk furnished with pens and pencils; a brass telescope; a
paint-box. Wrapped packages stood on the floor. The set of
island water-colours, not yet hung, leaned against the wainscot.

He saw that the table was still occupied by the scrapbooks,
the pot of paste, the scissors, tools of the private task from
which he had learned to avert his eyes. She had been at the task
today. An English *Times Weekly* edition lay open, with a page
cut from it.

He thought idly, "I wonder if she'll still keep the scrapbooks after Terry gets here."

He did not care any more. It was a sudden discovery, standing
there in the doorway, looking at the room. It was as sudden as
the death of inspiration, the dry, "Oh, what the hell?" taking the
whole fabric apart.

He saw that he was at the end of his hatred. Probably he had
been at the end of it for a long time; he hadn't looked; he had
taken for granted the fact that it still survived; the poison
blowing from England. And it was finished. Whether it owed
its end simply to a year's attrition, whether to the golden
peace of this time, he did not know. Perhaps it had died ten
days ago, with the deeper note of Celia's voice, saying, "You
did it. . . . You did that for me," and the rest of the words that

he could still remember, would always remember, the accolade of words.

He lit a cigarette and stared about the room. The sea wind fluttered the chintz curtains and the sunlight was strong; it winked on the brass telescope and the black japanned lid of the paint-box. A memory came back: of standing in a New York apartment, thinking, in a pale forecast of this moment's tenderness, that he was looking at the shell of Celia. What he saw here now was the shell of Celia's happiness.

Perhaps it was the habit of loving that could kill hate. Whatever it was, he knew that he could loiter and open the locked door in his mind.

He leaned against the lintel, hands in pockets, looking back. He could see the London house, the long room where he had waited for Carey. He could see Carey limping down the three steps, the look on Carey's face as he came to stab and end the dream. He could hear the words.

It was all quite flat; the colour and the dimensions had left the scene. He played it through like a gramophone record in his head and knew that its power was gone. Liz and his first lesson in loving, the song in the garden, the fast-fallen shadow; Carey in his shape of a smug avenging angel, Carey the winner; they were so dim beside this present that the mind yawned at them, said, "Oh, what the hell?" and set them aside.

A new wind of freedom blew.

"Thank you," Levitt said after a little while.

Utterly at peace in the discovery, he lingered. He moved to the table, stood looking down at the scrapbook. Tenderly, without any sensation of spying, he opened it. He saw that she had pasted into it Nanny's cable that confirmed the sailing-date. Tenderly and without any sensation of spying, he turned the pages back. Glane; Carlington; and now a shiny half-page cut from a magazine. He saw the head and shoulders of a man looking up at a statue, whose sharp exquisite shadow fell on white stone.

Levitt felt himself frown; his forehead wrinkling as though by its own will. It was a queer feeling.

It was chance, of course; it was nothing.

He turned more pages back, and came to a press-cutting from the London *Times*:

GLANE MEMORIAL PRIZE AWARD

He read the paragraph. He was still curious, still diverted.

He turned another page, and here it leaped at him, the same statue in plaster, a professional photograph; the cast was sideways on to the camera; the lines were sharp.

"Not possible," Levitt said to himself.

He looked away from it, looked back.

He went out and across the porch, into the house and up the stairs to his room. His jacket hung on the back of a chair. He took the wallet from the inside pocket and carried it down.

"I have to see," he said to himself. "I have to see. I may be wrong. When I put the one beside the other, they may look quite different. It is so long since I looked at it; I may have forgotten."

He came back to the table, to the open book. From the back of the wallet he drew out the folded sheet of paper, the thin sheet with the darkened edge. He spread it on the table, flattening the four creases carefully. He went on staring for a long time. Then he turned more pages of the book. He heard the sound of the car on the other side of the house. Still he could not move. Only when he saw Celia come past the window did he shut the scrapbook and push the drawing into his pocket. It was the same quick gesture that he had made in the London room when he heard Carey coming.

(iii)

Now there was the lamplight and the silence in the room, the gentle buffet of the sea outside and the book fallen on his knee. Celia said, "I think I'm tired. Any views about bed?"

"Be with you in a minute."

He looked up at her as she paused beside his chair. He made an effort. "Next week," he said. "They sail next week."

"Yes. You all right?"

"I'm all right."

"You look—" she stopped.

"Look how?"

"Sort of haunted. You have, all evening. Nothing worrying you, is there?"

He took her hands. "We're through with worries," he said. But he was seeing her through glass; he wanted to be alone. After a moment she kissed his forehead and went out.

At once he relaxed. He poured himself a glass of beer and returned to the arm-chair. The re-stating of the thoughts that he had had since afternoon began; he would have liked to write them down:

"That couldn't happen. At first I thought it could, because nobody has ever seen the winged horse, not even Celia. At first it looked like funny magic; and that was all right; it was crazy, but it was all right. Until I put the drawing down beside the photograph of the cast.

"I wish I still thought it was magic. I'd forgotten the thinness of the paper. It went through; of course it went through. You found those lines on the block. You traced them. It couldn't have happened any other way.

"But what went on in your head, Carey? Did you know it was mine? Did you say 'That's Levitt's horse'? You must have known. I'd been sitting there, waiting for you; at that table, with the drawing-blocks.

"Wait a minute. Justice; justice. Suppose you carried the block away from Celia's house, without looking at it . . . only found the imprint long afterwards. No; that won't do; those lines wouldn't stay. It couldn't have been long afterwards.

"No, Carey. I don't think I can get you out of this one. You knew it was mine; and you took it. Perhaps in your morality, it's all right, to take a drawing that isn't yours and to make a statue from it. Perhaps you don't think you owe it to me.

"And that is where you're wrong. And it isn't the only thing you owe me. You owe me the Glane Memorial Prize; you owe me all those pretty paragraphs; you owe me the fact that you're famous now, not just a dull competent craftsman. They build you big, those paragraphs. No; it was I who built you big. I began it. J. G. carried it on. J. G. liked the horse, didn't he, Carey? What happened to the boy with the fawn? I guess it's still in the studio, or somewhere down in the garden; but J. G. takes his Sunday mob across the lawn, between the yews, up those steps, to look at the winged horse.

"If it had been any other drawing I'd ever done, I wouldn't care. You could set up a statue from any old sketch of mine and I'd have no kick. But this one's different.

"It's the only beautiful thing I've ever done. I'd forgotten, until today, how beautiful it was. Don't ask me how it happened; I don't know how it happened. I never could before and my guess is that I never will again. It just came, that day; the day when I was utterly, completely happy. I sat there and my heart drew it; my love drew it; it is my horse.

"You took everything that day, didn't you, Carey?"

Now he felt the grin of the fox. He didn't want it to come, but he knew that it was there. (In the mirror; if you looked, only you didn't look in mirrors now.) He went on with the re-statement:

"I've stopped feeling as though you'd hit me in the face. I've had that feeling twice now. Once on the December morning; once this afternoon, after I'd put the drawing down beside the photograph. Thinking of the prize; thinking of the Royal opening of Glane; you'll wear a tail-coat, Carey, I shouldn't wonder, and the King will shake your hand . . . all that, I thought, and me just sitting here . . . Levitt who isn't Levitt any more. Levitt who draws an obscene little girl for a Boston comic strip and sells a cartoon on the side when times are good; Levitt who missed out on *Searchlight*; Levitt who's lucky to have a job at all; Carey up and Levitt down: so goddamned unfair it kills you. That's the way it felt when I was sitting at the table, looking at the scrapbooks. That's over.

"I'm almost grateful now; almost enjoying it. It's as if, somewhere inside, I always knew that you'd do this; always hated you for that St. Michael façade, that easy, golden-hero smugness; simply because, with the eye that I used to have, I could see through it. Remember our talk on the Ashford train, Carey? I sketched you on the menu; you didn't like what I saw. What did I see?

"I saw this coming, Carey.

"I saw the weakness, the shadow, the secret.

"That's what I realise now. And it makes me feel better about all of it. Wonderful, how much I can dig out of the old days, and feel better. I've been right back, since dinner, sitting here, remembering; even to a minute before I met you, a minute in the ship going to England. A story I told; Celia saying that you told it too, but without my embellishments; me saying, 'Truthful fellow, Carey?'

"Are you a truthful fellow, Carey?

"Let's apply the justice formula once again. Did you by any chance tell J. G., tell any of them—where you got those lines? No. If you had, Celia would know, and Celia would have talked to me.

"You could have written to me, couldn't you? Even if you didn't tell them. You've had a year and a half to talk in, Carey; and you haven't talked.

"It's quite a present you've given me today. Just as I'd stopped hating you, too. I have to make up my mind just what I'm going to do with this pretty present. I don't want to decide in a hurry. There's no hurry. I've got you, Carey. Maybe I always wanted to get you."

He shut his eyes. He did not like the way that it was going. He thought of the brief, earlier freedom, the new wind blowing, the knowledge that he did not hate any more.

"By God, he took that, too. He takes everything."

"Wait. He hasn't taken everything. He hasn't touched Celia; nor this house, nor your life here. Nor the words that Celia said to you ten days ago. They're safe. They're more important than anything. Don't endanger them. Go to Celia;

talk to her; tell her. Don't lock another door; don't let old darknesses in."

"Darknesses? This is light. Light on all of it. Light on everything."

"No."

"It makes me feel strong."

"Surely. That's the danger."

"I've been down so low in my mind—about me."

"You were safer down, weren't you?"

"Safer? What can hurt me in this? It's Carey who's going to be hurt."

"By you?"

"By the truth."

"Leave the truth to God, Levitt. For all you know, it's hurting him now."

"Like hell it is. He's a thief and he's on top of the world. He's going to get what's coming to him. I'll see to that."

(iv)

Upstairs in the bedroom Celia waited for him. She could hear the small, occasional noises from the room below; the creak of the floorboards as he rose; the steps coming back to the chair; then, after the silence, the creak of the boards again.

It made her feel alone, the unexplained vigil that he was keeping down there.

"What happened while I was out of the house? Why was he different when I came back? Why did he talk of Carey tonight? Carey and the Memorial Prize. . . . He never talks of Carey. Those short, abrupt questions and then no comment; just 'I see'; 'I get it.' Why did he want to know the story of the prize? Why has he sat so quietly, frowning, looking into a place in his mind and not liking what he sees?"

She was back at disquiet, at the Knave of Spades; at the dark thing. And this was cruel after what had happened so recently, to him and to her. After the sight of his courage, after the knowledge that he had taken his worst private hurdle for her sake; had gone out in the face of humiliation to see that justice was done.

Was there another private hurdle still to be taken? Yes, there was; always she had known it, without a clue to it. Another trial awaiting him, by which he must be broken, and perhaps renewed.

"And tonight, I think it is here."

Sorrowfully she weighed the new trust, the new honour, the respect that had made her look at him and think, "Now I can have your child."

This must not be destroyed.

Yet the quiet footsteps were destroying it; they were treading it down, as she listened to the creak of the boards.

Now the door of the living-room opened and shut. She heard him come up the stairs. She waited.

June, 1951, England

(i)

"AND here," said Baron, as he opened the garden door and strolled out on to the terrace, "is the place where peace begins. First thing I do every Sunday morning, stand here and praise God."

The nurse said carefully, "It's a beautiful view." He didn't like the nurse; if he dared, he would get rid of her tomorrow. The heart attack had been slight; no cause for anxiety, they told him. If it were not for the approaching ceremonies at Glane, he would have been back on the job in London a week ago. But he had to cosset himself a little, with Glane ahead. Not that it was bad fun, in this weather, to make Carlington his headquarters. He leaned on his stick, looking towards the green on the marsh, the blue dazzle beyond the green. His breathing still troubled him.

The nurse settled him in his chair on the terrace. Mather came out with the appointment list. The Sunday visitors were heavily restricted, but he could fill his day without them. He looked at his watch. "Tell that lily-of-the-valley I'm waiting."

"Mr. Lynn, sir?"

"Mr. Lynn. If he's still in bed, kick him out."

Gerald forestalled him, appearing now at the garden door. He wore a sky-blue sweater and coffee-coloured corduroys. His camera was slung over his shoulder. "Not late, am I, dear?"

"Of course you're late. What were you doing?"

"Standing at my window, praising God," said Gerald, with winsome acidity.

"You shut your trap."

"In fact I got to Mass. And about time too. How are you feeling, Baron?"

"Magnificent, thank you. Who could feel otherwise, in this glorious place?"

Gerald perched on the terrace wall beside him. "Fat, forty and still faunlike," J. G.'s mind commented. Aloud he said, "Sunday in the air; one can feel it, can't one? Sunday to me will always mean the church bells over the marsh."

Gerald looked at him slantingly. "I do wish you'd let me stick to my original idea and open the series with a portrait of you. That sort of remark has just the touch of phony charm I want."

"Phony charm," said Baron; "that's what I get for talking from the heart."

"Ah—but you can't put out its pulsings except in phony phrases," said Gerald, wagging a finger, "any more than I can. If my mother died tomorrow, I should be heartbroken; but the most perfectly shaped and printable comment would *spring* to my lips."

"Not to mention to your typewriter."

"Of course." He put his head on one side. "Baron, darling; change your mind. You're a natural for the series; the first Happy Man."

"Would you call me a happy man, Gerald, seriously?" He heard the wistful note in his voice.

"My dear, of course I wouldn't. Down below you're *seething* with Freudian serpents. I'm talking of the way you'd come out on the page." He waved his arms. "Why I Am A Happy Man, by James Baron. June morning. Golden success. Looking back down the long vista of a fruitful life. At peace with the world, and with my own family: the great family of the English people whom I have striven to serve."

"Quite sickening," said Baron, "and I rather cotton to it. But the whole purpose of the series, as you and I agreed, is to show that England is still a place where *young* men can be happy." (He had had some difficulty in dissuading Gerald from beginning the series with Gerald Lynn. "To my public I am a *frozen* twenty-five," Gerald had protested.)

"You run along to Anthony," Baron said. "He's expecting you. He and Liz will give you lunch. I don't want to set eyes on you till dinner-time."

"Charm, charm," Gerald sighed. He jumped off the wall, blew Baron a kiss and scampered away, the wide corduroys flapping.

"Here," Baron called after him. "You can go by that path, you know; under the wall."

"Yes, darling. But I wanted another look at the horse first; I'm full of the prettiest schemes." He went round the corner of the house and out of sight.

Having spied for the nurse, Baron lit a surreptitious cigarette. Gerald's prattle never upset him. It was only because he was not yet quite well that one phrase lodged and tingled: "At peace with my own family." Was it tact that had made Gerald turn that phrase so rapidly into journalese?

"My family . . ." Baron thought, "Tobias dead; Celia married to that gangster and living in America. Terry leaving us this week. Dear little boy; I shall miss him horribly."

("No, you won't," said the still, small, hateful voice inside. "That's just an act. You aren't so fond of Terry. He's Terry West; and the baby born to Liz will be Baby Carey. Not Baron. There'll never be another Baron.")

"If Tobias had lived. . . . No," he said to the shadowy mood,

"I won't give in to this. I'm a happy man; every bit as happy as dear old Anthony, with his glorious success and his marriage and the baby coming." He chuckled. "I believe it's pure happiness and nothing else that's making the fellow put on weight."

(ii)

Gerald Lynn strolled through the gap in the yews and crossed the lawn. At the top of the three white steps there was the white stone shell, like a shrine before the black cypresses, and the bronze horse standing in the shrine. Once again, its beauty halted him. As when he first saw it, he had the sensation that he was looking at something he knew well; a classic; oddly familiar, oddly compelling. "You have to stare, and go on staring; the way that you go on staring at the sea.

"*Most* curious, the look he has, of standing in the sky. When one thinks of a winged horse, one imagines him in flight, like all the conventional drawings, like the Mobilgas advertisements; clever of Anthony to make him stand still; he's more impressive standing still. Those lines are flying lines. The head is uncanny; I could *swear* those nostrils breathe." He stared at the burnished head, the glowing flank, the arch of the wings.

It was a rich patina; Anthony's own trick or the bronze-founder's trick? The velvet-brown, the coppery glint and the gold took the sunlight. "And like *cream* under the hand, it would be," Gerald said to himself. "But to pat this majestic beast would make me shy."

He took his camera from the case. There were enough photographs of the horse already; there would be more next week, after the Glane ceremony. But he liked to illustrate his work with his own photographs. He paced, choosing the angle.

"Hullo; how do you do, good-morning," said a voice behind him. He turned and saw Terry West. Terry had now, he thought, a merciless beauty; he never smiled; his eyes had heavy lids, like Celia's and J. G.'s; Celia's full lips; these gave him the look of a stone cherub.

"Why are you taking a picture of it? Do you like it?" The voice was soft and full, emphasising all the words, rounding them.

"Yes, I do. Very much. I hear you're off to America."

Terry nodded.

"I've just come back from there."

"May I take a picture, please?"

"Yes; mind if I hold it for you, though? It's a *very* peculiar camera. Now you press that little thing, there. . . . And when the picture comes out in the paper, you can tell everybody you took it. I'll send you one to America."

"Thank you very much. The horse has *been* in the papers."

"I know. But this one will be in an article about your Uncle Anthony. I'm writing the article."

"Will he mind?"

"I hope not."

Terry's eye wandered. He looked at the horse. "And he walks up and *down*, up and *down*," he said in a sing-song, talking to himself. "From here to *here* and from here to *here*."

"Who does? The horse?"

Terry gave him a look of contempt. "Not the *horse*, no; it couldn't. Uncle Anthony. Very early in the morning. I see him out of the window." He took a compass from his pocket and laid it in the palm of his hand.

"You're N.N.E.," he said.

"What d'you mean about your uncle walking up and down?" Gerald asked.

"I told you. In the morning, early. He walks from here to *here*; and from *here* to here." After another intense scrutiny of the compass, he said, "I must go now. I want to feed my dog." At the gap in the yews he turned and shouted suddenly, "*No time to play with the giraffe!*"

Alone, Gerald bowed a little to the horse and went. Crossing the end of the terrace, he waved to Baron in his chair, then took the path under the wall to the white gate.

He halted, looking at the cobbled yard, the coach-house studio with the wrought-iron sign above the door. Two white doves were flirting on the roof. "All very amiable," Gerald thought; "we'll have a picture." He took the snapshot and then knocked at the door.

"Hullo," said Anthony Carey.

"Looks like a great handsome butcher in that blue coat," Gerald thought. He walked in; the smell of plasticine hung in the air. There was a half-worked sketch on the stand, wax being built up on a small iron armature; it looked like a lion.

"All wrong, so far. Tame," Anthony said. "They want two lions for the new Eppersley building. Old Eppersley's on the prowl, but the lion, as you might say, isn't. Or not yet." He grinned at it benignly, hands on hips. He was most certainly the right choice for the happy man; Gerald had forgotten the enduring smile, the solid golden feeling about him. It was now several months since he had set foot in the studio and it impressed him again with its ample spaces, the completeness of its equipment.

"Go on working," he said. "I too will prowl." He made notes as he went; he studied the practical essential drawings, muscles of a leg, a forearm, a foot; the tools of the trade interested him; the articulated skeleton, the profuse collection of compasses, calipers, rulers and triangles. It was easy to make Carey talk shop.

"A sculptor," said Carey, "besides being an artist, ought to be a medical student, a mathematician and a mechanical engineer, with some of the talents of a cook, some of the knowledge of a metallurgist, and the qualifications of a steeplejack.

"In this day and age we're a bunch of sissies. All the phases have become separate crafts. Plaster moulding and casting, enlarging, stone-cutting and founding. There isn't one sculptor in a thousand, these decadent and enfeebled times, who can do all of them." He limped away from the working stand. "Take Cellini; the bumptious bastard could not only do all those things, but silver-smithing, gold-smithing, enamelling and stone-setting as well. He still had time for the girls—in a comprehensive way—and besides that he was a gunsmith and a cannoneer."

He went to the sink, scrubbed his hands, cleaned his nails, and lit a pipe. The sunlight was strong on his profile. "Queer, that little twitch of the eyelid," Gerald thought, "nervous thing. He was through the war, of course."

"Don't let's take Cellini, dear, please. Though it's all very interesting. What I have to take today is you."

"Oh dear," said Carey. "I knew it would be. I was warned. Honestly, I could murder J. G. for letting me in for this. I'm no earthly good at talking about me."

"Hold that pose," Gerald cried. "*Terribly* effective, with the cast behind you. Thank you. Now, don't be difficult. I'm the most painless interviewer; *practically* do it all under an anæsthetic. Don't you think the series rather a good idea?"

"I don't know about the series. J. G. just said you wanted to interview me. Give you my private life on a plate was how he put it."

"Well, yes; your *entrails*, in fact." Gerald perched on the edge of the drawing-table. "But the series—so good, I think. We're calling it 'Why I Am A Happy Man.' "

Carey said, "Oh," and continued to look benign, but unimpressed.

"I get so tired of all the gloom and doom, don't you? I've just had six weeks in America with everybody concluding, in the *politest* way of course, that we're finished. It occurred to me on the boat—surely there are *some* people in this country who are doing exactly what they want to do with their lives—not counting Socialists; I'm a terrible Tory and I'm sure you are. J. G. adores the idea, of course, provided I keep the right stress on private enterprise. What do you *think*?"

"Well, of course," said Carey slowly. "I see what you mean."

"And to have you for the first, ties in wonderfully with the Glane ceremony; can't begin to *tell* you, dear, how glad I'll be when Glane really is given to the public at last and I can stop writing about it. I feel as if I'd been going to have a baby for two years; as to which, *how* is Liz?"

"She's pretty well," said Anthony. "Let's go up to the house and find her; getting on for lunch-time." He stripped off his blue overall. "I could do with some food, too; didn't quite know what time you were coming, so I went to Early Service instead of the eleven o'clock."

"Am I in the presence of a *practising* Protestant?" Gerald fluttered.

Carey grinned still more. "You are, indeed. Does it worry you?"

"Not a bit, darling; fascinates me. Do tell me——"

"Can't talk religion, I fear," said Carey in the doorway. "Never could."

"No," said Gerald wistfully, "I was afraid of that."

"But if it's a recipe for happiness you want," Carey added as they crossed the yard, "I can give it to you in a nutshell. It's entirely dependent on living according to your credo."

This, Gerald thought, was somehow surprising; it was a good trite truth, but it was early in the game for abstracts. It was said briskly, finally and at once dismissed. "Pretty little house, isn't it?" said Carey, as they came under the arch from the yard. "Queen Anne. Been in the family since it was built."

"*Too* feudal. Is the churchyard *full* of Careys?"

"Stiff with them, yes." He led the way into a small white-panelled room. "Liz won't be long. Let's have a drink."

"I don't drink, isn't it awful?" said Gerald.

"Not awful at all. Highly worthy. Don't you ever?" He looked at Gerald admiringly, holding the whisky decanter in his hand; with his left cheek to the light, the twitching eyelid was visible again.

"Occasionally I dip my nose into a glass of champagne, but it's always quite fatal."

Carey said, "Afraid I like all the good things of this world; suppose that's why I'm getting fat."

"You have put on a little weight, haven't you? I'm always so glad when other people do. D'you diet at all?"

"Good God, no," said Carey.

"So difficult socially, isn't it?" Gerald said. "People act as though you'd shot them through the heart when you won't take potatoes. And of course not to drink is one worse. I spend my entire time in America having my mouth *held* open and drinks *poured* down. Liz, darling, how lovely to see you."

She was as beautiful as ever, as childish as ever. He found it hard to realise that she was married to Anthony. ("And really the baby doesn't *show* at all; of course it's early yet, and those long-legged people *don't* show.")

"Gerald," her voice had the comically mournful ring that he remembered. "How very nice for us to have you; I was afraid it would be one of J. G.'s opprobrious young men with bright keen news-hawk faces. *Did* you see Celia—first thing I want to know?"

"Not this time. Nobody does. She was up on her island, immured. I talked to her on the telephone."

"Oh, tell."

"She was very funny about a sauce that had just *divided*, or whatever it is sauces shouldn't do."

"Celia cooking," Liz murmured. "It's still profoundly mysterious to me."

"She seems very happy with her Levitt."

"Nice chap, Levitt," said Carey. "We hoped they'd get over before this."

"No drink?" Liz said to Gerald. "Oh, sad. I don't, you see, and this poor Carey was looking forward to having somebody to drink with. He has endless drinks alone."

"Shut up, darling," said Carey, good-humouredly. "You make me sound like a soak."

"By my standards, you are."

"Now Gerald will print that," said Carey, pouring himself another drink. "Among aids to happiness, Mr. Anthony Carey confidently lists alcoholism."

"It isn't about happiness, is it, Gerald?"

"Well, yes, dear; why not?"

"I never know how anybody can think of anything to say about happiness. Either it's there or it isn't, like a cold in the head. And I'm sure," she said moodily, "that you only really recognise it when it stops."

"Unlike a cold in the head," said Carey; his left eyelid went on twitching.

(iii)

"Well, now, that wasn't really so difficult, was it?" Gerald pleaded. "I'm almost finished."

Carey watched him; he was perched once again on the drawing-table in the studio, feathering through his notes. "The only thing that irks me a little is that it's almost too much of a floral tribute to Baron. I don't *want* to represent the old monster as your fairy godfather."

"But he is, y'know," said Carey, sucking at his pipe. ("I could expand that, couldn't I? I could tell you, Lynn, just how much I do owe to J. G.")

"Do you really mean that you weren't going to submit the horse for the Glane prize until Baron persuaded you?"

"No, I wasn't; that's quite true. It seemed to me a private thing—a family property, if you like. I meant it for Tobias. But J. G. overruled me."

"Well, I'm cutting that right out," said Gerald. "Next thing you'll tell me is that he designed the horse himself."

" 'Et's roight," said Carey in Cockney. "Came in here one morning and found him modelling away like a madman."

Gerald poised his pencil. "You've given me an idea. Can you remember your actual moment of inspiration? I mean, we know that it was originally inspired by the poem, but could you tell me just how and when you suddenly said to yourself, 'That's what I'll do'? See where I'm going, dear? I'd like to end on the *corniest* little paragraph, tying happiness to inspiration."

He waited with his pencil poised. Carey struck a match.

"I'd made several shots at the horse before, you know," he said. "But this one——"

He paused. In a moment of light-headedness he tricked himself into believing that he could open his mouth upon certain words once rehearsed, that he would tell this story.

BOOK V

"MY NEW-CUT ASHLAR"

(December, 1949—June, 1951)

"MY NEW-CUT ASHLAR"

December, 1949

(i)

THE door of the studio-room in Celia's house shut, and Carey stood alone; he wanted to go after Levitt. There must be something more that he could do or say. The last savage speech had not hurt him. He wrote it off as forgivable. Levitt would be sorry for the things that he had said; Levitt was all right; Levitt simply had the misfortune to love Liz; unlucky Levitt, lucky Carey.

"God, how he minds," Anthony said to himself. "Somehow I didn't expect it to be so bad. Persuading myself all the way up to town that he might be relieved; that it might have been a spur-of-the-moment mistake for him too. Wishful thinking; trying to make it easier for me in my own head."

He paced the floor. "Poor devil; and even though I mean that, it still sounds patronising. Of course it does. It can't not. I've won; and perhaps if it hadn't been for Levitt I'd never have won. Liz, the beloved donkey, might have kept quiet for years; and I might in time have got myself married to a second-best blonde." He could not help standing still, grinning at his future.

It was all improbable now; shadowy in his mind already, the moment of early morning, the urgent voice in the dark. He played it back, from her hysteria and his sleepy efforts to soothe her, through all the incoherent talk, to the words that came out at last with the tears: "You—you're the only person I'll ever love, and I don't care if I do shock you by saying it."

"Beloved donkey," he said again. "Oh, my love, my love. And if I were Levitt, I think I'd cut my throat."

He wondered what Levitt would do. "Hide now and lick his wounds, I suppose. Lucky, in one way; he's got a two months' reprieve from all of us. Would have been a little too tough to carry on in London and Carlington after this. He'll be hating me a lot less by the time he gets back. But I'd like to see him before he goes, somehow."

He could not telephone Liz yet. Levitt's pain and anger still seemed to be here, in the room, all over the room. He would have liked another chance to sketch Terry; nothing like work for putting one back on an even keel; but when Nanny opened the door to him, she had told him that Terry was in bed.

He wandered to the table where he had left the drawing-blocks and sketches. He switched on the lamp; the dun after-noon light promised fog; it had been misty on the road coming up. He saw that one block was pulled to the edge of the table; his pencils were scattered.

"Levitt using them?" he wondered. He lifted the block. It tilted and the light fell on strange lines; he could see a dazzled imprint here. It reminded him of prints that he had once seen in the snow. Ski-ing in Austria, he had found the heraldic trace of wings on the bright surface, the marks that the choughs had left.

He held the block at the same angle, closer to the lamp.

"Looks like a horse; a horse with wings. Who's been drawing a winged horse, I ask myself?"

He straightened the block and the horse vanished.

Sitting down at the table, he picked a soft black pencil and began to scribble to and fro lightly, across the page. Yes, here they came, the deep white lines, strong and clear below the surface scribble. He went on down the page until he had it all. Now it looked like a thin white carving in relief on dark stone.

"Lord," Carey said, "that's the horse, all right. As I wanted to make him once, for Liz, for Tobias. He's a beauty. That's the horse . . . as he ought to be."

"And look who made him," said an astonished whisper in his mind.

"Can't believe he did, though," Carey retorted. "This isn't Levitt's work, I'll swear."

"Of course it is. Who else could have done it? He was waiting for you. He drew on the top sheet and tore it off and the lines came through; it's thin paper."

Carey rubbed his forehead perplexedly. "Levitt . . . but it's asking oneself to believe that a chap who writes lampoons could write an Elizabethan lyric. Well, maybe he could; maybe he did." He studied the horse from all angles.

"Jealous, eh? I believe you are. Just because it was always your ambition to draw it. And it's perfect. It damn well is perfect. I can't stop staring. . . . Don't know what it's got exactly; some trick in the economy of line that gives the soaring look. Yet he doesn't soar. But he's standing on cloud, this horse."

After a moment he saw something else; he shaded the lower right-hand corner with the pencil. "Might be his signature; might not. It's a scribble of a sort. Well, good luck to you, Levitt; don't I wish I'd done it? You—who have said again and again that you couldn't draw anything beautiful if you tried . . . remember saying to me that if you were given the Botticelli Venus as model, you'd turn her into a leering whore?"

There was an illogical comfort in wondering suddenly if this were a copy; if Levitt had found it in a book; or in a museum, and drawn from memory.

"Why should I care? Well, I can see why. The Winged Horse is so much ours; can't help feeling that it belongs to all of us, to Toby and Celia and Liz and me. Here," he said to himself. "You'd better ring up Liz." After a moment's hesitation he pushed the tracing under the top page of the block. He would certainly keep it. As he picked up the telephone, he saw how quickly the fog had come down. The garden was gone from the windows; false night was beginning.

"Darling."

"Oh, Carey," he heard the gusty, contented sigh.

"How are you now, sweetheart?"

"I don't know. I spin in a haze. It *was* true, wasn't it? It did happen."

"If you're in any doubt," he said, "I'll remind you that we are engaged to be married."

"I will try not to be in doubt. I haven't told anybody, except Prince. What happened, with——" the voice stopped.

"With Harry?" He paused. "Well, I've seen him. I've told him."

"Hell," she said, "I ought to have done it myself; I can tell by your voice. I am gutless and worthless."

"Yes, darling."

"Was it awful?"

"Pretty awful," said Carey, having struggled to lie.

"Yes . . . I don't really know if I want to hear about it or not."

"Take off that hair-shirt, please. Anyway," he said, "those things happen. People get over them. Don't spend all night brooding. I love you and you love me."

"Very odd," she said. "Are you coming back tonight? There's thick fog here."

"Here too."

"Please don't drive in fog. I'll die of worry and this would be a pity now."

Anthony laughed. "I'll telephone the A.A. and see what the roads are like."

"Promise not to come if it's bad? I would far rather pine alone with soup."

"Pine you probably will, my pretty. Me, too. Shall I tell Celia? About us?"

"Oh, yes, I think. Give her my love. Will you stay there?"

"If she'll have me. Otherwise I'll go to the club."

"*Don't* get run over."

"I never do," said Anthony.

After he had got the report on the roads, he decided to stay. He went back to the table; he pulled his tracing out from below the top sheet of the block. He shook his head and smiled helplessly . . . "*Lord*, it's lovely. No need to be sorry for anyone who can do that." The thought sounded an echo; months ago, when he had stood in the cellar beneath his studio, looking at the cast that Jane Ireland had made.

"Would you like a cup of tea, Mr. Anthony?"

"Oh, hullo, Nanny. Yes, I think I rather would."

She said, "Don't you want more light in here? It's getting terribly dark."

He drank his tea. Then he began to work, with the tracing clipped to the board that he had been using for the sketches of Terry, and a series of dots on the clean paper before him. Once he had the measurements, he made a neat job of the view from the other side. Now he began to feel confident and gay. He sketched a possible front view. It had some authority, he thought. He had made careful studies of a horse's skull and kept them. There was a Greek horse that he liked; he would look at it again when he got back to the studio; make further sketches; then it would be a matter of getting to work with proportional compasses.

And then?

"Well, then it'll be time to tell Harry Levitt that I'm setting up the model for Toby's memorial from his idea. To hell with the boy with the fawn," said Carey. "This is it."

He sat there, grinning and excited. He unclipped the tracing from the board, seeing the shadow of his arm fall, large and black, across the lovely outline.

Then he heard, far down the passage, the slam of the front door. Celia had come home. He did not know what urgency was here now, making him fold the sheets quickly and thrust them into his breast pocket, as though he had something to hide. As soon as he had done it, he was perplexed. A dark cloud of depression came without warning, like a black tent dropped on his head; it muffled all happiness. He crossed the floor, limped up the three steps. He walked slowly down the unlit passage to meet Celia.

(ii)

Anthony took the thin white rag off the model and stared at
it. It was still secret. He had not thought it would remain
private and precious for so long. But these three weeks had
gone by to a galloping tune, to the Winged Horse tune itself.
The careless happiness reminded him now of the days in Paris;
days when he was a student at Julien's, confidently believing
that his name would go down to history with the giants. It
seemed to him, turning the revolving top of the stand, that he had
at last proved the truth of all that the younger, furiously-
diligent Carey had studied and believed. The old phrases were
back in his head, "Tools should be the extension of your
fingers", "Work by the shadows", "*Il faut attraper les accidents
et les convertir en science*"; all day he rediscovered the old
moods of the young man, and could not tell for certain how much
of the strenuous hope he owed to the horse in the making, how
much to love.

The studio was different. The short light of the December
days had become a challenge, and the studio itself the holder of
the secret, to which he hurried with the tune in his head when it
was still too dark to see clearly. He would stand at the door,
looking down its length, thinking that the statues he saw were
not his; the black marble puma, the wrestling men, stood with a
new authority, all their familiar faults lost in the kindly shadows
of early morning. Oh, yes, they were his, but with a difference.
It was as though he were staring at the truth that could never be
recaptured, the artist's dream in his head before he destroyed it
with his hands.

Then, intimidated, he would go to the new dream; and all the
way, so far, it had been magically preserved; the drawings on
squared paper, with the arcs and lines set about them by the
compass, were authoritative. He studied them now as he had
studied some Raphael sketches in the Louvre, a certain Leonardo
hand or the Leonardo skull in sections.

The jump from the drawings to the first model had frightened him to death. Looking back, he thought that that was the worst of it, that he had gone about it in a kind of nervous dream, the way that he had gone into action often during the war. (That was the day that he forgot to go over to Carlington for lunch and he remembered leaping like a trout when Foliot knocked at the door.) But his hands had stayed steady; his eyes had not failed him; the first model had survived; he could see it now; the little horse on the shelf above the work bench; the rough sketch was a delicate and faithful job.

And here on the heavy stand the last model, the thirty-eight-inch horse, was as good today as he had been under the tired, searching eyes of Carey last night.

"Good enough," Carey said. It was a source of pride to him that his remorseless technique had prevailed over the infernal excitement of making this thing. He was safe now. He had feared that the iron armature might stiffen and devitalise the horse; it was not so. He was tempted to work over it a little more; the base of the second wing could do with a deeper relief. He chose his favourite tool, a wire tool that he had mended half a dozen times since the Paris days; he liked its lightness in his hand, the worn wooden handle.

"Don't fiddle, chum," he said after a moment, and put the tool down. He lit a pipe and looked ahead. There was only one choice, and the choice was bronze. Ten feet of winged horse in bronze for Tobias. Not set straight against the cypresses, as the white marble boy with the fawn was set now. "He needs a niche; a plain white shell, like the plaster shrines you see in France. And I think," said Carey to Carey, "that he'll take an eighteen-inch pedestal above the steps. I don't want to lose that look he has of standing in the sky; and height will help."

> *"He had flame behind the eyes of him,*
> *and wings upon his side."*

He looked at the wings, still triumphant, the wings ready to soar to the sun.

"And now," Carey said to Carey, "it's time to show him to Liz." He dropped the thin white rag over the model again.

"Informal unveiling by Mr. Anthony Carey, three-fifteen, p.m."
He limped out of the door and across the cobbled yard. "Still a
mild winter," he thought, and that echo sounded as if from a
long time ago; these short weeks had cut off the past from the
present, made a new triumphant phase. He came on, by the path
under the wall; he made a detour by the formal gardens, went
through the cut in the yews, crossed the grass and stood for a
moment looking at the boy with the fawn. He felt forgiving
towards it today; it had a peaceable, a wistful beauty, after all;
the hand resting on the fawn's head was good enough. But under
the pearly grey light of afternoon, the black trees and the pearly
marble figures were grouped in sadness; even with the sunlight
they kept their quiet mood.

And for Tobias, as he had always known, this thing should
blaze; as a bronze horse in a white niche would blaze here by
spring.

He went down again to the terrace. From the windows of the
long room, he heard Liz playing, the same phrase repeated,
obstinately, in a perfectionist's rage that was making the same
small mistake every time. He strolled in by the garden door.
She played a crashing discord and leaped off the piano stool.
She was dressed in a red sweater and blue trousers, the clothes
that J. G. disliked for her. She looked enchanting, Anthony
thought, leggy and tremulous; the hint of the ballet dancer was
always there.

"*You have no conception,*" said Anthony, doing J. G., "*of the
effect of trousers upon a woman's body. They take away every
particle of femininity and leave a sexless horror.*"

"Dear love. Why not? Surely you do not wish to use my
femininity before tea."

"Don't be vulgar," said Anthony. "I never marry vulgar
girls. Come along." He took her hand. "The time has come."

"I may *see*?" she said, looking at him with enormous eyes:
"And what, I ask myself? The first hush-hush job you've ever
done."

"I *think* it's all right," Carey said as they went along the path
under the wall. "Had an awful terror when I started that it

might turn out to be just another dull Carey job."

"You are not to say those things."

"They're true, darling." He opened the white gate for her and as they crossed the cobbled yard he was wondering what her reaction would be to Levitt's part in this. She found it hard to mention Levitt's name. She had said, "It's something that makes me shiver inside; a thing that I'm so ashamed of I want to think it never happened; as if I had been sick in public, it was the worst thing *anybody* could do."

They came to the studio door. He could trust her, he thought, as he opened it, to see the merits of the horse while it was still in wax. She had helped him in the studio for long enough to acquire a semi-professional eye. He said, "Stay just there," and lifted the white rag off the model on the stand.

Oh, easy, he thought; no trained eye was needed to appraise this, to applaud this. The grandeur of the design overcame the dull, grey stuff in which it was worked. Beyond it the finished figures, with every gain of casting, cutting, size and patina, lagged, drooped, were nothing. The horse was all. From here he looked at it in full face; at the slim narrow head, the delicate forelegs, the curve of the belly and the fore-shortened arches of the wings. The magic persisted.

Liz said comically, "*Struth* . . ." and no more. She put out a hand that groped for a few seconds before it found the revolving top of the stand.

"Well?" Carey said.

She went on turning it.

"But you know," she said. "You must know. You don't need me to tell you."

"I think I know," said Carey solemnly. "But I'd like you to tell me, just the same."

"Love: I can't; not as it should be told. That just *is* the most beautiful thing you've ever done."

"Think he'll lose himself in plaster?"

"God, no. Find himself." She was dazed and abrupt, shaken. "I never saw anything I liked so much. Never; never; never. Our horse."

"Our horse."

Still in a trance, staring at it, she said, "How did you *get* that?
You've tried before. So many times."

"Yes, I have, haven't I?" And now he had thought that he
would tell her of Levitt's drawing, but he found that he paused;
after a moment he repeated, "Tried before, yes. . . . Then this
—just happened."

Somewhere in his head a brisk voice spoke; his father's voice:
"Anthony, that's not quite straight of you, is it? Own up,
now," and still he did not; Liz was speaking again, crowing,
hurling old words back at him. "No sculptor, Mr. Carey? Just
a monumental mason, Mr. Carey? Couldn't do a plaster head as
good as the drippy one that revolting Jane Ireland did last year.
Now let's have a little sense, shall we?"

Still he stood, transfixed. It would be so easy to say, "In fact,
love, I can't claim it as wholly mine; the original drawing was
made by Harry Levitt." What was stopping him? He did not
know. Now, as Liz hugged him, he felt queer because he was
letting the moment go by. "This poor Carey is a genius—I
always said so. Oh, and Anthony, it *is* the horse; Toby's horse;
he has flame behind the eyes of him all right. *And* those wings.
Marble? Bronze? Bronze, I'd say."

"Bronze, yes. Here are the drawings," he said, giving himself
another cue and knowing, flatly, that he might not take it. Was
it in unconscious provision for this hour that he kept the first
black tracing folded away between the leaves of an early drawing
book? It must be. Yet it couldn't be. He had started on this
thing, surely, without any intention of cheating Levitt.

He watched her head bent over the drawings.

"And here on this shelf," he said, "see the little one? You
can have him if you'd like——" She was frowning now.
"What's the matter?" he asked quickly. It suddenly occurred to
him that Levitt might have drawn that horse before, might have
shown it to her. She would be more likely to recognise it from
the drawings than from the model.

Liz said, "*This* ought to be the memorial; not the boy with the
fawn."

The little flare of relief shocked him. He hesitated; he said, "Well, of course that's been in my mind. I'd like it to be." ("But if I can't bring myself to give Levitt his due, I'm damned if it ought to be.")

"It's got to be. Wait till J. G. sees it."

He cocked his head on one side. "Liz, darling, I don't want J. G. to see it till I've cast it in plaster."

"Why not?"

"Well. . . . You know. . . . It might go wrong. Not sure, in fact, that I'm trusting myself to do that job. Think I'll get Ian Ferris down to help me."

"Even so," Liz said, dancing up and down before the little horse on the shelf. "You've got to show it to Ould Maister. Now. As is. I insist."

He came up behind her and planted his hands on her shoulders. "Why do you insist, pray? And who are you to insist, pray?"

"I am the proudly-peacocking bride of the gentleman who made this." She leaned against him, staring back at the stand. "For *absolute* beauty——" she said and stopped. "Oh, Anthony, don't be mean. He'll lose his mind with pleasure. Remember, on that hideous cruise, the sketches you made for the horse and how none of them went right?"

"Ould M.," said Anthony, "has got to wait. Once it's in plaster he may be allowed a view. And you keep that tiny flannel-mouth shut, see?"

"Not *tell* him about it, even?"

"No; please not."

Liz drooped. "If you want not, then not. But he'll be all sore and chafed when he finds out; you know how he loves to be in on the beginning of everything, how he loves to be told; and anything of yours—I'd be scared not telling."

"You forget," said Anthony, "that I don't happen to be scared of J. G." He kissed her. There was a feeling like a wrinkle now in his mind; the feeling that one had when an unpaid bill or an unwritten letter was nagging.

Liz stood, with her arms at her sides, back in her trance of absorption with the winged horse.

"Mr. Michelangelo Donatello Leonardo Carey," she said at
last, "and look, don't let's have any nonsense about the casting.
Let your professional moulder moulder; in his grave, if necessary.
You can do that; it's your thing. Why does this horse give you
jitters?"

He could say, "Because, you see, it isn't really mine," and get
back the minute that had passed. Odd, that it should be so
important; when he had all the rest of the day in which to tell
Liz about Levitt's drawing. Yes, that was comforting, no hurry,
he said to himself.

January, 1950

Carey awoke, saw that the time was only half-past six and lay
back in an effort to sleep again. This was the tricky moment. If
he did not sleep at once, he would begin to feel the absurd
weight of the thought that lay in ambush.

Its power perplexed him. It was as if the thought had stayed
awake while the seat of his reason slept; it acquired a mastery
of its own that did not at first yield to reason. Though, of
course, by the time that he had bathed and dressed and eaten his
breakfast, he was on top of it again. He was unused to a
troubled waking. And it was foolish to lie here with his eyes
shut, hearing the thought. It talked; it said, "You ought to tell.
Why haven't you told yet? When are you going to tell?"

"Oh, shut up," he said to it. "Let me sleep; what does it
matter?"

"If it doesn't matter, why haven't you done it yet?"

"Shut up; I must sleep. Ian and I were playing chess till one
o'clock."

"H'm. You've had plenty of time to tell Ian about that
drawing in these last three days, haven't you?"

"I'll tell him this morning; now will you be quiet?"

He turned on his side; a little better; a hint of peaceful
drowsiness. (Easiest of all, to write Levitt a note; that was the
thing to do; it was between him and Levitt, wasn't it? Yes, of
course it was.)

He slept again and dreamed vividly that his father still lived;

his father was in the next room and in the dream Carey rose and dressed and walked in to say good-morning to him. The old man raised his head from a book that he was reading; he looked at Carey with reproach, there were no words spoken, just the piercing reality of that reproachful look. It hurt him after he was awake.

Ian was finishing his breakfast. Carey had known Ian all his working life; he was the older of the two Ferris brothers, improbable characters, both. Ian looked like a butterfly-hunting professor in an out-of-date comedy; round head, thick glasses, small, ruddy beard and the kind of greenish knickerbocker suit that was becoming as rare as doublet and hose. Ian was a man of painstaking hobbies; sculpture and plaster-moulding went in with mountaineering, Greek history, and chess. Jock Ferris, the younger brother, was a numismatist, an expert in the chasing and patining of bronzes. Funny types, in Carey's view; but his Paris days had taught him to respect funny types who could do things with their hands.

"Sorry I'm late," he said.

Ian's moustache and beard closed over a large piece of bacon.

"Don't worry; I'll go ahead now." He had a high, whistling professional voice; the vowels almost cockney.

"Stay and talk to me; I'll make speed." His housekeeper brought fresh coffee. "Do you dream?" Carey said to the beard.

"Only when I happen to have something on my mind. I dreamed about your horse last night, for example. All the brass strips had fallen out on the floor and when I looked at them they were my teeth. I was extraordinarily worried. Not about the cast, about my teeth. I kept wondering how I should ever be able to manage with false teeth. All the more absurd because I've had false teeth for twenty years. Now really, Anthony, I'd like you to excuse me. I want to catch the twelve-ten if I can; going to de Fries' exhibition. It's the opening today. You ought to be there yourself."

"Can't stand de Fries, and I can't stand his work," said Anthony sunnily.

"Oh, my dear fool—the Bach of modern sculpture." Ian was

always evolving unlikely parallels of this kind. "The Beethoven of modern umbrella manufacturers," Anthony said to himself, giggling inside.

Presently he followed in Ian's track across the yard. It was cold this morning, frost glinting on the grass between the stones, thin ice on the puddles. The sunlight was metallic, the sky reddish behind the black trees. A mean, lowering day, he thought and did not know why; usually he liked a frosty morning.

They had kept the stove alight. The cellar smelt of coke-fumes, green soap and shellac. It was a chaos of tubs and buckets. Plaster splashes covered the walls. Ian, with his jacket off, was assembling the pieces of the mould. He hummed a tune; his hands, weak-looking, narrow hands, minced through the work.

Infinitely removed from the débris all about him, the winged horse, cast in plaster, stood on the solid work-table. He looked more fragile now—"out of his egg"—as Ian had said last night; he was new, gleaming, alive. Anthony leaned on the table, testing it with all his knowledge and all his powers of detachment, searching for a flaw in the cast.

"That's a very lovely thing," said Ian. "Make no mistake. You've graduated. Always thought you would, once you'd stopped being modest and awed." He moved about the cellar, tidying up, with the same odd blend of fuss and speed that he used while making the piece-mould. Brushes, cans, scrapings, wire, brass strips, twists of burlap, all departed before the quick, old-maidish hands.

"You don't need to do any of that," Anthony protested, still hypnotised by the horse.

"No trouble," Ian said. He helped Anthony move the cast on to the lift. Above in the studio Anthony hauled on the pulleys; up it came into the light. Ian sent the pieces of the mould up after it.

All the student's agony was here again. He remembered the first plaster cast that he had ever made: a head; he had left an air bubble in the cast and his thumb had gone through, breaking it. He had minded about it for a long time. He fussed more than Ian now, setting the horse on the turn-table.

Roping the mould with Ian, the thought, the masterful thought of the morning, came back. "Why don't you tell him?" He shrugged it away; it was less powerful now, though it was there. If it had not been there, he would not talk to himself inside. "Nothing odd about having a pro here to help with the casting, is there? Nobody could say that made the horse Ian's horse. So what's the difference with the drawing? You're just letting it become a bogey in your mind. Such a silly little bogey."

"Can't tell you how grateful I am, Ian," he said. "Come back to the house and I'll write you a cheque." Neither of the Ferris brothers had money. When he was younger this had embarrassed him. But Ian never hesitated to name his price and take the cheque, as briskly as any other tradesman. He always added his train fare, "and-let-me-see a fourpenny bus ride. Thank you, Anthony; and many congratulations. I'll want to see it. When it gets to Morris Singer's, ask Jock to show you that new acid compound of his. It's extraordinarily effective for golden-brown tones. Going to have it pointed up right away?"

Anthony hesitated. He had waited nearly two weeks before calling Ian in for the cast. Which was odd. And this too was odd, this finicking in his mind about the enlargement. "Oh, yes, I think so. I want the right team, of course; my usual team, for the big stuff. Haven't found out who's free and who's busy. I'll drive you in, old boy."

"Well, thanks again," Ian said in the station yard. He picked up his cheap fibre suitcase and departed. Anthony drove back down the Ashford road. He left the car in the drive and hurried across the yard to the studio.

Now it was worship, lighting his pipe and standing still; gloating upon the blue-white wings, the pure, straight head, the curved neck; the look of delicate balance that those four limbs had, the ethereal balance, the sky-standing look.

If only that dream would not come back. Extraordinary, how sharp it was still. His father had never in his life looked at him thus, that he could remember.

"Just because you've got it on your conscience, the lie. Damn it, I haven't told anybody a lie. I just haven't told."

("And if you can't tell, Carey, it would be better to take a mallet and smash the cast to pieces, now.")

It was a nightmare game that he played suddenly, glancing across to the work-bench, to the two heavy mallets that leaned against the wall. It had a demon quality of fun in it. He didn't like it, and he did. After a moment he shivered and said to himself, "You can't be well, you know. That's morbid and horrible. Get out of here and go and find Liz, there's a good chap."

But he sat on the step of the model stand, hugging his knees. The model stand, not being in use, was pushed down and away, under the second skylight, in the middle part of the studio. From here he saw the horse in a new perspective.

He was still gazing at it when the door of the studio was lightly tapped and opened at once: Baron's shadow moved across the threshold ahead of him.

The first thing that Anthony thought was, "He walks as quietly as a cat; Tobias always said so." Feeling the heat of his own skin, he said to himself, "Why am I blushing?" He sat on, stupidly, where he was, his hands hanging between his knees.

He thought, "Why doesn't he say something?"

Now the grey curled head, the small lithe figure in the dark overcoat, assumed in ten seconds a pose that was wholly condemning. The arms were folded; the chin jutted out. It was the implacable shape of justice standing there; imperial justice, Cæsar's shape. In another second the right arm would shoot forward, the thumb turned down.

Verdict on Carey? Verdict on the horse? But this was dreaming. He rose. Baron wheeled slowly.

"Anthony, my boy. I didn't know you were here. Saw your car go off——" his arm moved in a sweeping arc towards the cast; he shook his head helplessly. "Was this the secret?"

"Well, yes, it was."

J. G. chuckled. "Spying on you, eh? That's what you think.

Well, I was. And if you're angry, I don't give a damn. Just my disgraceful curiosity," he broke off. "My God, you've done it this time." He stared reverently; continued to stare.

"Like it, J. G.?"

"*Like* it. Look at me," said Baron simply. There were tears in his eyes.

"I think I got him," Anthony murmured.

"You got him, boy. Toby's horse." He took two short, prancing steps, halted and shook his head again. "Oh, *pure* beauty," he said. "Life; vigour; majesty."

("Now's your time. Tell him now. Get that tracing out of the book where you've so inexplicably hidden it and say, 'Look, here's how it began; with this drawing of Levitt's.' ")

"Genius, Anthony, genius," J. G. said. "No wonder you were keeping him a secret. A present, eh? To all of us. Am I forgiven? I had a queer sort of hunch, you know; couldn't keep away. Don't you dare tell Liz I came to spy." He gave Anthony's arm a great squeeze. "God bless you, you're a genius."

("Hurry up, Anthony. Tell him. I'm waiting." It was his father's voice.)

"That's the memorial," Baron said.

"I know; I thought so myself when I began."

("Go on now, can't you?")

"Nothing against the boy with the fawn, as you know. I'm delighted with it. But this, by God, this is for Toby. Marble?"

"Bronze."

"Of course. What else but bronze? . . ."

("Hurry now.")

No, not for a moment. Because J. G. was going to quote; he had puffed out his cheeks a little; his arm made another gesture towards the horse. His voice droned down to reverent quiet and he spoke the words like a blessing on Carey:

> "*My new-cut ashlar takes the light*
> *Where crimson-blank the windows flare*
> *By my own work, before the night,*

Great Overseer, I make my prayer.
If there be good in what I wrought,
Thy hand compelled it, Master, Thine . . ."

"If there be good," he repeated.

("Liz always said that he could hypnotise you if you let him; how many times have I laughed at that?") Yet for a moment it was true; the fierce light of admiration in the grey eyes compelled him, kept him silent, holding the stare when all that he wanted to do, or so it seemed . . . was to say—"I have to tell you how it happened," and tell.

Then Baron turned from him and stretched out his small powerful hands towards the white shape, saying, "Nobody but you could have done it; nobody but you."

March, 1950

Anthony came out of the National Gallery and walked through Trafalgar Square, looking for a taxi. It was the most amiable of early spring afternoons and he had spent an hour as he usually liked to spend it, but he was worried about his eyes; there must be something wrong with eyes that only stared and did not see. It was a queer little symptom, this. His eyes were trained cameras, used to pick up the masses of light and shade, the form and composition around him. Something had gone wrong today. Standing before the pictures that he knew, he had found his eyes merely noting, like dull reporters at a routine job. His mind had taken no message at all; his mind had fussed along automatically with another preoccupation. Now that he was out in the street, the people who passed him had clouded faces; the whole London scene was blurred a little. And he did not feel refreshed, as he had hoped to feel; merely tired and fussed and anxious to get back to the studio.

He found a taxi at the corner of the Haymarket. He was early for his date with Liz; it didn't matter; he could have a drink while he waited for her.

"Berkeley Hotel," he said to the driver.

When he reached the Berkeley and walked in by the Piccadilly entrance, he saw that the shutter on the bar was down. It was not yet half-past five. At the tables along the decorative channel between the swing-doors and the bar, the people already here were having tea; tea in thin china cups, little cakes and sandwiches. He found a sofa table empty and sat down.

"Tea, sir?"

"God forbid. Your clock's slow, isn't it?"

The waiter grinned at him; it was the same waiter who used to serve him here when he was on leave in the war. "Sorry, Mr. Carey; ten minutes to go."

Absurd, to want a drink so badly. "I never used to be a punctual drinker," Carey said to himself. "Tired, that's what. Work and wedding preparations mixed. Wouldn't be a bad idea to go on the wagon for a bit. Oh, don't be silly; you're talking like a drunk." The waiter brought him a copy of the *Evening Flash*.

He turned the pages. Still no sign of Levitt's American cartoon; it had been missing for some days.

It struck him as outrageous that he should be watching the silver-painted shutter of the bar instead of watching the door for Liz.

There it went now, rattling up and revealing the little lighted cave, the man in the white coat, the reassuring rows of bottles and glasses.

"Bring me a large whisky and soda."

In a moment he would be safe. It was not serious, this drinking habit; he was only cross with himself for the brief, last-minute hustle that happened in his mind every evening now. It reminded him of the scutter across open land under fire, to the fox-hole.

"It's got to stop," said Carey, pouring the drink down his throat.

He saw Liz come through the swing-door; she had her London look; elegant, exhausted, drooping under the burden of parcels that might have been stone weights; he went to help her.

"Darling, bless you. Take all. My fingers are sawn off by sadistic string; and I have shopping sickness. Ginger ale, please."

She sat down limply beside him.

"Poor darling. I wish you drank," he said.

"Drank? As for fish?" She was enlivened. "Mean you would like to see me roaring and hiccoughing and having delirium tremens?"

"I mean a drink would put you right in a minute."

"Indeed it would not." She pecked at the ginger-ale with small henlike sips.

"Well, I'll have another whisky, to balance," said Carey.

"Why do you like it?" Liz asked idly.

"Don't know. I just do. Gives one a kind of holiday inside one's head."

She looked puzzled.

"But do you *want* a holiday inside your head, my dearest dear? From me?"

"God, no."

"From work? Tell. Didn't you have a spiffing idle day? I pictured you carousing with your chums at the club and then strolling through delicious galleries while I suffered to death in Fortnum's."

"I had quite a good day. Fussing, though. Days off don't suit me. Think J. G.'ll be back this week?"

"Anthony——" She looked at him comically. "You sound as though you were dreading him. Touch of Baron fever? Not you, surely?"

"I wasn't his favourite character when he left, remember," said Anthony.

She said, "Darling, don't be an ass. He loves you to distraction. He was just a little bored because you were so slow getting the boys on the job at the studio. And you did take an awful time about it."

"You know why. I got worried about the money. Still appals me when I think what I've spent on myself and my job all these years. Gentlemen who are getting married can't afford so much fun."

"Oh, pooh," said Liz. "If you ask me, that's exactly what gave Ould M. hurty feelings; not that it takes much, I agree. But of course he meant to foot the bill all along."

"I didn't want him to," said Anthony, "and I still don't."

"Well, you'll have to swallow it down, I fear. And I didn't mean the whisky; false pride does not become you. It is Toby's memorial and J. G. commissioned it. Anyway, he'll be enraptured when he sees all that mayhem in the studio."

"Liz."

"Yes, my love."

"Have you heard anything from Levitt?"

"Goodness me, no," she said primly.

"Realise he'll be back any time now?"

"Well, all right." She stiffened; then gazed at him. "Is that what's worrying you? That J. G.'ll bring Harry back from America with him and the three of us will meet in agony?"

Carey said slowly, "No; not quite that."

"Well, what? As you know, I suffer from an impediment in my speech about H. L. But he will behave nicely; he has pretty manners. Not a word will be said. I brace myself for this meeting regularly, every morning when I wake, as for breathing exercises." She continued to look dejected. "Darling, don't tell me that you also have to brace; it's so unlike you; and it makes me feel guilty."

April, 1950

(i)

In the dream, Anthony was sitting perched on the heavy platform, above the turn-table in the studio. He was naked; Ian Ferris, with an assistant to help him, was pointing up the enlargement of the plaster model, and Anthony himself was receiving the points; the three steel needles were making the measurements of the horse on the skin of his chest and he understood that the finished design would go right through him to the back.

He could not quite understand the process, nor why Ian should have taken the place of the professional enlarger, who had been on the job for days now, nor what had happened to the big armature. But he could only sit still; Ian kept strolling towards him and checking the points, calling back to the other invisible figure; the horse itself was also invisible. He thought that it was J. G. who was helping Ian, but he could not be sure. The points hurt him, and he looked down at his chest. He saw black blood there.

"That's all right," Ian said to him. "It isn't your blood." The warm stickiness was disgusting, stickiness of something more obscene than blood.

He woke, sweating. He sat up, shaking off the peculiar horror; a horror unsharable, yet for a little while proof against the early morning light and the validity of the bedroom walls. "Ugh," he said to himself, "I haven't had nightmares since the war."

He thumped the pillow and lay down. The dream faded. Here was the morning mood; it had grown in power; it was no longer one small intrusive thought that nagged him for a while. It was becoming an inquisition; and today it had a panic urgency.

"Are you crazy? Why did you let it go as far as this? Look at the time you wasted; all the weeks and weeks that you've had; just that one little hurdle to be taken and you didn't take it. But it was *easy* then. You could have done it without thinking; why didn't you?

"Why didn't you show it to Liz? That was easiest of all. In the studio, that first day, when you showed her the model and the drawings? Why didn't you take that one black tracing out of the book and spread it out beside the rest and say, 'Here's where it began; with this drawing of Levitt's'?

"But of course you did that . . . you really did. You're back in the studio now, and you're doing that. There's just the thirty-eight-inch model there, and the drawings are on the table, and you're stretching your hand to the book where the tracing is. It's all right, thank God. You're telling her, showing her. None of this has happened. You've turned time back to there, and you're honest again, you're safe. 'Look, Liz; here's where it began . . .'

"Wake up, Carey; it isn't so. You didn't tell her; you haven't told anybody. And Baron's home from America, back in London; Baron will be here today. Bringing Levitt with him, perhaps. You've let him see Levitt, talk to Levitt. You could have written Levitt, cabled Levitt. You meant to. But you didn't. And you didn't tell J. G. before he went; you meant to, of course, that last evening before he left; one of the many evenings when you said to yourself, 'I'll tell him at six o'clock'; those awful days when you went on and on thinking about it until six o'clock.

"Six o'clock was the good time; the let-up, time for signing off, with a glass in your hand. Look at all the six o'clock chances you had with J. G. And after the first drink it didn't seem so urgent, somehow. It would do tomorrow. . . . And tomorrow the hurdle was higher. But you were still going to take it, at six o'clock.

"Until there wasn't a tomorrow left. And there isn't now; there's only today.

"Get up, Carey. It's the hour when factory workers rise; your studio isn't a studio any more, it's a factory. You've heard the hammering and the sawing and the swearing of the men on the job. You've seen the spikes set in, the joints bolted, the slats coming into shape, the shape of wings; you've seen the pointing machine at work, pointing up the lie; while in the smaller frame he sits, white and poised and perfect. The lie in plaster.

"How could he be so perfect, when Ian mixed your lie with the plaster, stamped your lie on each number piece of the mould? Why didn't he come out with a flaw? The flaw's there all right; it doesn't stay in the cast; it's built into the armature. There's a flaw in the framework, a flaw in every slat, they shell-acked the flaw and kept it in; they press the flaw in with the wax and they can't see it. They don't know it's there; but you do. And they're nearly done now. They'll be out of the studio tomorrow, with all their clutter, and you'll be face to face with the full-scale lie, ready to start the finish modelling.

"Only maybe you won't finish it at all now. J. G. isn't blessing any new-cut ashlar as from today.

"Kipling still, but different.

> " *'There's pleasure in the wet, wet clay*
> *When the sculptor's hand is potting it.*
>
> . . . .
>
> *but the pleasure felt in these is as chalk to*
> *cheddar cheese*
> *When it comes to a well-made lie.'*

"Not my new-cut ashlar, J. G., but my *'ring-fence, deer-park lie'*."

The factory was quieting down. It was less like bedlam today; he climbed through the mess and litter to get to the model; sawdust, shavings, slats and boards, cans of shellac, beer bottles, coats and tools. It was never possible to make them tidy up as they went along.

And now he stood at the base of the ten-foot model in wax. The frame was still around it. Price, his chief enlarger, was on the job, and the tow-headed boy who perched on a cross-beam and whistled as he worked. Anthony looked at the tow hair. It would be good to be able to climb inside that skull for a minute, live there, be the boy, untroubled and whistling; get a minute's peace. Good to be Price, too; poor little Price, with his cough and his invalid wife. His adversities came from outside; not from a self-tied knot within.

At the smaller frame, beyond the steel barriers of the machine, the third man Billy Lewis was at work for the last re-checking of the points, while Terry watched him from a yard away. Billy was an ex-Slade student; broke, devoted, industrious. Anthony had used him as assistant before and he would stay to help with the finish modelling. Good to be Billy, with his broken nose, his incredibly long arms, his one poor room in south London. Good to be Terry; you would find the most peace, of course, inside Terry's skull. Terry had a fistful of shavings in his hand. He would stand here as long as Nanny let him stay; silently watching.

"Nice day, Mr. Carey."

Nice day, indeed. Most suitable for J. G.'s return to co-incide with the removal of the machine, the clearing of the mess, the departure of Price and the tow-headed boy. They had worked hard and well; the cash bonuses and the beer had helped. They would leave the place in order, they worked as hard on the cleaning up as he did himself; Billy, too, though Billy didn't get beer or a cash bonus for overtime. When J. G. looked in here tomorrow morning, the studio would be itself again; only the white cast here and the ten-foot model.

"Extraordinary," he thought, as he climbed on to the plat-form, "how little has managed to go wrong; no major operation required, no going through to the wood; nobody's as much as scratched a thumb; never did a job begin and end so smoothly."

Even with the struts of the frame blocking his vision, and the tow-headed boy climbing around like a monkey, he could see that the wax model was remarkable. Wherever he looked, on head or wing or flank, he found a hint of excitement, of authority. The same magic luck that had held from the start went on holding.

It was only his, Carey's, luck that ran out today.

"Can't wait to get your hands on him, can you?" Billy was saying. "Don't blame you."

"I'll be back," Carey said.

Wherever he looked, he saw the spring. In the grass of his field there were the wild daffodils, overhead the chestnut leaves unfolding; the painted shapes of crocus in flower at the foot of the rhododendron bushes. He opened the white gate.

"However bad it is," he said to himself, "it's going to be over, done with. Remember that, all the time he's blasting you. You need never feel like this again after today. The knot inside you will have gone; the hurdle will be down; you'll be free of the lie. You'll be you again, even if you're you in disgrace.

"And any blasting, any disgrace will be better than this, this living with the knot tied inside you. Always, afterwards, you must try to remember how bad this has been."

He met Foliot in the hall. The imminence of J. G. was palpable; library door open, with fresh flowers ready; tension and brisk footsteps and the telephone ringing, Foliot alight like a Christmas tree.

"He'll be down, early; two-thirty at the latest; I should say we could safely expect him by two-fifteen or two-twenty. ("Unusually broad in her estimates today," Anthony thought.) Wonderful for a Friday, isn't it? Of course he can't wait to see Carlington. Says he feels he's been away a lifetime, not just ten days."

Anthony forced himself to ask lightly, "Who's with him, d'you know?"

"Just Mr. Peet and Mr. Micklethwait," she said. "And Mather, of course."

"All right. I want to leave a note for him." He went into the library, sat for a moment in front of J. G.'s desk with the sheet of Carlington writing-paper before him, wrote suddenly and vigorously:

"Welcome back, J. G. I want to see you right away, and I know you want to see me. I've got to pay off the chaps this afternoon. (Price & Co. are finished, and will be taking the machine away.) I may be stuck for a little while; you know what the clearing-up involves on a job like this."

His writing looked cramped, spiky. He added:

"Will you please telephone over to the house when you want me. Or, if I don't hear, I'll come the first minute I'm through."

(ii)

"We'll take Randolph's walk, shall we?" said Baron. He had changed into fluffy tweeds; he carried a stick; Prince panted and rootled beside him.

It was impossible to feel all right now. Throughout the afternoon the wires had been tightening. He could feel the odd surface-play of the nerves on the muscles of his face; he had even thought that his speech was affected by it as he greeted J. G.

Impossible to know, from Baron's affable briskness, what would come next. One just had to walk and wait, with the skin of one's face still twitching oddly. "Good to stretch one's legs a bit," J. G. was saying; the walk took them down the first field on Carey's side of the fence. After that you turned right, beside the stream and on into a deep lane; from there a field path twisted up towards the village. A twenty-minute walk.

Of course J. G. knew. It was not merely the effect of his own fast-ebbing courage that made J. G.'s words sound so strained. "Wonderful how everything's come on; not a daffodil when I left." And the sideways-shifting grey eyes were after him, chasing him. Looking into those eyes deliberately, he felt the authentic shiver that the others had described. He had laughed at it: the chemical effect of Baron's presence, as though he sent a cold, strong wave out from him, and now that you could feel it, you knew, for ever and ever, that you were weaker than he.

Incredible, with the sun glinting on the grass, the trumpets of the daffodils, the nostalgic wind blowing from other springs.

"Glad to have the chance of a talk," J. G. said. He swished at a bunch of plantain leaves with his stick. "Knew you'd be anxious. Celia write to you?"

"Celia . . ." He had forgotten Celia. Distracted for a moment, he found himself blinking again at the fact that he had betrayed her confidence. He still could not see how it had happened. J. G. had grilled him before, when he had given his word, grilled him without success. It had happened after six o'clock, of course, which was why, no doubt, he had given it so little thought since. Quite a long talk they had had, he remembered; all of four whiskies long. Guilt stabbed him.

"It's as bad as you said; and worse. She wrote to you?" J. G. repeated.

"I've heard from her," Anthony said slowly; "she didn't say much. I've been worried, of course, so has Liz."

They had come to the stile that led into the lane. Baron halted and put a hand on the stile.

"She's washed her hands of all of us, Anthony. Refused my help; insulted me. It's hopeless. Nothing we can any of us do. And it breaks my heart. She'll stay there in New York, go her own intolerable way." He compressed his lips; his heavy lids drooped; it was the puffed mask of condemnation. Anthony watched him, dazed by the temporary reprieve.

"No," J. G. said after a minute; he gave his long rattling sigh. "I can't bring myself to tell you—not even you, what happened. Either what she said to me or——" he paused and said, "No," again; a little smile came and went. "Funny, those things that one can't tell; that won't come out."

"I'm awfully sorry. My God, I'm sorry, J. G. What about Terry?" said a weak, placid voice that did not seem to be Anthony Carey's voice at all. His eyes were watching the play of the sun on J. G.'s hair; the light wind took the ends of the little curls on the temples and frizzed them.

"Terry stays here; thank God the child has a home; thank God for Carlington. Er, in fairness to Celia, that trust fund wasn't spent. Not that there's much of it, but at least the capital's safe. Chicken-food," he said. He played a sudden surprising golf stroke at a lump of dried earth. "But still." He swung the stick again. "Sacked Levitt," he said. "Another pleasant half-hour. He didn't take it well."

The sun stood still.

The same weak, placid voice echoed foolishly, "You sacked him? Why?"

"What? . . . Had to, Anthony. One of my mistakes. Been on my mind a long time; didn't discuss it; knew you were fond of him. Don't often make mistakes; when I do, they have to go. His work wasn't good enough."

The play of the muscles under the skin of Anthony's face had begun to subside; he could feel just one muscle that still twitched, the muscle of the left eyelid, winking. He had had it before, he remembered.

"His work . . . yes; it was falling off a bit," the placid voice echoed. His mind awoke out of its brief dizzy stupor; it said, "What the hell are you talking about? You know you don't think that. You thought Levitt's work was getting better all the time. Why can't you say so? Turning into a yes-man?"

J. G. set his foot on the stile. "I know you liked him," he repeated wistfully; "close to us all, at one time, wasn't he?"

"I did like him." The words sounded feeble, insincere, as though he had not really liked Levitt.

"Till you found him making up to Liz, eh?" J. G. was relaxing now; he said, "Well, that's over. He won't come back. Really, altogether, I had the bloodiest time. Wonderful to be home."

They were in the further field. Anthony saw the track of the path ahead; the familiar path, the familiar curve of green over the hedge, the slice of cottage roof, blue smoke going up from the crooked chimney. He felt weak, spent.

"Here," said Baron, as they topped the rise, "is where your father always used to stop and take those famous deep breaths of his." He stretched himself on tiptoe, inhaling and exhaling. "Dear old boy," he added on a prayer-note.

"Bless you, Anthony. You're a great comfort to me. If it weren't for you and Liz . . ." His words trailed off on another rattling sigh; then briskly, prancingly, he turned towards the village. "Back to the studio, eh, boy?"

The wistfully tender smile was there now; the eyes were wide and candid. He was a little benign creature with grey curling hair; a sort of Puck; a good kind godfather. Good old J. G. How had you—two fields back—been afraid of him? You could tell him anything.

The village street sloped downhill; they were past the inn, past the church.

"Queer about Harry Levitt," J. G. was saying. "Interesting, those little spurts of talent. Topical talents, one might call them, brought out by a particular climate of opinion. Then, when the climate changes, they seem to wither away. Levitt, now . . . perfectly of an era; the end of the war and the immediate post-war era. He's dated; he's a back number. Simply because the times are a moving target. A year from now, nobody'll remember his name.

"Unlike some gentlemen I know, with fine statues to their credit. They're for posterity, they are."

Anthony opened his mouth and shut it. There was nothing in his mind now but a laughing bewilderment; so foolish to have thought that the lie would be done with, today. He supposed vaguely that if the challenge had come, he would have met it decently. But already this morning's Carey, the Carey of earlier afternoon, looked like people whom he had once known and might not know again. His left eyelid went on twitching.

(iii)

It was the fifth morning of peace; a peace so resounding and continuous that he slept long hours. When he awoke now, the time was already half-past nine. He saw the spring rain on the window, beyond the window the green chestnut leaves slight and glittering. He saw his room.

"So grateful," he thought drowsily. "So happy. Stopped worrying. . . . Safe . . . . Like having been in pain for weeks and weeks, and now no pain." He shut his eyes, lay on in the luxurious cocoon, feeling every muscle of his body relax, just that little feathering movement of the left eyelid was there; it did not matter.

This was a disgraceful hour to lie drowsing; Billy Lewis would be up and dressed, ready for work. Another long, placid day in the studio was ahead, the studio that in its new return to order, silence and cleanliness matched his own mood. He thought back over yesterday; only a day of work and walking in the rain with Liz; of drinks, and dinner and music after dinner; Liz, Billy and himself idling through the evening, "*And there they fleeted the time carelessly, as they did in the golden world*". It was a day that had gone with the magical ease and smoothness of this new phase; as though for months he had been moving stiffly, painfully, and now marvelled at the return of co-ordination. His eyes were clear again and his hands steady.

Under the miracle of reprieve, it was easy to live. All that he must do, in the course of the next few weeks, was to write to Levitt. He had whole phrases of the letter ready; it had ceased to be a hurdle. He would find the address somehow; perhaps Celia could help there. No hurry.

"Come on, my boy, this won't do," Carey urged himself. "Up and out."

While he was shaving he studied the twitch of the left eyelid. It was almost invisible in the glass; it was intermittent. It went on for ten minutes or so and then stopped. "It's better, I think; didn't notice it so much yesterday. Queer, for it to come back. Not half so bad, of course, as it was the other time. Hardly shows."

He dressed and ran down the stairs, with the hopping slide that his stiff knee dictated; he called through to the kitchen, "Sorry, Mrs. Ryder! Overslept again." He wondered why Mrs. Ryder should find this new habit endearing; once again she beamed on him as though he had done something clever. Billy was still in the dining-room, his long legs dangling over the arm of a chair; he was doing the *Times* crossword.

"I'll go ahead," Billy drawled. "This grey light is what we need."

"Wait for me," said Carey, helping himself to fish-cakes.

Billy tapped the newspaper. "There's a story about the Glane Memorial prize. Interview with de Fries. No holds barred. You can submit a design; or a cast; or photographs. Closing date September. Why not try them with this here horse?"

"Oh, no," said Carey. "I couldn't do that. Glane's got J. G. all over it. Wouldn't be right or proper."

"The virtue," Billy said, "of you gentlemen with independent incomes has been remarked upon before. By a Greek, I fancy. All the same, it's highly mysterious to me."

* * * * *

May—June, 1950

(i)

"We commit him to the flames," Anthony thought. In the foundry, with the dirt floor and the dust-smeared windows, the streams of fire poured from the tilting crucible; the dusky figures, booted and swathed, went about their business; the green and gold flames flashed upwards under the cupola. The lie moved on.

There were three kinds of fire, the molten fire that poured, the green and gold flames, and the glow reflected on those thick, moving silhouettes. Beyond the range of the fires, traced with shadow, there was the mere industrial cavern; its function might, he thought, have been to produce munitions, farm tools or steel rails.

The foundry seemed, as it had seemed before, a place Olympian and secret, a place detached from him. There was always an excitement in this; it was the feeling of authority taking over. (Authority of the printer and bookbinder transforming a typescript; authority of the builder validating the architect's drawn plan; authority of the hand establishing the lie.)

Then there was the bronze horse, cooled, out of the pit; the horrifying transition horse; his outlines unrecognisable, interrupted by sprues, risers and jagged fins. There were blisters on his surface. He was a distorted thing. The first time that Carey ever saw this stage he had wrung his hands, thinking, "It is ruined."

Now he was used to it. He was used to the roughness of the team who came with heavy files; with hacksaws and chisels and grinding wheels. They straddled the horse carelessly. They chopped and banged at him, noisily striking off the horrors, like a pair of knockabout surgeons in a nightmare.

Still they had their power to put a little of the old panic into his throat. He could not watch them; the sight of a hacksaw on that head, the sight of a grinding wheel on its flexible shaft rasping across one of those wings, turned his stomach. His nerve did not come back until the chasers were on the job.

It was a relief to be up in the lighter room. This was sculpture again, not hacksaw surgery. Here was the cast for reference; here were the processes that he knew. And the men that he knew, Jock Ferris, brother of Ian, with his assistant.

Jock was unlike Ian; he was long and lanky, with a face as undemonstrative as a Scots hillside under sleet. The only point of similarity with Ian was the pair of nervous, old-maidish hands. Anthony could watch those hands driving their fine tools and not wince.

Now with a quieter mind he began to see the new horse, the stranger. He was a stranger as a woman you had loved last night was a stranger when you met her again. He had a personality of his own; he did not belong to you any more. This left you half-shy, half-incredulous. You hung around, pipe in mouth, unable to stop staring. In your mind, Anthony thought, there was a violent collision between distrust and pride.

"Coming along nicely," Jock Ferris grunted. He was on his knees by the base, working on the off hind hoof. He glanced over his shoulder at Anthony and chuckled sardonically; "I obsairve on your face the look of a young father confronting his first baby. 'Will that button of a nose ever be more than a button? And, heavens, the chin—is he going to have no chin at all?' And all the time the parental smirk, 'Did I really do this myself?' "

Anthony grinned. "Well, it always does feel like that," he said, watching the assistant perched between the wings, a frivolous jockey. Ferris continued to crawl about the base.

"Where's your signature?" he asked suddenly, "I don't see it."

(ii)

Two days before his wedding, they brought the horse to Carlington. It was a fine morning. He stood with Baron and

Liz, Nanny and Terry, watching the magic speed of the last phase. It all looked easy. There were the rollers, moving smoothly across planks that left flat marks on the lawn; then the planks slanted up the steps; then the two-way hoist on to the plinth, and it had happened. The eye, accustomed to the white, empty niche, blinked for a moment, taking the new thing in.

There were the men thanking Baron for his heavy tips, climbing into the truck; then only the marks of the truck wheels in the gravel and the flat marks on the lawn.

Nothing to do now; it was an odd feeling, Anthony thought; no more work on the horse. Jock had given him the acids, given him the first wash and waxing; the job was done. Still he found that he paced about inside his head, restlessly believing that there must be another stage.

He stood beside the plinth in the sunshine; he looked back to the day of grey skies and sad cypresses, and telling himself that a bronze horse with wings would blaze here for Tobias.

He was not the only one who now began to feel *désœuvré*, anticlimactic. Baron, having exhausted his superlatives, said wistfully, "I'd have liked some ceremony. Sentimental, perhaps; I'm getting old." He did the little shuffling dance with his feet and then slapped Anthony hard on the back. . . . "Enough ceremony coming our way Wednesday, what?" He patted the horse's flank and walked around the plinth, peering at all of it again.

Liz was at the foot of the steps, her head tilted back, staring on at the statue. Nanny was towing the reluctant Terry away across the lawn. Baron's quiet little question came suddenly, at Carey's elbow.

"Looking for your signature. Where've you hidden it?"

"It isn't signed, J. G."

Baron looked puzzled.

"I thought, for a private thing like this . . ." His words trailed. He gazed helplessly at the horse. The proud, burnished head looked over him, beyond him, away.

"Oh, nonsense," J. G. was saying; then the tender smile came: "How like you, Anthony."

"What's like him?" Liz asked, coming out of her dream.

"Modesty. Here carried to excess," said Baron; the smile slanted on one side.

"It isn't modesty," Carey protested.

"Reticence, then. You've got to sign it; Liz, don't you agree? His masterpiece . . ."

Liz looked at Carey before she said, "Oh, I don't know. If he does not wish to sign, why should he sign? This horse is not a cheque, nor the Magna Carta, nor again the North Atlantic Pact."

"Please don't be silly," snapped Baron.

"Honestly, J. G., it's too late now," Anthony said. "The signature should have gone into the cast."

At once he saw the face take on the puckered, thwarted likeness of a peevish child. . . . "It's disappointing."

"I'm sorry."

"Can't you carve it—chisel it?"

"Well—I suppose so. But——"

Baron's feet stamped on the white stone. "Can you or can't you, old boy? That's what I want to know."

"Well, of course I can. But it won't look too good. I'd have to chisel through the patina and the signature'll fairly shout. See what I mean, J. G.? It will be bright bronze—like gold."

Baron flashed back into good-humour: "Magnificent! Why shouldn't it be? That's exactly what I'd want it to be."

Anthony saw Liz watching him sympathetically. "You can carve it on the back of the base, Carey, dear; where its only message will be to the cypresses."

"Certainly not," Baron said. "On the side. Here. Eh, Anthony?"

"If you say so."

Liz knew that he was unhappy. She hugged his arm all the way to the house, in Baron's wake, singing mournfully:

> "So you'll *take* your little chisel
> and you'll *carve* it after lunch."

She halted him before they came to the cut in the yews. "Tell.

. . . You forgot all about signing it, didn't you? Hence look of guilt and rapid cover-up to Ould M.?"

"No, truly. I just didn't want to put it on."

"It was the smallest of scruples," he told himself; "what's the good of having scruples when you can't make yourself write to Levitt? You know you'll never write to him now . . ." He shrugged and surrendered, thinking, "So there was one more thing to be done, after all."

Presently he went up, carrying the chisel and the short, chunky-headed hammer. Despite his wretchedness, he still felt the glowing shock of pleasure as he reached the little lawn and saw it stand there. It made precisely the triumphant shape that his vision had given it on that grey day last year.

And now he knelt beside the base, his steady, co-ordinated hands driving hammer and chisel to make the legend: ANTHONY CAREY FECIT and the date in Roman numerals. Out it came, the lie in bright gold, with the little metal chips tinkling on to the stone.

He wiped it with a duster; he looked back over his shoulder; he was expecting to see Baron walk between the cut in the yews. Guiltily, glancing back again and again, he took from his pocket the small bottle of patining fluid and, with hurried strokes, brushed over the bright carved letters and numerals. The lie dimmed.

"I'll come back tomorrow," he said to himself, "and give it another coat."

September, 1950

(i)

It was the sort of party that Carey used not to enjoy, the mixture of stage and literary types with a sprinkling of titles; Gerald Lynn's party. He liked it now, because Liz was there. In the days before his marriage, he recalled, he would have come alone, equipped with a reluctance that would after several drinks subside and leave him with a roving eye. Chasing the possibility of *La Princesse Lointaine* through a hedge of glasses and cigarette smoke, he remembered, sighting the line of a neck, a mouth that laughed, a body that he could make himself want. All over, that phase, at least.

It was curious how often he was now compelled to add "at least" when he came to any unfavourable reflection upon his former self. "At least I don't do that now." It was encouraging to find a phase of his past conduct that he did not like, but the little rider "at least" added itself automatically. Funny mental arithmetic going on inside, Carey thought, and at once took another drink. The talk in which he found himself was not quite absorbing enough to keep his mind nailed. He found his eyes straying around Gerald's Victorian room in search of Liz. It was then that he saw Jane Ireland coming in with John de Fries. Jane made a comment on the past; not an important comment. He did not think that he wanted to talk to Jane; certainly he did not want to talk to de Fries; who stood now in the doorway looking at the party, with his air of surly appraisal.

De Fries always entered a room in this way; the stomach first; then the whole stocky intolerant figure. Beside him, Jane in her scarlet dress looked painstakingly pleased with herself; she might be in his bed tonight or she might not. Hers was an intermittent tenancy. De Fries had an improbable façade for a hunter, Anthony thought, assessing the neat, grey-brown head, the expressionless little face, the clipped moustache. He didn't look like a sculptor either; a Harley Street surgeon, perhaps, or a Tory politician, but not a sculptor. He was greeting his host. Now his eyes travelled, with a halt at a bosom on the way, to meet Carey's eyes. Carey bowed; de Fries always made him uncomfortable; de Fries did not return the bow, but said something to Gerald Lynn and at once Gerald came towards Carey.

"Come along, dear. John wants a word with you." Gerald wore a white waistcoat with his dinner jacket, and dark sapphire studs. Seeing that Anthony looked at the studs he cried, "I've got *everything* on tonight," and extended his arms, showing enormous cuff-links to match. "You don't hate John, do you?"

he asked wistfully; "he terrifies me, but I'm quite fond of him."

"He embarrasses me." De Fries always made it abundantly clear that he despised Anthony's work and Anthony with it.

He looked no more friendly than usual; Jane exuded a certain bitter sprightliness.

"What are you doing with yourself these days?" was the grunted opening.

"Working," said Anthony, finding, as ever, that all ease of manner deserted him in this company. "Finishing a job I began in the summer; a stone relief." There were interesting things to be said about the job, but they perished under the patent surliness. "House on Hampstead Heath," he added lamely, "belongs to a friend of J. G.'s. Beautiful old house, falling to pieces."

"Stone relief help to hold it up?" grunted de Fries, and Jane gave a determined, supporting giggle. "I was at Carlington Sunday; had lunch with J. G." His eyes wandered.

"Saw your horse," he said, his tone still uninterested, grudging. Into the silence Anthony heard himself launch the only question that he was vowing not to ask.

"Did you like it?"

"Mm. Yes. I did. Great improvement on anything you've done before. Isn't it? What?"

"No reason to hate you especially for phrasing it like that . . ." Anthony reminded himself. The twitch of his left eyelid began to be tiresome.

"J. G. tells me you're submitting it for the prize."

"Does he?" said Anthony. He could not imagine why J. G. should say so. And it seemed unlikely that de Fries, chairman of the R.B.S. Committee appointed to judge the Glane Memorial, had suggested it to him, however much he liked the winged horse. In another time Anthony would have said, "I'm afraid he's got it wrong. I can't go in for that. We've discussed it already." But in these days there was always a little thinking to be done where J. G. was concerned, a little weighing-up, a little wondering; you told yourself that this was because he was now your father-in-law.

"Well?" de Fries barked. "What about it?"

"I haven't quite made up my mind," Anthony said carefully.

"Better make it up, then. Closing date's coming along."

"Is it? I haven't really thought about it much; haven't read the rules or anything."

"Rules printed. All over the place. You can read." His eyes wandered again.

"Be very silly not to try for it; damn silly," he said next. "What's stopping you?"

"Just," Anthony fished for the words—"Oh, certain family aura about Glane, after all. I feel——"

"Feel J. G. might rig the committee for you?" De Fries was, beyond a doubt, at his most offensive, and the short laugh, the dig at Jane's ribs, did nothing to diminish his effect.

"Naturally not. I meant——" Anthony began, but de Fries interrupted him, said, "Well, you'd better hurry up. Read those rules," and, suddenly sweeping Jane out of his path, cruised with deliberation towards the bosom at which he had stared earlier.

Jane looked at Anthony and laughed.

"What's funny?"

"Just John on the prowl," she said gaily.

"I'm sorry, Jane, I don't find anything about him funny, as you know."

She said, "It's only an act; all of it. But then you never did like acts, did you?"

No reason, he told himself, why this should make him miserable, no reason to stand silently staring at her, with the search beginning inside.

"It was, if you'll recall, your total inability to put on an act that sent me back to John." She added, "But seriously, Anthony, that's the most beautiful piece of work. And the old boy wasn't fooling. I've seldom seen him bowled over; he doesn't bowl easily. And he wasn't prepared to like it. In fact he couldn't have been more bored at first when J. G. invited him to see it. Why the wink?"

"Smoke in my eye," he said.

(ii)

While he worked on the job at the Hampstead house, Anthony occupied one of the two spare rooms on Baron's floor at the Savoy. Today, since Liz had gone back to the country, he did not hurry to return. J. G. had said that he would not be free till six o'clock.

Anthony had enjoyed the day; high up in the September air, balanced on scaffolding, with the bag of tools slung over his shoulders; a steeplejack's day, and all London spread out in haze below the Heath. (No chance to think except with your hands that drove chisel or pitching-tool across the stone.)

He had a cup of tea at a Hampstead tea-shop and idled home on top of a bus, tired as any other workman. The luxuries of the Savoy suite were soothing. He had a hot bath, changed his clothes, and drank two whiskies before the summons of Mather sent him to the third. He was always careful not to have more than two before a meeting with J. G.

"Hullo, there," Baron called from the recording machine. "Help yourself. With you in a minute." He dictated smoothly. "So, while regretting that I have not at the moment any opportunity of helping you, I hope for you a happy solution to your difficulties." He snapped off the switch and rose. "Begging letters always upset me. I don't know why," he said. He looked tired tonight, Anthony thought; he wore his office clothes, black jacket and striped trousers.

"Make it a stiff one, Anthony boy. I've earned it. You too, eh? I didn't realise you were going to be alone here tonight or I wouldn't have made a dinner date. Thought Liz was staying up. Good party last night at Gerald's? Uncivil of me not to look in, but I was too damned tired."

The perfect cue; why the impulse to stall, to postpone the question? This happened to him often now, for no reason. The simplest words got stuck. Not that this particular issue was entirely simple. But it was not difficult to say, "I saw de Fries at Gerald's party." He worked at it, with the help of the third whisky. "Oh, and I saw John de Fries," he ended. Baron's eyes moved quickly.

"Who? . . . John de Fries—oh, yes; he was at Carlington last week. Took him over to Glane; brought that ex-girl friend of yours with him." Baron paused. "Did he tell you how highly he thought of the winged horse?"

"In so far," Anthony said, "as that kind of phrase fits his vocabulary."

J. G. chuckled. "Rude little man, isn't he? Act, of course. Take it from me, John was deeply impressed. Deeply impressed." The eyes went on watching Anthony.

"Look, J. G., he said something about entering it for the prize."

"What? . . . oh, yes, we spoke of it. You know, old man, I've been thinking; you'd better get rid of those scruples of yours, hadn't you? After all . . . why not? That's as tough a bunch of judges as you could find. They won't show anybody any favours."

"It isn't that." Anthony turned his glass in his hand. "I'm not saying for a minute that I could win, but——"

"De Fries thinks you might. And they've had one or two entries that he finds quite impressive."

Anthony muttered, "Let me off, J. G., will you, please?"

He saw Baron's fingers begin to tap.

"It may seem silly, but I just shouldn't feel all right about it." ("And that's true enough; I shouldn't. But it sounds as though I felt all right now . . .") From a great way off, he glanced reflectively at the time when he had felt all right; it was like looking at another person. "In the time of my innocence," he thought, dreamily—"the time that isn't there any more. The time when I didn't have this—this wound in my mind." J. G.'s voice pulled him back.

"What's all the agony about, eh?" Then his face softened. "No, I can see what it's about. You're too honest to live, you always were. Just like dear old Randolph." He was at his most gentle and wooing now. "But truly, Anthony, you mustn't. I can see what shadows your mind; easy to read as a book; you always were. You can't get it out of your head that if you won that prize, you'd have won it with my help. Eh?"

He rose. "Here, let's have another drink, shall we? . . . No, I'll pour them, don't like being waited on all the time, makes me feel like an old man." He crossed to the sideboard. "Mind you, I admire your independence; always have admired it; could make life a lot easier for you and Liz if you'd let me . . . ought to have your own little place in London, you know." He came back, carrying the glasses. He remained standing. Twin wreaths of grey and blue cigar smoke rose about his head.

"I didn't make the statue, Anthony, after all. . . . It's the statue that'll win the prize, not J. G. Baron's son-in-law." He cocked his head on one side and his eyes were bright.

"Going to tell you something," he said, "think you'll see why. Randolph was the straightest person who ever lived, wasn't he?"

"Yes," Anthony said, "I think he was."

"I helped Randolph once. And it meant a great deal to me that I was able to do it. More perhaps than any single act of friendship ever meant to me. And it made nothing but a bond between us. Remarkable thing. I've parted with a lot of money in my day and lost a lot of friends by it."

"Money?" Anthony said, startled.

"Money, yes. You know," he said, "when people take money from you, they get ashamed; think you're remembering it all the time. First they take too much trouble with you, then they fade away. Your father never let it make the slightest difference."

The quiet words were quite unbelievable; Anthony's first thought was, "How many times in his lifetime did I hear him say, 'We don't owe a penny to anybody'?" He gazed at J. G. incredulously. "I don't understand. You mean Daddy owed you money?"

"I do not. It was a gift. He came to me for help and I gave him help. I was proud and glad to."

("Partly the drinks that make me feel like this; dazed.")

"But what happened? When? He never told me."

Baron's feet performed their little shuffling dance, a pleased little dance.

"Of course not. That was one of my stipulations. He wanted you to know. But I didn't; it seemed to me that you might worry about it—as boys do about those things; worry, and feel obligated."

"When was it?" His voice, he thought, sounded abrupt, rude.

" 'Twenty-nine," Baron said. "He'd only just retired from the army and gone into business. You may remember the Stock Exchange crash; the Hatry crash, we called it. Your father was on the board of several companies. Every one of them failed. By November of that year he hadn't a penny."

" 'Twenty-nine," Carey thought, "that's twenty-one years ago. I was still at prep school; Mummy was alive."

"And of course," J. G. was saying, "the farm was nothing but a liability, even then." He blew smoke rings, a whole line of zeros, thick blue zeros, scudding across the air. "Don't you think the less of Randolph, now. That isn't the point of the story."

"How much did he borrow?" the rude voice rasped.

"Not borrow, please. And I'm certainly not telling you. Quite a large sum, that's all you need to know. Let's say that I invested in him; and a good investment it turned out to be." The smile was dazzling; then it went. "Anthony, don't look at me like that—as if I were a stranger."

In fact, Anthony thought, he was not looking at Baron at all; he was looking at the memory of his father and seeing the stature diminished. He saw the upright carriage, the square shoulders, the easy military manner; he heard again the casual references, "Not quite straight, you know"; "Bit of a shyster, I always think." And the maxims, "I've a horror of debt, Anthony; and I want you to feel the same." The kindly warning before he went to Paris, to study at Julien's: "It's a good allowance, old boy. But if you find it isn't enough, don't run up bills. Just let me know how much you need to keep yourself straight."

(Straight. Straight. Straight. "You'll go straight, always." "Come straight to me and tell me." "If anything happened to me, you'd always go straight to J. G., wouldn't you?")

In a sudden appalling change of perspective, he saw the willingness of his father to share him with Baron as the gesture of a debtor; the semi-adoption, which he had never questioned, neatly, horribly explained. ("So J. G. bought me; bought us both; bought father's friendship . . .") He ranged bitterly over old ground; over the sale of the farm and Randolph's later, dignified stipulations. "We're solvent, Anthony; we don't need to be rich," and he himself thinking, "How right Daddy was. We'd have been serfs to J. G." He remembered congratulating himself that he wasn't one of the Carlington yes-men, Baron's property, on the other side of the wall.

"It's a queer feeling," he said. "I'm sorry if I'm stupid. But it's hard to realise that you've been keeping us for years."

"No, no, *no*." J. G. looked horrified. "How can you say such a thing? Randolph made that—er—slice of capital the foundation for some remarkably sound investments. He had a talent for it, you know. Courageous too. One might say that what he brought to the world of finance was the gift of a clever soldier's strategy. How often in life is it given to any of us to give a good man a chance?" The face with the wistful smile seemed to be asking a kind word.

"It was bloody good of you to do it, J. G.," he said slowly. "Don't think I'm not grateful. It just makes me feel queer somehow. I'd like to pay it off, gradually; if you'd let me."

J. G. shut his eyes, puffed his cheeks in pain. "Please. You are not to think of it. You would be robbing me of something very dear to me. I beg you not to say that again." He opened his eyes; there were tears in them. He stretched out his hands. "Don't you see—you hurt me?"

"I'm sorry."

"The only reason I told you was to show you that a great gentleman could accept help of a far more palpable character than the mere—mere shadow of a name . . . and not let it do one thing to spoil a close and lasting friendship. So, when it comes to the Glane prize——"

("*Click! As when the trap shuts, you're inside the den!* Is that the hurt, malicious slanting of my mind? As I see it now, you only pulled the story out at this moment to show me, in the subtlest way, that I'm not in a position to say No to you. And you're right, J. G.; I'm not. I think I wasn't before; without this extra weight thrown into the scale. . . . But now. . . . Funny thought, that we owe you everything.

"But I still can't believe it. I still can't believe that Daddy was living a lie all those years.")

The thought shaped and pointed; he shook himself. "All right, J. G. I'll think again. Bless you. Mind if I take another drink?" and presently he was saying to the kind wistful face, the face of the wounded Puck, "But of course not; I swear it's not going to make the smallest difference between us."

May, 1951

(i)

The nearest that he came to telling was on a day that began quietly, with no warning of difference from other days. There were now long intervals of comparative peace, wherein he could feel that he was learning to take the lie for granted, just as he took his stiff leg for granted. It was a damage to him, as the knee was a damage. It set him a little apart from other people, but the worry was not persistent. When he was tired, it became acute and the familiar spiral began: with clouded vision, with an incredulous blink at the persons about him who were whole; the small stab of wonder that he had ever been whole like these, free like these. After that beginning he could tell where the thoughts would go; there was no stopping them. They played back the story, they gave him all his chances again, they cursed him for his silence; they played forward in prophecy to the moment of justice still ahead, and this they sketched in nightmare detail. When the mood was bad, it could last a whole day without a let-up; at the end of the day he would not be able to remember precisely what he had said or done; even the moments alone with Liz were veiled by looking inward.

But today did not promise to be like that.

Soft summer rain fell and the marsh was hidden. He worked under daylight lamps; he was engaged on a series of drawings for the new Eppersley building. He was the right sort of tired, he thought; having slept badly at first, then heavily and dreamlessly; now he felt limp, placid; it wasn't one of the jittery mornings after too much whisky. In these days he scored the better mornings with a faint sense of triumph.

He jogged along contentedly until midday; Liz had spent the night in London and would not be back before afternoon. He could not remember whether J. G. were coming today or tomorrow; this nagged at him. Life was so much easier without J. G. Everybody had been telling him that for years and he had never agreed. The tension, the side-stepping, the careful attitudes, once mysterious and absurd, were now his own habit. It had been coming on him, he realised, before the story of his father had made it an inescapable routine. J. G. returned to that story now and again; perhaps he was uneasy for having told it; perhaps he felt obliged from time to time to ram it home. You could not tell which and it did not matter which. Automatically now you covered the shrinking repugnance inside you; you said heartily that it was a wonderful thing for J. G. to have done, that of course it had made no difference, that you were, on your father's behalf and your own, eternally grateful.

The worst of it was that it could impart (this only when you were really tired or full of hangover) a look of unreality and falsehood to every memory of Randolph. Even the least ambiguous of his words or actions would lose by it; so that you thought, "Phony" and hated yourself for the thought.

He could have found some ease, perhaps, in talking it over with Liz; but, with a speed that puzzled him, it had entered the ever-expanding private territory; the place in his mind where he was alone. Odd, to acquire secrets easily. Once, when he met deviousness, it had baffled him.

Certainly it was better, all of it, when J. G. was not here. Now, looking at his watch, Anthony needed to know whether he would come today. He switched off the lamps and went out of the studio.

There was a break in the clouds, a break in the rain. The wind was high; the blossom was beginning to fall; scattering on the path at his feet. The ruffled green leaves swung and shook drops on his head. Over the marsh now there shone a crooked, fanciful sunlight, with the mists shredding and a white gleam of sea behind the ghost of the water tower.

As he came to the terrace, he heard Prince barking, and the sound of a car's engine shut off. He went round the house to see if this were Baron. It was not Baron. The car was a long, American car, and the woman who stepped out of it was alone. He saw a smooth dark head, a face of familiar beauty, a smile that was a little bemused as though this person were under a spell. He recognised her; she was Catherine de Lille.

"Hullo," she said. "You're Anthony Carey, aren't you? I *am* glad to meet you."

She said it wistfully; she made it sound as though there had been a conspiracy to prevent their meeting. He stood off in his mind. Because he knew her legend, and because of Tobias, he wanted to stare. The effort of not staring made him shy; he took in details of the façade, the lighted look of the skin, the paint on the lips, a jewel, the pattern of a *crêpe de Chine* scarf.

From the eyes he got the impression of somebody for ever in repose; there was an endless calm behind the eyes; she gave him too long a look for conventional good manners; she had obviously no reservations about staring and still it was not an offensive stare; decades of security had gone to make it natural, he told himself, a lifetime of self-acceptance, a lifetime of being loved.

"I wanted to meet you, too," he said.

"Well, you see, I am in England so little. Or I would certainly have come before. This is the first time in two years." She looked at the garden. "It is lovely, isn't it? Rain in England; I suppose you dislike it?"

"No, I don't. I like all weathers." He saw her looking at the house. "Monstrosity," he said, "but one gets fond of it. I don't know if J. G.'s here; I'll find out."

"He isn't," said Catherine de Lille, "he's in London; we talked. I told him I was driving down to Dover and I wanted to see your winged horse on the way."

"The horse; how nice of you," said Anthony formally.

"Will you take me to see it?"

"Yes, rather." He limped beside her, across the courtyard, between the walls of yew, over the lawn. The rain had stopped; the grass glittered. There he was, ahead and shining, mailed with drops of rain. "Gave him a good wash the day before yesterday," Anthony said.

"What d'you wash him with?"

"Hard soap and ammonia. Then I wax him when he's dry."

"It sounds almost too intimate a procedure for that beauty; I've seen the photographs," she said. They came to the smaller lawn.

She stood still at the foot of the steps, silent, taking her time. He looked at the horse and his eyes began to be cloudy; the white niche, the triumphant outline, the glow of dark brown and gold departed. It belonged to him now less than ever. It was not itself any more; it was a letter on thick white paper, with the names of the R.B.S. Committee printed above and the signature of John de Fries. It was a paragraph in *The Times*, a column in the *Flash*, a page in the *Sun*. It was the Glane Memorial Prize and the Glane Memorial.

It was its own replica, still at the foundry. "So many doors have shut on it," he thought, thinking of it molten in the tilting crucible, molten in the furnace. "So many hands have worked on it, not my hands; you would think by now that the first black tracing was of no importance at all; the hands that have poured and cast and welded, other men's work, the people with whom this making has been shared, might—you'd think—have removed all authority from that. But they have not. I can think of them, from Ian Ferris making the first plaster mould, past Price and Billy and the tow-headed boy at the armature, all the way to Jock Ferris with his queer chemist's brew, putting the acid on cold. And they don't tell the lie. They do not add to it nor make it less. The lie was there before they came. And it's still there."

It was a quiet panel of thought; it did not torture him today. It was simply present, the cool, detached condemnation.

Beside him, Catherine de Lille said, "The photograph does him less than justice; so much less."

"Thank you."

The horse looked down at them; the sunlight was stronger now; lifting the ripple of the feather pattern on the wings; the hints of muscle and vein came up, liquidly gold; on the white stone the shadow sharpened.

"Tobias would be very pleased with you," she said conversationally, not making a dirge of it.

"Bless him, I hope he would."

"It's a magnificent patina; how long have you had him up?"

"Nearly a year, now."

"I remember watching Père Limet in Paris; do you do it like that? Use a blow-torch?"

Anthony grinned. "I don't do any of it; it's done at the foundry. In fact a man called Jock Ferris put the first acids on; he's something of a magician. Not a blow-torch. It's better for the bronzes that stay out of doors to work on cold metal. Patining's an expert job."

"Did you want him to be the Glane Memorial?"

He looked at her, surprised. She had spoken lightly; she was still gazing at the statue.

"Well, no, I didn't. What made you say that?"

"I thought J. G. might have persuaded you," she said.

The voice had an overtone of knowledgeable friendliness. While he was making up his mind to reply, she added, "To me, if I were you and I had made it, the winged horse would be entirely and completely Tobias' winged horse. I'd want it for nowhere else and for nothing else. Glane . . . well, I am sure that Glane will be a most respectable achievement. But surrounded by a public fanfare that hardly matches the mood of this."

"Yes, it will be." The twitch of his eyelid bothered him suddenly. This was the voicing of his own thought; yet, most disturbingly, he felt that he could not now assent; he did not seem to have the right to express an honest view. "But J. G. always wanted a fanfare for Tobias," he reminded her, "from the beginning."

"I know." She turned from the steps. "That's understandable. And I don't believe that Toby would mind. He'd have clamoured against it, of course. Hypocrisy, he would have said. He was still so young that he could only see the virtues and the vices as they really are."

"As they really are," Anthony repeated, "what do you mean by that, Madame de Lille?"

Catherine paced slowly on the grass. "I mean that it's only in youth that one has the extreme luxury of seeing right and wrong like the figures in an allegory; detached, clear angels and devils. At that stage of—of spiritual virginity, they are recognisable. They're outside you—in perspective. After a time they mix and cloud and come inside, particularly the devils. And the older one grows, the more one forgives, which is good, and condones, which isn't good."

He felt hypnotised; he heard himself say, "In the time of one's innocence . . ." She looked at him with a hint of laughter. "Well, the sooner *that* time ends, the better," she said, surprising him so that he stopped, saying violently. "*Why?* Why should it end? You've just said——"

"I know. I've said that it was easy, in youth, all of it. I didn't say that it should go on being easy."

Anthony pulled his pipe out of his pocket. For the first time in months he was drawn wholly into an argument. "But innocence—or at least guiltlessness, which is somehow, in my view, the more adult version of the same thing——"

"It isn't the same thing at all," said Catherine de Lille. "How can it be? You can be tempted and guiltless. Innocence seems to me to preclude temptation. And the sooner one meets temptation the better."

"Oh, why?"

"Don't sound so sad about it; you don't need to agree with me."

He laughed. "Well, why?"

"Because the longer it's postponed, the worse trouble it makes. Remember what came into the room that was swept and garnished?"

Now he could not be sure whether she were laughing at him; it was hard to tell from the look in those untroubled eyes.

He said, "If one goes on being innocent and un-tempted for too long—that's dangerous?"

"I should have said so, wouldn't you? Fighting only comes with practice after all. If you've never had to fight, nor trained in fighting—but you know that, as a soldier." She halted at the gap in the yews. "Why are you perplexed? I'd have thought that it was obvious—a cliché."

Anthony was silent. He was accustomed on the bad days to find himself pulled up by chance phrases—in a detective story, a sermon, a novel, any phrase that touched even remotely on his problem. He would sit staring at it, feeling accused alike by a comment on lying or a comment on truth; by a reference to dodging issues or a reference to facing them. But he thought that the present storm in his mind was not the same. He was applying her words to Anthony Carey, less from a sense of guilt than with a sense of startled relief. As though, he thought, she had given him a hint of how it happened.

She looked back at the horse and he followed her eyes.

"Thank you very much," she said, holding out her hand. "I hope we'll meet again."

"Oh, please don't go. It's too quick. Won't you come into the house? Come to my house; have some coffee or a drink."

"I mustn't or I shall miss the boat."

"Please."

"I'm sorry, Anthony Carey; I'd have loved to, but I can't. Are you ever in Paris? Come and see me. Bring Liz."

"I want to talk to you now," he said, sounding to himself like a stupid and obstinate little boy. She shook her head, smiling regretfully. They came to the car in the courtyard. "Come to

Senlis. Take a rest after the Glane trumpetings. Promise? Both
of you. I am always there; you only have to telephone."

He watched her step into the car; she waved to him as she
drove under the archway. "Why in the name of God should I
think that I could tell Catherine de Lille? It's insane, but I
believe that if she had stayed another moment I would have told
her, without the slightest hesitation." Perhaps he was fooling
himself. He went into the house, found out from Foliot that
J. G. was not expected until tonight, and returned under the wall,
with Prince fussing at his heels.

"The Glane trumpetings," his mind echoed, and he added,
"if it weren't for Liz, I'd really like to die before then; I swear I
would. Well, nothing odd about that, is there? Every coward in
history has felt the same."

He got his car out of the garage and drove to meet Liz.

(ii)

"Such a pretty afternoon," she said, "let's drive. Let's go to
Glane."

"All right, that would be fun."

"You know," said Liz, "one of the nicest things about you is
that you never argue or protest that you have letters to write or
say, 'Oh, You Don't Want To Do That Now.' It *is* the most
endearing characteristic. I think the first time I ever knew I
loved you was when I wanted to go in the graveyard and read
the tombstones and eat veal and ham pie from the village shop
instead of going home to lunch."

"Did I fall in with this mad carnival?"

"Yes; and paid for the veal and ham pie, and we read every
single tombstone."

"You were," said Anthony, "a most gloomy little girl."

"I still like reading tombstones. *Hannah Broker*," Liz
crooned, "*She was greatly loved*; my favourite thing. Will you
put that on my tombstone, Carey, dear?"

"No, darling, because I intend to die first."

"*You dare*——" said Liz furiously.

The marsh had its sun-bleached, historic look today; the fragile blossom, the shadows on the light green grass, the bone-white fences, and the sheep that grazed reminded the eye that the land was old. When they came to the foot of the low hill where Glane was built, they saw the new thing signalling to them.

Once its lines had been vertical lines; it had stood up like a little castle on its knoll; the new Glane made horizontal lines of yellowish stone; McLeod's architect had attempted no fake restoration. He had laid out on the original cruciform a modern village. In the sunny quiet, it had an atmosphere of its own, not of the past, but of now; the wide green at the centre had the feeling of a college quadrangle; a star of stone pathways led to the naked plinth.

Anthony was reminded, as they stood and stared, of certain moments on their honeymoon in Rome when he was for ever looking from a beautiful thing that had been there a long time to this profile beside him. Liz was changing, he thought; there was a new calm here, not the calm of Catherine de Lille, a much younger and more dedicated calm; he found—as he had found in Rome—that he was studying the line of eye-socket and cheek-bone and neck, the flesh that belonged to him, with more curiosity than he could give to stone or bronze or painted canvas. She said, "I have a terror that this horse will look too small," and added, "his place is really Carlington, in his niche, is it not, Carey, dear?" She turned to him. "Why are you staring at me?"

"Because you look thin in the face."

"Haggard, as for witch?"

"No; delicate, as for dryad."

She looked away. "That inn sign's a stinker," she said.

"No, it ain't," said Anthony. "You'd kick far more if they'd done a Ye Olde job. Want to have tea here or in the town?"

"At the sad hotel? Harry's hotel . . ."

"Harry's?"

"We went there once," she said evasively; then she took a step towards the plinth. "In fact we went there on the day that I told him I would marry him; I see no reason to be reticent. I have no fear of him any more."

The words dropped a shadow. "No fear of him any more," Anthony's thought repeated, "No fear of him any more." The sword over his head was Levitt, the nearness of Levitt; not yet a physical nearness, but the threat who had moved up, come within striking distance, married to Celia, bound to return.

The marriage was one of the sign-posts on this seemingly endless journey, the most ominous sign-post yet. He did not know how he had lived so placidly in the company of its shadow since last year. Except that one became used to any idea, even a sword over one's head, when it stayed hanging. As they walked back through the village, he remembered the morning that the news came; Liz with her eyes several sizes larger than usual, greeting him at the dining-room door when he came down to breakfast, "I am on my way to get a feather in order that you may knock me down with it. And I couldn't be more pleased and nor could they." As usual, she had begun her story at the wrong end, so that it took him some time to discover that Celia was going to marry Levitt. He must have acted well; he had been a good actor for a long time now.

For weeks after that moment he had dreaded the letters with the American airmail stamps. It seemed impossible that there would not, one morning, be a letter from Levitt, a letter threatening him, questioning him. Celia must talk to Levitt of the winged horse, of the Glane prize. Liz sent faithful press cuttings and he dared not dissuade her.

But the letter never came. "Perhaps he's forgotten that drawing; perhaps he destroyed it long ago," was a familiar poultice to apply to his anxiety; he was near believing it on the quieter days. But on the bad days, he would remember Levitt saying, "Can't draw beautiful things ever. I'd have turned the Botticelli Venus into a leering whore."

On the bad days it was easy to remember all that Levitt had ever said to him; he came in panels of dialogue and the words had always an echo of honesty. In memory, he looked like a man hunting honesty; his hound look was still vivid; hound profile sniffing on an unfamiliar scent.

And now, Carey thought, the routine of the mind's side-step was almost perfected. (Liz, looking up from the writing-table, saying, "Send your love to Celia and Harry?"; the artless enthusiasm with which he joined her cry, "Oh, I *wish* they'd come home." And the time when, at her request, he had tried to break through J. G.'s angry, enduring silence, and beg for money for Celia and Harry; it had taken him four whiskies to do it and J. G. had shot him down without effort. And signing his name on the card for the Christmas presents, "With love to Celia and Harry from Liz and Anthony." And studying the snapshots that Celia sent from the Vineyard. He had become used to Levitt, wearing a grin and a pair of swimming trunks, in a small leather frame on the writing-table.)

There were aspects of relief to it, of course. There was the knowledge that at least he would have some warning of Levitt's coming. The earlier bad days had planted him with a certainty that he was going to run into Levitt on a street corner in London, and several times he had thought that he saw Levitt walking towards him. That was over; that had been at its worst in the period when he still kept the faint hope that he might sit down and write the letter beginning:

"MY DEAR HARRY,

"I've been meaning to write for ages. Do you remember doing a drawing while you waited for me in Celia's house—last winter?"

"Anthony——" Liz said sharply at his side. He awoke.

"Sorry, darling."

She said, "You haven't done that for days. Didn't you honestly hear me?"

"No, my love."

She stood still beside the car, looking at him tenderly. "What *is* it, exactly, that happens?" She had asked him before.

"I don't know, quite," he said, as he had said before, "I just go off into a dream. What were you saying to me?"

"Saying we'd go home, please, and not the sad hotel. Nothing to do with H. Levitt, I appear to be tired."

"Then home we go."

They drove away, and he saw her turning back to watch Glane vanish. She sighed.

"In fact," she said, watching the marsh, "I am not tired. I suddenly thought that I could not tell you in the sad hotel. And I have to tell you, because it is becoming a slight burden on the soul. And these are better out than in." She laughed. "Celia would call it hair-shirt. But I must. I owe you trouble, Carey, dear."

"Trouble?" He spoke lightly; he did not look at her, looked ahead, seeing the white road, the thorn bushes luminous with their flowers, the green flats.

"I do worry about you, darling. As you know. Not sleeping and getting borne down by work, and the twitch in your poor eye. So I took a step; don't be cross."

"Of course I'm not cross. What sort of a step?"

"I told a doctor about it. In London; Riddell, the neurologist; you've met him at Carlington."

"Ah," said Anthony. "Yes, I remember him." He said, "Your idea? Or J. G.'s?"

"Well, but of course my idea. I do not discuss my husband with J. G.," she said primly.

He hid his relief. "Oh, I just thought that as he was J. G.'s chum. . . . Well, you're very sweet. What did you tell Riddell?"

"I told him all, and said what I've said to you, that I thought you were having a delayed something or other from the war. He says it does happen."

"I've told you," Anthony said comfortably, "that there's nothing to worry about. And I assume that Riddell charged you five guineas for saying the same thing."

"Would you see him?" she asked wistfully.

"Oh, darling—yes, some time, if it goes on. But honestly——"

"He thinks you should."

Anthony chuckled. "What does he think'll happen next? Do I start twitching all over and falling about?"

"Please, love, I beg you not to mock this serious matter. Of course he didn't say it was a serious matter."

"No, well, it isn't."

"He wanted to know if you had had a shock, or if there were anything on your mind. I said only work."

"Work's easily explained," Anthony said, "anybody who got two commissions that size, right on top of each other and both with a deadline—ask Riddell how he'd like to tackle the Eppersley building and the Erndle fountains at the same time. Bless you, my love, I'll see him. I promise. Once I've got those designs set up."

She sighed. "Must you wait? It would only take a day. You don't want to spend the rest of your life taking those drippy sleeping pills, do you? These are the perquisite of the tense and the highly strung. Riddell says that too much drink is not good, by the way."

"I have yet to meet a doctor who says it is," said Anthony.

Another green packet of press-cuttings had come with the afternoon post. He looked at them, drinking his second whisky, while he waited for Liz to come downstairs. He saw his own face, an old picture, taken in uniform. The caption was "SOLDIER-SCULPTOR", and since the newspaper was one in J. G.'s provincial chain, the column underneath was long and leisured. After referring to the Glane award, it retold the story of his earning the decoration at Anzio. "Former Commando Major," was, he thought, an incomplete epitaph on today's Carey. "Former Commando Major; present neurotic, liar and cheat." The threat of Riddell worried him, and his eyes clouded again, so that he read the rest of the press-cuttings without taking them in. He saw the faces of the Anzio men; the grimy, bleeding faces and his own hands that tore at the cave-in on the hillside while the shells screamed over him. Those faces came back sometimes with a look that they had never worn, a look of reproach.

He refilled his glass. He heard Prince thumping down the stairs and got up to open the door for Liz. She had changed her suit for a black dinner dress. "Hullo. . . . You are very formal tonight, Mrs. Carey."

"I felt formal." He watched her move to the sofa under the lamp. She sat down, keeping her back straight, with one hand placed lightly on the sofa on each side of her. The Queen Anne room with the white panelling, and the furniture that was of the period, made a suddenly fit background.

"More trouble?" Anthony said, watching her.

"I trust you will not think so. It occurs to me that anybody else in this day and age would have told when hopes began to dawn. But first I was shy and then I thought what death, doom and destruction there are in anticlimax; more than in anything else, really—don't you agree?"

"Agreed," said Anthony, "but you have yet to tell me what you are talking about."

"All is now in order," she said. "I am going to have a baby. I hope it will give satisfaction, but of course," she added mournfully, "one can never be sure."

(iii)

They were listening to the Emperor Concerto and playing Canasta. He had no coherent thoughts about the baby; he had told himself for years that he wanted children and now that the prospect of a child was here, his thoughts stopped nostalgically at the other Carey, the Carey who was past and dead, Carey without the knot inside him.

"I fear," said Liz, "that you have now given me the pack." She picked it up and began to sort the prizes.

"Not to mention the game," said Anthony, throwing down his cards. "Hardly worth scoring, darling. You're miles in the lead." He got up, kissed the top of her head, turned off the gramophone and went to the sideboard. "Only beer," he said to the unspoken comment.

"Soon you will be fat," said Liz. "Well, I can't talk; so shall I be. Oh, *why* not eggs? What shall we call this child? I really am extremely glad to have told you. Now I have, I don't know why I didn't before. I tried to several times, and the words got stuck."

"I know that one," he said tranquilly, coming back with the glass of beer. She looked at him, large-eyed.

"Do you? I should have thought no."

"Everybody knows that one."

He saw that she was watching his eyelid.

She put the cards away, went to the sofa and lay down. He came to sit beside her. "Having two things to tell was bad," she said, "that's why I feel exhausted. One's enough, heaven knows."

"One's enough; you're right."

"You speak with authority, Carey, dear. Are you keeping a secret sorrow hidden, as for knife in bosom?"

"No, darling. Did Riddell put that into your head?"

She said, "I should always understand if there were things that you couldn't tell me."

"Bless you. But that," he said, "is because you are still a kitten. As you grow older, you'll know that people who love each other should have nothing they don't tell."

He watched her face, the long neck stretched back on the cushion, the chin pointed upwards.

"Are you sure? I still think they might. Not that I have hideous depths within, myself. I don't believe there's one small, regrettable item in my life that isn't known to you. I always ran to you with everything, didn't I, my darling?"

"You did."

"Even with Harry Levitt," said Liz.

He was silent, remembering that dark morning. It was the beginning of everything that had happened to him, everything good and everything bad. He went back to Catherine de Lille's words, "What came into the room that was swept and garnished?" ("What was there of me, before December, 1949?") Liz was saying, "Never, no matter how long I live, will I forget the feeling. Knowing that you loved me, that I needn't go with Levitt; walking back down the path in the sun and the cold, singing the Winged Horse at the top of my voice. Out of prison and into Paradise, that was. I love you so."

"And I love you." He held her close. "And it frightens me because I don't deserve you."

She said, "Oh, foolish Carey."

"You come first, whatever happens," he said.

"Nonsense, I am a poor thing. But I'll tell you this. If you had murdered six wives in secret, I'd still love you."

"In fact it was only five," said Anthony.

Like this, with their arms around each other, he thought that he could tell her and not be afraid. But the moment went by, with all the other moments, and he did not speak.

June, 1951

"I'd made several shots at the horse before, you know. But this one——" Carey said. He paused.

Perched on the table in the studio, Gerald Lynn was still looking at him inquiringly. Carey wondered for how long he had been silent. His thoughts had rushed all the way from that first moment, standing alone in Celia's studio-room, to here.

"Do I remember my actual moment of inspiration?" he heard himself repeating. "Now, do I?"

He was aware of the load, the box; sometimes it came in this shape, shape of a heavy iron box whose corners pressed outwards against his skull; the load in your head that you could not put down.

He smiled at Lynn. "Lynn's all right," he thought. He did not mean that he liked Gerald Lynn. The words had come to have their special sense, their private sense; he added to them the usual rider, "He's all of a piece; whole; free. No battle going on inside."

There was nothing odd in wishing to change places with a middle-aged pansy. It was the familiar bend of thought; the wish to live for a little time in somebody else's head, and be at peace.

"Honestly, I don't, Lynn. I do remember trying to get him

right when I was cruising with J. G.; just after Tobias died."

"*No*," said Gerald, tapping his notebook, "you've given me a *biography* of J. G. already."

("I have told you nothing.

"I could tell you that J. G. bought me long ago; that he planted this fact, the fact that I belonged to him, when I jibbed at the Glane prize. He set the trap. I'm in it now.

"I could tell you that J. G. has made me his heir; heir to the common stock of fear that others have inherited. That my father inherited. He was afraid of J. G.—or he wouldn't have lied to me. I could tell you that I'm afraid of him now; afraid of his shadow. I remember his shadow, fallen on that threshold—just beyond where you're sitting, Lynn—as it came once to spy on the winged horse when he was still in plaster.

"I could tell you how J. G. took my father away and gave me a liar in exchange; how he helped to take away the man I once was and give me this liar in exchange. Yes, he runs neatly through the pattern, as he runs through everybody's pattern.")

His eyes wandered to the table, to the sets of proportional compasses lying there, Baron's gift; to the heavy stuff on the further floor, rollers and turn-tables, Baron's gifts.

"All right, we'll scrub J. G.," he said.

"Always remembering," said Gerald impishly, "that I'm employed also by the big rival. I'm not exclusive to the Baron group."

Carey knocked out his pipe. "That worry you, ever?" he asked. "Working for two sides?"

"Never," said Gerald briskly. "In a way it's simpler to have a double mortgage on your soul; helps a sense of proportion. You can't remember *anything* about the moment of inspiration, dear?"

"Well, no—just that it began with a rough outline drawing—don't know what's happened to it now."

("In fact, chum, it's just under your elbow, you'd be surprised; shut up in that old sketch-book of mine. I haven't destroyed it yet.")

"I do remember waving good-bye to the big wax model, at that door, when the truck took it to the foundry. That's corny enough, isn't it? Waving to one's own work."

("And as I waved, I saluted the lie in wax on its way to become the lie in bronze.")

"Oh, and when he came back in bronze he reminded me of a story out of the war, in Italy. Chum of mine, who was in Florence when they began to bring out the treasures hidden from the Germans, saw a Donatello horse come back down the Lung' Arno on a tank transporter, with American troops driving him."

"Charming," Gerald interrupted. "We'll say you saw that yourself."

"I didn't, old boy; I couldn't have; I was out of the fighting long before they got to Florence."

"Dear me, you *do* suffer from scruples, don't you? It's quite a pretty story. But it doesn't tie happiness to inspiration, does it, exactly?" He feathered back through the pages of his note-book. "Oh, yes; look, let's end another way. Remember this, what you said this morning, dear? 'Happiness depends entirely on living according to one's credo.' Could you define the credo?"

"Mine? I don't know that I could." The twitch of his eyelid worried him. "*Nothing* like a credo, really, is there?" Gerald was urging. "Do try."

("Give you my case-history instead, any time. Because it *is* a case-history, of a sort. Odd things happen.

"Take the time I had to go back and see my old school; I didn't have any damn' reason for going, just took a train one afternoon; I thought it would help, can't think why. Didn't try to see anybody I knew; wandered around the houses, went up the staircase in what used to be my house; peered into the room, said 'Sorry' to the boy who was there, went to the playing-fields and watched the football, hung about in the library, went home.

"All the time I was doing that, I had two lines of poetry in my head. Housman's poetry:

'The youth I did not value
and will not have again.'

"It nearly drove me crazy, not being able to remember the first two lines. But when I tried to look up the poem in the collected Housman it wasn't there. And I never have found it. I suppose I made it up.

"There was the tart-ish, would-be-intellectual girl who looked like Jane Ireland; she was the daughter of those friends of J. G., I worked on a stone relief job on their house in Hampstead, last autumn. It was just after J. G. had told me about giving my father the money. I slept with that girl, slept with her, of all the idiotic, unnecessary things to do; I'd only been married four months. And I love Liz.

"It wasn't that I was particularly drunk. She said something that made me think she knew and understood what I was going through in my mind; something lofty and elaborate about the crucifixion being integrity—or one's integrity being the crucifixion; I can't remember; it is the kind of phrase that I despise and she is the kind of person I despise, but for twenty-four hours I thought she was my salvation and I ended up the twenty-four hours in her bed.

"I hate that. Because one can't say any more, ever again, 'It isn't the sort of thing I do.' The trouble with this worry in your head is that it changes you, not into one different person but into a whole series of different people, not nice people, any of them.

"Sometimes, just silly people.

"There was the time when a man who used to be in my company raised Cain at the regimental dinner last year. Somebody was attacking the Jews. This boy is only half-Jewish anyway, and none of us knew that; he doesn't look it, and his name isn't Jewish. But he had to speak up. Speak up is a considerable understatement. He talked for half an hour, getting whiter and whiter and angrier and angrier, and we were all highly uncomfortable; afterwards everybody said that it was shocking bad manners and that he could have kept quiet, and who cared if he did have Jewish blood?

"And my answer was that he cared and that he would have felt like a coward, sitting there, letting some chucklehead talk about 'Kikes' and pretending it didn't touch or concern him. He *had* to say it. And he fascinated me so much for being able to say it that I thought he must have some secret philosophy I might learn. I invited him here for the week-end. And of course I never got around to asking him about it.

"We hadn't a thing in common, he's something or other in Imperial Chemicals, one of those wildly well-informed scientists with a passion for political argument. Liz said not to have him again, please, she couldn't understand a word he said.

"One makes clutches all the time, clutches at the past, clutches at other people, clutches at words. And for a moment they help, and then they drift by. . . .

"Drift into that queer cloud. The blurred look that faces have now, that's a maddening symptom.

"And the absentmindedness that makes me not hear when people speak to me.

"And going out at early morning, when I can't sleep; walking round the statue. Tobias is there, with me, then. But he despises me.

"Quite a good interview, this one, Lynn, would it be? Why I Am A Happy Man, by Anthony Carey. It's sad for you, you're not getting it . . .")

He paced, hands in pockets. "My credo. Well, there's not much to it. I think I respect truth and courage more, the older I grow. They seem to be the basic principles. They interlock, of course; without fear there's no untruth. I imagine that every lie ever told has been based on fear. Every important lie. Or—d'you know something?—I don't believe there's such a thing as an unimportant lie."

"Go on."

"No, I can't," said Carey abruptly. "That's all."

"You *looked* as though there were going to be much more."

"No," said Carey. "Roughly, I believe that if you live according to your lights, you can't go wrong. Even if they are, by other people's standards, odd or incomprehensible lights, it doesn't matter. You get to know what they dictate to you, and you have to steer by them. Otherwise you're sunk." He sat down and stretched his arms over his head. He looked beyond Gerald's shoulder, at the first white cast of the winged horse on the pedestal. He recalled wanting to take one of the two heavy mallets and smash it to pieces.

"You've been an *angel*," Gerald was saying, "let's have just one more picture beside this lion of yours. Take a tool, dear; more effective."

There was a knock on the door. Liz said, "Darling, sorry; cable. It went over to Carlington with a sheaf of J. G.'s. Has Hollywood bought the movie rights of the horse, would you say?"

"Perhaps Walt Disney wants it. Probably something from Celia," he said. He opened it; saw that the origin was Gander, Newfoundland. He was aware of Liz, framed in the sunlight at the door, of Gerald putting his camera back in its case.

He read the message.

After a moment it seemed wholly expected, a summons that he had been awaiting; the last thing and the worst thing.

"Don't know if you remember that I was hoping to catch the four-ten to Ashford and that if I met you at Celia's house in St. John's Wood it couldn't be later than three o'clock. We'll keep the same rendezvous, I think, on Wednesday of this coming week, that's the Twentieth. Same place, same time, see?"

It was signed *H. L.*

Slowly Carey folded the cable. He found that he could smile at Liz and say, "Nothing interesting, love. Just a rather dull gent from the Modern Art Museum in New York; he's been threatening a long time. Wants to see me this week."

(*"Oh, I say, how quick and clever; you're good, aren't you?"*)

He slipped the cable into his breast pocket. The chill at his finger-tips and the deafness in his ears were uncomfortable. He said, "Time for a drink, isn't it? Come on, Gerald." As he limped across the cobblestones, he wished he could be sure that his head was not shaking. It felt as though it were nodding up and down, like the head of an old man.

BOOK VI

AND I RIDE

(June, 1951)

AND I RIDE

(i)

LEVITT climbed off the bus at the Abbey Road corner and walked down the avenue. The leaves were thick and green on the trees. There was the London light, the London quiet, the feeling that he remembered. He saw changes here: seams of new brick mending split walls; new paint; new window-panes. He had not thought that his memory of each house on the way to Celia's house would be so clear. They came, one by one, just before his eyes found them.

It was easy to turn time back, to restore the other afternoon. The pictures came scurrying out of their hidden place. He saw himself striding fast, with his head lifted, and the song keeping him company.

It was interrupted suddenly in his head by the words "Cobbett's Wen"; he remembered Baron's sneer and his own retort to Baron, "London is more mine than yours." Yes, he had looked with love on this street, this city, that winter afternoon. Now summer was here and hate was here. He came to the garden. He had spied upon the house yesterday, walking up from the other main artery road at the end of the avenue, pedantically saving the exact walk of the original afternoon for now. It was an unexpected reversal to find this house in decay. Once solid, in a neat garden, flanked by shabby neighbours, it was today a roofless shell of walls in a dusty space. A square white board announced the name of the contractors on the job. The three houses below it were also coming down. On this site, another board told the avenue, a block of flats would be built.

Leyitt strolled across the wreck of the garden. He stepped over a pile of planks and came to the doorstep. There was no front door; it was odd to walk through the house and look up and see the sky over your head. Looking down, he saw footprints in the white mortar dust, workmen's footprints or Carey's? He was five minutes ahead of time, but so might Carey be. He thought that Carey would be.

He went on down the passage from the front hall. At the end of the passage, there was the frame that had been the door. He could see the sunshine striking down into the dusty shell of the studio-room. He came to the top of the three steps.

The windows were out, of course, and the far door. The gallery was torn down; you could see the scar where it used to be. The walls were stripped and the floor thick with dirty scrapings of wallpaper and plaster. It did not feel like a room any more; it was a sort of abandoned patio, full of sunlight and dusty motes flickering, with the green untidy back garden pressing at the long window-frames. Anthony Carey rose from his seat on the window-sill. He limped into the middle of the room. He said nothing. He stood there, looking at Levitt.

His image clashed so sharply with the image in Levitt's mind that it was easy to return the stare in silence. "Oh, poor Carey, look what's happened to you. Still handsome, of course, but St. Michael's running to fat, isn't he?" The skin of Carey's face was redder. The features were a little thickened; one eyelid twitched in a steady wink. "Why that eye?" Levitt said to himself. "You never used to have that eye."

"Mess, isn't it? Lucky, in a way, that they're pulling it down, though. Otherwise we mightn't have got in," Carey said. His voice was unchanged, deep, charming and gentle. He smiled. "Nowhere to sit, I'm afraid, except in the windows."

Now that it was here, Levitt wanted to make it last; he had planned his opening moves and he made them, with his eyes still fixed on Carey. He put his hand in his breast pocket, took out the drawing, unfolded it, held it up at the level of his chin between fingers and thumbs.

Carey looked at it, nodded and said, "Well; what can I do for you?"

"Not much," said Levitt. "I thought you might like to see it,

that's all; you never have seen it. I'll keep it, if you don't mind."
He folded it and put it back.

"It's mine, after all, isn't it?" he said sunnily, taking the
envelope out of his side pocket. "But here's a present for you; a
photograph of the drawing. Had the photographs made in New
York. Good, aren't they?"

Carey stood with the photograph in his hands.

"Very good," he said in a casual voice.

"Got plenty more," said Levitt. "Signature's come out nicely,
too."

Carey put the photograph in his pocket. The silence held.

"You know more about these things than I do, Carey; and I
haven't seen the statue itself, only pictures of it. But I'd say that
anyone—seeing the drawing—would recognise the lines,
wouldn't you? Even somebody who didn't happen to be the
artist."

"Yes," said Carey evenly. "I think it's obvious. That side
view's unmistakable."

"It came through on to the block, of course."

"Yes, that's what happened."

"When did you find it?"

"Just after you'd gone."

"You knew it was mine?"

Carey looked at him indulgently. "Whose else could it have
been?"

"Well—yours, as it turns out," said Levitt.

Carey said, "See what you mean."

"Tell anybody?" Levitt asked.

"No."

"Ever think of telling anybody?"

"Yes. I've thought a lot about it, as a matter of fact." He
pulled his pipe out of his pocket; his movements were slow and
dreamy as though he were thinking about something else. He
was irritating. Levitt heard his own voice rasp on his next
words, "Did it ever occur to you that this drawing might mean
something to me, might matter to me very much?"

"Well, yes, I thought it probably did. Remember your saying

you couldn't draw a beautiful thing; that you'd have turned the Botticelli Venus into a leering whore." He put the match to the pipe and strolled back to the window-sill and sat down; he settled himself comfortably, leaning his back against the frame, pulling up one knee and hugging it, only half-turning his head towards Levitt. "On some days," he said, "I can remember pretty well everything you ever said to me. Yes, I believe I guessed how much the drawing meant to you."

"But you still stole it."

"Yes. I still stole it."

"Why?"

Carey said, "Ah, if I knew that, I think I'd have the answer to everything. I've had hints, of course, clues, now and again. But they don't add up. I've tried to work it out, but the whole answer doesn't come."

"It's been on your mind, then?"

"Very much on my mind." He turned his head away, looking into the garden.

He puffed at his pipe. "What surprises me," he said reflectively, "is that you didn't see it earlier; I was expecting to hear from you after Liz sent Celia the first pictures."

"Celia doesn't show me anything that comes from England."

"Oh? Really? That explains it, then." Carey looked stupid now. "Why not, if I may ask?"

"Because," Levitt said, "I've never wanted to see or hear. I shut you and England and Liz and Carlington up inside me, because that was, at one time, the only way I could keep sane. And I went on doing it. Lonely for Celia. It would take somebody with her self-discipline to let me alone, not to try to break in, don't you think?" He was surprised that he had to say this to Carey; it was off the point and it wasn't Carey's business.

"She's got guts," said Carey. "How did you find it at last? I'm interested."

"I began looking at her scrapbooks in the Vineyard one afternoon last week; it was an afternoon when I decided I'd stopped hating you. That's why I could look at them. Very funny."

"Did you tell Celia?"

"No. Said I'd got a piece of unfinished business over here and she must trust me. She does trust me, too."

"Nice, to be trusted, if one deserves it," said Carey.

"You're damned stupid," Levitt said angrily. "You always were."

"Mm——" said Carey—"case of arrested development in some ways, I'm afraid. Really does seem like the action of an imbecile when I look back on it. It snowballed, you see. The beginning was so small. I shaded over those lines of yours from sheer curiosity; made them come out white; it looked like a stone carving already. I'll show you the tracing; still got it in my studio. Meant to bring it with me, as a matter of fact, but I forgot. Stupid. I get blanks these days."

"And you decided then and there that you'd pretend it was yours?"

"Lord, no," said Carey. "I meant to tell you at once. I never was satisfied with that boy-and-fawn marble job I did for Toby; thought this was the kind of winged horse I'd always wanted. Made sketches—side and front; scaled them up and then started modelling in plasticine to see how it would go."

"And it went?"

"And it went," said Carey. "Snowball, you know. Growing all the time. First I was going to tell somebody in a minute, Liz or J. G., and I was going to write to you; and I didn't; kept putting it off. Gradually got more used to the idea; never quite used to it."

"It was too pretty a thing to part with, after a bit, though?"

"Sort of," said Carey. "Yet I don't really know. I find it all very hard to understand."

"So do I," said Levitt, acidly. He paced beside the window. "J. G. pretty pleased with the horse? Liz like it? Did J. G. have to rig the Glane prize for you? Or did it win on its merits? Interesting, that the ceremony's coming up. I really was fortunate to find the picture at this minute, wasn't I?" He went on talking to the dreaming, expressionless face. "Don't you think I was, Carey?"

Carey took his pipe out of his mouth. "What do you want?" he asked; his voice sounded sleepy. "Money?"

Levitt laughed, he stooped, and scraped some plaster off the sole of one shoe. "You'd pay me to keep quiet?" he asked, looking up.

"Is that what you want?"

"How much would you pay? I'm pretty broke."

"I know you are." Carey looked more awake now, awake and sympathetic.

"I don't get good jobs any more," Levitt said, "no Glane prizes or fat commissions for me. I draw a comic strip for a Boston paper. And I'm pretty tired of living on a shoe-string. And there's more to it than that." He placed himself in front of Carey, looking into the blue eyes; the eyelid twitched on steadily; he wanted to tell it to stop.

"It muddles me," said Levitt, "to be in the s—— when I'm a better guy than I used to be. When I was something of a heel, I got on fine." He had not expected to say this to Carey, yet it was now not only easy but important to say it.

"Everything in my life's all right, except that," he said. "I've got Celia, and that's the best thing in the world. But I'm not much use to her; I can't give her any sort of life; I'm nothing any more; just a second-rate cartoonist. Why? What happened?" He shrugged his shoulders.

"What did happen?" Carey asked gently.

"Nothing of any importance to anybody but me. I grew up; I learned to behave. I stopped lying, and I loved somebody more than I loved myself. Something good ought to have come out of it. Well, J. G. sacked me, and I went down, and I've gone on going down. As far as work goes, I've never had a break since. And I'd be very much astonished if I ever did again. . . . But I drew the winged horse, see? And you stole it." He stared past Carey's shoulder into the sunny garden. "It would be reasonable for me, wouldn't it, to want money?"

"It would," Carey said.

"Well, as it happens, I don't. Does that make you feel any better? I guess not; you haven't a hope of buying me off. I wouldn't mind blackmailing you, I admit. Occurred to me in the plane on the way over, that I could probably get a sizeable cheque out of you before I published the story. Unfortunately, I don't seem to be geared for blackmail. You ask me what I want. I want the truth to be told; that's all."

Carey's smile turned down at the corners, as though Levitt had said something painfully foolish.

"Why's that funny?"

"It isn't funny."

"Well, then, here's my plan. I'm not telling you how much of it I've carried out." He came to sit in the window-frame, he straddled it, one leg dangling over the sill outside; he faced Carey.

"One thing that struck me right away was that the Baron group wouldn't use this story. J. G. would kill it. No matter what he thinks of you for having done it, he'd still protect you, protect his family, protect himself and those pretty Glane Souvenir supplements that'll be on the news-stands quite soon. I'm right, aren't I? No talk with him could possibly include a request to publish the drawing and the story, could it?"

"No, I see that," said Carey. "Why don't you give it to the big rival? Let Gerald Lynn write it up? He works for them. He'd be a good person to handle it; he's just done an interview with me for J. G. and he wanted to know how the horse happened; where I got my inspiration. I couldn't tell him. You could."

The coolness of the suggestion threw Levitt off balance. He could think of no retort to Carey's calm. Carey said, "I was with Lynn the day I got your cable; giving the interview. Title might amuse you, 'Why I Am A Happy Man'." He knocked out the ashes from his pipe.

"So what?" snapped Levitt.

Carey did not answer at once. Then he murmured, "You're unhappy because you're suffering from an injustice; you want your rights; that's fair enough." He frowned. "But when you were, in your words, something of a heel, you say you got on fine. Did you, *really*?" The bewilderment of the face was naïve; the question had a schoolboy quality.

"Sure, I did," said Levitt. "I was big stuff then—you remember?"

"But was it all right inside?" Carey persisted.

"I never worried, if that's what you mean. What is all this, anyway?"

"Doesn't matter," Carey said, "except that I've forgotten how to be happy. . . . And you're the first person I've said that to," he added, smiling and sleepy-eyed. An odd remark; odder still, the fact that Carey's left eyelid had suddenly stopped twitching.

"What did you tell Lynn, then? How To Be Unhappy Though Famous?" Levitt mocked him.

Carey shook his head.

"Well—what d'you want *me* to tell Lynn?"

Carey looked lazily into space.

"I'll be seeing J. G. today, of course," Levitt said.

"J. G.? Even though he won't publish the story? . . . Yes, I think I understand why." He paused. "J. G.'s ill, you know. He's pretty bad. Went back to work too soon after a heart attack; they're keeping him in bed at the Savoy."

"I know that. I've got my date with him. The fact that he's ill isn't likely to soften me up, if that's your idea."

"No, it isn't my idea. Just wondered if you knew," Carey said.

"I'll show him the drawing."

Carey nodded.

"And just in case he grabs it and tears it up, well, that's why I've got the photographs. Three of them." He climbed off the window-sill. "And I've typed up the story quite prettily; three copies." He strolled towards the doorway. "I put a covering note on each," he called back over his shoulder, "suggesting that whoever reads it calls on you for comment before publication." He walked up the three steps. "Just where those stories and photographs are going is my business. Have to safeguard myself against any really drastic action by Baron, don't I?"

He hung there, waiting for Carey's answer. None came. "Well, thanks," said Levitt to the bowed fair head and thoughtful pose. "Good-bye."

Carey rose from the window-sill, limped into the middle of
the room. He looked at Levitt. He rumpled his hair with one
hand; he said, "So time's up," and drew his hand down quickly
across his forehead, holding it over his nose and mouth. Levitt
heard the great gulp of the sob behind the hand; then Carey
turned from him blindly and went out through the frame of the
garden door.

(ii)

"Looking back over the past two years," Baron said into the
recording machine, "we can be justly proud. But it would be
better to salute the achievement that is Glane in a spirit of
humility. We might, at evening when the ceremonies are done,
recall to ourselves these words:

> *'The tumult and the shouting dies,*
> *The captains and the kings depart . . .'*

"Wait. Cut." The two lines, now that he heard them,
sounded a ring of *lése-majesté*; they sneered at the Royal
Daimler driving away.

"Recall to ourselves these words, which bear especially upon
any monument raised by man:

> *'Still stands thine ancient sacrifice,*
> *A humble and a contrite heart.'* "

He snapped the switch that held the machine. He was not
satisfied. He never could dictate leaders lying down.

His large bedroom with the Chinese wallpaper was trans-
formed as far as possible into the likeness of his office; there was
the machine, there were the two telephones, the noiseless typewriter, the constant flow of messengers, the files and the fuss.
But the office façade was punctured all over the place by flowers
of an ornate and formal sort. The people who sent Baron flowers

ran to gold baskets, tall fierce lilies, spear-headed roses with long stalks; to satin bows girt about rigid, expensive plants in pots.

They kept coming. He did not like them; he was expecting all the time that the nurse would unwrap one great tent of white waxed paper to reveal a wreath. People like that ordered flowers like that over the telephone, and the next thing you knew, there'd be a wreath; or a cross; it could easily happen.

He was not uncomfortable. The occasional cough in his heart was the only hazard and he could stop it at once with the pills on the table beside him. The august specialists would not commit themselves. But he went on believing he would be well in time for Glane.

He was only fussed, he told himself, because of Levitt. Damn Harry Levitt for appearing out of the blue at this moment, of all moments. He tried not to let it fuss him, but he could not help thinking "Levitt again——" with peevish hate. It was so difficult to put Levitt into the focus of Now. He belonged to the past. Levitt the scapegrace, Levitt the smart-alec, Levitt the promising upstart who had failed to maintain the promise, these were still irritatingly available to the mind's eye. Their only successor was Levitt the impudent fly whom he had swatted in New York. The mind's eye still blinked at the Levitt who was Celia's lover. And from November until today, when asked to contemplate Levitt the son-in-law the mind's eye had stayed obstinately shut.

Even if he had been feeling well, Baron thought, the forcing entry would have disturbed him. He could not understand it; could not fathom the insolent urgency, the gay voice that said, "I've got something to tell you." One would have thought that if Levitt came at all, he would come to fetch Terry, but Terry had sailed yesterday. How could Levitt afford this flying visit? It made no sense. "But it would make less sense for me not to see him; I'd just lie and fuss. What's wrong? Can't be anything wrong with Celia, unless he's stalling. He said Celia was fine. Yes, Mather?"

"Mr. Lawrence Peet and Mr. Micklethwait are outside, sir. Miss Calhane will be here in a few minutes and I wondered——"

"I don't pay you to wonder. What's that page-proof you've got there?"

"Mr. Lynn's article for Sunday, sir."

"The Happy Man, eh? Let's look at it." He felt a little soothed. Lynn had done his usual pretty job with the article and the photographs. "Thank God for Anthony," echoed in Baron's heart as he looked at the figure posed beside the unfinished clay. "It's Anthony's hour of triumph, just as much as mine."

The two subordinate shapes stood at the end of his bed: Lawrence Peet lounging fastidiously; old rocking-horse Micky rubbing his hands and nodding his head. It was amusing to see them change with the arrival of Doris Calhane; each making a sudden statement of sex. It was like the clicking of the troops' heels for the entry of the officer, Baron thought; at the summons, "Female Flesh!" (trimmed with orchids) they came to the salute, each in his separate manner. Poor old Micky's face radiated a fatuous beam; he bowed and he rocked; he capered to an arm-chair and wheeled it nearer to the bed for Doris; he stood back, still beaming. Lawrence Peet lost his smile, stiffened, pulled down his waistcoat, gave her the benefit of his features in blank repose. It was the young man's challenge, the disinterested parade.

Doris, if she could see either of them, through those false eye-lashes, apparently took them for furniture. She let her body do the work—as she sank into the chair with a lyre-shaped swing of the hips, a boot-and-saddle gesture that placed one hand at her belt and dropped the left knee over the right; the left leg hung motionless. "Best legs in Europe," Baron thought, "and, which is more of an achievement, in America. If I still cared about legs . . ." He greeted her as though he still cared about legs. He remembered her at a farewell party in his stateroom, sailing from New York in '49. Who else had been there? Grant Parker, he thought; Celia; Gerald Lynn; Levitt? Certainly Levitt had been on board, coming to work for him. "But I don't think I invited him. I'm getting horribly hazy these days; it's not so long ago." He was watching the clock for Levitt; he let Doris do the talking. Here it was, now.

"Mr. Levitt, sir."

"All right, bring him in. My American son-in-law," he explained to Doris. "You remember Harry Levitt, don't you, boys? Now, nobody's to run away."

As Levitt crossed the floor, he brought the past with him. Some traces of the later, English-type Levitt still lingered, the well-cut, shabby suit and the hand-made shoes. But the tie was elaborate; the short hair-cut, the smooth, gangster's walk, and the assured sparkle combined to reproduce Levitt of New York '49.

He took Baron's hand, stood beside the bed, looking down at him. "How does it go?" he asked gently. His eyes were livelier even than Baron remembered; he had arranged his face for sympathy, but he was still very gay about something inside.

"It doesn't go badly," Baron said, "I'll be up in a day or two." He could not get it into his head that Levitt was married to Celia. Try as he might, the picture would not set. This man sounded only the echoes of a mistrusted employee. (He remembered calling Levitt the Knave of Spades.) Very inconsiderate of God, again. But God was an inconsiderate fellow; you were used to that idea by now.

"Just a flying visit?" old Micklethwait was asking, Doris crooning, "Honey, how *can* you fly, now there are all these beautiful boats?" and Levitt replying, "Beautiful boats take beautiful time and beautiful money." Lawrence Peet murmured, "Hate aeroplanes," making it sound as though that finished that.

When the three began the tactful break-up, the mass move, Baron felt a moment of panic. He was not ready to talk to Levitt; he had not decided who to be.

"Hell," he thought, "I'm making him too important." Now there was a stooping cloud of Lanvin scent as Doris kissed him, then Lawrence's tight, friendly little bow and jaunty wave of the hand. ("Lawrence getting a bit above himself these days; wants watching.") Now Micky's warm moist grip and it was over. They were gone. He was alone with the Knave of Spades.

"You're damned unexpected," he said when the door was

shut. "Did Celia send you? What's this about? Getting old
. . . don't like surprises."

"I'm sorry. But this needn't worry you, unless you let it."

"Celia all right? Really all right? I don't need soothing. If
you've bad news, fire it out." He folded his arms in their scarlet
silk sleeves; he jutted his chin.

"No bad news from her, I can promise you; Celia's well; and
as beautiful as ever."

"Never thought she was beautiful," Baron said. "Charm by
the bucket-load; beauty, no."

"You've a poor eye," said Levitt amiably. "But she's happy
as a clam, waiting for Terry on the Vineyard. She sent her love."

"Her love, eh? Didn't send you?"

"No," said Levitt. "I'm here on my own hook. A bit of
unfinished business came up."

"What? . . . Unfinished business? With me?"

"Well," Levitt said, digging his hands into his pockets,
"some of it's with you."

Baron frowned. "Your son-in-law," he said to himself.
"Oh, nonsense . . . Carey's your son-in-law. This fellow's just
a thorn in the flesh, a printer's error, a pesky nuisance."

He sighed. "Well, you'd better sit down and tell me about it.
Help yourself to a drink; they're all there, on that tray. If you
don't see what you want, ask Mather."

"I don't believe," said Levitt, "that I'll take a drink, thanks
very much." He sat down in the arm-chair that Doris had
vacated; he cocked up his right foot on his left knee; he was
silent.

"Doing all right over there now?" Baron asked, feeling compelled to begin.

"Well, yes and no," said Levitt cheerfully. "Got a steady job,
small job. I'm not the toast of the town. Funny to think that if
it weren't for you, I might still be the toast of the town."

"What? . . . If it weren't for me, eh?"

"Why, sure. If you hadn't lured me with your siren-song,
I'd still be sitting on velvet with Parker Publications. But
don't think I grumble. I don't. I'm darned grateful to you."

This was disconcerting. "What the devil have you got to be grateful to me for, I'd like to know? Give me one of your cigarettes, I'm not allowed to smoke."

Levitt rose, handed him the cigarette, gave it scrupulous measure with his lighter and sat down again.

"Grateful to me, eh? What for?" Baron repeated.

"All of it," said Levitt. "Goes way back. Fun to trace things back. Exquisite satisfaction when all the pieces fit." His fluent hands played an imaginary concertina in the air, then brought their finger-tips together. He looked over the top of them at Baron.

"I used to be afraid of you," he said. "Why was that, d'you imagine?"

"Lot of people are," said Baron, savouring the thought; "very silly of them. You didn't come all the way from New York to tell me that, did you?"

Gently smiling, Levitt shook his head. Already Baron felt tired; his eyelids were heavy. He looked at the alert, mocking face and thought, "Celia's husband; she loves him. They've got away, both of them."

"I don't mean anything to you any more, do I?" Levitt asked.

"What?" It was just the sort of question that he most disliked. Levitt knew that he had heard it; he did not repeat it. He said, "Well, I did once. Quite high up on the list of Baron's young men one time, wasn't I? Then I slipped. Just how, d'you recall? When did you start hating me?"

"What? . . ." This question was worse still. It had a thrusting indecency.

"I said, when did you start hating me?"

Now he could feel the aggressive winds; they blew from the unwisdom that wanted things in black and white. Only the wise knew that there must be neither black nor white, but safe, uniform grey. He stalled on his answer; he pushed the pillows up behind his head and raised himself. To smoke was good, but they were right about its not helping the feeling in his chest. He gave a rattling sigh.

"Don't really know what you mean, Harry. Nothing to

add to what I said to you when we parted company in New York. Your work went down; you lost your bite, your grip. You know that. You weren't good enough. It's been borne out by everything that's happened to you; everything you've done."

"Not quite everything, as it happens," said Levitt, "but let that pass, for a minute. It wasn't only my work, J. G., was it, that troubled you? Didn't I come a little too near? Fit into the family a little too cosily? Competing—shall we say—in Carey's field?"

It was the arch indecency; he could distinctly recall feeling just this about Levitt; he was outraged by Levitt's crudity in mentioning it.

"Anthony Carey," he said, "is a part of the family; a very special part. He's more than a son to me. None of us could ever feel as much for anyone as we could for Anthony."

"Celia could, thank God, and did," said Levitt gaily, "and more. Never mind. That *was* the trouble, wasn't it, Baron, really? I came too near. Check?"

Baron put out his cigarette and folded his hands; he looked at their neat shape, at the small brown blotches of age upon the delicate, wrinkling skin. He stretched the fingers and saw the power in the hands. "Maybe you did, Harry," he said; "it doesn't matter now."

Levitt nodded. The dark, hound profile lifted inquiringly. "But Carey," he said. "Different. Great guy, Carey . . ."

"Wonderful boy," said Baron; perhaps it was the cigarette that brought this sense of anæsthesia, of drowsy surrender.

"Were you always so fond of him, or did it grow?"

"What? . . . It grew." He played with the drawn-thread-work on the hem of the sheet. "I've always felt that Anthony was headed for great things . . . and now . . . proved. At Glane——" he stopped. "Funny. Anthony really means more to me, in one sense, than my children do; he seems to belong to me more than they ever did."

("And, damn you, Harry Levitt, I could tell you why. I bought his father out of a bad patch of trouble. I staked the family. I kept them going. I paid Randolph up. The old boy would have been in prison if it hadn't been for me; soft-pedalled that to Anthony of course—soft-pedalled it all. I paid the bill—all the bills. I kept the Careys for years.

"Why? I liked them; I admired them. They were gentlemen, and I wasn't. That's terribly important, if you come from nothing, d'you see? I loved being able to do it for them. It made them mine. But you keep out of this, Harry Levitt; it's none of your business.") He said, "Open that window behind you a little, will you? Hot in here; and I'm getting tired. What d'you want to tell me?"

Levitt looked diabolical. "Great guy, Carey," he repeated. "Better guy than I am, no?"

Baron said, "Better guy than either of us."

("And I blackmailed him. That's the thing in my life that I'm most ashamed of: putting that pressure on Anthony, opening his eyes to the fact that it was I who called the tune. Telling him, after all those years of silence. But I had to do it; once de Fries said he could win, I had to do it.")

"Yes," Levitt said thoughtfully, "assuming of course that one knows what sort of guy one is."

In Baron's mind, the coloured pieces of a kaleidoscope shook and shifted. He went on looking at them; little dazzling chips, the things that he knew; hints and clues, proofs and threats; evidence, corroboration, the myriad separate parts that must never meet, lest they should form an unbearable whole.

The irregular heartbeat quickened, until it became the familiar, panting pain in his chest; his heart coughed and loosened it. He stretched his hand for the pills. Levitt was there to pour the water; Levitt was leaning above him, solicitous, kind; the raffish intruder with the fancy tie and the devil's face.

"All right," Baron said. "Nothing to fuss about. Give me a minute." He lay back, resting. "Celia . . . that house of Celia's on the Vineyard . . . went there once; can't remember it for the life of me."

"It's a grey frame house," Levitt said, "looks like a little ark; on a plateau of rough grass—can't call it a lawn, really; white window-frames; flagpole at the edge of the grass; steps going down to the water."

"Hmm," said Baron, "what's she do with herself all day?"

He watched the Knave of Spades. The eyes were still smiling; kindlier now; the lines of the mouth softening, or perhaps it was his own limp, peaceful tiredness reflected in Levitt, making Levitt appear to relax. Levitt sat down again in the chair beside the bed.

"Do with herself? Carpentering; cooking; painting; taking the car to pieces and putting it together again; you know Celia. She's been awfully busy getting it all ready for Terry." He rested his elbow on his knee, his chin on his hand, still smiling, though his forehead frowned. "Keep seeing her the way I left her; on the grass, flying the aeroplane."

"What aeroplane, for God's sake?"

"A toy one," Levitt explained. "She bought it for Terry; she loves it. It's like a kite, only better. Kind of tricky to launch it into the wind, but once it's up, it flies high; like a silver bird. Don't know why it sticks in my mind, her standing there alone; arm up above her head, holding it, watching it fly. She looks——" he paused "—contented. Solitary. Person you want to hold out your arms to and yet can't touch. . . . Except you know you can—really . . ." He broke off. "Hell, what started me on that?"

"Celia," Baron said. "I know what you mean; she's all of a piece . . ." He could see her as Levitt had described her; wearing a shirt and trousers, probably; the arm up, the sun on the fair head, the look of being alone and absorbed.

"Only person," he muttered, "who's always had the clue to me. Reason why we fight, of course . . ." He was almost ready for sleep now; the pills did that.

"Clue to you?" Levitt asked; the expression of his face was still gentle.

"Mphm," Baron grunted.

("You'd like to know what it is, wouldn't you, Harry Levitt? Well, you won't. And it's too damned simple. Clue to me is I'm scared. Always have been; all my life. Celia knows that.

"Scared of what? That's the first question you'd ask, isn't it, Harry, you who were scared of me once? And that answer's damned simple too. Scared of the truth. What else is there to be scared of?")

"You're tired, aren't you?" Levitt was saying.

"I've told you I'm tired," he said pettishly.

("And what I haven't told you . . .

"For people like me, the Truth's the light that is too strong to bear. How could I bear, if I really faced it, the truth that nobody's ever loved me? And that I'm not worth loving? The truth of the things I've done? I've hated; hated my own flesh and blood; I've played dirty tricks all my life; even a trick on Toby's memory; even a trick on Anthony; can't stop myself, it seems. You'd probably say the way I treated Celia was cruel; and you might be right. How could I bear *that* truth? Answer, I couldn't; nor the truth that I'm a screaming, pitiful little runt of a coward inside. . . .

"Could you bear it, eh? Wonder what you'd say if I asked you that? Wonder what you'd do, in my place. Maybe what I've done. Turned myself over the years into the plausible likeness of a great family man and a great fighter. I do it damn well. Think of the obituary notices. Hope they'll let one read those, on the other side, but one can't be sure; just like them not to. 'Fleet Street Titan'; 'Rough Diamond'; 'Heart of Gold'; 'Nature's Gentleman'; 'Dynamiter'; 'Pioneer'. That's what they'll say. That's what they think I am. And there are intervals, do you know—only of course you don't know, because I'm not telling you—when I believe it myself. Have to.

"But the intervals, I think, get shorter. Not sure I'll be able to fool myself to the edge of the grave. I'll try. By God, I'll try.

"Well, Harry Levitt, what's got into you? Weren't you here to tell me something? Why do you just stand there, letting me look at you and think my secret thoughts? You've not come all this way for nothing, not if I know you.")

He raised himself a little. "I've told you I'm tired," he said again, "but not too tired to hear what you've got to tell me. You said it was important."

There was a long silence. Levitt had risen; he stood, digging his hands into his pockets, his forehead still wrinkling, the look on the face alternately rueful and amused.

"Get on," said Baron sharply.

"God damn you," Levitt said, without rancour, "I can't do it after all."

(iii)

"I don't believe it, it can't have happened; it didn't happen." He went on saying this in his head as he walked. The time was a quarter to six, and the Strand was full of people going home; the shabby London crowd, foreign to him yet; standing solidly in line for buses, herding past him towards the Tube, streaming into Charing Cross Station. Traffic jammed and horns blew lazily, not with the urgent rage of the hooting in New York streets, but with an occasional plaintive chorus.

He was aware of the hot, bright evening, the smell of dust and petrol, of a sky where carved clouds hung in motionless beauty.

"I don't believe it. I didn't let Baron get away with that. Just because he was ill; and tired. I didn't let him swing it on me. I couldn't.

"Why? What the devil happened? Was I sorry for him? ("Sending a man to do a boy's work," the far voice of Celia echoed.)

"Hell, I wasn't. Of course I wasn't. He's as slippery as ever, as tough as ever. What difference does it make, that he's ill, that he loves Carey—that he made me talk about Celia? I've no pity for Baron.

"For Carey, then? Was I sorry for Carey? After all this? B——s. I've no pity for Carey. Carey's a weak sister. Carey just burst into tears and ran. J. G. will find out about Carey fast enough; even though I won't be the one to tell him.

"And why not I?"

He had no answer; no answer to the man who had sat in the air-liner, mile after mile aloft, thinking only that he was coming here to do this; no answer to the man who had written the carefully-worded cable in Newfoundland; no answer to the man who had stepped down on London in the grim mood of an avenging angel; who had spent two days in his Bloomsbury hotel, planning his words, tapping up the story for the Press, walking London alone, waiting for Carey. That man would not believe this moment.

"Came three thousand miles to take a fence—and ducked it," he said to himself.

"I'll go back. Now. Tell him. Now."

He stood still on the pavement. He had come to the corner of Trafalgar Square; he saw the red buses sweeping past him; the white fountains that poured upward at the sun; the lions, the tall dark column against the sky.

"No. That isn't the important thing. What's important is to get the story out. Telling J. G. was just my private fun. Okay, coward, you had your chance, and you missed out on it. You'll damn' well get on with what matters now. Take a drink, get in a taxi, go to Gerald Lynn. Carey's right; that's the man."

He turned down Whitehall. He went into a dark little public-house where he used to drink when he worked for the *Flash*. He stepped straight into the past. It was the same, with its smell of beer; the hunting pictures on the wall, the polished brass, the parrot in the cage, the mixed Cockney voices. Here another Levitt had stood with a glass in his hand, thinking about Baron.

He didn't like it; it put him back in thrall. Baron was still Baron. After two years of voyage and discovery, the granite goblin had not stepped down from his niche. Baron had won.

He saw the tired, pagan face on the pillow, the little crooked smile.

"But he *can't* win. It's the truth that wins; it must be. I proved it, with Grant Parker, a month ago. It's the truth that wins."

He drank the warm drink and it made his mouth twist.

"We'll see to that, won't we?"

He took the drawing from his pocket. He looked at it. This was enough. If he had only done this in Baron's room he could have said the words. He held it stretched between his hands, staring; the scruples vanished; the authority of the thing that he had made cast them out.

"I must have been crazy," Levitt said to himself. He put down his glass, paid for his drink and went.

He walked, looking for a taxi. He felt as powerful now as he had felt this afternoon, on his way to Carey. As he gave the address to the driver, he remembered Lynn's house; the party for Catherine de Lille; Tobias running down the steps ("Cover my well-shaped and flying tracks"); the look of the profile moving away inside the car's lighted window. A long time ago, he thought. The traffic was clotted around Westminster; England became unreal again. He did not believe in these towers, this bridge, this river. They belonged to memory, not to now.

The taxi came into Victoria Square. Here was the red door, the dolphin door-knocker, the square brass plate announcing Gerald Lynn. As he waited, he found himself looking down the steps, following Toby's dash to the place where the car had been.

The manservant said, "If you wouldn't mind waiting a moment, sir. Mr. Lynn's on the telephone."

From the room at the top of the stairs, he could hear the voice, the light murmur and the sudden shrill upward skirl; then the manservant came back.

"This way, sir, please."

The room was the same; with the emphasised Victorian furniture; here were the shell pictures, the antimacassars, the Buhl desk. Gerald Lynn sat at the desk, still talking on the telephone; he had put up his feet on a beaded footstool. He raised a gay hand in greeting. "With you in one minute. Do sit down." He said to the telephone, which he was cradling between neck and shoulder, "Mr. Harry Levitt, no less, has just walked in."

There was a crackle of comment from the other end. Gerald listened with an air of martyrdom. "Yes . . . yes . . . *yes*. All right, such *words*. . . . Twenty minutes. . . . Dear, I'm not a V-Two; there is such a thing as *transit*." He slapped the telephone down on its bracket and leaped to his feet, holding

out both hands. The face of the dissipated angel was alight; the
sun behind his head made the thin gold hair into a halo.

"I can't tell you how glad I am to see you—nor how *little* time
we have. Your angle, at once. From the beginning. No, from
the end; I've a passion for the story that bites its tail, as with
fried whiting. Do you sit, stand, or pace, dear? Whichever you
wish. But please—the speed of a prairie fire. They want to go to
press." He seated himself at his typewriter. Levitt stared at him
stupidly; he felt a stiffness coming over his face.

"They have to make a block, too; that photograph's enchanting. Done in New York? *Bang* on the front page, of course. It's
the Baron angle that *slays* them; they're begging me to sign it,
and I utterly refuse. *Noblesse oblige* after all. Not that he won't
guess. Stop my chatter, will you, please? I'm too excited. *Hold*
me down and tell me all."

The stiffness became a cramp that hardened round Levitt's
jaws; his lips stuck; a foolish, grating voice forced itself between
them.

"I don't understand."

Gerald said, "Oh, darling, *don't* be obtuse. I've been Glane's
midwife for two years; how could I sign this? Not that I've
attacked Baron; I've simply told the story, as instructed. But
you do see—with Glane this week, and the horse having been
whooped up in all the Baron papers till you'd think it was the
Winged Victory—it is lovely, of course." He began to giggle.
"Know what? I was just going to ask you if you'd seen it."

Under Levitt's silence, his smile faded. "What's your trouble,
dear?" he asked crisply.

"Carey's told you."

"Well, yes, *natch* as they say on your side. What else do you
think I'm talking about? He's been here all the afternoon. Only
left ten minutes ago."

"You said—the photograph. You've got the photograph I
gave him."

"Certainly. Are you offended? He wants it back; but it's got
to be published. It's *evidence*, dear, as well as decoration and
drama; you do see that? Now, *quick*. When did you first find

you'd left your stable door unlocked? Shall we say that?" he asked archly, beginning to type. "Rather fun?"

"No," said the same foolish voice, "we won't say that."

Gerald's eyebrows lifted. "Angry? Yes, of course. It *is* monstrous. I was disarmed, I suppose, by poor Carey. Coming to confession. Bliss to have this sort, without fear of libel. Look, dear. . . . Try not to be angry. By tomorrow evening there'll be nobody who doesn't know it's your horse. *Ex*-quisitely timed, you see. On the button for the Glane ceremony. But talk, please. Don't pull any punches."

Levitt frowned, moistened his lips, lit a cigarette. He said, "I have nothing to say."

Lynn's hands fluttered above the typewriter. He cocked his head on one side and half-closed his eyes.

"It *is* a line, of course. Cold dignity; implacable justice. Yes, it *is* a line. But is it the best we can do, dear? We must ask ourselves that."

"Cut," Levitt said, "I mean it. It isn't a line. I have nothing to say."

After a moment, Gerald shut the typewriter. "I see you haven't, but you *do* rather break my heart."

"I'm sorry."

"I can't honestly see, dear, why you came, if you were going to take this stand."

Levitt was silent.

"Didn't you trust him? Was that it? You wanted to be sure he'd *really* told me? You needn't have bothered. I never saw a victim so ready to be cooked; insisting on being cooked. And at once. He was afraid J. G. might stop the story somehow. And it had to be told, he said. I understand it, in a way. Poor dear Carey. *Can't* make out why he did it, can you?"

"Ah, if he knew that," Levitt murmured, "he'd have the answer to everything." The only person he could see was Carey; Carey was all over the room; Carey who had got here first.

In his ears, Carey's naïve voice repeated, "When you were something of a heel, you say you got on fine. . . . Did you, *really*? . . . But was it all right inside?"

It wasn't; not with Carey. That was why he had come. Hard to do, Levitt thought; come to this limpidly malicious creature and say the words. Not confession to a priest nor a friend; just the straight sale of your guilt to the Fleet Street buyers. "You couldn't have done it," said Levitt to Levitt.

He had ceased to be angry. It was too logical to make him angry. Baron had said it: Carey was a better man than he was. The last piece of a complex pattern had fallen into place and made the pattern simple. In its simplicity, it showed that he, Levitt, was most arbitrarily saved from an act of self-destruction.

He stared past Gerald's head, across the fringed curtain at the window, to the grey London houses in the evening sun. He saw that since he found the photograph in the scrapbook he had been fighting to get back the past. He had struggled to recapture the snarling fox of a Levitt whose skin did not fit him any more.

That Levitt, he thought, would have made his killing. He would have bargained with Carey for money before he made it. He would have thrown the story contemptuously in Baron's face.

But he had failed to bring that Levitt to life. At this attempt he might have succeeded; might have conjured him, here in this room. And now he was robbed of his chance. Robbed by Carey.

("You take everything, don't you, Carey?")

Robbed by Carey.

Saved, by Carey.

With an effort he brought himself back; he smiled at Lynn; his voice was different and placid when it said, "I'm sorry. I really have nothing to say."

"Perhaps you will tomorrow. Where can I get you?"

"Don't think you can. And now run. Your masters will be waiting." It was in his mind to say, "Any good my asking you not to publish?" but he saw what would happen. They would publish, and quote him as asking them not to, make a noble figure out of Levitt. A little too late. It was Carey's day.

Lynn snatched his copy from the desk. . . . "You wouldn't like to read it? In the taxi, with me? . . . No? Rather *odd*, dear, aren't you? *Must* run."

As he shut the red front door, Levitt still saw Carey; saw him walking away from here, having done it. He thought, "Where did he go? What will he do?"

(iv)

Carey shut the red front door and walked away. He crossed Victoria Street and turned to the right; when he came to Eccleston Bridge he turned again, to the left this time, over the bridge, walking south, walking fast.

His first thought was that he had no thoughts. This was like waking from an anæsthetic. The awakening made him look back along the afternoon, to the moment of the sudden sob in his throat, the turning away from Levitt with the tears pouring down his face. "Haven't cried for years and years," he thought dully. "Must have looked funny to Levitt. It was the end, of course; that's what did it. You don't see those things coming, at the time. I must have been in a state of shock from the minute I got his cable—shock on top of strain . . . months and months of strain, and then, after the shock—well, I cried, I think, when I knew I'd got them out at Anzio."

He walked through Eccleston Square, with the great gap on the left where the bombed houses had been; he went on down Belgrave Road. He had no idea where he was going; he had no idea what time it was, what day it was. His body and mind took the same impact of relief. This was peace. Peace going on and on; inside him and about him. "If there were such a thing as a silence that sang," he said to himself, "it would be this.

"The padlock's off; the chain's broken. There's no more knot inside; no more heavy iron box inside my head. It's out; it's over; it's finished.

"And why, in the name of God, since it feels like this, couldn't I do it before?"

He looked at the front of a public-house; at a small news-agent's shop; at a dustbin and a black cat that danced out from behind the dustbin. "Hullo, cat," he said and stooped to play with it. He looked at its pushing head, at its boxing paws. His eyes felt new. For a long time they had been clouded, blurred, seeing nothing in true focus.

The magical clarity persisted. All that stood up about him was bright and sharp and detailed: the shape of the cat, the lamp-post, the perspective of narrow, squalid houses stretching out of the square. He was at leisure to look at things, to look out, not in. He realised now that his left eyelid was no longer twitching and he wondered when it had stopped doing that. He walked on.

He crossed the last seedy square, with its stucco, its gaps, its peeling paint; he came to the tramlines and turned left at Mill-bank. He walked on the riverside.

He tried to look ahead, to see what would happen. He tried to see the story as they would print it, to see the result of the story; to see what would come out of this, for Glane, for J. G., for himself, but he could not. His mind kept leading him back to the moment of telling it; the moment when he opened his mouth and said the words to Gerald Lynn; standing beside the overmantel in the strained Victorian room.

"Hullo; I came to tell you something. Remember asking me about my moment of inspiration? Well, it wasn't inspiration; it was a theft. I stole the design of the winged horse from this drawing of Harry Levitt's. Here's what happened."

The words had come smoothly; Levitt had magicked them free of their prison.

"*Carey, for God's sake . . .*" It was the voice of somebody who no longer mattered, somebody outside the walls of this calm; he had no power. He was not Anthony Carey; he was the spokesman for the frightened people.

"Look at it, can't you see it? The way they'll play it up? You could have kept it back, couldn't you, till after the cere-mony? Think of the unveiling of the statue—now. What will happen now? 'The Glane Trumpetings'; what tune will they blow now, those trumpets? Carey, for God's sake, do some-thing. Stop the story.

"Think of J. G. . . . Will he ever speak to you again? He'll be your enemy for ever. After he's lashed you from the crown of your head to the soles of your feet. How can you face him? You know what it is to be afraid of him—as you never knew before, as you never were afraid before."

Carey grinned. "No, I don't know what it is to be afraid of him; not now. I don't know how to be afraid again. I'll take what's coming. From J. G. From all of them. It's easy. It doesn't compare with having those words locked inside; that was fear. This isn't. The words are said. Fear's over."

He came to the bridge, to the towers of Westminster. He could go on walking for ever; this was all that he wanted to do, to walk and hear the silence that sang.

"But Liz," said the voice of the spokesman outside the walls. "How can you do this to Liz? Liz who has trusted you and loved you; you were a rock for Liz. She'll never trust you again. For Liz, you are taking away the roof, the walls, the floor. Can you face that and still not care?"

"Yes," he said. "I can. Liz will understand. Liz has seen the thing happening to me and she will be glad, for me and with me, that it's over.

"Taking away the floor and the walls? Oh, nonsense—I'm destroying nothing for her; I'm putting something back. I pulled that house of safety down nearly two years ago, not today. I rebuilt it today. She has been living not with safety but with danger. Living with a liar; with somebody cursed; with somebody who wasn't really I."

On that thought he halted. He had crossed Westminster Bridge and he stood on the Embankment, still on the riverside. The sky was gold and the water took the light in long gold flakes. A brown barge went past; he watched it.

"Somebody who wasn't really I. He was afraid and he has gone. I'm back. Levitt brought me back. Levitt knocked the shackles off the prisoner, set the Truth free, gave me myself again. I'm back; this is I. And Liz is safe with me."

He breathed deep and what he drew into his lungs was the new wind of freedom. He walked on, exultant. He did not notice that his feet were taking him straight to Baron's doorstep; he knew only that he was walking free. Now he could hear the beat of the wings, and the words kept him company. They shouted to the sky:

> "And once atop of Lambourne, down toward
>   the hill of Clere,
>   I saw the Host of Heaven in rank, and Michael
>   with his spear
>   And Turpin out of Gascony and Charlemagne
>   the Lord
>   And Roland of the Marches with his hand
>   upon his sword
>   For the time he should have need of it
>   and forty more beside.
> *And I ride!*"

(v)

It was a workman's train that Levitt took; a slow train that left Cannon Street at five. It was half-past seven when he reached Ashford; there was no taxi in the station yard; he walked, under the misty sunshine of the day's beginning.

The look of the town puzzled him, as the towers of Westminster, the bridge and the river had puzzled him. It was something that he had put away, stored in memory. It must still be there. Surely it was now only in memory that he stood before the shop window where Tobias and Liz had loitered, more than two years ago, on the first day that he came here? Surely it was a ghost-Levitt, haunting the town? The real Levitt must be asleep, in the house on the Vineyard; in the room that looked on the sea; asleep, with Celia beside him; he had sent his spirit over on this job.

He came to the corner, by the traffic lights. He thumbed a lorry that was headed for the Carlington road.

"I'm only going as far as the village," the driver said.

"That'll do; I can walk it from there."

He watched the marsh come; the widening fan of sky, the

fields that stretched to the sea. There was the white fence, running between Carey's land and Baron's; the bulk of Carlington itself rose above the trees; then as the road wound inland, it was lost. They were at the village now.

"This'll do me fine," said Levitt. "Thanks a lot."

He met nobody on the road. When he came to the gate of Carey's house he halted for a moment, looking into the garden. He passed the gate. Here was the red wall, the archway. He went in.

He heard the sound of his own feet on the gravel; no other sound but the bird-song overhead. He went through the cut in the high black walls of yew; the grass was wet and shining; he kept on looking at the grass; if he looked up he would see it now; but he was shy of looking up. He kept his eyes lowered until he reached the steps.

He raised his eyes, to the white niche and the bronze horse. He went on staring, in the silence that the statue imposed.

He had not thought that it would make this silence. It was humbling in its beauty, in the soaring magic that his pencil had given to the old lines long ago. It was wholly faithful to that first dream.

'This I began . . . This Carey finished.'

He looked at the solid masses of light and shadow; at the muscles that had the validity of flesh, at the curved belly, the delicate legs; at the poised miracle of the four feet standing lightly, at the burnished head and the triumphant wings.

> "*He had flame behind the eyes of him*
> *and wings upon his side.*"

Slowly he mounted the steps; he laid his hand on the bronze flank.

"Good-bye," said Levitt.

He had to linger for a moment, looking down over the garden, over tiers of lawn and terrace, down over the marsh to the sea. Hard across his eyes there rode the picture of another sea; of a rough lawn and a figure standing solitary, with the arm raised above the head; the sun glinted on the fair hair and on the silver toy flying.

"All right, darling," he said softly. "All over. Ended. I'm on my way back to you. Wait for me."

He ran down the steps; he paused once to look back at the statue. He went on, across the grass, between the yew hedges, out of the gate and down the road.